WEEPING WATERS

Karin Brynard

WEEPING WATERS

*Translated from the Afrikaans
by Maya Fowler and Isobel Dixon*

Europa
editions

Europa Editions
214 West 29th Street
New York, N.Y. 10001
www.europaeditions.com
info@europaeditions.com

This book is a work of fiction. Any references to historical events,
real people, or real locales are used fictitiously.

Library of Congress Cataloging in Publication Data is available
ISBN 978-1-60945-446-3

Brynard, Karin
Weeping Waters

Book design and cover illustration by Emanuele Ragnisco
www.mekkanografici.com

Prepress by Grafica Punto Print – Rome

Printed in Italy at Arti Grafiche La Moderna - Rome

For Rien

WEEPING WATERS

1

The call came through just after two.

He was at his desk at the police station, having his lunch of vetkoek and mince. Washed down, as usual, with a mug of strong black coffee. Three sugars.

He was almost done when the phone rang.

One of the constables on duty in the charge office. "There's been a murder," the man gasped, "two dead. A farm killing. Woman and child. White. On Huilwater farm, about forty kays out on the Upington road." And then, "The caller's still on the line. Would the Inspector like to speak to him?"

Inspector Albertus Markus Beeslaar shoved the vetkoek aside.

A man's voice, shaky and hoarse. "Too late," he kept repeating, "a madman . . . a devil . . . "

The voice broke off.

"Like animals. Both of them, just slaughtered. Blood. On everything. Everywhere."

He said he was *standing* in it. Then the man began to sob, stammering about being too late.

It took some coaxing to get a name out of him. "Boet Pretorius," he eventually answered. "From the farm next door."

The child was barely four years old. "Four, just four," he said, over and over again.

"Where's the woman's husband?" Beeslaar asked this several times.

"There *is* no fucking husband," was the fierce reply. A foreman, yes, but he was nowhere to be found.

Where was he phoning from?

There was a long silence, as if the man had to think about it.

Then, "Good God, man! Get out of the house, *now*," Beeslaar ordered. "Wait outside. I'm on my way."

For a moment Beeslaar didn't move. So much for a peaceful life on the platteland, his dream of a quiet small-town post. He threw the vetkoek into his wastepaper basket and told the constable on duty to send more backup to Huilwater. He rounded up two colleagues and got a car. The Citi Golf. The only one available in a carpool of two. No air con, a hundred and eighty thousand on the clock.

They squeezed in, ready to tackle the forty kilometres of dirt road.

Sergeant Pyl had to take the back, with Ghaap in the passenger seat. Beeslaar crammed his own two-metre frame behind the wheel. Cursing under his breath, as he did each time he got into the tiny car: the steering wheel too close to his knees, the seat too narrow, no legroom, his head against the roof, leaving him feeling hemmed in and pissed off. This afternoon was no exception. He was in a foul mood already, even before they hit the road that led to the murder scene.

But all that didn't irritate him as much as the fact that he was still struggling to find his feet in this post: real city boy, ill at ease in a world of farmers and cattle and farm roads and sand and snakes and blazing-heat-without-air-con. He'd barely arrived, blissfully under the impression he was heading for a quiet job in a peaceful backwater, when the shit hit the fan and started flying in all directions.

He arrived right in the middle of an unprecedented wave of stock theft. And either he wasn't a detective's backside any more, or he was dealing with a super-sophisticated mafia. Because he could find neither hide nor hair of these crooks, no matter how hard he tried.

The farmers were at their wits' end. And furious, because

they were being nailed. Everyone wanted results, arrests, while he was having a hard time telling his arse from his elbow, let alone rounding up a cunning bunch of stock thieves.

And then, just a fortnight ago, two farm workers were brutally murdered on Vaalputs. They must have caught the thieves in the act. The remnants of a flock of sheep, some with throats cut, others with hock tendons slashed, had lain there, bleating and bleeding to death, all goddamn night. Till the farmer discovered them the next morning and put them out of their misery. And only then found the bodies of the workers, the Jacobs brothers, underneath the carcasses, trampled to shreds by the panicked beasts.

And he, Albertus Markus Beeslaar, sat there like a damn fool. With everyone looking to him, the new guy with so many years of experience. Big Man from the Big City. Schooled by the cream of the crop of Johannesburg's old Murder and Robbery Squad. But here he was now, blowing around like a lost fart. With not a clue about what to do next.

If only he had caught the thieves, the Huilwater woman and her child would still be alive to—

He narrowly dodged a pothole. Bumped his head, berated himself—stop brooding and focus on the road: the potholes were the size of chest freezers.

With half an ear, he listened to Sergeant Pyl behind him—the hyperactive one, who couldn't keep his trap shut for a second, even if he had to shout to make himself heard above the din of gravel clattering against the chassis. There was lots of gossip, he said, about the single woman farming on Huilwater. An eccentric artist from Johannesburg. And the Griqua girl she was adopting, and that weird Bushman farm manager of hers. Pyl's voice was virtually drowned out as they rattled over a corrugated stretch of road, so that Beeslaar couldn't always follow the thread.

Half an hour of shuffling, shaking and head-bumping. Pyl

prattling on doggedly from the back. Ghaap, his long, skinny body folded up like a stick insect on the seat next to him, was thankfully less talkative. Then they finally found the turn-off to Huilwater and stopped at the back door of the farmhouse.

Boet Pretorius was sitting on the back steps, his large figure hunched over. There was blood on his clothes. Stains on his knees and forearms. Even in his hair. There was vomit on his shirt, and a dark smear on the hand that was clutching a cigarette.

Around him a wordless gathering of men: farmers from the district, driven in from God knows where.

Who'd sent word? Beeslaar wondered fleetingly. Pretorius?

One was still hovering in the kitchen doorway, his face pale and frightened. Probably went in to satisfy a macabre curiosity, Beeslaar thought as he headed for the group.

"Beeslaar," he introduced himself, "and Sergeants Pyl and Ghaap. How many of you have been inside?"

He got his answer in the form of downcast faces, hands fumbling with a hat or a pistol at the hip.

"Christ," he muttered, and walked past them.

The man at the door quickly stood aside. "There's no one left," he told Beeslaar, who took a moment to comprehend what the man was trying to say.

"From now on, you all stay clear of this house," Beeslaar barked. "This is a murder scene, not a fucking freak show!" He swallowed back his anger and then tried again, more evenly, "Please see to it that nobody leaves this place before I've talked to every one of you! Understood?" He waited sternly until they assented. Then he turned and went inside the house. Over his shoulder he ordered Pyl to man the back door—no one, apart from the forensics team from Upington, was permitted—and Ghaap, meanwhile, should start taking statements and round up some officers to find the farm labourers.

*

It was a particularly gruesome scene. In twenty years with the South African Police Service, he'd not witnessed anything like this. He saw the child first. In the first bedroom. Lying on her side, in a pool of blood. He could see the blood was fresh—a few hours, at most.

The woman's body was in a second bedroom. She was sitting on the floor, her back against a chair. Her arms hung loosely, hands relaxed, palms open to the ceiling. Like a rag doll propped upright on a child's bed. But without a head. Or rather, from where he was standing in the doorway, he couldn't see one. And he didn't want to get too close—he'd wait for the team from Forensics. Not that this was a pristine murder scene, exactly.

The two bedrooms and the passage were covered in bloody tracks from the farmers traipsing in and out. Beeslaar felt his blood pressure rise.

The forensics team from Upington turned out to be one bloke. "Sorry I'm so late," he said, introducing himself as Hans Deetlefs. "Without my GPS I'd never have found the place!" He looked pretty pleased with himself and his GPS, this man with the fresh face and big specs. He was a short man, but clearly minus the accompanying syndrome. And he seemed smart. Already kitted out in his plastic coveralls and shoes, bag of tricks in his left hand, camera hanging from his neck. "Welcome to the wild North West, Inspector," he said, blinking his little eyes in a self-satisfied way. "I hear you're all the way from Joburg!"

Beeslaar mumbled a response, in no mood for chitchat.

Cheerily, Hans Deetlefs unpacked his case and deftly set to work, pointing out a detail to Beeslaar every now and then. Such as the fact that the woman's head *was* actually there. Quite simply, her throat had been cut so deeply that her head fell backwards into the hollow of the seat. Together, they inspected the chaos in the bedroom. The drawers had been pulled from the wardrobe and emptied onto the floor in a tangle of underwear, scattered items of jewellery and cosmetics, and the mattress half dragged from the bed. As if someone had been searching for something. A low bookshelf lay upended and several books were spattered with blood; this had apparently happened before the killing.

"She must have sat watching," Hans happily declared. "Bet you a hundred bucks they fed her roofies before murdering her." He blinked up at Beeslaar.

"I'm not a gambling man," Beeslaar grunted.

The blood was everywhere: walls, floor, bed. The woman's long summer dress, light blue, was stained black. And outside, the front stoep too was a mess, with three sheepdogs and a mongrel lying in pools of blood.

Deetlefs wasn't much bothered by the fucked-up state of the murder scene. "Shit happens," he said with an irritating grin as he blinked again. His words were still hanging in the air when more shit threatened: Sergeant Ghaap appearing in the doorway without foot protection, glowing cigarette in hand.

"Inspector, the guys outside wanna know if you can . . . umm, how long it's going to take. They want to go."

Beeslaar began counting to ten, but didn't even reach three. "Fuck off with that cigarette! And then go and tell that bunch outside: if they want to spend the night in the cells, they should just try and leave here!"

When Beeslaar was finally satisfied that he'd seen everything, he left Deetlefs to it and stepped outside for some fresh air. And to listen to Pretorius's story.

But there was a commotion and more violence threatened.

The farm manager had arrived. Before Beeslaar could stop them, a group of young farmers pulled the man roughly from his truck and onto the ground, ready to beat the hell out of him. And then shoot him. Ghaap, Pyl and a couple of their col-leagues had to break it up.

Adam De Kok was his name. An interesting figure, the Bushman foreman that Ghaap had mentioned. He'd been in town all day—with the Huilwater housekeeper, Mrs. Beesvel—doing the weekly grocery shopping and collecting stuff from the farmers' co-op. Beeslaar took them aside, walked with them to the manager's house some thirty metres from the main homestead. They settled on the back stoep, where Beeslaar spoke to them both. But they were both shocked, knew noth-ing—the poor woman could hardly talk, she was so distraught. She broke down, speaking in gasps between sobs, about "her little ones," "the evil world," "too late," "bad people." The evil world indeed, Beeslaar thought, as De Kok comforted her.

There was little point in pressing them further right now. De Kok said he would take Mrs. Beesvel—Outanna, he called her—inside for a cup of sweet tea, while Beeslaar stayed on the stoep to finish the questioning. He had the rest of the workers brought to him for interviews. Same story from each one of them: "saw nothing," "heard nothing." All of them were clearly beside themselves. Two more had to be fetched from a distant camp where they'd been repairing fences. And apart from the fact that they were also clearly shaken, they too knew nothing.

Then Beeslaar moved on to the waiting farmers. Starting with Boet Pretorius.

"Went into town this morning, just the usual, co-op and bank. Quick burger at the Dune, left at about half past one. And on my way back . . . " He grimaced. "I'm on the farm next door, Karrikamma," he said. And no, he hadn't noticed any strange or unusual vehicles around here, or along the way.

"I just wanted to stop by, the house is so close to the road, you know, you can just quickly pop in."

Seven o'clock, almost five hours later. Deetlefs had just given the green light for the bodies to be taken away. The ambulance guy, an unwashed fellow with wine on his breath, had a hard time loading them up. The closest available pathologist was in Postmasburg.

The yard was suddenly quiet. The farmers gone, the one-man team from Upington gone. Ghaap and Pyl on their way back to the station with the ops guys.

Beeslaar was alone. Sitting on the back steps, where he'd found Boet Pretorius earlier that afternoon. Looking out over the yard, at the two giant blue gums shading the back door. A lane of white karees separated the manager's house from the main house.

A big zinc dam stood at the front of the house, a windmill alongside, its pump straining, screeching as it drew water, its blunt blades a metallic grey against the sky. Dusk was falling. The setting sun flared red in the fine dust that hovered over the yard.

Beeslaar felt slightly nauseous. Not just because of the bloodbath he'd witnessed that afternoon. It was the water. He'd been in this godforsaken place for two months, but still couldn't get used to the brackish water, water that turned soap to scum and left chalky limescale rings in every glass. His body yearned for the stale swimming-pool flavour of Joburg tap water.

He tried putting Joburg out of his mind. It was a different life. He was here now. On this farm, in this heat.

Sweating like a pig. And thirsty, always thirsty.

But he also knew that now, sitting here, this thirst was the very least of his problems.

2

S ara Swarts looked for a tree, some shade, in front of Number 3 Driedoring Street. Yvonne Lambrechts's house, Tannie Yvonne, as they called her, not a real aunt, but a friend of her mother's from way back, and one of the few people in the district she still knew.

It was Tannie Yvonne who had called her yesterday with the news about Freddie. And the child.

"My sweetheart, you've got to be strong now. There's terribly bad news."

It hit Sara like a lightning bolt. Freddie . . . and *like that*.

And a child. The girl she'd wanted to adopt. She'd even sent a photograph. At the time, Sara had hardly even looked at the picture. Another of Freddie's crazy "projects." Not yet over, the thing between Freddie and her . . . Oh, God.

Sara turned off the ignition and got out. Tired of thinking. Right through the night. Kilometre after kilometre of merciless road—all the way from Cape Town. Thinking, and regretting. All along the West Coast to Vanrhynsdorp, then east and north again. With Freddie on her mind all the way. And the issues she'd had with Freddie, those final bitter words . . .

Up the ridge of the plateau, towards the Hantam. Then Bushmanland, vast and flat. Two, three hours' drive between one sleeping town and the next. The straight road a tunnel through the dark. Here and there the flare of an animal's eyes, or a greyish something scurrying across the road. Jackal. Mongoose, a buck. Not another living soul to be seen. Just the black night and the two beams of light her lit-tle Corsa cast onto the never-ending black tar. At sunrise she saw the first quiver trees, wild silhouettes dancing against the dawn. And then the red dunes in between haakbos and grasslands, the camel thorns with their characteristic umbrella shapes. For the first time since receiving the news she felt real again. Here, back in this familiar world, as if the night had been some harrowing nightmare where she'd stumbled through a dark maze, in search of . . . who knows what.

She knocked on Tannie Yvonne's door and was met with hysterical high-pitched barking. The door had scarcely opened a crack when three small fluffy dogs rushed at her, jumping up at her calves.

Tannie Yvonne embraced Sara without a word. She was still in her pyjamas and smelt of talcum powder and sleep. Dry-eyed, Sara stared over her shoulder at the familiar corridor and lounge.

"Come in," she said, "I'll make us some tea."

"I should probably go to the police first," Sara protested.

But the older woman took her firmly by the arm and led her through the house, to the back stoep. "It's still cool here. Stretch your legs a while, I'll bring the tea. I've made it already. And you need to eat something before you start this day."

Reluctantly, Sara sat and looked around her. At the cement stoep with its corrugated-iron roof, the pot plants smothering the crowded space, the battered cane chairs with their limp cushions. She felt anxious: sitting down for tea seemed a waste of time. But maybe it would be better to collect her thoughts before she headed for the police station. Perhaps she should take a bath first, change her clothes. Brush her hair.

She looked down at her bare legs and feet. She was still wearing the denim mini she'd worn to work the day before. Her flip-flops were probably still in the car. There was a coffee stain on her T-shirt. She licked a finger and rubbed at the mark listlessly. Then she took the elastic band from her hair, lowered her head, gathered the hair up, and tied it back in a ponytail.

Half an hour later she headed for the police station, which was within walking distance. It was a tiny town—one long main road, tarred, with a handful of dusty dirt roads criss-crossing it. The police station was on the main road, half a block down from the Driedoring Street turn-off.

Sara walked briskly, aware of the heat already gathering on the tar. And it was still early. Just after eight, the last time she had looked. She stood for a moment on the steps in front of the police station, smoothing the creases in her skirt with damp palms. Then she took a deep breath, pushed her sunglasses onto her head, and went inside.

"My name is Sara Swarts," she said to the female constable at the counter. "I'm here about the . . . er . . . death of my sis-ter. Swarts. Frederika. She was . . . m-m-m . . . yesterday . . . "

Sara swallowed as she saw the dismay and sympathy in the sturdy policewoman's eyes. Her short, combed-back hair was streaked with silver. Sara wondered how much this woman—Kgomotse, said the name tag on her chest—had seen in her years.

"Hai!" the policewoman said with a concerned click of her tongue, "just wait, ma'am. I'm calling someone quickly." She put out a hand, gently touched Sara's arm on the counter—as if she were afraid Sara's courage would fail her. With the other hand she picked up the phone and said something in Tswana.

A moment later a slim young man appeared in a doorway to the right. "Go with him, ma'am," Constable Kgomotse said softly, "he'll take you to the inspector."

The man led Sara to the door of an open office. "Miss Swarts is here," he said quietly and turned to Sara, indicating she should enter.

Sara shifted the shoulder strap of her bag, removed the sunglasses from her head, and walked in. It was a large room with steel cabinets lining one wall and windows overlooking the hot main road on the other. She walked towards a giant of a man who struggled out of his chair to greet her.

"Beeslaar," he mumbled, half crouching over his chair, his one hand pressed against a red tie, until Sara took a seat opposite him.

"Thank you, Sergeant Pyl," he said to the young man who had fetched Sara from the front desk. The sergeant hesitated, an inquisitive glance lingering on her, before he disappeared through the door.

"I appreciate you coming in," the inspector said, sounding rather breathless. "I was actually on my way to Mrs. Lambrechts's. I'd heard you were here. Small towns . . . " he explained with a smile.

Sara nodded.

"May I offer you some coffee?" With a big hand he gestured towards the tray standing on one side of his desk: two cups and a thermos flask on a finely crocheted cloth, along with a floral-patterned saucerful of ginger biscuits. Sara declined, then changed her mind.

"Thank you," she said softly.

The policeman hoisted himself from the chair, this time more successfully, and unscrewed the red thermos cap with stiff fingers. He poured the strong, black fluid with a slightly shaky hand.

How much milk and sugar? he wanted to know. She asked for two, but he put in three, stirring slowly, placing the cup in front of her. The saucer of biscuits he placed next to her cup before carefully taking two for himself.

He was even taller than she'd thought at first, she realised. A rugby lock in days gone by, perhaps, who had let himself go as he approached forty. His black hair was receding, salt and pepper at the temples. There was perpetual thunder in his face, she could tell. It was pale, painted in heavy, dramatic strokes: big, straight nose, thick black eyebrows in a permanent frown. His mouth was wide, but softer, and he had a strong angular jaw, with a clefted chin.

He cleared his throat and stirred his coffee, briefly appraising her from below his heavy brows.

"My sincerest sympathies," he began. "Do you feel . . . um, up to this? You must have driven all night?"

"Yes. I couldn't get a flight from Cape Town to Upington at such short notice." She leaned forward slightly, struggling to hear him. His muffled speech suggested a man of few words, not much given to talking. Or maybe her ears were still blocked from the nine-hundred-kilometre drive, especially with the racket of the last stretch of dirt road.

"There are a couple of formalities I'd like to dispense with first," he said, dragging a brown folder closer. Sara took a sip of coffee. It was unexpectedly hot. She swallowed quickly, feeling it scald its way down her throat.

"You drove the whole way by yourself?" More statement than question. He didn't wait for an answer, assuring her that he'd be brief.

"You're the deceased's only relative?" His voice was slightly louder, as if he felt more at ease now that the niceties were behind them. He started writing.

"She was my sister."

"Her full name?"

"Frederika Cornelia Swarts."

He nodded without looking up, and wrote the name down in a crabby scrawl.

"Freddie for short," Sara added, and the policeman looked up for a second.

"Her date of birth, place of birth?"

"Huilwater, the farm where . . . where it happened. We were both born on the farm."

"Year?"

"She was born in 1976. Freddie was thirty-three." She'd just had a birthday, Sara remembered with a pang. And she hadn't even phoned her.

She looked up, saw Beeslaar watching her from under his eyebrows again. His gaze had softened.

"You still feel all right with proceeding?"

Sara blinked yes, her one knee twitching nervously. She crossed her legs.

"The farm. Huilwater . . . " He looked at the form in front of him. "Was it your sister's property?"

"Family farm. She stayed on after my father passed away."

"When was that?"

"About eighteen months ago."

"Your mother?"

"Died. About twenty years ago, 1989, around then." She swept her hand over her eyes, embarrassed that all of a sudden the exact date escaped her. "But Freddie, well, she's really from Johannesburg. She had a job there, she was an art teacher. And just recently, before my dad fell ill. And when he got sick . . . "

Her throat constricted. That's where the trouble had started between her and Freddie.

Beeslaar made a note on the sheet of paper in front of him. When he was done, he asked, "So there's no other family?"

"No. Or I suppose, maybe. My father had a brother, but he died years ago."

"Your full name, date of birth?"

"Johanna Susara. The 9th of May, 1978." She gave the address of her flat in Cape Town's City Bowl. And her work address.

Beeslaar gave her a swift glance, frowned. "You work for a newspaper? A journalist?"

"Yes, I cover environmental affairs."

He put down his pen, picked up his coffee and looked at her over the rim of his cup.

"The child, your sister's child, Klara Boois. I believe she was in the process of adopting the girl?"

"I really know very little about her," Sara said quickly, and shifted her legs again. "I mean . . . " She stared at the desk in front of her. How to say this without sounding like a heartless bitch?

The policeman took another swig of coffee. During her silence, he carefully picked up both his biscuits between thumb and index finger, dipped them into the coffee simultaneously, and stuffed them into his mouth in one big bite.

"What I mean is that Freddie and I, this last while, we didn't . . . have much contact."

His eyebrows rose as he chewed and swallowed. She saw a flash of interest in his olive-green eyes.

"I mean that we . . . " She looked down at her hands, but found no answer there. The red nail polish, she noticed, had been chewed off.

"What I mean is that my sister and I kind of fell out two years ago and I . . . we didn't have any contact after that." She could hear herself swallow. It seemed ridiculous, her rage at Freddie for persuading Pa to refuse further hospital treatment, to stay on the farm. But it seemed righteous then, justified. Now it suddenly seemed so pathetic. Selfish, really. She realised she had just been scared, not wanting to face his death. She'd run away when they needed her the most.

When she looked up, she saw Beeslaar staring at her intently, his gaze unreadable.

"Inspector, who did it?" she asked. "Have you got a suspect at least?"

He appraised her a moment longer, his tongue probing his cheek. "It's still very early." He pulled at his collar, as if it was pinching him. The red tie seemed to be permanently askew.

"What we do know, is that at this point we're looking at a robbery that seems to have gone awry, if I can put it like that. Apparently a few things are missing too, but not much. Some dresses, the chain your sister wore around her neck. It had a small silver cross, apparently."

Ma's silver chain. Delicate, with its simple crucifix.

"Anything else?" she asked.

"We were hoping you could shed more light on this. So far, we understand that the gold band your sister wore on her middle finger is missing, possibly a few other pieces of lesser value, it's hard to be sure, but her jewellery box was definitely rifled."

Sara was no longer listening. "Farm murder," she murmured, only realising she'd said the words aloud when she saw the policeman's frown.

"Er . . . yes. We actually don't use that term any more." His voice was deep but melodic, rising from the depths of his drum of a chest. "What I mean is," he scratched at his throat, "it remains an appalling crime. I don't for a second mean to say that it isn't. But it's no different from any other violent crime. It . . . "

Sara stopped listening. She saw Freddie again, that last day she'd left Huilwater. She had kept following Sara, pleading, as Sara furiously packed her bags and flung them into the car after their blazing row about Pa. Freddie stood at the car window, her hands on the metal frame, as if she physically wanted to prevent Sara from driving off. All her explanations as to why it was better for Pa to die on the farm. Sara shouting at her, "But Pa doesn't *have* to die!" Freddie shaking her head, tears dripping from her chin onto her dress. "*Stay*, Sara, stay with us. For Pa's last—" Sara putting the car into gear and lurching off. Freddie running after her. At the farm gate she stopped, a slender figure in her long, loose-fitting blue silk dress, golden curls blown upwards, weightless in the dust.

The policeman had stopped talking, she realised. "What

exactly *did* happen, Inspector?" she asked, hoping to break his questioning gaze.

His eyebrows relaxed. He spoke, hesitation in his voice. Sara suspected he was providing minimal information. Even so, she couldn't help imagining some thug, some monster, with Freddie there, all alone on the farm. Demanding she hand over money and firearms—Freddie with her slight frame, her slim arms, her small hands. Sara was always the strong one, the wild one. Loved riding bareback, never thought twice about punching a boy. But Freddie, despite her nickname, was delicate, a downy thistle.

"Do you think my sister suffered any pain?"

He tugged at his tie, trying to loosen it.

"We suspect she might have been heavily drugged before she was murdered."

"Drugged!"

"There was no sign of a struggle, Miss Swarts. No indication that she tried to defend herself or offer any resistance. She wasn't tied up or anything. At this stage we suspect that she knew the attacker or attackers and let them in herself. That maybe she unwittingly—she and the child—ingested a drug that made it impossible to fight back."

"But she's . . . what exactly killed her?"

"The neck wound. The post-mortem isn't done yet. Naturally, we're working as quickly as we can, but, well, at this stage we're convinced that's the cause of death. Hers and the girl's—the carotid artery—severed with a sharp object." He glanced down at the file again, frowning deeply. "Do you know whether there might be someone who had a reason to want her dead?"

Sara realised she was gaping at him. Then she slowly shook her head.

"But I thought . . . Tannie Yvonne, Mrs. Lambrechts, said it was the stock thieves. She says—"

The eyebrows knitted. "Well, yes, your sister might have

been one of their victims. We've had a wave of stock theft—sheep, cattle. I'm talking large-scale. By people who know what they're doing. People with very sophisticated methods, an organised syndicate, maybe, with a good intelligence network. They know exactly where and when to strike. And they are merciless, it seems. Cunning. Two weeks ago they killed two people from Vaalputs, so—"

"You mean they had their throats cut too," Sara heard herself say.

It felt so unreal, she almost wanted to laugh. But there she was, Sara Swarts. With a knee that had started twitching again like a wind-up toy with a will of its own. And she was talking about Freddie. Gentle, dreamy Freddie, with her sharp yet quiet sense of humour, her unexpected cynicism and distaste for convention and pretension.

"But why Freddie, Inspector? What did she ever do to them? God knows, she . . . I don't think there was that much left to farm with, even. My father had started selling off the livestock before he died, I guess it's quite a small herd of cattle now, some sheep. Not sure."

The policeman straightened his shoulders. "We think it was simply a violent robbery. Remember, the house is right next to the main road. The gate is always open. It's an easy target. And these people are opportunists. But I don't want to get fixated on the stock thieves. It's just that there are very few farm attacks in this district. Even livestock theft used to be rare around here—especially on this scale. But that's not to say we're ruling out other possibilities. So I have to find out whether you know of any other people who might bear a grudge against your sister."

In an effort to get the image of Freddie in that long blue dress out of her mind, Sara brushed the hair from her eyes. She felt tired, too tired to talk. "Ja, it's like I said, Inspector. For the last . . . nearly two years, we weren't talking. But I just can't imagine . . . Freddie is—was—really wasn't the kind of person to make enemies."

"The farm labourers. I assume you knew some of them? The manager? The older woman who worked in the house?"

"Outanna!" Jesus, she'd clean forgotten. "Is she all right? I mean, nothing happened to her, did it?"

The policeman pursed his lips, looked down.

"But she raised Freddie and me . . . " The words dried up, and suddenly her throat felt swollen and sore. She clenched her teeth. "She did everything for us. She brought us up. My mother wasn't well."

"And the manager? De Kok?"

"No, I don't know anything about him at all. He must have come later."

"You think your sister hired him, possibly after your father's death?"

"Well, my father had been talking about selling back then. I think to a neighbour."

"Pretorius? Boet Pretorius?"

She shrugged. "He never got that far. The cancer grew too quickly. And, well, I don't know what happened after he died." She looked down at her hands again, ashamed of what this man must think of her.

"The workers?"

"As far as I can remember, there were two families, but it's like I said . . . Do you suspect any of them? Or the manager?"

He tugged awkwardly at his collar again, then took a handkerchief and wiped the sweat from his temples. Yet Sara felt strangely cold.

"We have no suspects yet, Miss Swarts. But at this stage it seems that the attackers knew that on Wednesdays the workers were off for the afternoon, with the manager and housekeeper in town on business. Your sister and her daughter were probably home alone on Wednesdays.

"It could be that the attackers watched the house for a good long while. The house being next to the road and all."

"Was Freddie raped, Inspector?"

"No, Miss Swarts. No, she wasn't. But it looks to us as if the attacker, or attackers—"

"Tell me straight, Inspector. It's better that way."

Again he tugged at his collar, gazed out the window at the heat shimmering off the tar, and then turned back to her, "It looks as if they wanted to leave a message. The way they left her. Her body was propped up against a chair. In her bedroom. In a seated position. And her hair had been cut short. Cropped to the scalp."

He paused for a moment and watched her, as if he wanted to see whether she really was as strong as she made out. "Nothing makes sense when it comes to this kind of attack. But I assure you, we're working at it flat-out. There are plenty of people with access to the farm. And your sister had several children under her care at one stage."

"God, I don't know anything about that. What do you mean—children?" Sara felt, for the umpteenth time, as if she had burst into a stranger's nightmare. Freddie, with an adopted child. Apparently four years old. Klara. And a foreman. And the strange children . . . This was a Freddie she didn't know. Would never know.

"According to my sources," said Beeslaar, "she used to foster some youngsters. Mostly from labourers' communities in the district." He waited for a reaction, then went on. "You obviously didn't . . . " The handkerchief came out again. "Sorry," he said. "The heat . . . I'm not from around here. Still getting used to it."

"But who could have borne such a huge grudge against her?"

"That's what we're going to find out, Miss Swarts."

"Can I see her?"

"Yes, of course. The autopsy still has to be concluded, hopefully before tomorrow. But you'll have to drive to Postmasburg. We had to take her there—the closest available district surgeon."

"I'll drive," she said, getting up. "I have to see my sister."

3

Beeslaar had just seen Sara Swarts off when it grabbed hold of him.

He'd felt it coming during their conversation, but put it down to the heat: the pounding heart, that stifling feeling, the sweating.

He said a quick goodbye and almost fled back to his office. He had to catch his breath, keep his head. He hadn't had a panic attack since Joburg, and had hoped he'd left them there. But now, this murder investigation.

It was the child—each time a child was involved.

His hands shook, and he felt something pressing on his lungs, making his muscles twitch—across his back, under his right eye. His face and back were dripping wet.

He took a deep breath. It's just anxiety, the shrink had told him, you can control it.

Eyes closed. Inhale. Hold for four counts, and exhale.

Stay with the breath, it will relieve the anxiety.

A jumble of images flitted through his mind. He saw the child at Huilwater, the cut throat, the blood, her eyes half open, looking at him.

They were the eyes of another child, the one in Hillbrow . . . no, the other two: shot—lying in their beds like a pair of dead pups.

Why are you always too late, Beeslaar?

He got up. He had to get out of the office. He wanted a cool spot, somewhere with air con.

A few minutes later he flopped down on a stool at the Red Dune, diagonally across from the police station. The place was dark. And, merciful Jesus, it was cool. The barman, Oom Koeks Koekemoer, presented him with an ice-cold Coke.

"Hot enough for you, Inspector?"

"Like hell itself, Oom Koeks, like hell itself," he said.

Sitting in his dark, cool corner, the thought suddenly hit him: Pretorius, the previous afternoon, when he'd called to report the murders, had spoken about being "too late." Someone else had, as well.

Then he remembered: the old housekeeper. She'd said this too.

4

An unfamiliar car was parked in front of Tannie Yvonne's house, a brand-new BMW 4×4.

Sara's heart sank. She didn't have the strength for this. She'd just managed to escape the suffocating concern of an old farmer and his wife on her way home. They'd greeted her by name, but she had no recollection of them. We knew your mother and father very well, the woman said, we were glad when Freddie came back to the farm. There are so few young people in the district, and a person doesn't know these days what will happen to the land when the old folks pass on. But that such an awful thing should happen . . . Where will it all end?

The old man had held his tearful wife's hand in silence. It's terrible, the way things are going these days, she rattled on, a person isn't safe anywhere any more. People, in their own beds . . . Her husband hushed her. For a moment the three of them stood there, searching for the right words, eyes downcast. "Just say if there's anything," the woman offered. Sara thanked them—maybe too hastily—desperate to get away, dreading all the sympathy she knew still lay ahead, the clumsy attempts at consolation. She remembered it all too clearly from her mother's funeral long ago, the mundane comforting in the face of death. Maybe even more so with one so sudden and violent. A murder, a farm murder, affected everyone in a community like this. Everyone. She could see it on the faces of these two old people. The fear, the realisation of a nightmare in their midst, as though the primal fear we all carry had loomed up from the shadows of the subconscious to confront them.

Murder. How many people in this country face news like this daily? Hundreds? She'd read somewhere there were fifty-six murders a day. And a murder out on the farm is the greatest nightmare of all—an idyllic rustic life, isolated, far from help, ending brutally, unexpectedly.

"Sara, my dear?" she heard Tannie Yvonne calling from the back stoep as she entered the house. "We're back here."

A woman with a fine face and large tired eyes got up from her chair as Sara stepped onto the stoep. She looked like she was stepping out from a Queenspark advert, all pastels and golden hair. But not quite. She lacked the femininity of a Queenspark model, that rounded fullness. She was too skinny, sinewy-skinny.

"Nelmari Viljoen," she introduced herself. Her handshake was firm. "I'm so, so sorry about your loss. It's a tremendous shock." She held Sara's hand for a moment before letting it go. "Freddie used to talk about you so much." She sat down.

"I'll get you some tea, love," Tannie Yvonne said, getting up. Sara had wanted to offer, but felt paralysed. Something rubbed against her neck and she turned around, startled. The leaf of a delicious monster, a huge dark-green thing reaching out from the nest of plants behind her, seeming to admonish her.

She shuddered and moved the chair forward, then sat down again.

She felt the woman's eyes on her, didn't know what to say. This woman: another phantom from Freddie's life, materialising.

She'd talk a lot about Nelmari. Back then, even before she moved to the farm. It had been Nelmari this and Nelmari that, ad nauseam.

Sara and Freddie spoke regularly then—most often on Sunday evenings, when off-peak calls were cheap. They'd phone each other whenever anything happened, not long conversations, but enough to know what was going on in each other's lives. Like the time Sara was promoted from the general news team, leaving behind the donkey work of chasing ambulances and road accidents, covering the unveiling of monuments and tedious social events. When she was finally promoted to the environmental team.

But the major changes were in Freddie's life. She held her first exhibition somewhere in Melville, a modest affair at a friend's house—where she met someone who convinced her she should be a full-time artist. Freddie had sounded entranced. She's a businesswoman, she said excitedly. One of Joburg's top businesswomen. And she wanted to introduce the world to Freddie's work.

Freddie was ecstatic. And the next thing Sara heard, she'd resigned from her teaching post to concentrate on her art.

"It's so unreal," she heard Nelmari say next to her, startling her from her reverie. "I simply can't believe it. Not Freddie. She, well, she was like . . . she was my best friend. I don't have any family, you know."

Sara had no idea how to respond, looked away.

"You've just been to the police," Nelmari said. She sat with her legs crossed, hands in her lap.

Sara wanted to say yes, but couldn't form the word. She didn't know where to begin with all the questions she had about Freddie. This person, after all, was closer to Freddie than anyone she knew.

"Do they have any leads yet?" Though breathy and warm, Nelmari's voice was tense.

Sara shook her head, cursing her muteness.

"Is there something I can do? Help you with, perhaps?"

"Thanks," she heard herself whisper. Then, more loudly, she said, "I mean, there's nothing I can think of now. I only just got here. I don't even know yet myself."

"I still have to go see Inspector Beeslaar myself. He asked me to help locate the foster kids, to find Klara's mother and so on," said Nelmari.

"Tell me about Klara."

"There isn't much to tell. Her mother worked picking grapes on one of the riverside farms. An alcoholic. Drifted around doing odd jobs. At one stage she disappeared. I don't even know if she's still alive. There's no father, as far as I know. I mean, the mother didn't exactly know who he was. Klara was an FAS child. Foetal Alcohol Syndrome," she explained. "She landed up with Freddie a year ago—straight out of hospital. She'd been badly neglected, malnourished. Freddie got permission to take Klara into foster care for a while. She really grew to love her, and started offical adoption proceedings."

Tannie Yvonne arrived at the door with a tinkling tray and Nelmari got up to give her a hand.

"Heavens, Yvonne, I didn't realise you were making some for me too. I'm in a hurry, actually. Things are really hectic. We're about to start building at Red Sands, and everything's on a knife edge now."

"Ag, it's okay, Nelmari. Sara and I will have it," the older woman said.

"I might come by again later. Everything is in such a state, and as it is I've been away the last two days."

She reached for a pale-blue leather handbag—the same shade as her shoes—and stood up. A diamond glittered at her neck, and she wore diamond studs in her ears, Sara noticed. On her fingers, a sapphire solitaire and a simple gold ring. A designer watch hung loosely from her wrist.

"Sara," she said, looping the bag over her shoulder, "I'll come by again later this evening. In the meantime, please don't hesitate to call if you need anything. I'd really like to help. It's the least . . . " Her eyes glittered with tears.

Sara managed a hoarse "thank you" before Nelmari gave

her a peck on the cheek and disappeared into the house, her perfume lingering behind her.

"I didn't realise she looked like that," said Sara, watching as Tannie Yvonne slowly poured tea from her cup into her saucer.

"Yes," she said, blowing ripples on the tea to cool it, drinking from the saucer. "She isn't exactly the type you'd expect around here. She's so neat, so groomed. But she has a head on those shoulders, I can tell you that." She poured the last of the tea into the saucer and put it on the floor for the dogs. "A better friend you surely couldn't find. She and Freddie really were like—" she paused, "sisters."

The word hissed in Sara's head.

5

Beeslaar caught Oom Koeks's eye. It was too early for spirits, but he was certainly ready for the Tafel Lager—which was handed to him in a white mug. He took a sip and sank gratefully into his corner. He liked the gloom in here. He was still struggling to get used to the strange over-exposure of small-town life. The never-ending greetings, the interminable pleasantries. The extravagant pleasure with which the farming community had welcomed him—as if he were the messiah they'd all been waiting for. Still, he could understand it: there was little excitement here, just a handful of constables sorting out the winos and the wife beaters.

The last detective had left two years before—he'd taken a package. So, in more serious matters the Upington branch stepped in, with all the accompanying frustrations.

Until Beeslaar arrived. Then two constables were kicked upstairs to him, with new ranks and all: Johannes "Janus" Ghaap and Gershwin "Ballies" Pyl.

Hell, he missed the city. Especially on days like this. He missed its anonymity, the vast facelessness you could just disappear into.

His cellphone chirped. Sergeant Ghaap saying he was back at the office. Quite something, this Ghaap, he thought as he ended the call. Still keeping his distance from Beeslaar, two months down the line. Spoke only when he had to. A bit of a closed book. Born in the district, he spoke slowly, his Northern Cape accent flattening his Afrikaans As and Os, as if the corners of his mouth were permanently attached to his ears with a pair of rubber bands.

Beeslaar smiled at this, slipped the phone back into his shirt pocket, and glanced over the edge of his glass at a chubby young man who had just ambled in through the swing doors.

Polla Pieterse, he saw, and slid down in his seat. He'd soon learnt to give Polla a wide berth. A big blond fatso who farmed alongside his father and brothers, he was one of the reasons Beeslaar preferred to avoid the bar over busy weekends, especially in the evenings. Because for guys like Polla—and there were plenty like him—a white policeman was either a bosom buddy or a sell-out. And he'd make his view loudly known, especially after a stiff drink or three.

The man had barely sat down at the counter when a woman called from the door, "Polla, where's your buddy?"

It was Nelmari Viljoen, but she didn't come in, just stood at the door of the Red Dune. The only bar in a hundred-kilometre radius, the place reeked of beer, and with its touristy African-style decor, it clearly wasn't the kind of place for a woman like her.

An interesting woman: pretty, but not in any way flirtatious. A businesswoman, and a successful one at that. A self-made millionaire, apparently, with irons in every conceivable fire. An estate agency here, one in Upington, and one in Kimberley too. But her flagship business was in her hometown, Joburg, he'd heard. With the Northern Cape being punted as the next tourist mecca, after Cape Town and the Kruger Park, she was sure to be first in line for commission on all the property that changed hands for new developments and playgrounds for the rich.

"Sorry, Miss Viljoen." Polla rolled his Rs, spoke in a slow drawl. It made him sound like a slow-witted child. "Don't know where he's got to. But while you're here, can't I order you a little something?"

"No thanks, I have work to do. Please tell Buks I'm looking for him."

Buks Hanekom was a young farmer, recently returned to the district to take over his father's farm. A clever chap, at first glance, but Beeslaar suspected his heart wasn't in farming. He spent far too much time in town, at the Red Dune in particular.

They said he was racking up debt. Maybe he'd already sold the old man's land to Nelmari. That would make sense; not much money in farming around here any more, he'd been told.

In his two months here, Beeslaar had had to learn a good deal about the area and local farming operations. The land, he knew, could handle sheep and cattle, but the lack of water and the unreliable rainfall made it high risk. The only farmers who made money were those close to the Gariep—towards Upington—who farmed grapes and stone fruit. The rest were just small-scale, or they'd turned to hunting and game tourism for the foreign market. He knew of one or two of these guys, farther into the Kalahari, towards Namibia. And, of course, there was Boet Pretorius.

His thoughts turned to the chaos in the farmhouse the day before. And that poor lovestruck fool Pretorius. Someone, somewhere, had mentioned he and Freddie were planning to get married . . . What was he "too late" for?

"Yes-yes-yes, what do you say!" The jovial voice interrupted his thoughts.

It was Buks Hanekom, his stocky body brimming with energy and enthusiasm. He walked in as if he owned the place, gave a satisfied grin as he caught his reflection in the Castle mirrors behind the counter.

"Howzit, Paulie-boy?" he said, slapping Polla between the shoulder blades before hopping onto a bar stool next to him.

"No, kwaai, boet," Polla answered, his face a happy moon. In contrast with Polla Pieterse, Hanekom was well groomed, his striped blue shirt tucked neatly into khaki shorts. Expensive Australian walking boots, and matching leather hat. Ray-Bans. His red-brown moustache and hair were neatly trimmed.

"Pour my good friend here your coldest Castle, Oom Koeks," Polla gushed, and the barman silently stooped to open the under-counter fridge. "On my tab."

He had to get out of here, Beeslaar decided, before they saw him and started getting chatty. Everyone wanted to add their two cents' worth about the case. And everyone had a gripe to air.

He hesitated, about to drain his glass, when Hanekom cornered him.

"Afternoon, Inspector."

He stuck out his hand and Beeslaar glumly heaved himself up for the greeting.

"Any news yet?"

"We're making progress, yes."

"I just want you to know we're behind you all the way," he said.

Beeslaar raised an eyebrow in acknowledgement.

"We've rounded up a whole bunch of guys from the old commando. Informal, you know. But we've been out patrolling the whole district since last night. We really want to help. We'll bring any suspicious persons straight to you."

"Suspicious persons? What are you talking about, Mr. Hanekom?"

"We can't allow this . . . this atrocity. Can't you see what's happening here, Inspector? Suddenly we're being told all white-owned land is stolen land. Then come the robbers. Robbing us blind. They start terrorising and murdering our workers. And then they start looking for the soft targets, our women and children. It's nothing but a blatant attempt to wipe us out, get us off the land."

Beeslaar said nothing.

"Do you know how many farmers have been murdered in this country?" Hanekom's face reddened. "I'll tell you. Two thousand, if not more. More people than were killed in the Angolan war! And I can tell you one thing: we're not going to sit around twiddling our thumbs, watching our people being murdered off their land!"

Beeslaar picked up his glass. He had better drink something cool before he lost his temper. This was just what he needed: a bunch of men with far more hormone-fuelled emotion than brains. He took a sip, put the glass down, slowly and deliberately.

"Mr. Hanekom, I can understand that people are upset. But this is a police case now. And we're doing everything—"

"Upset! That's not quite the word, Inspector." He stooped over the table, his face so close that Beeslaar could smell his cherry chewing gum. "We've become a target, you know that, hey? We, the farmers of this country, and it doesn't look as if anyone could give a flying fuck. All those people overseas who yelled blue murder over apartheid. Where are they now? You know, it's only news if it's a white man supposedly abusing human rights. But I've got news for you: we aren't going to sit quietly and watch while our people get slaughtered in their own homes."

Beeslaar leaned away. "Look, Mr. Hanekom, I'm not sure exactly what you're threatening. But if you take the law into your own hands, you're breaking it. And then you'll have *me* to deal with. I can understand that people want to see quick results. But it's the police's work—"

"Ja-ja. In the meantime our farmers are dying like flies. And it just couldn't bother you lot. I'll say it again, we've had it up to *here*. We're being beaten down bit by bit. And we're not allowed to do anything. Shut up, and yes sir, no sir. Our God-given rights to defend ourselves and our homes are being taken away, one after the other. Our guns are being taken from us, the commando system's kaput, and now there are laws that can force us off our land Zimbabwe-style."

"That law hasn't been passed."

"For now. But you and I know it will come again. Because it's part of a bigger plan to force us whites off the land." He took a breath, "No one is going to take away our democratic right to protect our people and our possessions. That I can promise you."

Beeslaar had had enough. He stood up, nearly tipping the glass over. Drawing himself up to his full height—all 1.95 metres of it—he took quiet satisfaction as Hanekom stepped back. Who said size doesn't matter? he thought, knocking back a last gulp and banging the glass down on the table.

"I have to go now, Mr. Hanekom," he said as calmly as he could. "I have work to do. And if my deductions are correct, you have an appointment yourself. With Nelmari Viljoen. So let me give you some good advice. You and all the ex-commando boys should just go back home and leave the policing to the police. Okay?"

With that, he walked over to the counter, gave Oom Koeks a twenty-rand note, and told him to keep the change. Polla Pieterse was left gaping.

Behind him were two new arrivals, men who cast their eyes down as Beeslaar walked past.

What was it, he wondered as he strode through the swing doors, that flickered in Hanekom's eyes when he'd mentioned Nelmari Viljoen?

6

F riday morning, not yet eight o'clock, but the sun was already white hot.

Beeslaar wiped his brow with a handkerchief. Christ, when would he get used to this heat? Worst of all was the relentlesness of it—every goddamn day. A "cool" day in these parts was apparently anything below forty degrees. And people reckoned this was rather a tame summer, what with the odd thunderstorm giving relief.

His two colleagues, sitting across the desk from him, appeared unfazed by the weather. Eland blood, that's what they had. He'd been told by a local that this majestic antelope was able to cool down its blood, preventing its brain from boiling. Or something like that. Unless it wasn't the eland after all? Could be a bloody kudu, for all he knew. They all looked the same to him.

Beeslaar peered from under his brows at the two men sifting through their notes. There were patches of raw skin on Pyl's neck where he'd scraped some pimples with his razor. He was young, barely twenty-three. His slight stature, along with the oversized suit, made him look even younger. A short-arse with an overdeveloped Adam's apple.

But quick, and keen.

Johannes Ghaap was a year or so older, but his body told a different story, as if he'd already done a lot of living. He had a dark complexion and a tall, strong build, with a fleshy face and a dented nose. Looked like he'd had his fair share of bar fights.

Unlike Ballies Pyl, he wasn't wearing a suit, didn't give a damn about convention. His usual outfit consisted of khaki trousers, a short-sleeved shirt and a pair of sturdy boots. He was unhurried, cool, looked bored most of the time. And unlike Pyl, who constantly fidgeted, Ghaap's movements were deliberate, slothlike, as if everything was an effort. People called him "Jah-nis"—the name stretched out, so leisurely, as if the quick triple syllable of "Johannes" might somehow offend him.

Both of them rookies with zero experience, and he now had the pleasure of training them. Beeslaar the nursemaid—Nanny McPhee minus the moustache.

"Okay," he said, "what do you have for me?"

Pyl picked up the stack of papers he'd placed neatly on Beeslaar's desk. Only to put them down again. Some fluttered to the ground. He dived after them. Then he tore a page out of his notebook and frowned at it.

Beeslaar sighed inwardly.

"Go down yesterday's list, Sergeant, starting with De Kok. You went back to him and checked his alibi. By the way, please remember, both of you, we write short, clear reports from the information we gather. And for the love of God, don't forget the time and date. And you don't leave the report in your book. Everything goes in the murder file. Every day. Just like I explained."

Pyl cleared his throat and began, "Yesterday morning at oh-nine-hundred hours I was at Huilwater, where I saw Mr. Adam De Kok at his home. I asked him . . . "

"You don't have to read out the statement, just give the main points, Sergeant."

Pyl's Adam's apple bobbed up and down a couple of times. Then he continued, "I questioned him again, Inspector, but his story hasn't changed. He was in town the whole morning and only went home after two in the afternoon. Oubaas Bekker from the trading store has confirmed that De Kok was at his shop at about eleven. He dropped off the old lady—the house-keeper, Mrs. Johanna Beesvel. Apparently De Kok and Mrs. Beesvel do the farm's shopping there most Wednesday mornings. The people at the co-op have confirmed De Kok was there. Jan Regopstaander, senior salesman, says De Kok was loading up some draad . . . "

"Loading what?" Beeslaar was baffled by Pyl's Northern Cape accent.

"Draad—fencing, mos. That's what the two workers, Lammer van der Merwe and, er . . . " He rustled through his papers. "Dawid Tieties. That's what they were busy doing the afternoon of the murder—fencing. You remember, Inspector? De Kok and I went to fetch them from the camp where they were working, so that they could give their statements. Nè?"

As Beeslaar waved his hand impatiently, Pyl put the page aside and went on. "De Kok was loading up fencing that was ordered a month before. And dose—I've got the name here." He leafed through his notebook. "Where's it? Okay, here: Terimi—I don't know how you say it. It's for worms, for sheep worms, or something."

"Just go on, Pyl, otherwise we'll still be sitting here at midnight."

"Right. And he loaded up two twenty-five-litre cans of paraffin and a drum of diesel. He also filled up the bakkie with petrol. Old Oom Niklaas Vegter, at the pumps, says he thinks De Kok left there after twelve. Then he went back to the shop to pick up Mrs. Beesvel and the week's groceries."

Jesus, if Pyl decided to read that list out too, Beeslaar was going to jump out the window. But he reined in his impatience and said, "Good, and the rest of the story, you got that confirmed too?"

Pyl leaned forward. "De Kok did go back to the shop, like Mr. Bekker says. He bought some personal things too, toothpaste and—"

"Right, right, so De Kok's story checks out. Thank you, thorough work. Where did he go afterwards?"

"The bank. Him and the old lady. Mrs. Januarie, the bank manager or whatever she is—she's the only one there, you know—she confirmed they were there with her. And she remembers the time, because it was just before she had to close up for lunch and it was quite busy in the bank because there were lots of farmers in town that morning, and she was worried she'd have to chase everyone out before closing time, and the farmers get cross if they have to wait till two o'clock when she opens up again. Pretorius was at the front of the queue, very impatient, she said, and she helped him just before she closed up to go eat." He paused.

"But De Kok, Sergeant. What about De Kok?"

"Er . . . yes, he was one of those she turned away and so he was back again just after two, and he asked for bank statements for the farm accounts and drew money from his personal account, and applied for a new cheque book—"

"Yes, yes. What time did they leave?"

"Soon afterwards, because, you know, nè, they got back to the farm just after we arrived."

"What do we know about De Kok?"

Pyl glanced at Ghaap, but there was no reaction, so he carried on. "I don't really know him much, but people say he grew up wild, though you wouldn't know it looking at him these days, and also because he's so full—"

"What do you mean, 'grew up wild'?" Beeslaar interrupted.

"No, I mean, you see, he's an opregte Boesman. His people are from the deep desert, there, Botswana-side, and they say he was still wearing skins and eating ants until just the other day. Now they say he eats with silver knives and spoons. Which he got from overseas. And he acts all stuck-up, you know, all fancy-like, he's too good for poor people, hanging out with the white people now. And just the other day he was still a true baboon."

Clearing his throat again, Pyl carried on. "I've already talked to the workers on the two farms next door. Those farms aren't as close to the main road as Huilwater, so they don't often see strangers. But they're scared, Inspector, they're scared."

Beeslaar tapped his pen.

"It's the white people . . . " Pyl looked at Beeslaar with big eyes, until the inspector gestured at him to go on.

"They say yesterday some white farmers were going around, questioning all the workers. I heard this from people next door to Huilwater, and also from ones across the road. It looks like they've got guns and they are treating the people kind of rough. Have you heard anything about it, Inspector?"

"I know about them, yes." He gave a brief account of his altercation with Hanekom. "Right or wrong," he said, "emotions are running high. And Wednesday's thing, on top of the stock theft and the murders of two weeks ago—it stirs up feelings."

Question is, he thought to himself, where do you draw the line? How far do you allow things to go before you step in? Arresting Hanekom now would just whip up emotions even further. Especially if he himself—the only white face at this station—were to do it. If you're too tough, you're the white cop trying to crawl up the black bosses' arses. Leave things be, and you give men like Hanekom the impression they can carry on regardless. And the black bosses paint you as a closet racist.

"It's the commandos," Ghaap suddenly said, abandoning his doodling that had been occupying him. "I think it's ever since the commandos were disbanded that the farmers have been so moerig."

Beeslaar mulled this over: the farmers' resentment at the loss of their apartheid-era civil-defence units. Then he said, "Ja, probably, but it's not the whole story. And that's where we come into the picture: me and you and Pyl. These people feel they're being squeezed from all sides. By the economy, by politicians and by crime. And you've seen the damage our lot of stock thieves have caused, how many farmers have been financially wrecked because of it. And now it's come to murder. The Jacobs brothers a few weeks ago. And on Wednesday, the mother and child at Huilwater. So."

He looked at the two men in front of him, wondered if he was wasting his breath, but pressed on. "The commandos are an old issue. Like the politics that went along with it. But the bottom line stays the same. Firstly, we can't allow vigilante action here. People are looking for a quick fix, and they want to fight. But—and this is my second point—the quickest way *we*," he pointed at himself and at each of them, "can defuse this thing, is to put the perpetrators behind bars. And in the meantime we make sure no more innocent people get hurt. So, Sergeant Pyl, did you find out yesterday if there was any kind of intimidation or bullying going on?"

"No, Inspector. Nobody's talking. They complain the boere are rough, but nobody's prepared to lay a charge. Also . . . " He seemed to be putting his thoughts in order, "What I meant to say . . . There's other stuff scaring the people. They say it's the, er, Bantus. And they're saying the Bantus are going to kill the lot of *them* too."

"I hope you tell them this thing is not about race. It's crime. Plain and simple. These kinds of attackers are nervous, inexperienced robbers. And if they feel threatened, they kill—doesn't matter who comes along—and often it's a labourer. But whatever the case, it's not a question of race."

He punctuated his point with a brief silence.

"What about feelings towards the deceased?" he continued. "A grudge, maybe, someone who felt hard done by? Maybe she chased them off the farm? Someone owing her money?"

"No, Inspector. She had a good name among the people. I also went looking for the drifters and the karretjiemense. They spend their nights at the roadside with their donkey carts, you know, so they see everything. But I couldn't find a soul. Maybe it's all the angry farmers charging up and down—you just don't fuck with a bebliksemde boer. Never mind one that's swinging a rifle."

Ghaap came to life again. His voice was deep and gravelly, like an old smoker's. "Huilwater's people are talking about other things that scared them too."

"Like what?"

"Witchcraft, the tokoloshe, stuff like that." He opened his notebook and looked at something he'd written down. "They're talking about someone visiting the farm, the kind of person that throws bones, stuff like that."

"A sangoma? What for?"

"Couldn't say. They're so scared that every one of them has packed up and left the farm. Now they're sitting with the Chicken Vale lot in town, with the coloureds. Mrs. Tieties, she's the woman that works in the kitchen at Huilwater with Mrs. Beesvel, you see. She says that's where all the trouble started." He was quiet a moment. "But you don't get much out of them either. They're still all mixed up and deurmekaar about Wednesday's stuff. But from what I've heard, a sangoma came, a few months ago. They didn't like that at all. But De Kok and the old lady, Mrs. Beesvel, said they shouldn't worry. That it was just the lady farmer and her funny ways. She just wanted to make a painting of him, they said, with all his bones and beads and goeters. Said she liked the old ways, Miss Swarts. But she was wrong if she thought that old witch doctor could keep her safe . . . "

"And what happened to him?"

Ghaap shrugged. "Who knows? But old lady Beesvel—to me she looks *really* scared when I ask about it. Almost hysterical. She keeps saying she saw it coming. Evil. Blood. Over and over. But she doesn't say what or how."

"Do you know if she's had any medical help?"

Ghaap shrugged, "I don't know, Inspector."

"Is she also in town now?" asked Beeslaar.

"With her sister, Sanna van Wyk, over in Chicken Vale."

"Stay close to her. These housekeepers always know things. She may be the only one who really has an idea of what's been going on at Huilwater. Ask the sister if she can take her to the clinic. She needs to get well—she's got to talk to us."

Ghaap looked up and said, "Don't know if this is something or nothing, but I was in the township late afternoon, Mma Mokoena's shebeen, while you were gone to Postmasburg. I wanted to hear if anyone had noticed any strangers, you see, the stock-theft problem. Then someone mentioned Mma Mokoena's rich Joburg boyfriend. A Minora, they say."

"A *what*?"

"Sharp-sharp, like a blade. No one knows anything about him, except that he's throwing money around like mielies. Might be nothing, but that's all I've heard about strangers around here."

"Good work," said Beeslaar. "Could be our first lead in the stock-theft case. And God knows, we need something desperately. Those buggers are making fools of us. Sergeant Pyl, I want you to do your rounds *again* today. You take the Golf and go for a drive—"

His phone rang. The Swarts girl was in the charge office and wanted a quick word. "Hold on," he told the two men opposite him. "I'll be back in a minute."

7

Tannie Yvonne had offered to accompany Sara to the mortuary in Postmasburg. Before they set off on the hundred-and-twenty-kilometre journey, they stopped at the undertakers in town.

"I'll go in so long and ask if there's someone who can see us," said Tannie Yvonne. "You can wait out here and catch your breath. You looked like a ghost when you walked out of that police station."

Sara was grateful for her calm presence. She was scared of what lay ahead. The policeman had warned her: Freddie might look very different from the way Sara remembered her.

The thought of Freddie dead was still unreal. Everything around her felt unreal—familiar, but strange: the oppressive sun, the cicadas shrieking relentlessly. It felt as if it came out of your own head, that ringing. The town's desolate streets, the withered trees—the municipality seemed to have decided to stop watering them at some point. Here and there a hardy karee tree clung on, but the blue gums and syringas stood like skeletons. Across the street a ragtag group hung around in the shadow of a shop verandah, watching her with interest. So typical of country towns, she thought, the clusters of people hanging around in front of the bottle store or general dealer. Skinny, dirty creatures with worn-out shoes and tatty clothes. The women crowing with laughter at some remark, their mouths wide open and toothless. Or shouting drunken abuse at someone down the road.

Today their lives had been intensified somehow by someone else's murder. As Sara got out of the car, they stared with open curiosity, muttering among themselves, with one woman jutting a chin in her direction as she harshly shushed her wailing children.

Sara gave a tight smile, nodded a greeting, and deferentially they all inclined their heads. Then she walked over to Van Zyl & Van Zyl Funeral Services.

8

Beeslaar mopped the sweat from the back of his neck before sitting down at his desk again. He had just said goodbye to the sister of the deceased. She was on her way to Postmasburg and wanted to know where the mortuary was. He'd have offered to accompany her if it wasn't so bloody far. Just driving there and back would have gobbled up more than three hours of his day. And he'd already spent the whole of the previous goddamn day there for the autopsies.

The Swarts girl seemed to be made of stern stuff, he thought. And though she was small—just a touch over one and a half metres—she was not as delicate as her dead sister.

But this morning she'd seemed off-colour. Her green eyes were red-rimmed, dazed, as if she'd spent the night staring at something terrifying.

Beeslaar stretched out his arms and supressed a yawn. His chest was still tight—the combination of the heat, a sleepless night, yesterday's autopsies, the tension, perhaps. Making him yawn repeatedly, like a dying chick.

He leaned forward, elbows on the desk, his chin resting on his hands. Back to business.

"All right," he said to the two sergeants. "Where were we? Motives. What does the murder scene tell us? Let's look beyond the obvious for a moment, past the easy target and the stock thieves. First thing we ask: What does the murder scene tell us?"

"Revenge," said Pyl. "Like, like . . . that guy in the Free

State. The one we read about in *Rapport*?" He gave Beeslaar a questioning look, but didn't wait for an answer. "It was a hell of a big story. Ugly. Definitely revenge, an eye for an eye. The son of a labourer, see. The farmer killed the father a long time ago. Or that's what people thought, because the man just vanished one day. Never to be seen again. But the family kept believing it was the farmer who did it. Meantime, the son grew up. And one day he came back and ambushed the farmer. First he strangled him. Then he cut open his stomach. And then he took him and hung him from the windpomp upside down! The farmer was still alive when someone found him there. But then he died." Pyl's eyes leapt excitedly from Beeslaar to Ghaap. "An eye for an eye, and a tooth for a tooth," he finished triumphantly.

"Well, right," said Beeslaar, somewhat disconcerted. "That might be a good place to start. The murder scene tells us a story, a history. It tells us what happened. And it also tells us what didn't happen, so let's start with that. For example: the woman was not attacked by strangers. That's clear. Yesterday's autopsy confirmed it. There are no signs she fought back, or of any other trauma such as a blow to the head. It's as if she sat down willingly for the perpetrator. Did she take drugs? I don't think so. There wasn't even a Disprin in that house. And why would she have drugged the child too, *and* the three dogs? Next question: Who was it she knew well enough to let the person in willingly? Our stock thieves? Let's assume the answer is no. Okay, who then? Who were the people who came by regularly? Let's start with them."

He turned to Pyl, instructing him, "Start with a list of the foster kids. Who are they, how old are they? Everything. Did any of them have a reason to feel hard done by, unjustly treated? And remember, everything comes back here."

He tapped the file that was open in front of him. In the old days, they'd called this dusty brown docket a "donkey." This one was still slim, just a handful of A4 sheets with statements. The fingerprints and crime-scene photos were still coming. Also the autopsy reports. And more statements, case notes, reports.

How many of these damn things had he compiled in his life? Mountains of them.

And the flood of adrenaline when you have your man and you get to hand over your donkey, fat and flawless, into the hands of a state prosecutor. That hunger, that flame, undimmed by lack of sleep, dismal pay or the hours of drudgery in compiling reports to build up a file like this.

Where had that flame gone? Was it even flickering now?

"All right. Now we've got statements from each of the farm lot. They've been checked and cross-checked. And everything checks out?"

Ballies Pyl nodded enthusiastically, but Ghaap stood immobile.

"What about the computer, did either of you look at it?"

Ghaap gestured towards Pyl. "He's the expert."

"Ja," Pyl said, "I went through it. I think they only used it for bookkeeping, because that's all I could find. No Internet, so no email. Just rows of numbers showing stock sales and so on."

"Right. Then we broaden our search. I'll be talking to Pretorius again today. And hopefully a few other people who regularly visited the farm. Ghaap, you stick to the old lady, Mrs. Beesvel. We'll meet up here again sometime today—let's say lunchtime—and compare notes. We need to get to the next question: the chaos in the woman's bedroom. Was it just a random search, or were the perpetrators looking for something in particular? Why did the victims have their throats cut? Why did the child have to be killed too? But we mustn't lose sight of the link with the stock thieves. Keep turning over every stone you come across. Ghaap, you go talk to the old auntie, I want to know everything that went on at that farm. And try and get hold of your Minora man—your sharp guy from Joburg."

Ghaap merely looked blank, but Pyl scribbled furiously.

"Any questions?"

"The drugs," Ghaap said in his slow, deliberate manner. "I'm talking about the drugs the victims were given. You won't find that kind of stuff around here. Our people's poison is still alcohol and dagga, nè? The cheapest. Some tik, at best. And ja, sometimes you'll see a white pipe, but even Mandrax is hard to find around here. People are too poor for hard drugs."

"But you never know what Mma Mokoena's fancy boy might be peddling here, huh?"

"What drug do you think it was?"

"I'd put my money on roofies. It could take months before we get something on paper from the lab in Pretoria. In the meantime, I'm pretty sure the Postmasburg doc's prelim will confirm it."

Pyl looked puzzled.

"Rohypnol," explained Beeslaar. "The date-rape drug. It paralyses the victim, but without knocking them out. Just remember, these murders are now priority number one, but we don't lose sight of the two previous ones, or of the stock theft."

As they started gathering up their things, Pyl reminded Beeslaar of the TV team on its way to do a story on the murders.

"You talk to them, Sergeant Pyl."

"Me!"

"Yes, you. I have other things to do. You just tell them we're making good progress and we're leaving no stone unturned in our investigation, et cetera, et cetera."

"But—"

"And then you refer them to Superintendent Mogale in Upington or the official spokesperson in Kimberley, okay?"

"But it was the media guy in Kimberley in the first place—"

Beeslaar leaned forward and Pyl recoiled.

"Listen, I don't have time for the bloody media. Wherever they stick their noses in, things turn messy. You just tell them there are no suspects yet, but we're following various leads. And that's it. If they give you shit, refer them to the super."

"O Jirre, I forgot!" Pyl sat up again. "The super—he phoned early this morning and asked that you call him back as soon as possible. On his cell. He says he's on his way here."

Beeslaar waved the two men to the door.

Once they were out, he allowed himself a deep sigh. The superintendent. Nice. Just what he needed to brighten up his day.

9

Sara closed her eyes a moment, allowing them to adjust to the dimness of the funeral director's office. It was typical of these old buildings, she remembered, this darkness. They were built in the days before electric fans and air conditioning, when small windows and thick walls were the best defence against the heat.

Tannie Yvonne was talking to a woman at a desk. All around were funeral wreaths, and coffins were on display on the floor.

"Oh, my dear girlie," the woman said when she spotted Sara. "My deepest, deepest sympathy for your loss." She approached with outstretched arms, and hugged her tightly. "It's so terrible, so terrible. I knew your mother and father when you two were still tiny little things," she said into Sara's hair. When she stepped away, she wiped at her nose and eyes with a scrunched-up tissue, took Sara by the arm and led her back to the desk.

"One feels so defeated," she said once they'd sat down. "I just said to Yvonne, a person isn't safe anywhere any more. And where do you run to? We can't *all* go off to Australia. And a government that allows these crimes! They just couldn't be bothered. Because we're white, of course. They keep saying we're a rainbow nation now, and the past is forgotten. But they leave the criminals to kill off the lot of us, one by one." She picked up a cigarette from an ashtray and took a drag, her eyes closed as if she were sending prayers to heaven.

Sara tried to think of something to say, but her mind had stalled.

"My son in Pretoria has been hijacked twice. Each time they took off with his car," the woman continued, blowing smoke from her nose. "Only thing the police have to say is he should be glad he's still alive. And, Lord knows, one *is* happy. But what kind of life is this? The last time his little boy was with him in the car. The child is so traumatised. He doesn't eat, doesn't speak, wets his bed. And my son . . . " Again she inhaled, her eyes closed, her mouth a wrinkled red pout. Then she stubbed out the cigarette and took a receipt book from a drawer.

"You don't have to worry about your sister and the poor little one, you hear. We'll see to it that they get brought back from Postmasburg, and we'll take care of all the funeral arrangements. You don't have to worry about a thing. In whose name do I open the account?" She opened the book and moved a sheet of carbon paper into place.

After what felt like an eternity, everything had been noted and signed, and Sara could flee.

They sat in silence for most of the drive to Postmasburg, with Tannie Yvonne pointing at a signpost here and there to say something about the farm owners. As they got closer to the town, the landscape changed. The red sand and thorn trees gradually gave way to a whiter, limey soil studded with stones and dwarflike trees—witgatwortels, Sara remembered: shepherd's trees. Her father had always said that the early farmers made coffee from the roots. Farther along, the landscape changed again: shrub veld with black dolerite rock—hence all the iron and manganese mines in the region.

Dear God, it felt like a lifetime since she'd left this place.

How many years had it been? Each Christmas, that dull ache she couldn't give a name to. She had missed . . . What?

Certainly not the farm. Not the bad-tasting brackish water.
Not this unforgiving landscape. Not Pa. Their awkward telephone conversations once every few months had been difficult
enough. Hardly a motivation to spend Christmas in this place.
Freddie had made the effort more often. But she—she'd made
excuses. Maybe it had been the one good Christmas she'd
missed. There had been a tree, and Ma and Pa had been cheerful, and nobody had been ill. Ma had been her old self again,
fully present, exuberant even. And there had been gifts, and Pa
saying they'll eat proper braaivleis like boere. No turkey, none
of those English dishes, no steamed puddings with coins inside
that could break the kids' teeth. And Ma quipping that den-
tists need to make a living too, and Pa saying they could make
a living off the rich, there were enough of *them*. Their
Christmas tree had been a thorn-tree branch, there were no
pine trees around here. Ma had painted it white, and Freddie
had decorated it with ribbons and angels they had made out of
paper . . .

At Postmasburg, they followed the signs to the hospital,
where Sara found parking in the shade of a blue gum.
"You're sure now, child, that you want to look at her?"
asked Tannie Yvonne.
"I have to. I want to see her with my own eyes," Sara said,
but without much conviction, as she opened her door.

10

It was the best-looking farmstead he had ever seen. Not that he was an expert. His notion of lovely or ugly was formed in the mining towns of the East Rand, all that brick and slasto. And after that, the police street in Fordsburg. But not even that could completely blind him to beauty.

And it *was* beautiful, Beeslaar decided as he got out of the car. A wide wrap-around verandah, several chimneys suggesting a multitude of fireplaces inside, the outside walls a pale sandstone. The garden was shaded by a row of blue gums, the bark of each tree peeling away quite artistically. A big fountain. A fan-shaped stairway leading up to the wide verandah.

Very grand.

The double doors of glass and wood swung open, and the gigantic figure of Boet Pretorius stepped outside. Looking a lot more imposing than he had at Huilwater in the aftermath of his gruesome discovery. Dark-blond curls, amber eyes, the Camel Man in farmer's guise. Minus the moustache.

His handshake was hard and calloused. He led Beeslaar to two large rattan easy chairs and a low coffee table with legs of polished gemsbok horn on the verandah.

"Your place is really something," Beeslaar remarked once they had taken a seat.

"Ja," Pretorius said, his gaze far off. "A lot of sweat went into it."

For a while the two sat, surveying the landscape of sand and grass the shade of a lion's mane. Nearby blue gum trees were blue-grey under the onslaught of the sun.

"How long have you been here?"

"About four, five years."

"But you're not from around here?"

"No, hell, I didn't inherit; I had to buy my way in here. I hear you're from the Joburg area too?"

"East Rand."

"Hmm, yes. My father was a miner in Benoni." He smiled wryly.

"I have a few routine questions," said Beeslaar, taking out his notebook.

Pretorius was impassive.

"Wednesday. Where were you that morning, and why did you head out to Huilwater?"

Pretorius sat up and looked askance at Beeslaar, a frown on his face. "But I have *already* answered your questions." Annoyance flickered in his eyes.

"I know, but you weren't really up to it then."

Pretorius looked away. When he spoke again, his voice was weary. "I was at the co-op, I had to go to the bank. Wage transfers for my labourers. I was the last one to be helped before lunchtime. I had something to eat at the Dune, left around half past one. It's about a half-hour drive. But you know all this!"

"How many workers do you have?"

"Look, I don't have any labourers' families living on the farm. That was one of the conditions when I bought the place. The families living here had to be resettled and compensated. I didn't want to be landed with all the usual social problems. I brought my own people in. Loyal, faithful, all hard workers. They're here on their own, no wives or children. No domestic violence, no borrowing money. I don't allow a drop of alcohol. And I hand-picked them myself. Pay them nearly three times the norm."

Nobody's fool, decided Beeslaar. A man with a plan, and he'll bust your balls if you get in his way.

"As I was saying," Pretorius continued, "I went to the bank, but there were problems with one or two debit orders. Then I went off to the co-op. And on my way back I stopped off at Huilwater. And, well—you know the rest."

"Right. And you're still sure you didn't notice any people or vehicles on your way there? Cars or trucks along the way, nothing like that? And the farmyard itself, when you got to Huilwater, what did it look like? What were your first impressions?"

"First impressions. Man, I'm telling you, I saw nothing and no one. And there wasn't anything like a first impression. I just came driving along. Not a soul about. The place was quiet. Completely quiet." He lowered his gaze.

"Your labourers," Beeslaar said. "How many of them are there?"

Pretorius sat up and took a deep breath, as if he was emerging from a trance. "Seven. Almost all of them Sothos. I prefer it that way. They don't mix with the locals. And one—my manager—I recruited from an agricultural college in Kimberley. Apart from them, I have a housekeeper, Mrs. September. She's the foreman's mother."

"What line of work were you in before?"

Pretorius looked at him sharply. "Irrigation."

"So there's money in that?" Beeslaar gave his surroundings an appreciative glance.

"Not if you're a snot-nose nincompoop selling crappy little sprayers and spitters to some old man with a patch of lucerne. But that's how I started out. Ever heard of McGallum Water Works?"

Beeslaar shrugged.

"I built it up from nothing. Started working for old man McGallum as a rep. Bought him out eventually. I spent my days in a shirt and tie, selling. Any damn thing that could pump or spray. Submersible pumps, turbine pumps, cylinder pumps, borehole pumps, you name it. Pipes, tanks, dam-building machinery. I dealt in everything. And by night I installed the stuff. Myself. I don't trust another man when we're talking about my name on a product."

"How long ago was this?"

"I started in the Free State, about fifteen years ago, but eventually I was doing business all over the country. I had it good. After '94, there was a lot of change. Labour laws, minimum wages, that sort of thing. More and more farmers started mechanising. And I was there to sell them the machinery. But really I wanted to farm for myself. And the moment I got the right offer I sold the whole caboodle, came here and bought this place."

He sat thinking about it a moment, but then concluded, "And that's it."

"And that's how you brought in your own workers," Beeslaar continued.

"I can vouch for each one of them. They're not your usual dirt-poor unskilled workers, the type who might steal to pay off their debts. These are men with ambition, working alongside me to build up this place. Steal? No, they sure as hell don't need to."

"You seem very certain."

"I'll stand by this. My people are far more than ordinary farmhands. Some of them spend their evenings studying to become field guides and conservationists. Once this business is established, they won't be spending their days fixing fences and running around in overalls. They'll be working with the guests. No, man, you're wasting your time if you think you need to check them out."

Beeslaar chewed at his lip. "And what about the manager?"

"The same. Him and his mother. They have family in Kimberley they visit once a month, but they don't mix with the people around here. Besides, we're far from the main road, there's the security gate, the intercom, everything. Strangers can't just come wandering in here."

"I'd like to talk to your workers anyway."

"I'm telling you. If they'd seen something, I'd know about it."

"Still . . . " Beeslaar tapped his pen on the back of his note-book. "The stock theft of the past couple of months—you've had no losses?"

"Nothing, no."

"Why has everyone around you been targeted, but not you?" He had to ask this, though he already knew the answer: security. Karrikamma had been thoroughly fenced off. Game fencing, electrified, the works.

"There are too many soft targets around me," Pretorius confirmed. "But if you want to see my people, they're out in the veld today. It'll take a while to call them in."

"What do you have in the sheds over there?" Beeslaar pointed at the three big corrugated-iron sheds about three hundred metres away. They looked new, each with large slid-ing doors and cement aprons.

"Tools, poles, cement, stuff like that. It's all temporary. I'll have to get rid of them once everything's done. I have a lot of fences still to be electrified, drinking holes to make for the game. They're an eyesore, so as soon as I'm ready to open for guests, they'll have to come down."

"Did you know the deceased well?"

Pretorius didn't answer. He took a cigarette from his shirt pocket and offered one to Beeslaar, who declined. Pretorius lit up and exhaled with a hiss. "Well enough." He said nothing more, his eyes downcast.

"Did you have a good relationship?"

Pretorius took another sharp, deep drag of the cigarette and then crushed it in an elegant glass ashtray.

He looked briefly at Beeslaar, then turned away. When he started speaking again, his voice was hoarse.

"She . . . Man, let me just say it straight. I loved her, that's no secret, but . . . We, ever since she got here, we had a good relationship. We were close friends, you could say. And I hoped it might become something more, but . . . "

"Why were you there on Wednesday?"

Pretorius ran knobbly fingers through tight, sandy-coloured curls.

"I wanted clarity. About where she stood."

"Did something specific give rise to that?"

"Man, I just wanted to talk to her."

"Was there someone else?"

His eyes narrowed. Then he shook his head—more disbelief than denial. But he said nothing.

"When you called on Wednesday afternoon, you said it was too late. What did you mean by that?"

"What?"

"On the telephone. When you called to report the murder. You spoke to me and you said you were too late."

Pretorius frowned, rubbed at his curls again.

"Jeez, did I say that? I guess, well, if I'd come earlier I could have stopped—"

"Do you think anyone had reason to want her dead?"

Another deep, slow inhalation. "Look, she had a soft heart. Very soft. But she was stubborn too. Like her father. You never knew him, but—"

"Might this stubbornness have led to some friction?"

He got a shrug as answer.

"What about the manager—De Kok?" asked Beeslaar.

Pretorius pulled a face, as if tasting something bitter. Then he snorted. "Ha. What a fuckup. Look, let me be honest with you. I don't like the guy. I think he's arrogant, too big for his boots, if you know what I mean. He was on first-name terms with Freddie and so on. But that's still no reason." He reflected a moment, running his tongue across his lips. "But if it was him, he's a fucking idiot. An arrogant idiot. He's the first person one would suspect, no?"

Beeslaar didn't react.

"Oh hell, what do I know? She was going to sell the farm until he appeared on the scene. I was interested myself, but my finances, well, this place eats money. But Freddie changed her mind all of a sudden, hired him as a manager. God knows, I hear he's got enough money to buy his own farm. But you probably know more about that than I do."

"Go on, tell me?"

"Don't know much myself. His people were genuine Bushmen. San, rather," he corrected himself. "And from what I understand, he started school late. But he's very bright, passed matric and all. Studied, and then took off to the Middle East. He worked for the oil sheikhs. Took care of falcons or racehorses, that sort of thing."

"The fact that she changed her mind about selling—how did that affect you?"

"Not enough to want to kill her, Inspector."

"What do you farm here?" asked Beeslaar.

"Game."

"Hunting, or what?"

"It'll be the biggest private game reserve in the whole of the Northern Cape, an exclusive hunters' lodge. Guests like Prince Charles, rich Americans. Eventually my place will link up with the Kgalagadi Transfrontier Park. My land stretches to the Botswana border already, but I'd like to go up all the way to the park—so that the animals can move about more freely. But . . . " His voice was flat.

"Would Huilwater have to become part of your reserve?"

"Eventually, yes. But I'll say it again: not enough to want to kill Freddie. Not that way. Not any way."

Beeslaar got up. "I or one of my men will be back later this afternoon. We'll speak to your people then," he said, and slipped the notebook back into his pocket.

11

Hang up. I'll call back!" Beeslaar shouted into his cellphone as the car clattered along the road. The connection was poor, cellphone networks weren't prepared to spend money on towers around here. There wasn't
enough of a customer base—too sparsely populated. So the
signal was limited to the odd hilltop.

Beeslaar headed towards a thorn tree at the side of the road
and hit the brakes. He punched in Ghaap's number and
waited, his elbow on the opened window. Apart from the tick-
ing of the cooling engine, it was absolutely silent. An odd sort
of stillness, he thought. As if it had personality. A presence,
almost, like somebody standing too close to you in the dark.

"Sergeant Ghaap here," the slow, heavy voice interrupted
his thoughts.

"You were looking for me."

"Inspector. Just wanted to let you know, there's someone
who saw the trucks."

At last, thought Beeslaar, another sighting of the cattle
trucks that had been noticed around the time of the thefts.

"When?"

"Three nights ago. On the R1706."

"The Huilwater road," observed Beeslaar. "Plates?"

But he knew he was asking in vain. The information thus far
had been vague, poorly followed up, and the file he had inherited was a mess. What the farmers needed here was some sort
of a formal monitoring system—some kind of permanent

neighbourhood watch to keep a close eye on traffic, keep radio contact with police stations. Some of the older farmers were already talking in that direction, Beeslaar knew.

He wanted to help, but he needed more time, had to earn more trust, and above all close this damned case. Then there was the problem of politics: farmers who suspected him of being anti-white. These recent murders—especially Wednesday's—were fuel to their fire.

"Who's your source?"

"The source?"

"Fuckit, Sergeant Ghaap, who told you this!"

"I know, I know. I'm looking for his name. It's a guy from the co-op. I just know him by his nickname, Tros. His real name is Willie. Willie Draghoender."

Beeslaar had never heard the name before—some strange reference to a chicken, he thought—and wondered fleetingly if Ghaap was pulling his leg. But there were many strange surnames out here, most of them referring to a tribal past.

"Good, good," he said to Ghaap. "Be sure to get everything from him. We want the time, description, number, which direction they came from, whether they were full or empty. Any distinguishing signs, logos, paint chips, dents. Did they look like the other trucks that were spotted? Everything. And, oh, phone Jan Steenkamp of Loeriesvlei, the chap from the Agricultural Union, and ask if he knows anything about a case of theft on Tuesday night—the night before Huilwater. I have one or two things to see to, then I'm coming in."

Where were the trucks coming from? It was as if they appeared out of nowhere before an attack. And a cattle truck was a big thing. Where would you store it? If they were coming from far away, surely someone would have noticed them. So far they had been spotted only twice: a convoy of trucks— two, three of the things at a time. Once by someone who nearly smashed into them late at night. He swore they'd been driving very fast—without lights. The other time it was a farm worker—same story with the switched-off lights, at high speed. The rest of the reports were rubbish. Someone saying the vehicles were under a spell, became invisible. There was even some poor fool who reckoned they were UFOs.

Beeslaar smiled at the thought. That same fool might be stark raving mad. But for all he knew, it could just as well have been a bunch of little green men they were dealing with here.

These guys were smooth operators, for sure. The whole thing stank of a syndicate. One with enough money for equipment and intelligence. How else did they know where to strike? How did they know how to navigate this maze of dirt roads? They had to have good inside information. But from whom? Between him and Pyl and Ghaap they had spoken to each and every one of the region's karretjiemense, as well as other migrants doing odd jobs here and there. But nothing. Maybe they'd looked in the wrong places. Maybe they needed to check the permanent workers more closely. There must be an informant somewhere.

An even bigger mystery: why here, of all places? Far from everything, from the big illegal meat markets. Far from Johannesburg, not to mention Cape Town. Kimberley was the nearest biggish city. Still, Kimberley was chickenfeed compared to the urban areas of the Rand, or the even more densely populated areas of the Vaal Triangle, Greater Johannesburg, Gauteng. So where was the outlet for this stolen stock?

Beeslaar tapped his index finger on the steering wheel.

In front of him, a swathe of grassland stretched as far as the eye could see. He passed a thorn tree, chuckled at the giant nest in it—all those sociable weavers, hundreds of them, living in what looked like a huge haystack that had been blown there by the wind. This really was a beautiful corner of the world, he had to admit. And strange. You needed true grit to survive here, people said. One year you'd wash away in a flood, and for the next six, everything shrivelled up. And then the locusts would arrive . . .

And now the syndicates. What kind of person steals live-stock? Were they a different species to drug thugs or stolen-car merchants? Or was it just the goods that differed?

Animals take time to load, they're difficult to transport, and the trucks can easily be spotted. And you have to travel on dirt roads—endless gravel. Some as smooth as tar, others sandy, or rutted with corrugations and potholes. Most roads are unmarked. Made only for the people who live here, who know where they are and where they're going. Who wouldn't run around in circles, as he so often did. Somewhere, there had to be an insider in this business.

Be that as it may. The rules of the game remained the same, whether it was city crime or rural: top-notch intelligence and the very best equipment. And nerves of steel.

He just needed to pull himself together, get a change of per-spective. Everything here was pretty much the same as in the city—even the office conditions: the old lot gone, the vacuum filled with inexperienced, untrained youngsters. Low morale, communication straight out of the school of Chinese whispers, wankers with rank.

Speaking of which . . . He remembered with a jolt that he still had to phone the superintendent.

12

Own your own piece of the Kalahari at Red Sands: Sunshine 365 days a year. Breathtaking sunsets. The rare desert lion . . .

Sara stood with her hands behind her back, gazing at the advert. With her mouth open, she realised after a while, and snapped her jaws shut. The massive poster covering one whole wall, window and all, was inviting people to invest in a piece of bare land just beyond Upington. Or at least, to her it had been a patch of barren veld up to now. Sand and dust and rock.

Nelmari Viljoen was peddling it as paradise.

Red Sands. Dear God.

The pretty receptionist suggested she take a seat, but she kept looking at the poster. She'd been feeling strange for the past forty-eight hours, though strange had just morphed into downright weird. Nelmari's office was one great praise song to the Northern Cape.

DISCOVER THE GREEN KALAHARI! read the poster. Pictures of camel thorns with those huge weaver bird nests, the green belt of the Gariep River, sweet wine from desert grapes, the Augrabies Falls, wild dogs, a giant dune, desert lions against a lurid sunset, Kimberley's Big Hole. And beneath the wall of praise, a scale model of a golf estate surrounded by the red dunes of the Kalahari—Red Sands.

Sara sat down on an easy chair covered in cream leather. An ottoman, peachy pink and also in leather, served as a coffee table. Glossy books about the Kalahari and its wild animals lay there on display. Opposite were two cream sofas smothered in suede scatter cushions.

The building was once an old house, but the interior walls had been knocked out, the floors covered in a laminate of blonde wood. Subtle lighting gave the place the feel of a luxury cinema. Clearly, big money had been spent here.

"Nelmari's on her way," confirmed the pretty girl, her honey-brown eyes inspecting Sara discreetly. "Can I offer you something so long? Tea, coffee, something cold?"

"No thanks. I could really just come back later. I just thought, erm . . . "

She was small, the girl. Heart-shaped face, almond eyes and skin like caramel. Evidently born and bred in the region. But she looked very different from most local Griqua girls: make-up just so, fashionable miniskirt, short hair chemically relaxed and dyed light brown.

She and this very elegant place looked like something from another world—as if stranded here en route to New York, blithely enduring the dust and sand and tough thorn scrub until they could move on to where they belonged.

Nelmari appeared at the front door. She looked hot and flurried, her cheeks red from the heat.

"Iced tea, please, Charné," she called out as she approached Sara, her arms outstretched. "Sara! Sorry you had to wait. Let's go to my office." Her voice was warm, husky, a sensuous breeze. She took Sara by the arm and led her through a door set into the gigantic mural.

I'm walking right through Kimberley's Big Hole, Sara thought.

Nelmari closed the door behind her and took both Sara's hands in hers. Her eyes looked even bigger today. And wearier. "I'm really sorry I couldn't come along to Postmasburg this morning. I would so have liked to see her, to say goodbye.

Freddie was . . . " She let go of Sara's hands, turned around quickly and walked to her desk, fingers brushing at her cheeks. She took a tissue from a box on the desk and blew her nose, then dabbed at her eyes.

"Sorry," she said with a shaky smile. "I forget, you know? It's as if it didn't happen. As if she could walk in here any moment. But the simple fact that you're here, standing there . . . And if I feel like this, I don't want to know how you must be feeling." She faced Sara directly. "And with me not thinking straight, everything's going wrong today. Starting with the building work in Upington. The builders phoned early. The municipality has ordered all construction to stop. Everything. Just like that. Can you believe it?" She looked at Sara with big eyes, like a child that has just heard the tooth fairy doesn't exist. "They say we don't have the necessary permits. Lord, after everything we've been through. It's costing me millions!" Her voice was still soft and low. Singsong, as though she was reading a story to a toddler.

She showed Sara to a three-seater sofa. It stood to one side, part of a small, tasteful sitting area. The sofa was sixties retro, upholstered in a light fabric. There was a matching easy chair and a coffee table of light birch. Sara took a seat on the sofa, with Nelmari on the chair opposite.

"Tell me," she asked, and took out a long, slim cigarette, "how did it go this morning?"

"It was pretty tough." Sara wanted to say more, but again she couldn't find the words.

Nelmari blew a thin plume of smoke towards the ceiling. "And you? Are you okay?"

"Fine, yes. I'm okay." Despite the heat, she noticed, Nelmari still looked elegant. Her hair drawn back into a chignon, the trouser suit a cool white with ice-blue piping.

"I'm glad I went," she said eventually.

"They say it's easier if you get to say goodbye. You know, to accept it all. That's why I wanted to go too." Her voice cracked. "What, er, how does she look? I mean, you *saw* her?"

"Yes. It was horrific, really. She looks terrible. It's as if her hair—it looks as if someone used a pair of sheep shears. It was hacked off. So brutal. Her scalp torn . . . "

Nelmari gave a little whimper, screwed her eyes shut.

"Sorry," mumbled Sara.

"No, no. I'm the one who should apologise. I'm so damn pathetic with this kind of thing," said Nelmari and took a long drag of the cigarette between her shaking fingers. "I just pass out, you know. When I see blood." She flicked her ash into the porcelain ashtray, closing its lid. "Do you know when they'll be done? For the, er, funeral?"

"No idea. I'd like to drive out to the farm this afternoon. I should probably go pay my respects to the people there. Especially Outanna. And see what's missing. For the police. I was wondering if you . . . "

"Of course, Sara. Anything. I feel so bad that I couldn't join you and poor Yvonne this morning. And you've already driven so far—on your own. I'd like to come. Even . . . even though it's hard."

"And can I ask you something about Freddie? Things were pretty rough between the two of us, as you probably know." She didn't wait for an answer, just bumbled on. "Do you know why she decided to stay here? I thought things were going so well for her in Joburg. She'd started making a name for herself, hadn't she?"

"Oh yes, absolutely." Nelmari's gaze was sharp again. "She was just incredible. From the very start. I organised a big exhibition for her—in Rosebank. And jeepers, I could hardly believe it myself. It was going so brilliantly. Just about all the Gauteng newspapers were writing about her. And then there was an article in a women's magazine. With the most beautiful photographs. You probably saw it."

Sara smiled. Yes, she had seen it—but quickly, on the sly, in a café. She hadn't even taken the trouble to buy it, and she didn't tell anyone about it. None of her newspaper colleagues, not even Harry, her best friend these days.

"'The Girl with the Golden Brush' was the title of the article," said Nelmari.

Her eyes shone at the happy memory. The way a true sister would react, thought Sara. So pleased, so proud.

"I don't know what it is about her work that touches people so." She thought for a bit, then carried on. "They said she points people to the things that terrify them—us—subconsciously, the primordial stuff still stirring within us. All those fears and fantasies."

She spun the ashtray, looked up, and asked, "When last did you see any of her work?"

Sara was caught off guard, fumbling for words.

"Ag, never mind. I don't think it had really changed that much, still the naïve pictures you will remember. Almost childlike." She smiled crookedly. "But the moment you step closer, they punch you in the gut."

Sara was clearly nonplussed, and Nelmari gave an arch laugh. "I know, I sound just like an Omo ad," she said. "But I'll show you her portfolio. Then you'll see for yourself. I collected all the articles, the reviews and a list of who bought paintings. I had two television shows lined up to do something on her later this year. When her next exhibition was ready." She inhaled sharply, as if coming back down to earth. Her eyes wandered to an invisible spot on the coffee table. "Maybe they'll still do something. An overview, a profile, perhaps."

She went quiet. The cigarette in her hand had burnt all the way down, a long worm of ash threatening to fall.

"What did Freddie make of all the fuss?" Sara asked.

Nelmari didn't answer. Her face was rigid, desolate. Then

she leaned forward and stubbed out the cigarette. "Yes," she said wearily, "and her work sold, hey. We couldn't keep up."

"And more recently? Here on the farm? Was she still painting?"

Nelmari looked up. "Oh yes. We are . . . were working on a big exhibition in Joburg. Yes, she was painting, that's for sure. Which was one of the reasons why she decided to stay. At first I wasn't really convinced. Her market is in the city. The events, the media. We were sort of at loggerheads about that . . . " Her voice trailed off.

"How was she really, Nelmari? Was she happy? The last time we had a decent conversation was when she was still in Joburg, before Pa got ill."

Nelmari brushed a strand of hair from her face. Then she moved the ashtray, positioning it in the centre of the table. "I think she was. Happy, I mean. It was as if she suddenly—she was suddenly an *artist*, you know? Sort of . . . driven. Before, just after she stopped teaching, she struggled to work full time. She said she felt guilty painting all day."

"But it's thanks to you she took the plunge, wasn't it?"

Nelmari gave a coy smile. "Oh, I was just a catalyst, really. I just *knew*, the first time I saw her. When I saw her work, I knew she'd be a big success. And the last while, I think she started believing it herself. She worked flat-out, stopped answering the phone. She was moody sometimes. Irritated if you disturbed her. Emotional, even. But she was working. And that's the most important thing. So," she shrugged, "yes, she was happy."

Sara examined her fingers, the chipped nail polish. She had so many questions, but her head felt empty.

"I only hope the police do their job for a change," she heard Nelmari say.

"Nelmari, *who* would do something like this? *So* hateful, so cruel?"

"Oh hell, Sara, I don't know. I suppose it's the stock thieves.

She was just an easy target, I imagine." She got up, walked to the door and called out, "Charné, have you gone all the way to Tzaneen to fetch that tea?"

But Sara was no longer in the mood for iced tea. She wanted to leave. Flee.

God knows where. One thing she did know was that whatever she was looking for, she wouldn't find it here with Nelmari Viljoen. Maybe it was nowhere to be found. She didn't even know what it was anyway. Forgiveness? Some connection to Freddie?

It was too late, anyway. Far too late.

Slowly, she drove back to Driedoring Street. She stopped for a cool drink at the café, paid hastily and fled from the inquisitive stare of the girl behind the counter.

At Tannie Yvonne's house she parked under a big tree lower down the street, flung the door open to let in some air, and punched a number into her cellphone.

"Sara," she heard Harry's voice, breathless, on the other side. "God, it's impossible to get hold of you. Did you turn off your phone? And did you get the messages I left with Tannie Lambrechts?"

There was something about Harry's voice that always made her feel better. He was just one of those people. Lively, fit, energetic, well-balanced, a naturally enthusiastic extrovert. Not in a naïve way, just wholesome. And it was contagious. They had become friends when he moved into her apartment block in Cape Town, when she discovered he was a journalist too, but freelance. He was like your gay best friend, always there when you needed a shoulder to cry on. Except that he wasn't gay—he was constantly trying to convince her he'd be a much better guy for her than the arsehole she'd been seeing. And she had to admit, he did have a sexy laugh.

"Sorry, Harry. I was kind of busy."

"So how are things, hey?"

"I was at the mortuary this morning. In another town."

He waited for her to say more, but she was at a loss for words again.

"Do the police know anything yet, Sara?"

"No. I don't think they have a clue yet. As far as they could tell, nothing much was stolen. Some clothing, possibly, looked like the wardrobe had been ransacked. And some jewellery, her ring and a necklace of my mother's that Freddie inherited—Outanna says she never took it off. Nothing major. There wasn't much to steal, anyway."

"The newspapers here have gone kind of big with the story. Pics of your sister, and so on. Maria Bosch phoned me. She's looking for you. They're working on a piece for Sunday's paper. She wanted your cell number."

"I hope you didn't give it to her."

"Not without your permission, my dear. But you'd better steel yourself. It'll be a high-profile story. With your sister, you know? You never really told me much about her."

High-profile. As if that would bring Freddie back.

"Sara?"

"I'm here, Harry. I thought farm killings weren't news any more, on the decline."

"You thought wrong. It's just that they no longer make the papers. But your sister, well, it's different with her. To put it bluntly: she was attractive, young, and an artist. The newspapers say she was a philanthropist, did good work for the community. People find that fascinating. And the dust hasn't settled over the Wonderboom murders yet."

Sara remembered the case, the soapie actor who'd recently been killed in a hijacking along with his wife. The whole country was still in uproar about it.

"Here in Cape Town people have been talking about a march to Parliament. Sara, are you there?"

"I'm here. And I hear you. Just please help me with the newspapers. I'm not up to it. Not even for Maria. She's nice and everything, but still."

"Is there anything else I can help with? I've already been to rescue that poor dried-up fern on your balcony."

Sara smiled. If only more men were like Harry—not at all like those bastards she'd dated in her life. Keen, up to a point, but then the other women come crawling out of the woodwork. With her last boyfriend, the "other woman" was his own wife. And Harry, broad-shouldered, comforting Harry, had been there for her.

She noticed the big police inspector parking his car outside Tannie Yvonne's. "I have to go, Harry."

"One more thing. How long are you going to be away?"

The question caught her off guard. "I don't know. Why?"

"I have an assignment. Still just a possibility."

"And?"

"It's kind of tricky. *Sunday Times Magazine*, UK. They're looking for a photo essay on, er, farm mur—"

"Jesus, Harry. You can't mean that? How could you even consider it? And you want me to believe they approached *you*? Out of the blue? The minute your best friend gets into her car to drive off to the farm, for her sister's funeral—"

"Hang on, Sara. It's not just about that. They're looking for something broader. The empty countryside, the depopulation of the platteland, the whole land issue. The question whether Zimbabwe could happen here too. Really. And you know how long I've been waiting for a break like this."

Sara snorted.

"Really, Sara."

"I have to go, Harry."

"Sara—"

"I have to go. I think the police want to talk to me. You do what you need to. Bye."

She sat there for a long while after ending the call. Thinking about Harry. Harry and his big break. It was true, he'd been trying hard for a long time. He was doing well enough, but he was really looking for a foot in the door with the overseas magazines. They paid ten times as much. Harry wanted to combine his love of photography and his writing. His dream was to have a handful of regular clients, American and British travel mags, *Condé Nast*. A story like this could just be his big break.

She'd call him back later, once she and Nelmari had been to the farm. Her stomach lurched at the thought. She wasn't sure she had the stamina for this. But she had to. She owed it to Freddie, she hadn't been any kind of support to her at all. Freddie had taken over the farm, while Sara had turned her back on it, upset and angry as she'd sat there in Cape Town, brooding over it all. And Freddie all alone here, trying to make a new life for herself. A new life that someone else—hell, what kind of person would kill someone like this?

Who on God's earth could slit the throat of a person like Freddie?

And slitting a child's throat? A stock thief? No, impossible. The way Freddie was killed—God, it seemed so *personal*!

Grabbing her handbag, Sara took the keys from the ignition. She was thinking in circles, her mind buzzing like a blind fly. It was all too late in any case.

And she was being roasted alive in this oven of a car. She had to get out, even if it meant facing up to that giant of a police inspector.

13

Yvonne Lambrechts fussed over drinks in the kitchen as Beeslaar sat waiting in the lounge.

He used the opportunity to look around. Photographs on the wall, old portraits, among them an old black-and-white of a bride and groom. Must have been the old lady herself around fifty years or so ago. Another picture: the same groom, years later, in a cowboy outfit. Smiling at the camera, hat at a rakish angle, cigarette dangling from his mouth—all dashing, a real Humphrey Bogart. But his eyes looked weary, there were deep lines around his mouth: life had clearly turned out differently, all youthful expectations dashed. Alongside this, two prints of puppies with large mournful eyes that seemed to mimic the cowboy's disillusion. There were other dogs in the room too: an array of porcelain ones on a shelf, and on the walls, some framed pictures of various mutts.

Compensation, probably, for the lack of pictures of children, Beeslaar thought.

He heard her heavy, slow footsteps coming from the kitchen.

"I just have a few things to clear up, if you don't mind," he said as she appeared at the door. Taking the cool glass of juice from her, he asked, "I'm trying to get a better picture of Freddie Swarts and thought you might be able to assist?"

"Of course, Inspector, anytime."

They sat down.

"I take it Miss Swarts isn't here?"

"She's with Nelmari, Inspector. They want to drive out to Huilwater this afternoon. To see if anything else is missing, anything you might not have noticed the other day. And I think Sara wants to speak to the workers. You know, on a farm like that it's not just you and your own family. You're responsible for a lot of people."

"I thought the workers had all cleared off," said Beeslaar.

"Gone? All of them? I didn't know that." She looked at him in disbelief.

"The two labourers' families left yesterday. As far as I know, they've joined other family here in town. Apparently only the manager and one old man are left."

Yvonne clucked, then said, "Strange that they haven't come by yet. I suppose you can't blame the poor people, Inspector. You know, those two families have been on the farm for donkey's years, for a whole generation. They were like one big family. I can only imagine how upset they must be. And scared. If someone could be murdered right under your nose like that . . . "

Her eyes were small and watery in the fleshiness of her face. She dabbed at them with a crumpled tissue.

Once she'd regained her composure, he asked, "Who visited Miss Swarts most often on the farm? You see, we really have to talk to everyone."

"For myself," she said after a second's thought, "I haven't been going out there so often lately. My hip makes the driving difficult, you know, what with the clutch and all those hills . . . "

Beeslaar grimaced, a gesture of understanding.

"But Freddie wasn't the most sociable person either. I often went out there when she used to take in the foster children. Heavens, Inspector. You know, there's so much wretchedness among the poor in this district. Sometimes I think it's just too much, it's too much."

Her eyes misted over again and she struggled to control her quivering lips. Then she sniffed in annoyance.

"Please, forgive me. I'm not always this weepy. It's just so horrible, happening to someone like Freddie, to her of all people." The emotion overwhelmed her.

Beeslaar shifted uncomfortably in his chair.

"I think," she started again, "I think the person who went out there most often was Nelmari. She was on the farm just about every day, offering help and advice on the kids. A good person. And she has all the right contacts, knows lots of people in high places, you know—I mean people in government and so on—and she's been able to open many doors for us."

She was silent a moment, thinking.

"And Boet, of course," she continued.

"From the Karrikamma farm?"

"He was there often—especially in the days before Dam arrived, the foreman, you know, Dam De Kok. I think Boet helped Freddie a lot in the days when she was still planning to sell. Came to pick up livestock and took them to auction for her and so on. He has a good head for business. And a kind heart. She came to rely on him." She took a sip of her juice, wiped her mouth with the back of her hand. "Oh, and there were other people too from time to time, I suppose. But it was those two, I think, who were there just about every day."

"What kind of person was she, Mrs. Lambrechts?"

"Freddie?"

"Yes. All I know about her is what I hear around town. And some of it isn't very flattering. People said she was a bit, how shall I put it, eccentric?"

She clicked her tongue dismissively. "Oh, people! There are good people in this district, but God knows, there are others. Never satisfied. Doesn't matter how good they have it, they complain. And they feel threatened by everything. Even poor Freddie."

"What do you mean?"

"Because she was different."

"Different?"

She glanced up at the ceiling, as if she was carefully assembling the right words.

"Right from the start, Freddie wasn't too bothered with the white people here. Not that there are many left, in any case. The young ones leave and the old ones die off. Oh, well. She came here to take care of her father, initially. And somewhere along the line she started helping with the feeding scheme I run in needy areas around town. We have one in Chicken Vale and one towards the shanties of Emzini. And after Flip—that's her father—passed away, she stayed on to settle things on the farm. She continued helping me, and focused on the children, especially."

Her tone altered slightly, as she faced Beeslaar squarely.

"And then at some stage she got involved with the local Griqua tribe who wanted to reclaim tribal land. The land, you know, that their forefathers apparently owned in the area. You can just imagine how that went down around here. People talked. There were rumours she wanted to sell Huilwater to the Griquas. But that was just nonsense. The whole thing petered out, as far as I know. But apart from this, Freddie was just plain different. Actually, they're all like that. The whole family, I mean. And, well, people don't like strange ideas around these parts. And the Swartses didn't make it easy for anyone. They're stubborn. The whole lot of them, once they've got something in their heads. Old Flip, the daughters, every last one of them. Stubborn as mules."

Beeslaar took a sip of his juice. It was surprisingly nice, definitely not from a carton. Fresh apricot and peach, sweet as honey. He downed the lot.

"Well, you didn't really know her father, did you, Inspector? Or her mother, for that matter. But Freddie was a carbon copy of her mother, Tilla. An artist herself, but she was too weak for this world. When Tilla fell ill that first time, they sent her to a clinic for treatment. Nerves, you see. The children were still little. But Flip went and fetched her and brought her home. Against all the doctors' advice. He said he'd fix her himself. And he did. That hard man nursed her like a baby."

Beeslaar put his glass down carefully. "But Freddie wasn't ill, like her mother, I mean?"

"Oh, no, no, Inspector, there was nothing wrong with Freddie's mind. Look, her mother and I were friends for years. Like sisters, you could say. I knew her well. But I also knew Freddie. And because Freddie takes after her mother, people easily make that assumption. But Freddie was just different, her own person. Painting was her life. And when she didn't paint, she opened her heart to children. But most people find that difficult to grasp."

"And her paintings?"

"Man, I must say I didn't always understand what she was doing. Half the time I found the stuff a little, well, unsettling for my taste. It was almost as if she could see more than the rest of us, you know? Her grandmother on her mother's side was born with a caul, as they say—could see the dead. Apparently she found it a dreadful burden. Now, I don't want to say Freddie saw the dead, but she was intelligent, always looking at people, observing them. I think that's what made her paint. Just don't ask me what it all means."

"Did she get on well with the staff? I mean, she's a woman. Not everyone's happy working for a woman."

"Oh, nonsense, Inspector. Yes, Dam is a man and all, and he might look a little strange to some people, with his braids and the little beads and so on. But he knew his job. There were no problems, as far as I know."

"Apparently he has money. Why work for a woman if he has money?"

She looked at him uncomprehendingly.

"You're asking the wrong person. I wouldn't know if Dam

had a lot of money. But I can tell you this: Freddie trusted him completely. He ran the farm, and Freddie could carry on with her own life. I know, because I often asked her. Once she even said Dam was a godsend."

"Really?"

"She probably meant she could trust him with everything. You know, she was very depressed after her father died. And selling a farm isn't the same as selling a car. A farm carries many lives. And you have to ensure that everyone and everything is cared for properly before you let it go. Also, I don't know if there was any debt. She had to deal with all these problems. But then Dam arrived, and before we knew it, he'd turned everything around on that farm."

Adam De Kok, knight and saviour, Beeslaar thought to himself.

The man's alibi was rock solid. But he certainly wasn't your average foreman. On first-name terms with the employer. His Arabian trips. He appears out of nowhere, practically takes over a beautiful, single woman's farm, she views him as a "godsend."

"More juice, Inspector?"

"No, thank you, that was very nice."

Somewhere in the house a phone rang. She motioned him to wait and hurried off. He heard her answer from an adjacent room, her voice raised expectantly in greeting. Long-distance, he thought.

"Who?" she said loudly. And after a while, "Bosch? Okay, Sunday . . . I'll tell her. Yes, she's definitely not around. I'll tell her."

The front door opened. Sara Swarts stepped inside and greeted him.

Her cheeks were glowing from the heat. Strands of thick, straight hair clung to her neck and temples. She flicked the hair over her shoulders with an irritable gesture and wiped her hand across her forehead. There was a mist of sweat above the sweep of her eyebrows.

"The temperature gauge is at forty-three!" she said.

Beeslaar awkwardly agreed that it was hot. She was actually very attractive, he noticed: olive skin and prominent cheekbones above an angular jaw. Her eyes were a pale green, creating a dramatic contrast with the dark hair and eyebrows.

"Er, everything go smoothly in Postmasburg?" he said.

"Thank you, yes. When will you be . . . done with her?"

"It shouldn't be much longer."

She excused herself, wanting to change into something cooler.

Yvonne Lambrechts had no sooner finished the call than the phone rang again. Local call, because this time she answered the phone in a normal voice. "I understand. No, it's quite all right, I'll explain," he heard her say a number of times.

Beeslaar was just about to open the front door to leave discreetly when Sara appeared again. Barefoot, wearing a pair of denim shorts and a white T-shirt. She'd tied her hair up in a ponytail. Her limbs were slender but well shaped, athletic.

"I'm driving out to the farm with Nelmari this afternoon," she said, taking a seat on the armrest of the sofa.

He noticed chipped nail polish on the fingers holding a pack of Camels. Beeslaar felt a sharp craving—the first in months. Camels were his brand. One of the things he'd had to give up to keep his life together.

"Is that okay?"

For a moment he didn't know what she meant.

"To go into the house?" she prompted.

"Yes, yes. We're done there. I'll get the house keys back to you."

"It's okay, I still have my own set."

"I'm sorry, but Nelmari can't join you," Yvonne Lambrechts

said from the doorway. She came over to Sara, greeted her with a touch to the cheek. "She says she's got urgent business to attend to."

Sara left the engine idling—ready to drive off again at any moment. Then she turned it off, got out. She stood before the homestead, which lay before her, quiet as the grave. Nothing stirred. It felt as if it had been abandoned for years, the silence was that deep, that all-encompassing. Just like the heat. She glanced at the avenue of drab karees that separated the big house from the new, smaller one—the house Pa had built for his retirement.

She walked slowly, the gravel crunching under her flip-flops. She stopped, uncertain, fighting an urge to turn around and run, drive back to town. Tannie Yvonne had warned her after the inspector left—there were no people here any more.

The labourers had all moved to town. All the more reason to be here, she decided. Somebody had to see that everything was in order, that the animals were taken care of. God, the animals—that's why it was so quiet. She'd forgotten the dogs were dead too. She kicked off her shoes, clenched her teeth and walked to the back door.

The screen door creaked, as it always had—the spring needed oiling. She opened it, allowing it to rest against her back as she unlocked the back door. The top half swung open with a high-pitched squeak, revealing the cool, quiet darkness inside. She pushed at the bottom half of the old door with the ball of her foot, a habit that had earned her many scoldings in the past. Sarretjie, a lady doesn't *kick* a door open like that! Yes, Outanna.

Her eyes instinctively searched for the pale phantoms behind the back door—the milk buckets. They were placed there every afternoon after milking, covered with muslin against the flies.

But all she saw was a plastic bucket with a bunch of rags hanging stiffly over the edges. A mop with a long handle, its cotton strands hard and dry, leaned against the wall—someone must have used it to clean up afterwards. Outanna? Maybe once the police had finished on Wednesday. She shuddered, the sensation crawling down her neck and arms.

Dear God, Freddie.

It took all her willpower to cross the threshold.

She inhaled deeply, walked past the scullery and pantry into the kitchen.

Everything looked familiar and strange at the same time.

The old coal stove still stood in the corner of the kitchen, on the left. Unused for years, it now provided storage space for pots and pans. Next to it stood the gas stove that Pa had installed. On the other side, two old gas fridges, empty, their doors open. Outanna must have emptied them and turned them off. The rest of the room looked unchanged: granite sink and cold-water tap below the window on the opposite wall, large kitchen table in the centre of the room. Against one wall stood an old nineteen-fifties-style Formica kitchen cupboard, its clock still dumbly keeping time.

On one of its open shelves stood a photograph in a wooden frame—Freddie with a little girl laughing on her lap. Klara, Sara guessed, the name an unfamiliar sound in this sad house. Mousy hair formed a downy halo around her head. Her black eyes were slanted like those of a Siamese cat, her mouth hung open, moist and rosy. If you didn't know, you wouldn't be able to tell there was something wrong with the child.

Had been. That something *had been* wrong with the child. Why kill the child, for God's sake? Even worse, a brain-damaged child. How depraved could you get!

The inside kitchen door was open, as it always was. It gave on to a wide passageway with doors leading to the rest of the house. To the left was a door to the formal dining room. And ahead, along the opposite wall, was the door to Ma and Pa's old bedroom. In the far corner of the passage, Pa's old desk was still standing, though the computer had been replaced by a newer model. To the right were two doors—one to the bathroom and one to the second passage, which ran past the lounge to the front door. From it, two doors led to two separate bedrooms—hers and Freddie's, their old rooms. The rooms where Freddie and little Klara . . .

The passage door was open too. They never bothered to close doors before. Never locked anything.

She approached cautiously, refusing to look down the passage. A dark smell emanated from it, like bad breath. Sara opened her mouth so she didn't have to breathe through her nose. Gingerly, she pushed the passage door shut. Latched it and dragged a kitchen chair up to it. She wedged the chair back under the door handle. She realised it was a ridiculous thing to do, but did it anyway.

The floorboards creaked under her feet, sounding out harshly in the silence. She was walking on tiptoe, she realised. She went along the hallway to her parents' bedroom and opened the door slowly. The room was as spacious as she remembered, with large sash windows and a door leading to a bathroom on the left. To the right, there was an old-fashioned French door, complete with glass panels and doorknob at knee height. It led onto the verandah—which wrapped around the entire front of the house.

Sara stepped in cautiously. Two easels holding paintings loomed before her. She pushed aside some heavy curtains. This was Freddie's studio, it seemed. The double bed was still there, but a table with art supplies had been brought in—old jam jars with used brushes, paint-spattered rags, tubes of paint and pieces of frame. There was a delicate smell of turpentine hanging over everything. She looked at the two paintings on the easels—landscapes with strange beings floating around.

Against the wall by the windows there were more paintings, stacked upright. She stepped closer and flipped through them. More landscapes. Then she paused over one at the back of the stack. It was a kind of self-portrait. Freddie in a red dress. She was sitting on the floor with her legs stretched out in front of her, her back propped against a wooden chair. There was something in her hands. Sara leaned in closer. Freddie was holding something out to a stick-like figure in the foreground, as if she were offering it to him.

But her hair! It drifted around her head in golden clumps. It had been hacked off.

In horror, Sara remembered what she'd seen at the mortuary that morning: her sister's crudely shaven head.

God, no!

She took the painting and carried it over to the window.

It wasn't a red dress, she saw. It was blood pouring from a gash on Freddie's chest. And it was Freddie's own heart that she was holding out to the alien figure.

A mantis, she realised. A praying mantis.

Lord, what could it mean? She could feel her heart beating as she put the painting down.

It couldn't be a coincidence, surely? The painting looked like—exactly the way the policeman described finding her here. What could it mean? And why? God, that was way too farfetched!

On the other hand, it hadn't been unusual for Freddie to tear herself to shreds in her work. Sara remembered the first time she'd done so. She'd painted a woman with her head ripped open, streaks of blood spattered across the paper. "Mother racks her brains over us," she'd written underneath, quoting a phrase their mother always used. Ma had still been alive. Said she'd throw the child's brushes into the fire if she ever painted anything as horrible as that again. Pa kept quiet as usual, while Sara nearly choked on her giggles.

But her giggles soon stopped. Freddie's painting proved to be a kind of prophecy: Ma's long periods of depression, the clinics.

Sara slumped. She didn't have the strength for this.

The image of Freddie on that cold mortuary table swept over her. The vulnerability of her beautiful face.

A sound. A creaking floorboard, perhaps.

Her heart thumped. God, she was a sitting duck.

Anyone could overpower her here. She was completely alone on the farm, and the back door was still open!

For a while she stood dead still, too scared to breathe. The sound had come from the kitchen.

Then she heard it again.

14

Warily, Beeslaar took a seat on the sofa in Nelmari Viljoen's office. The thing looked as if its spindly legs might collapse under him at any moment. He looked around, unashamedly curious, noting the expensive elegance, the breezy contemporary colours and the icy sighs of the air conditioner.

And opposite him, on a salmon-pink easy chair, the slender figure of Viljoen herself. She wasn't his type. Too thin. All eyes and hair. Flat as a pancake.

But he could understand, perhaps, how she'd rev the engine of a beefcake like Buks Hanekom.

"She was my best friend, Inspector. And I have no family, you know?"

"Who would have visited her most often?"

She lightly tossed her hair back. It was in some sort of a twisted bun when Beeslaar entered, but she had let it down and shaken it free. The tips of her ears peeked through, like a pixie's.

"Well, me, I suppose," she said with a slight frown. "You could say we were like family. I discovered her, you know? Sort of managed her. She relied on me. I organised her first big exhibition in Johannesburg, as well as the next one, that we— that we'd planned for later this year."

"What state were her finances in?"

Nelmari arched an eyebrow. "Goodness, you're direct, Inspector."

Beeslaar said nothing.

"Well, she's never been wealthy. When I met her, she was earning a teacher's salary. And later, here on the farm . . . Huilwater isn't the type of farm to make anyone rich. You've seen for yourself, the state of the place. And then she appointed the foreman too. Initially I helped with the farm accounts. Freddie was a lost cause when it came to finance. Typical artist."

"Debt?"

"Surprisingly, no. You have to give her that—thanks to her father, of course. He died debt-free. I don't know of a single farmer who doesn't live off debt. But the profit you make out of a farm like that—well, it's pathetic."

"Enough to afford a manager?"

"Not really."

"So what did Miss Swarts live off? Her painting?"

Nelmari picked up a pack of cigarettes. Her slim arms were fairly muscular, he noticed, the veins pronounced on her bony wrists and hands. She lit up and blew smoke at the ceiling, daintily, her lips rounded. "No, Inspector, you'd have to be a Kentridge or perhaps a Marlene Dumas before you can start living off your art."

Neither of the names rang a bell, but Beeslaar let it pass. "So?"

She said nothing, but looked at him meaningfully.

"You supported her?"

"That sounds rather crude. Let's just say I invested heavily in her."

"And now?"

She didn't answer immediately. "And now the hardest day of my life has come." She looked away, wiping at the corners of her eyes.

Beeslaar gave her time to compose herself. Then asked, "The manager, Mr. De Kok. How well do you know him?"

She inhaled, then simply said, "I don't know him well."

"Do you know what his relationship with the deceased was like?"

"Oh, she was completely happy with him. I think he did his work well enough. He took over everything on the farm. Even started doing the books, kind of pushed me out."

"Would he have any reason to want to harm her?"

She looked pensively at the burning cigarette.

"You're asking the wrong person, Inspector. I'm not particularly crazy about the man."

"How so?"

She looked at him directly, then turned away quickly. "Oh, I don't know. It's difficult to put my finger on it. I don't think he's an easy person. Sometimes he made me feel like an outsider there, unwelcome."

"Were he and the deceased ever at loggerheads? Did they argue?"

"Why do you ask? Is he a suspect?"

"I just want to get an idea about the circumstances surrounding the deceased, Miss Viljoen, that's all. So, do you know if they got on well?"

"No. I mean, I didn't really have much to do with him. But I think Freddie was satisfied with his work. Other than that, I'm afraid I have no idea what he gets up to in his spare time. I know he has a thing for birds of prey. Personally, I find it a bit strange—cruel, even, to catch a wild animal and keep it tied down like that."

"And the rest of the staff?"

"What about them?"

"Might there be someone who wanted her dead? Someone with a grudge?"

"Oh. No, I don't think so. But you never know, do you?"

"What about the youngsters she took care of? I understand you were quite involved in that?"

"Those kids were young—most of them under ten. But there was one—Bully or Bongi, something like that. An angry, difficult child. He was barely twelve, but already had tattoos, one of them in the shape of a watch. He looked like a bit of a skollie, a real little troublemaker, never said a word. But Freddie—oh, dear, naïve Freddie. She said he was just a bit handicapped. That he had some speech defect. Nobody could trace his parents. He drifted around. Lived off the rubbish dumps, you know the story. I don't know what happened to him. But if you ask me, he's either in jail somewhere or he's joined some gang. So, sorry, but that's all I can really remember."

He made a note. Then, "Is Buks Hanekom one of your clients?"

She sat up, surprise on her face.

"Buks? Why do you ask?"

"I know you were looking for him yesterday."

"Oh, business," she said with a wave of her hand.

Beeslaar persisted. "Does he want to sell his land? I thought his father was still alive."

She smiled, mildly reproachful. "Gosh, Inspector, I can't see what this has to do with Freddie's death."

He returned the smile. "Everything may be relevant in a murder case, Miss Viljoen. And I think it's for me to decide if it's relevant or not. Hanekom has pretty strong feelings about these murders."

"And I, Inspector, am not obliged to talk to you about my business. Superintendent Mogale in Upington is a personal friend of mine. And I don't think he'd like your tactics."

Her eyes sparkled defiantly, challenging him.

Beeslaar didn't take the bait. There was no point in getting involved in a pissing contest—this woman and the super were quite friendly, he'd heard.

He tried a different tack, "Talking about land—Freddie Swarts was involved in a land claim, no?"

Nelmari Viljoen smiled, obviously pleased to have won the first round. "It started as an art project, I think. Freddie wanted to paint the old chief of the local Griqua tribe. But then she got carried away. She became obsessed with the plight of the Griquas. Their landlessness, their poverty. It was typical of her." She sighed lightly. "Anyway, she asked me to help with a claim. My lawyers looked the documents over, but unfortunately they didn't qualify—the tribe, I mean. I eventually convinced her to let it go. And then she started with the children. It sort of evolved from the Griqua thing."

"And how did that go down with people like Hanekom?"

"Well now, how would *I* know that, Inspector?"

Beeslaar got up. "Just one more thing, Miss Viljoen."

"Call me Nelmari, please." She got up too. Her perfume drifted over him, a hint of tropical flowers.

"There are people," he said, "who claim your Green Kalahari project is struggling. Is that the case?"

She smiled coolly. "Do I look worried to you, Inspector? I don't know about you, but I find that people often talk way too much about things they know very little about."

A moment's silence. When she spoke again, her voice was soft and light. "Like the way people talk about why you left Joburg."

He wasn't going to bite, he decided. But he was suddenly aware of the subtle hiss of the air conditioning and an iciness in the air.

"You didn't answer my question," he said.

"Is it relevant?"

"This is a murder investigation, like I said. Everything is relevant."

"All building projects go through stages, Inspector. But I can assure you this one is fundamentally sound."

"And do you still have the business in Johannesburg?"

"Oh yes."

"Also real estate?"

"Yes. Chiefly industrial. I have a residential section, but the focus is industrial. Selling as well as letting. That's my main business, really, and it's a well-oiled machine. I have a good man managing it. Personally, I only go up for a week each month. To see if everything's still standing."

Beeslaar walked to the door. She didn't accompany him. When he turned to say goodbye, she was already back at her desk, phone in hand. She gave him a wave as he pulled the door shut.

When he stepped outside, he almost welcomed the fierce heat.

15

Yes, it *was* a floorboard creaking—as if someone were transferring their weight from one foot to the other, very carefully.

Sara listened. There. She heard it again. The sound came from the kitchen. She would have to do something. Screaming wouldn't help, there was no help at hand. She looked at the lock on the bedroom door: no key. Oh, God.

And then—something scraping, a drawer being pulled open.

Where were the knives kept? Her heart was pounding and she could barely hear over the buzzing in her ears. Attack was her only defence. Grabbing a piece of wood from Freddie's paint table, she rushed out of the room and down the passage to the kitchen.

"Who's there!" she shouted, stopping dead in her tracks in the kitchen doorway.

A man lurched backwards at the sight of her. A book fell from his hand, loose scraps of paper fluttering across the kitchen floor.

The two of them gaped at each other.

"Who the hell are you and what are you doing here?" she screamed, the plank poised in the air, ready to strike.

"Sorry, sorry, sorry. I'm sorry. I didn't want to scare you," he said. "My name is Buks Hanekom. I saw a strange car parked outside, and the shoes lying in the yard. And the door was standing open, and I wanted to take a look."

"Are you the manager?"

He appeared dumbfounded, and then comprehension washed over his face. He smiled cautiously.

"No. No, I'm from Wag-'n-bietjie, two farms that way." He gestured with his head, on top of which was perched a brown leather Stetson. He had a luxuriant auburn moustache. And ice-blue eyes.

Sara lowered the plank and looked at the book on the floor. It was a recipe book, her mother's. He bent over quickly and picked it up, gathering together yellowed sheets of paper—handwritten recipes, or clippings from magazines—slipped between the covers over the years.

He put the book down on the kitchen table, carefully, as if it might leap to the floor again. "I saw the back door was open and then, er, the book was lying on the edge of the shelf like that, it looked as if it was about to fall off, and—good heavens, you must be Sara!"

Before she could react, he stepped towards her for a handshake.

"Pleased to meet you." His palm was unexpectedly soft and damp. Stepping back, he clasped his hands in front of him, earnestly. "I would like you to know that the whole community is deeply shocked over what happened here."

Sara put down the plank—part of a picture frame, she now saw.

He rattled on, "And I want you to know, if there's anything that I or any other neighbours can help you with, just say the word. We're all standing by you. In times like these we have to help each other."

The annoyance and alarm she still felt made it difficult to reply.

"We won't rest until we've apprehended the culprits. We've been out on commando, the whole district. Since Wednesday already."

"What do you mean? Are you with the police?"

"No." He laughed. "I mean us farmers. We've organised ourselves. Most of us did military service way back, and were in the commandos—before the government decided to ban them. But we can still mobilise a search party within minutes. We're all connected by Marnet, in our houses and in our vehicles."

She remembered Pa first getting to grips with the radio network—glad to be able to send out a quick SOS and get a reaction faster than by calling the police, what with the unreliable old manual exchange and patchy cellphone reception.

"In the provinces where there are frequent farm attacks, these systems often help you round up assailants within twenty-four hours," he said.

"Except in a case like this?" She couldn't help it. It slipped out.

He smiled faintly, though his unusually pale eyes showed no amusement. "Up till now," he admitted, and shifted on his feet.

As he did so, Sara saw the pistol holstered on his hip. "But we suspect the murderer is somewhere around here, right under our noses." He glanced out the back door.

He clearly meant to indicate that it was someone on the farm. The manager, perhaps?

"Do you have a weapon?" he asked abruptly.

Murmuring no, Sara gestured him towards the door.

"You can't survive in this country without protecting yourself. Not any more." When she didn't react, he said, "Would you like me to stay here until you're done? The sun is setting. It'll be dark soon."

"Thank you, but I'll be quite a while still. I have a few things to do."

He pulled a card from his back pocket and pressed it into her hand.

"My phone number on the farm, my cell number, everything. You can phone or radio any time of the day or night." He tapped the pistol on his hip meaningfully.

"Do you know how to use the radio?"

She shrugged dismissively, but before she could stop him, he had taken her by the arm and led her back inside the house, promising that it would take no more than a few seconds.

The radio was in the passage, mounted on the wall next to her father's desk. After what felt like hours, she was able to lead him back outside.

"Ja, well," he said, "Now you know how to use it. You must shout if I can help, you hear?"

"Thank you very much, Buks. I'll call if I need to."

"Times like these," he said, "we have to stand together." He took her hand and squeezed it before getting behind the wheel and tipping his hat at her. The big Hilux roared, and he pulled away.

She watched the vehicle until it turned onto the main road.

About to go back into the house, she glimpsed a figure standing motionless in the clump of trees separating the farmhouse from the outbuildings. She couldn't quite make it out, and for a moment she wondered whether she'd imagined it. But then he moved, coming towards her with quick steps.

The man was slim and slightly built, wearing khaki shorts and a T-shirt, and handmade velskoene without socks. "Afternoon," he said and put out his hand. "Dam De Kok." His handshake was firm and dry. "I'm the manager here."

For a moment they stood looking at each other. Then he lowered his eyes. "I'm sorry about your sister. About what happened here. Terribly sorry." He met her gaze again. Something burnt in his eyes, an emotion she couldn't fathom.

Barely her height, a touch over a metre and a half, his slender frame was perfectly proportioned—broad shoulders, narrow hips, muscular calves, the legs of a sprinter. His hands were rough and calloused.

Noticing a lamb that had trailed after him, she raised her eyebrows enquiringly.

"Her name is Lottie," he said with a smile. "One of the dozens of lambs Freddie hand-reared. And probably the naughtiest."

She bent to touch the lamb, looked up at the man. His hair was in cornrows, each ending in a thin braid secured with a coloured bead, all tied back in a ponytail.

He had the heart-shaped face typical of the people of the region, high cheekbones and a sharp chin, small ears. His skin was a light cinnamon, with premature crow's feet by his eyes, and frown lines on his sunburnt forehead. A man of the veld through and through, she decided. San. Every bit of him.

"Can I offer you something?" he asked. "Or are you in a hurry?"

His voice was easy, the Rs a light burr. There was something mesmerising about the sound, like gentle, rolling waves.

"I think I do need something," she answered. "And I don't think I'm in a hurry. Actually, I wanted to come see . . . The police want me to help with a list of stolen items, but . . . " She looked back at the farmhouse. "I'm not sure I can help them."

He appeared to comprehend this perfectly.

"Ag, really I just wanted to come out here," she continued. "I saw Freddie this morning."

He inclined his head slightly.

"Nelmari Viljoen was supposed to come too, but she couldn't make it in the end. And now that I'm here . . . "

"You gave Buks Hanekom a nice big fright." A smile lurked at the corners of his eyes.

"I guess you heard me screaming, hey? He sneaked into the house like a burglar and opened a drawer. I thought he had a knife—but it was just an old recipe book. Anyway, I didn't know there was anyone still out here. I thought everyone had gone, Dawid and Lammer, all the women and everything. Outanna too. Are you here alone?"

"No, Oom Sak is here too."

Oom Sak had been living on the farm his whole life. Worked for her father, right up until his seventieth year.

She followed him in silence as he walked in the direction of the house beyond the trees—Pa's retirement home. It made sense, actually, it was close enough to the farmhouse, but also private, screened by the trees.

He bent down to pick up the lamb that had been trotting after them. It bleated softly and settled into the crook of his arm, clearly used to it.

Sara felt a sudden heaviness in her heart. Why, she couldn't say. But perhaps she should be less sentimental and more careful, damn it. This man was, after all, suspected of the merciless slaughter of . . .

Oh God, her sister.

Freddie was dead.

In all the fear and flurry, she'd almost forgotten that.

16

H ow's it going?" asked Beeslaar, walking past the charge-office counter en route to his desk.

The trainee constable, Shoes Morotse, quickly put the phone down. Tall and muscular, he sported a sliver of a moustache.

"Afternoon, Inspector," he said with a barely perceptible hiss. There was a small gap between his front teeth.

"Girlfriend still love you?"

The young man bashfully scratched behind an ear. Beeslaar smiled, but said nothing. The constable's surreptitious phone calls to a tempestuous girlfriend were common knowledge. His boyish smile was apparently wasted on her.

In the corridor, Jansie Boois came charging at him. She was the one-woman nerve centre of the small station, doing admin, sorting maintenance, manning telephones. She had a basket with a lunch box and crochet work on one arm, her handbag on the other. On her way home for the weekend. "Inspector, there's a stack of messages for you. Do you want me to help quickly before I go? You remember I'm leaving early today? I have to help get the hall ready." She was a member of some cultural group that had invited an Afrikaans singer to perform that evening.

"You doing the high kick tonight as well?"

"Oh, you," she giggled, pushing up her glasses with a pale index finger. Then she stretched her eyes wide. "The superintendent has phoned twice already. All the way from Upington." She waggled her finger at him. "Naughty."

Beeslaar pulled a face. "I'll call. And you burn up that floor, hey! Do the Macarena!"

Superintendent Leonard Mogale's irritation was all too obvious. "You're a very important man, Inspector. Far too important for the likes of me, right?" His voice was a dark baritone and he spoke in a drawn-out monotone, each word carefully enunciated.

"I thought you said you were coming here, sir, so I wanted to gather as much information as possible. To fill you in personally, sir."

"Something came up." He could hear the superintendent's chewing at the end of the line. Did the man never stop eating? He already looked like a baby hippo. Barrel belly, fat face. And then there was his brusque manner, which had earned him his nickname, the Moegel—a combination of Mogale and mugu.

The superintendent swallowed, gulping as he did so. "But I don't expect I have to explain my movements to you, Inspector, thank you very much."

"Yes, Superintendent. I'm sorry. It's just, we're a bit thin on the ground, only one vehicle."

Mogale growled his dissatisfaction, his voice vibrating like a diesel truck. "I hear you, Inspector, and my heart is bleeding for you. But *you're* there now, aren't you. The Great White Hope of Johannesburg!" He laughed to take the sting out of his words, but Beeslaar knew there had been unhappiness surrounding his appointment here. Mogale would rather have had one of his own people, someone to help put his stamp on all the smaller stations in Upington's surrounding districts.

"But Great White Hope or not, in this part of the world we do things differently," he said. "Here we work together, we don't ignore each other. You with me? From now on I want a report from you every day. Starting Monday, when I'll see you and your docket here in my office, first thing."

Beeslaar bit back his rising protest. It was almost a hundred and twenty kilometres to Upington. A whole bloody day screwed. With him none the richer, and the Moegel certainly none the wiser.

Mogale was getting into his stride. "Because I'm looking like a fucking monkey here, man. My own director wanting to know what's going on, the commissioner breathing down both our necks. The politicians, the opposition, the bloody farmers with their agricultural unions. And the press. And I'm sitting here like a mampara. Completely in the dark, because Inspector Beeslaar is too busy to phone and update me."

He paused, allowing the rebuke to sink in, then continued more calmly, "How are things developing there? I hear there are white farmers walking around with guns, intimidating people."

Thanks a lot, Sergeant Ballies Brown-Nose Pyl, Beeslaar thought bitterly to himself.

"That might be a little exaggerated, Superintendent. The people are upset and full of fighting talk. But that's as far as it goes."

"I don't like this one bit. There's already been war talk in the newspapers. I don't want trouble like that on my watch."

"At this stage they're just a few isolated individuals. But I'm keeping an eye on it. And I wanted to ask: While you have the commissioner's ear, please push him for the letter?"

"Letter? What letter?"

"The letter for the lab in Pretoria, Superintendent. We need a letter from the commissioner saying this is a high-priority case, so we don't have to wait nine months before we get the results of the victims' blood tests. The letter to—"

"You can drop the attitude, Inspector. I know perfectly well what you're talking about. I'm working on it. Now, am I going to hear anything about this case, or must I ask someone else? Pyl? He looks like a useful young man. Or do I give the case to my men here in Upington?"

Beeslaar ground his teeth. Men like these, who'd joined the

Service just yesterday, home every afternoon by five. Promotion every time they coughed. And then the men like *him*—years of sweating blood, fourteen-hour work days, no weekends, no overtime, no rest till a case is solved. Health completely buggered.

But promotion? He could forget it. For the rest of his life.

His skin colour weighed, found wanting. Too light.

"We're questioning people at the moment, Superintendent. Taking statements, gathering fingerprints. We're working our way through everyone on the farm, the neighbouring farmers. There are no obvious suspects yet. But today we received information that might just tie our stock thieves to the murders. It hasn't been verified properly yet."

"What information?"

"The night before the murders, their vehicles were noticed in the area. But, like I said, we still have to follow that up properly. For the rest, we wait. The autopsies have been completed, we're waiting for the report, and for the final fingerprint checks. The blood tests—if the commissioner can manage to organise priority status—will take at least two months."

"Well, all right then. In the meantime, you stay on the lookout for vigilante action from the farmers. And for fuck's sake, keep me updated!" Mogale said and killed the line.

Beeslaar threw down the phone.

He patted the file in front of him, frowned at the pile of pink slips with Jansie's scribbled messages. He grabbed the lot, scrunched them up and hurled them into the air. But the wind from the fan next to his desk caught them all and flung them back at him.

He sighed, picked them up one by one and smoothed them with the palm of his hand. Then he got up, closed the file and put it in his drawer, locked it and put the key in his pocket.

It was five o'clock. Chaila time in the new SAPS.

And he was sorely in need of a drink.

17

T here's no end to that bladdy thing this evening," Yvonne Lambrechts exclaimed. But she didn't get up to answer the phone.

Instead, she put her hand out and folded it around Sara's. "I hope you get some sleep tonight, my darling."

Sara was in bed already. She'd taken a cool shower when she got back from the farm, and then went straight to her room. Tannie Yvonne had come to say goodnight. Sara felt like a child about to be tucked in and told a bedtime story. It felt strangely comforting.

"I feel as if I could sleep for a week."

"The whole world phoned tonight. That Bosch girl from the Sunday paper twice, actually. She said you know her. I said to her, try and understand the circumstances here. Lord, I don't understand how people can be so insensitive."

"Ag, she's just doing her work, Tannie Yvonne. I spoke to Harry, my friend in Cape Town, this afternoon. He said that the papers will be going ballistic with this story. So, Maria's just doing her job."

"He also called again, this Harry. I told him it was no use trying your cellphone, there's no signal on the farm. So, tell me, does he work with you?"

"He's my neighbour. We've been friends for years. I look after his plants when he goes away and he does the same for me."

"Oh. Actually, I don't really know who's allowed to get your number."

"Don't worry. Maybe tomorrow I'll have more strength to answer it myself. Have you heard from Nelmari?"

"She phoned too. She was very sorry that she couldn't go with you. I think you'd better call her tomorrow."

Sara stifled a yawn. "She's just too busy. She has the best intentions, but . . . Anyway, how well do you know Dam?"

"Not very well. I know Freddie was very pleased with him."

"He's a little strange, don't you think? He's so, I don't know. So . . . It's as if he belongs somewhere else. Otherwordly. You wouldn't expect him on a humble old farm in the Northern Cape. But he walks around in vellies that look as if he made them himself—and no socks!"

Yvonne stroked Sara's hand.

Sara shifted, leaned her head on an elbow. "Did Freddie ever show you her paintings? I mean, the stuff she was working on."

"I'm not sure I understand her work so well," the older woman said.

"You sound like Ma. But I think, the way I feel now, her paintings are too hectic even for me. There's one especially. It's a painting of Freddie herself. But . . . the hair. She painted herself just the way . . . just like we saw her this morning, you know?"

"Ag, no, my dear. Are you sure?"

"Yes. But you know what Freddie was like . . . "

"So. You think she saw it coming? Like your Ouma Nettie?"

Sara sat up, her back against the pillows. "I don't know. But it's weird, that painting. It's a self-portrait, with a big gash in her chest. And her hair . . . It's been cut off, with just a few clumps left. She really looks just like, well, this morning."

"Come, come, child. Try to sleep now, we'll talk again tomorrow."

Sara turned out the light and rolled over as soon as the door closed, but she was awake. It wasn't just Freddie's painting that was weird—the whole day had been off-kilter. Starting with Freddie in that place. And Nelmari, with her exotic office. But the strangest—no, the most surprising thing—was Dam.

Man of the veld and English lord all rolled into one. On the one hand he was as down to earth as a Kalahari meerkat. But then he was also proud, almost superior in his manner, the kind of confidence you don't often see in a farm worker. Even the way he poured the tea—as if he'd been to a finishing school. He wasn't effeminate. Just—what? Refined.

He'd invited her to sit on his little stoep, then produced a baby bottle and a towel and told her to feed the lamb while he went to the kitchen to make some tea.

Over tea, they'd made small talk—when she'd arrived, where she was staying, when she planned to go back, where she worked in Cape Town, whether she lived alone. She'd asked about the farm, whether he and Oom Sak could manage everything by themselves. He'd said he would speak up if the need arose. But he believed they could carry on for a while— without Dawid and Lammer and the rest. There was one cow that needed milking, and a few hanslammers that needed bottle-feeding. Luckily the cow was nearly out of milk, so he would send her back to pasture in a day or so. And the lambs had already been sold. All he had to do was deliver them. Lottie included.

After a while he'd excused himself to see how Oom Sak was getting on with the milking. He had topped up her cup before he left. On returning, he'd suggested a cold beer, which they'd sat sipping on the stoep until the sun began to set in a reddish haze.

"How well do you know that man who was here earlier?" she'd asked cautiously. "Buks Hanekom."

Dam had looked away.

After a while, he'd said, "That was his second time here today. I don't know what his story is, what it is he keeps looking for here. But it seems to me he's already made up his mind that I've got something to do with the—with what happened here."

She had to bite her tongue—she'd been burning to ask more questions.

"I guess you can't blame him," he'd said, "of course they would look at our people first. And it doesn't look good—with Dawid and Lammer and the others taking off like that. Me as well. I put up a fight on Wednesday when they wanted to take my fingerprints."

The sky had transformed into an orangey dusk, and Dam had turned his attention to two birds of prey in the backyard. He'd put on a thick elbow-length leather glove and said she could walk with him to fetch the birds and bring them back to the stoep, where they slept at night.

The smaller bird had been a Southern Pale Chanting Goshawk. She'd been sitting on her stand, a jess tied to her leg, and allowed him to stroke her blue-grey chest lightly with the back of his forefinger.

It was almost magical, Sara had thought, the silence, the soft twilight, the glow it had cast on him and his fabulous creatures, and the bond between him and the birds.

"Hold on, Princess, we're nearly there," he'd murmured. The bird had tugged gently at the leather jesses on her foot. He had found her in the veld a week or so before, he'd said, emaciated, half dead. She was still young, probably pushed out of the nest before she had learnt to hunt.

Dam had held his gloved fist out to the bird and waited for her to climb onto it. During the day, he told Sara, he let the two birds sit outside on their perches—if he was around. The jesses were long enough for them to move about on the perches, but not so long that they'd get tangled up and injured.

"Just need to fatten you up a little more," he'd coaxed as he waited for the goshawk to hop onto his hand, "then you're on your own again. Let's see if you can catch something this time."

When she'd eventually stepped onto the glove, he secured her jesses between his thumb and forefinger, carried her to the cage on the stoep, and then went back for the bigger one.

"Howzit, old pal?" he'd said in a low voice.

A Martial Eagle, he'd explained, as she stood admiringly before the bird with its dark plumage and yellow eyes, its crown of feathers shimmering on its regal head.

The bird had pecked at Dam's hands as he untied the jesses from the stand and secured them to his gloved wrist.

"He doesn't trust me one hundred per cent yet. I found him in the veld with a crippled wing. He must have flown into a fence, or maybe a power line. But he's almost himself again."

The eagle had pecked angrily at the glove, spreading its wings for balance. For a moment it blocked out the sun, casting a large shadow. But Dam's feet were planted firmly.

"Come, old boy, time for bed. Sun's going down." He'd waited for the bird to calm down and climb onto his fist. "Good boy, Krakus."

Almost dwarfed by the bird, the man had walked to the house with measured steps, skilfully coaxing it into its mew before covering it with a blanket.

Dam had hung the glove on a hook and took his pipe off a shelf, slowly tapping it and filling it again. She felt mesmerised by the man and the birds, the ritual she had witnessed—as if she were a sci-fi tourist who'd got lost in a time warp.

Just then, Oom Sak had come walking in from the lamb camp. He'd washed his hands with a bar of blue laundry soap, before coming over to greet her. He'd been on the farm for decades, for as long as she could remember. Hesitantly, he'd apologised for the other folks' absence—they were scared, he'd said, clearly concerned that she might think they'd just callously upped and left.

"It's all right, Oom Sak. I understand," she'd assured him.

Dam had invited her to eat with them, though warning, "It's a simple meal."

They had sat in the kitchen and Dam produced a cold leg of lamb. It carried the scent of rosemary and wild herbs, and he served it with a stout loaf of bread, and mint water in large round wine glasses. She hadn't eaten properly since Cape Town, she had realised.

Sara had carefully posed questions as they ate. But her host had been reluctant to talk about himself. "I grew up on a farm," he'd said, "deep in the Kalahari. My people were labourers there."

"Brothers and sisters?"

"No."

Each time he'd delivered his short answer, he first finished chewing, and set his knife and fork down with care. The owner of the farm, a man he called "Oubaas Van Jaarsveld," had sent him to school in Kimberley shortly before he turned ten. To get some "proper schooling," he had explained.

She had wanted to know so much more. Like, how had he turned out so differently? But how do you ask things like that?

"Tannie Yvonne says you worked in the Middle East before you came here," she had ventured. "For some rich Arabs?"

Oom Sak had given a snorting cough, and for a moment she was afraid she had probed too deeply.

Dam had taken his time chewing, put down his cutlery and wiped his mouth with a linen napkin. A smile had flitted across his taut features, she'd noticed with relief.

"I grew up in the veld. 'Wild'—just like people say. My grandfather, Oupa N!xi raised me as a Bushman, when that was still possible—before everything changed. I wanted to become a vet, but there was no money. The oubaas, the farmer, tried to help me get a bursary. But in those days it wasn't as easy for," he had given a bitter smile, "the previously disadvantaged." He'd picked up his knife again, smoothed a pat of butter over his bread. "The old man helped me find a job—and I studied accounting after hours. Got a diploma, at least."

"And the birds?"

"It started in Kimberley. I met a few guys from a falconry club, did my apprenticeship with one of them. Later on he went off to Dubai. And I followed."

"Is that how you ended up with the rich Arabs?"

He'd laughed.

"No, I didn't actually work for the 'rich Arabs.' I worked for a Brit in Dubai who employed a bunch of falconers—still does, in fact. Our job was to keep the luxury hotels pigeon-free."

"With the falcons?"

"Right."

"But how? How did you end up here?"

"I got tired of that kind of life. And I'd saved up enough to come back. So that's that." He had put a teaspoonful of jam on his bread and held out the jar, saying, "Last year's quinces. We made it ourselves—nice and tart, not too bitter."

The conversation had turned to the state of the farm—how many sheep there were, what game.

Oom Sak hadn't said a single word throughout the meal.

Afterwards, all three of them had cleared the table and washed the dishes in silence. But the silence had not been uncomfortable.

There was something about Dam, she thought, a kind of unaffected serenity that immediately put you at ease. You wanted to stay close to him. His soothing presence made you forget about yesterday, softened tomorrow's cares. Peace in the here and now. This, despite the horror of what had happened just two days before. Right there, only a few paces away.

In the big house that had once been her home.

18

At the desk in his study, Beeslaar irritably closed the Huilwater file. Ghaap's report of his interviews with Boet Pretorius's workers were so vague and woolly, they sounded as if he'd sucked them out of his thumb. And they were incomplete: nobody's address or ID number had been recorded. He'd have to go do it himself—take the statements all over again. And he'd have to drag Ghaap and Pyl along again, so that they could see how it was supposed to be done. Look and learn.

But he wasn't going to get worked up about it now. What he should have been worried about was his own negligence. There was a hole the size of a crater—the whole bloody Vredefort Dome—in the Huilwater manager's alibi. And he should have spotted it first. There it was, large as life, right there in the excruciatingly detailed document Pyl had compiled on De Kok's comings and goings. God almighty, right down to the fucking toothpaste the man had bought from the supply store. But one thing was screaming for attention—the hour between one and two, for which there was no record.

This, Pyl—greenhorn that he was—hadn't noticed. Even worse: he, the Great White Hope of Johannesburg, with all his experience, had missed it too.

The man had been at the bank until one o'clock—that much was evident from Pyl's report. And the bank, of course, closed for lunch. The old woman who had been in town with De Kok, Mrs. Johanna Beesvel, did have a record of her movements over this hour. She was with a group of other old people. They'd sat under the pepper trees of a vacant plot near the general dealer's. Previously, it had been the site for a monument to the Voortrekkers, but that had been pulled down by the new government. People sat there during lunch hour, waiting for the shops to re-open.

Dam De Kok, however, the enigmatic manager of Huilwater farm, was not among this group. He was at the bank at closing time, one o'clock, and again at two. But where was he in-between? Was an hour enough for him to drive the forty kilometres out to Huilwater, to dose his employer and her daughter and all the dogs with a Rohypnol concoction, slit their throats, change into clean clothes, and drive back again? At two o'clock on the dot he was back at the bank, Tannie Bella Visagie, the teller-cum-manager, confirmed. And it *was* Rohypnol, Willie Prinsloo, the Postmasburg doctor confirmed. All they needed was the stamp from the foot-dragging lab coats at the national pathology unit in Pretoria.

Beeslaar yawned and turned out his reading light.

The study was immediately shrouded in darkness. Best that way. Leaving the lights on, he had discovered in his few weeks here, attracted millions of goggas—bugs of all shapes and sizes. Nasty, stinging, biting things. The mosquitoes were okay. He'd learnt to live with them. But hell, there were a lot of creepy-crawlies that freaked him out. Completely.

And they wouldn't just leave you in peace. Oh, no. Ran up your legs. The very thought made his skin crawl. He brushed at his calves as he got up.

Mug of tea in hand, he walked through the darkness and out onto the stoep. He wanted to sit for a while in the cool evening air before going to bed. Maybe it would help to make him drowsy. He was still struggling to sleep. And when he did sleep, he kept waking up. A nightmare every time.

Friday night. Jansie Boois's concert in the church hall was long over, and the town was quiet. Just the far-off hubbub from the township.

Joburg felt very far away, with its dark soul, its throbbing menace—like Gotham City in a Batman movie. But this case had suddenly brought it closer—that city with all its darkness. And Beeslaar wasn't sure he was strong enough to deal with it.

Wednesday morning, the very day of the Huilwater murders, he'd been out in the district with Jan Steenkamp, from the Agricultural Union. They were calmly having coffee and a chat. Steenkamp had suggested he organise a meeting to discuss a farm-watch system. Beeslaar left, feeling good. And the next moment he was standing in one of those rooms again—a room filled with blood and death, the smell of fear.

And then: Ghaap with his burning cigarette in the passage next to the bedroom, right on the goddamn murder scene. He wanted to klap the man. Yelled him right out the front door. If he'd been twenty years younger, the idiot would still be lying in hospital now.

He himself, he'd learnt the old way, the hard way. From the bottom up. As a trainee detective, someone shoved a wad of donkeys into his hands. "Your docket is your Bible. And you work it until you're done. *Done*, as in, case solved. We don't close dockets, we solve them." Then he was paired up with an old boy, Bliksem. Short for Captain Blikkies van Blerk, Murder and Robbery, his nickname true to his thunder-and-lightning reputation for force and directness. He didn't waste words. Gave your statements one look and tore them up. "You think the prosecutor is going to understand this crap? Start over!" Everything Beeslaar knew, he'd learnt from this man. "The murder scene is your Holy Ground. Holier than the Virgin Mary's very own bra strap. You don't even *breathe* on it until forensics and the movie guys are done. You don't smoke, you don't traipse around with your mampara feet, all you do is make sure the victim is dead already. Then you fuck off, and you make damn sure no one else comes near the scene!"

Oom Bliksem. Had his turn at the Truth and Reconciliation Commission in the end. And now he was out of the Service. Him, and a whole generation like him.

Beeslaar sighed deeply and took a slug of lukewarm tea. Doesn't help to be bitter. He had to adapt, stay calm.

And these two new pups were learning, just as he had learnt.

He yawned and stretched, hearing his joints crack.

Hell, it was quiet. There were no people around, not in this part of town, anyway.

The town had been emptying quickly, the story of many a country dorp. It had started with the schools, post-'94: white people packed up, complained standards were dropping now that everyone had to integrate. Wanted to give the children "better opportunities." Then the exodus had begun. The doctor, the lawyer, the bank manager. The officer in charge of the police station.

All disappearing, one by one. Then the doors started closing: library, golf course, tennis club—the lot. Until all that was left was the liquor store and the co-op. And a handful of old-timers. While the number of unemployed in and around the town rose.

Beeslaar pushed his cup away. Time for bed.

As he stepped into the house, his blood froze. Something was scuttling down the passage, fast, disappearing into the lounge. A red roman. That's for bloody sure. Those huge, hairy spiders. Big as a man's hand and fast as lightning. Evil black heads with sharp pincers.

He rushed to the kitchen where he grabbed the insect spray, a feather duster and a broom.

He crept back to the lounge.

But all was quiet. No rustling or scurrying. The brute was probably skulking under the furniture somewhere.

Beeslaar steeled himself and took a cautious step over the threshold when something brushed his calf. Startled, he jumped, bumping his head on the doorframe and whacking furiously at his legs. He cursed—it was just the feather duster, and he'd almost frightened himself into a coma with it. But the fight had gone out of him. And his head ached like hell.

He slammed the lounge door shut, fetched a towel and rolled it up to block the crack under the door. If there was a red roman in the lounge, it'd just have to stay put for the night. He'd make a plan with it tomorrow. He'd had more than enough for one day. In the bathroom he wet a facecloth and draped it over his head, then headed for bed.

He lay on the cool sheet, all of a sudden overcome by spasms of laughter: how spectacularly he had lost his battle against the red roman! And how Sergeant "Ballies" Pyl had battled with the English language when the reporter from the TV news team had interviewed him about the case, "We will not let any stone lay still until the perpetrators are behind the bars," he had said into the camera.

Inspector Beeslaar fell asleep with a smile on his face.

19

S ara rolled over for the umpteenth time. She simply couldn't sleep. Outside, a thunderstorm was brewing, intermittent blue-white flashes illuminating the room.

The storm unsettled her, the lightning flashes making her flinch. It seemed to be targeting this house, the heavens directing their wrath specifically at her.

Images of Freddie filled her mind, her hair flying in the afternoon dust on that last day when Sara left the farm.

She tried calming herself, tried to think of the peace of the previous evening on Dam's stoep, as they'd all sat in the dark with mugs of tea. She tried to recapture that feeling of serenity.

Dam filling his pipe, completely absorbed in the task after offering Oom Sak his tobacco pouch. The old man had taken a pinch of tobacco and made himself a roll-up from a scrap of newspaper. The aroma had evoked a thousand childhood memories: early winter mornings, before school; the smell of the dry yellow grass; Oom Sak and the others standing outside, their warm breath billowing in the chilly air, waving in greeting as she and Freddie made their way to the main road shivering, their legs bare beneath their short school uniforms. She and her sister would jump up and down to keep warm while they waited for the school bus. Were those happy days? The two of them, so dependent on each other. Ma becoming more and more of a slumbering phantom. Had they realised how different their lives were from those of other children? Perhaps

Freddie did. Hence her long silent spells. And the sketchbook she carted around with her wherever they went. Now she was a phantom too.

As Dam and Oom Sak had sat smoking, she'd sipped at the comforting tea. Underneath her sadness, she had relaxed for the first time in two days, as if she had returned home after a storm. The night had been fragrant with eucalyptus. And the peppery smell of the karee trees, the sweet scent of the acacias in the yard. The stars had been spread across the heavens, a glittering reef of light.

"I'd forgotten how low the stars drift in this Northern Cape sky," she'd said aloud. For some time, all three of them had sat with upturned faces, staring into the night.

"They are the hunters," Dam had said. "Every one of them. The big ones—the shiniest ones—they are the hunters. Look at that one there," pointing with the stem of his pipe at a star hovering on the horizon. "He's one of the biggest. He hunts in the shape of a lion. He hunts in the furthest, most dangerous places. 'Tsa!' he calls. That's the call of the hunt: 'Tsa! Tsa-a-a!'"

Oom Sak had chuckled at this.

"But there's *one*. He's an even braver hunter. You won't see him now. He hunts so far away, so deep into the danger zone, you'll see him only when he returns home in the early morning."

"Who is he?"

"He's the one who chases the night away as he comes walking back home. He's done hunting, but his bow and arrow are still out, always at the ready. When the small creatures of the night hear him, they run away quickly. All you see is red dust rising as he comes walking up the sky, bringing the daylight with him."

"And his name?" she had urged after a while.

Dam hadn't answered, just sucked at his pipe. Storytime had evidently come to a close.

"Come, I'll walk you to your car."

She had sat up, jerked back to reality. "I don't want to go back to town, Dam. Can't I just stay here?"

"Here?" He'd looked at Oom Sak, and then back at her. "I'm not sure if that's wise. But I do have a spare bed and enough bedding."

Sara had got up slowly. "No, I'm talking nonsense. For a moment I'd forgotten about everything. I'll just leave."

In her rear-view mirror, she'd seen the gentle glow of Dam's house beyond the trees.

20

S ara had raided Tannie Yvonne's kitchen for cleaning products. Handy Andy, Domestos, Mr. Muscle. Two buckets, cloths, scrubbing brushes.

The older woman had desperately wanted to come along. But Sara had held firm. She had woken that morning with the clear knowledge: she would go and clean up that farmhouse. Scrub it down. Room by room. She was going to wash it clean. Set things right.

Call it crazy, as Tannie Yvonne had, or call it survivor's guilt, in Harry's words.

She just knew she had to do it. On her own.

Sara turned at the rusty signboard that still said HUILWATER: FLIP AND TILLA SWARTS. She drove through the gate, down the familiar dip, the car bouncing across the cattle grid, till she came to a halt under the old blue gum tree at the back door. She got out and started unpacking, digging around for the house key in her bag.

But as soon as the back door creaked open, her courage abandoned her. She put everything down and sat on the back steps. Around her, the yard was littered with blue gum twigs and shredded leaves stripped by the night's storm. The earth had been swept flat by the driving rain, and the trees and shrubs glistened, washed clean of dust. It was early, but already hot. A light crust had formed on the rain-smoothed earth. It cracked when you walked over it.

She sat until she felt calmer, then got up, carried the cleaning things into the kitchen, and lit the gas stove for tea.

While she waited for the kettle to boil, she walked through to the passage. The chair she'd wedged under the front passage door the previous day was still in place. For a long time she stood looking at it. Then she forced herself to open it and turn on the lights.

The smell was stronger with the door open. She hesitated for a moment or two, then took a deep breath and walked in. To her relief, everything looked normal. And clean. There was no sign of violence or blood, Outanna or whoever had been there had done a good job. The doors to Freddie's and the child's room were still shut. She lingered in front of Freddie's door, reached her hand towards the doorknob, but couldn't go through with it.

In a little while, she decided. After she'd opened the rest of the doors and windows to let in some light and air.

She struggled with the front door. It wouldn't open. She jiggled the doorknob, even gave it a light kick. But it didn't budge. She'd have to walk around—try from the outside.

She went back to the kitchen and out the back door, stepped around the house to the front stoep.

It was only when she pulled the outer screen door open that she saw why the door had refused to budge. Strips of leather had been wound tightly around the copper doorknob. Tiny little tortoise shells, blackened bloodied chicken's feet, and the hooves of a goat or small antelope were suspended from them. She gasped and stepped back, the screen door slipping from her grasp and slamming shut.

For a moment she stood petrified, then she scanned the yard, but there was nobody there. She leaned in closer and examined the ghoulish ornaments through the mesh. It looked like a sangoma's handiwork. Witch doctor stuff.

Sara turned around and ran over to Dam's house. She hammered on the back door, but there was no reply. The door was locked. In the yard, though, she saw the birds on their perches:

he must be close by. She called out—no answer—and ran to
the shed a little further on, shouting his name all the way.

Oom Sak came out of the shed at a trot, panic on his face.

"Miss Saratjie!"

"Where's Dam, Oom Sak?"

"He isn't here!"

"Where is he? He must come right now!"

"O Jirretjie!" The old man looked beseechingly at the heavens, then he stuck a thumb and index finger into his mouth
and whistled loudly.

"Da-a-a-am!"

He waited a second, cocking his head, listening for an
answer, then tried again. "He's just left," he said over his shoulder and whistled once more. "He must be somewhere nearby."

Eventually, Dam came running from the veld. Sara led him
and Oom Sak back to the main house and showed them what
she'd found. Oom Sak stepped back sharply. "O Jirretjie!" he
exclaimed. Then he mumbled an excuse before disappearing
in the direction of the shed. Dam, on the other hand, gave it
one look and slammed the screen door shut again. Then he
turned around and gazed out over the veld with a strange light
in his eyes, still panting a little from the run. She tried to follow his gaze, but saw nothing.

"Do you think they're still here?"

"I don't know. But are you okay?"

"I'm fine. What is this stuff, Dam? Why is it here?"

He averted his eyes, merely said, "When did you get here?"

"A moment ago. I wanted to start early. Shouldn't we go
and phone the police?"

He pulled a face.

"How did it get here? Who would put this stuff here?"

Again ignoring her questions, he scanned the surrounding
area, examined the shrubbery.

"What are you looking for? What is this? It looks like the

stuff witch doctors use. Or what? No, dammit. I'm going to phone the police. Right now. Come," she said and started walking towards the kitchen.

"Wait," he said.

She stopped. "What?"

"Never mind. You go phone so long. I'm going to walk around the house to see that everything's all right."

The telephone was in the dining room, the small, dim room next to the kitchen. Still the old black wind-up model. It had its own little table, a nineteen-fifties design. By the time she had the operator on the line, Dam's footsteps sounded in the kitchen, and she heard him taking the kettle off the stove. She'd clean forgotten about it, walked right past it. It must have boiled dry by now.

Once she'd finished talking to the police, she went back to the kitchen.

Dam held a mug out to her and she thanked him. "The police are on their way," she said and took a seat. "I spoke to Inspector Beeslaar. He's coming himself. He asked that we please don't touch the stuff. Also that we don't walk around the house unnecessarily, don't leave tracks. We must just wait until he gets here. He especially wants to speak to you."

As Dam blew on his tea to cool it, he peered over his mug at her.

"You think I shouldn't have phoned the police?"

"You did the right thing," was all he said.

21

Beeslaar had just walked every square inch of the farmyard, and his flip-flops were caked with mud from the previous night's rain. He rinsed them under a tap at the back door.

He had found a few more of the grisly thongs with their animal bones and hooves—some at the farm gate, and others on a corner post of the boundary fence a short distance from the house.

Ghaap and Pyl went with him, both silent and a little sheepish, having just suffered Beeslaar's wrath about the disorganised state of the Huilwater dossier. Even Pyl was quiet for a change. Between the three of them they could find no tracks—all traces had been washed away in the downpour.

"Did you find more?" Sara asked, standing in the kitchen doorway.

She was pale, her skin like wax against the black frame of her hair. There were flecks of gold in the green of her eyes, Beeslaar noticed as he straightened up from the tap. And she seemed even smaller today, all eyes and hair.

"Let's go sit down," he suggested and followed her into the house, shoeless.

She put the kettle on again and came to sit opposite him at the kitchen table, her clasped hands resting on the faded check of the plastic tablecloth. "Inspector, what *are* these things? And why are they here?"

"You didn't notice anything strange when you were here yesterday? Or this morning, when you arrived?"

She bit her bottom lip. "Do you think it's . . . that maybe it has something to do with what's happened here? With Freddie?"

"I really couldn't say," he said.

He was dismayed at the forlorn look in her eyes—those eyes should be sparkling, he thought.

"Inspector, who did this to my sister, to the little girl? So much *rage*, it looks like. Even killing the animals. It's all so extreme. And now these grisly things too. It's as if something evil has been let loose here. What's going on?"

"This kind of crime is often brutal, Miss Swarts. We see a lot of it, not just on farms, but in the cities too. But that stuff this morning—I'm not sure. Looks to me like the mark of a sangoma, throwing the bones, that sort of thing. Have you had any contact with the labourers yet?"

She sat up. "Why do you ask?"

"And the manager?"

"He has no idea what it's all about."

Beeslaar nodded. So, De Kok hadn't told her anything about why the labourers left or why the old woman had fled to town.

"Tell me. Do you know whether your sister ever consulted a sangoma?"

"Freddie? Hell, no."

"And the housekeeper?"

"No. Outanna is a churchgoer. I mean, it's not that people who go to traditional healers aren't religious, but as far as I know, the Griquas don't have witch doctors. She liked her herbs and potions though. She and Freddie both."

Beeslaar got up. "I'll get to work on this, Miss Swarts. In the meantime it would be better if you weren't alone on the farm. I'll be here for a while still, just going over to Mr. De Kok to have a word. But please phone me if there's anything, okay?"

"I'll be all right, thank you. Both Dam and Oom Sak are here, so I'm not alone."

"Nevertheless," he said and walked to the door.

She stayed seated, smiled wanly when he said goodbye and left.

22

S ergeant Pyl was having his hand bandaged in De Kok's bathroom when Beeslaar arrived. A bloody handkerchief was draped over the edge of the bath.

One of the birds had nipped him. "Those things should be caged," muttered Pyl as De Kok prepared to dress the wound.

Poor Pyl. It just wasn't his day. He'd already been teased about his broken English on last night's TV news. "Dem stones, dem stones, dem *turning* stones," some constables had sung as he walked into the charge office. And now he'd probably need a tetanus shot too.

Beeslaar decided it was best not to ask what he'd been doing with the birds in the first place. All he said was, "I'll wait outside on the stoep."

As he walked through to the kitchen, it struck him how simply the house was furnished. The easy chairs in the lounge were in good condition, but old and mismatched, as if they'd been bought second-hand. What caught his eyes were the books. Lots of them. The bookshelf was stuffed, and piles of books were stacked around the rest of the room. He gave them a quick glance, saw a familiar name here and there, Antjie Krog and Breytenbach. The man read poetry! The rest were bird books. On one of the shelves lay several ornamental daggers with curved blades and richly decorated hilts. On one wall hung a painting of a bird of prey, with smaller framed photographs around it. More birds. De Kok himself was in one, a serious expression on his face and a bird on his gloved hand.

Another photograph showed an olive-skinned man sitting on a white horse, a falcon on his wrist.

In the kitchen, on a cupboard next to the stove, stood a wooden stand with chef's knives, and rows of herbs and spices were arranged in a handmade wooden rack. A small basket held strips of leather, an awl, a short knife and a pair of scissors. Rolls of thin wire hung on hooks on the wall, probably tools for making jesses and hoods for the birds.

He went out onto the stoep and sat on the low wall, waiting for the first aid to be completed.

When De Kok and the two sergeants appeared, he gestured to the manager to take a seat at the table.

"Tuesday evening," he began. "Where were you, Mr. De Kok?"

The manager didn't look at him, but stared at the Formica tabletop, expressionless.

"Here," he said after a while.

"Is there anyone who can corroborate that?"

De Kok shook his head, pursed his lips.

"So if you walked to the main road and got into a vehicle there, nobody would know?"

"What are you talking about?" He looked up at Beeslaar, a touch of annoyance on his face.

"Just answer the question, Mr. De Kok."

"I don't know."

"You don't know. Right. Where exactly were you before you came to work on Huilwater?"

"Dubai."

"And? What did you do there? And for how long?" He glanced at Pyl, who was standing behind De Kok, studying his injured hand. Beeslaar motioned to him to take notes. Nothing wrong with his writing hand.

De Kok shifted in his chair, the movement small, barely perceptible.

"Jimmy Steele was my employer," he said at last. "He runs a falconry business in Dubai. I worked for him for the last couple of years."

"Jimmy Steele. Who's he?"

"A Brit. His company is called Desert Falconeering."

"And for how long was Mr. Steele your employer?"

"Five years. I was one of six falconers working for him. He had contracts with all the city's big hotels. To control the pigeon plague."

"Pigeons, really? Catching them?"

"Not catching them, Inspector," he said stiffly. "We hunted them. Keeping them off all the glass-fronted buildings. It's expensive to keep them clean. Each of us was in charge of one or two buildings, where we had to fly our birds twice a day. Scare off the pigeons."

"And before Jimmy?"

"I was in Oman."

"And your employer there?"

"What about him?"

"His name, for instance, Mr. De Kok."

"He's a businessman. He had a number of falconers working for him, taking care of his birds. He lives in Muscat, the capital. But we falconers lived in his other home, outside the city, where he keeps horses and birds."

"His name, Mr. De Kok."

"It's a long name."

"Look, we can go to the station and continue this conversation in the interrogation room if you like."

Pyl and Ghaap shared a sideways glance. He knew, and they knew, that they didn't have the luxury of an interrogation room.

"Mohammed bin Khamis al Dheeb."

"Thank you. Is that the man in the photograph in your lounge?"

"Yes, but what does that have to do with this business?"

"Call it pure curiosity. And I'd like addresses too. Jimmy Steele's, to start with. And your Mr. Mohammed alla-whatever. And then you tell me about your relationship with your boss here, Freddie Swarts."

De Kok sniffed lightly. "She wasn't exactly my *boss*. We had a different kind of relationship. More of a partnership. I managed the farm for her while I was looking out for some land of my own."

"Ja? I hear you called her by her first name."

The manager's eyes darkened, but he said nothing.

"When was the last time you saw her alive?"

"But I have already answered all these questions."

"Just do it again; I'm a thorough kinda guy. My colleagues here too. So?"

"The last time was the previous afternoon."

"Not the morning? You didn't have to report to her?"

De Kok pursed his lips again, then said, "She left me alone. I managed the farm. So she could carry on painting. I just informed her or consulted her now and again. And let her see the accounts."

"I'd like to see the accounts too. You won't mind if I take them along?"

"It's all on my computer."

"No problem. We'll take it along now. Inspector Pyl here is our computer expert. Oh, and while you're at it, your heavy-duty-vehicle licence."

"My what?"

"I know you have one. I'd like to see it, make a copy for my file."

Clearly exasperated, De Kok gave a shake of his head.

Beeslaar persisted, "The stuff on the front door of the farmhouse. What's all that about?"

"I don't know."

"Did *you* put it there?"

"No."

"You're sure?"

"Of course I'm sure. I don't have anything to do with it."

Beeslaar turned slightly, leaning his back against a pillar as he sat. He drew his feet up onto the wall of the stoep. He looked out over the farmyard. At the two birds of prey sitting on their perches close to the big trees, turning their heads heavenwards from time to time. What were they looking for? Their lost freedom?

"I think you know who put that stuff there, Mr. De Kok. And I hope you know that it won't help to lie to me. Sooner or later I'll find out. Of that I can assure you."

De Kok kept staring at the table. As still as a pillar of salt, Beeslaar thought. But he didn't look tense. On the contrary, he possessed an almost animal-like tranquillity. Like a cat: apparently idle, but all senses alert.

"Where were you on Wednesday afternoon between one and two?"

De Kok's eyes narrowed.

"Mr. De Kok?"

It was dead quiet on the stoep. Even Pyl had stopped scratching at his notepad and looked expectantly at the man with the beads in his braids.

"Just in town. Sitting in my truck, waiting for the bank to open."

"I think you're lying. Not even a mad dog could stand this heat, never mind sit in a truck for an hour. Now, I'm asking you one last time: Where were you?"

"In my truck, Inspector. And no, there was no one with me. I wasn't talking to anyone on the phone. There was no one in the street. Just me. In the heat. In my truck. And no one to confirm it." He glanced up at Beeslaar. But there was no challenge there, no attempt at playing the smart-arse. It was as if he were entrusting the world with his unquestionable integrity.

Beeslaar found himself mesmerised by the gaze of this strange man. Then he shook himself out of it. "With your permission, Mr. De Kok, I'm going to search your house now. Until I find something that confirms to me that you're lying. And then I'll lock you up and throw away the key."

He walked past De Kok, into the house. "Come on!" he bellowed at his two dazed colleagues.

23

S ara reluctantly returned to her task. She carried the cleaning equipment to Freddie's studio. She took out the Mr. Muscle spray and studied the fine print on the back: TOUGH CLEANING ACTION, LOVES THE JOBS YOU HATE. Ja, right.

She looked around the room. Apart from the easels and canvases, it wasn't very different from when Ma and Pa were still alive: the big double bed, the dressing table with its ornate mirror and Queen-whatsisname legs, the drawers that used to smell of Ma's Oil of Olay face cream. The mustiness of old talc.

The big drawer on the right that once held her bloomers, pantihose and scarves—all tangled in a messy nest. Ma certainly wasn't the tidiest woman in the world. And in the other drawer the brushes and hair curlers and pins and whatnot. She remembered Ma muttering curses, one hand holding a curler in place, the other scrabbling for a hairpin in the chaos of the drawer.

Pa's wardrobe, on the other hand had been a military parade ground. The underpants folded in perfect squares, one for every day of the week. A row of handkerchiefs. He didn't use them for his nose—just to clean his glasses or to dab at spills and spots on his clothes. On one shelf, a copper tin with nail clippers, a pair of cuff links with a horseshoe design, an old war medal that had belonged to Oupa. Next to that, a wristwatch missing its leather strap—also Oupa's. He'd always kept it wound up, its time accurate. So that his father might somehow stay the course, perhaps.

She opened the wardrobe doors carefully. As if Pa's clothes would still be there.

But they were gone.

Instead, the space was bursting with Freddie's art paraphernalia—paint-smeared cloths, pieces of sandpaper, old ice-cream tubs with used tubes of paint, rolls and scraps of canvas, masking tape. In the hanging space, large stretched canvases were stacked upright. Some were still blank, while others bore the first soft pencil strokes of a new design.

How terribly absent Pa was, she realised. Vanished, along with the intimate signs of his insular inner world. As if he had never been there at all—like the faint traces of Bushmen on the farm. Just a hint that remained. An arrow tip in the sandy soil, tiny fragments of ostrich-shell beads. Nobody to weep for the San. Generations of them, hunted down like animals for hundreds of years—by white and black alike. Only the land endured, impassive, irrespective of whose blood flowed over it. The rocks and sand and the lingering red sunsets remained, unchanging. Though the original people of the veld were gone forever.

And who would weep for Freddie? Just a handful of individuals left behind to remember, keeping the memory of loss alive. But even they disappear, eventually. All that's left is the wind. And the sand. And the rock.

With Freddie's erasure from this place, Pa had also edged towards oblivion. Freddie bore the last traces of him. Daddy's girl. The apple of his eye, perhaps because she carried within her Ma's spirit—silent as the veld, her emotions invisible as the waters that wept below the land's surface at Huilwater. She had the same turquoise eyes, the same slender frame as Ma, the two of them frail as newborn lambs.

Sara felt the sadness welling up in her throat, and she closed the wardrobe. But then immediately opened it again as something caught her eye: the edge of a painting, right there at the back. She flipped through the frames. Each one of them, she noticed, was some sort of self-portrait. Every one macabre: buttercup blonde hair curling around the head, wild and sensual—becoming a noose around her neck; a blonde bride with a crown of thorns and a bloodied veil; another—pregnant, a pile of white bones in her belly.

The last one was a large portrait, almost as big as she was. Sara tugged at it—a Kalahari landscape. A typical scene, thorn trees and a seething sun. Above the horizon floated a giant snake with yellow eyes and a glittering diamond on its forehead. Its jaws hung open like a crocodile's, and on its tongue lay a blonde woman with a crucifix on her chest, as if she were some kind of sacrifice. In the foreground, a long, winding row of couples stood waiting in pairs. Men in old-fashioned suits with top hats and tails, and naked women with long feathers between their buttocks. Several of the women had no heads. Creatures with strange insectlike legs moved among them.

How grotesque, thought Sara. But then she saw that the snake was also carrying a rider—a male figure.

It was Dam! Sitting there triumphantly with an eagle on his hand, wearing a traditional leather loincloth.

Bloody hell, Frederika, had you completely lost your marbles? What could a painting like this mean?

Sara put the canvas down and picked up the one she'd seen the previous afternoon—Freddie with bits of hair floating around her head, the exposed scalp, her own bloody heart dripping in her hand . . .

She raced outside. But the policeman's car had already gone.

24

Beeslaar and his two colleagues were driving down a low hill when his phone chirped. An unfamiliar number, he saw.

But when he answered, there was no one at the other end of the line. He stepped on the brakes and the car juddered to a halt over the corrugations and loose gravel.

"Hello!" he said, louder this time.

"Reverse," suggested Sergeant Pyl. "You'll get better reception higher up."

Beeslaar waved at him to shut up. He could hear something, only just. Breathing.

He turned off the engine.

"Who's there?" he called. "Hello!"

A click, then silence.

Beeslaar searched his call log, found the number. But he didn't call back. It was a landline. Joburg.

How many people had his new cellphone number? Less than a handful, surely. He had made a clean break when he left Johannesburg two months ago. With places, possessions and especially with people. He had no family left, a handful of friends. Apart from two or three ex-colleagues, he'd only notified a few people—for his medical aid, insurance, the usual official bumph. They were all listed in his contacts.

But not this number.

Deep down, he knew, though. He knew the name. His heart had said it already. His mind, however, refused to listen, beat the name back into oblivion.

Beeslaar pushed the phone into his pocket and flung open the door. He walked up the road, back towards the hill. He continued over the the crest, until he could no longer see the car. Then he stopped. Eyes closed.

When the pounding in his chest had stopped, he turned and headed back.

Sergeant Ghaap was standing under a tree, smoking, when he got to the car.

"Give me a cigarette," Beeslaar brusquely demanded.

An astonished Ghaap complied. Without a single word.

25

H ello, Oom Sak. Do you know where Dam is?" Sara asked when she reached the back stoep of the manager's house. The old man was sitting alone, smoking. He gestured towards the veld.

"Has he been gone long?"

Oom Sak squinted at her, shook his head.

Sara walked up to a fence, then stopped and scanned the nearby koppie, the veld. She couldn't see him, but called nevertheless. Several times. The dense silence of the veld pressed in on her.

"Here I am." His voice, behind her.

"Good God, Dam, where were you?" Startled, her words rung out sharply.

"Has something happened?" His voice was quiet, and though he looked at her, it was as if he was staring through her.

"Yes, there is something." Unsure, she searched for words. "I thought the police were still here. I actually wanted, well, to show them one of Freddie's paintings. And when I saw Beeslaar had left already . . . "

Dam stood motionless, hands by his sides.

"Did Freddie ever mention . . . Do you know if she ever had premonitions?"

Barely perceptibly, his mouth tightened.

She tried again. "Did you know you were in one of her paintings?"

He turned his head away.

"Dam?"

"I know of the painting you're talking about. But that's all."

"And the other one? The one where she—the one that looks like the murder scene?"

He did not answer.

"Won't you come take a look, please? It's there, in her studio."

Dam did not move.

"It looks as if she knew exactly how she was going to die. Are you sure you've never seen it?"

"You're probably reading too much into it."

"But really, Dam. That picture. It's precisely how she died."

"That's ridiculous. And I think you'd better go back to town. It's dangerous wandering about here—especially on your own."

"Don't say it's ridiculous. The painting is a self-portrait. You can see it clearly. And it shows how she was murdered. Exactly. The hair, the wound. Everything. It looks as if she *knew* what was going to happen to her. There's nothing else you can *read* in it. Come see for yourself!"

"I'm not going to look at paintings now. I've got work to do." He turned and walked away, towards the veld.

"What's going on with you, man?" she shouted after him. "Are you scared, or something?"

Dam stopped in his tracks and turned towards her. His face like dull parchment. "You'd better go back to town, to Mrs. Lambrechts. It's not good for you to go digging around here like this. It's upsetting. And it's not safe. I can't hang around here to look after you. There are animals that need food and water. I don't have any help now."

"I'm not going away. And I'm not going to let myself be chased off the farm like this. I'm here to clean up the house. And I'll decide for myself when I want to leave, okay? Or do you want me gone? Like with Freddie?"

Dam looked at her in shock, as if she'd hit him. Then he turned and walked away.

Sara groaned and closed her eyes. Her stupid temper.

"Dam!" she called after him, but her voice broke.

He had already disappeared into the veld.

Tannie Yvonne and all three dogs came to greet Sara at the front door.

"Old Koos from next door said you can go take a swim in his dam any time," said Yvonne when the dogs' noisy jubilation had piped down. "He had it cleaned out this morning, specially."

She swam in her underwear. By the time she finally emerged from the cool green water, the dusk had deepened to a murky purple. She wrapped herself in a towel and hopped over the low wire fence into Yvonne's yard again. She took a shower, washed her hair, and changed into a clean T-shirt and shorts before joining Tannie Yvonne on the stoep, barefoot.

"A whole lot of people phoned for you today. I left the names next to the phone," she said.

It was a long list. Various unfamiliar names—possibly people from the district calling to sympathise. There was a newspaper or two, including the one Maria Bosch worked for.

She fetched her cellphone and punched in Harry's number.

"Have you managed to cool down a bit?" he wanted to know.

"Just took a splash in the neighbour's cement dam."

"So, you're not angry any more?"

"Angry? Me?"

He laughed. "So I assume I can go ahead and do the story for those Englishmen?"

"Ag, it's all right, Harry. You do your story. It was stupid of me to get so worked up in the first place. Would you please put my plants in the bath before you leave?"

"Rescue mission complete. I've already fetched them and put them in here with mine. Dalena down the hall will take care of them all while we're gone." Then he asked, "How was your day?"

She wondered where to begin. So many emotions in just one day: fear, anger, confusion, sadness. And regret, hanging over it all.

"I'm beginning to wonder about this murder, Harry. And about Freddie—"

"What do you mean?"

"Whether it really was another farm murder—in the true sense of the term, I mean. Intruders, and all that."

"Sara? What are you talking about?"

"Look, I'm serious, Harry. I went through Freddie's paintings today, and there's one of her, a kind of self-portrait. But it's exactly—she painted herself almost exactly like she, like, well, Wednesday." She exhaled, frustrated.

"What do you mean?"

"She painted herself, you know. Exactly the way she was murdered. She's sitting against a chair, her body carved open. Covered in blood. And her hair is exactly . . . Just the way it was. I saw her . . . yesterday morning. It was cut off in clumps. Clean off. And in the painting it's exactly like that. It's almost as if she knew."

"That can't be, Sara."

"What if she knew someone wanted her dead? And that they—"

"Sara. Hold on. That's just not possible. If she knew someone wanted to kill her, she'd have gone to the police. Not put her suspicions into a painting. Surely she wasn't crazy, hey?"

"Harry, I'm telling you. The painting—"

"Have you spoken to the police?"

"I wanted to, but they'd left already."

"What do you mean?"

She told him about the voodoo stuff at the front door, how she'd wanted to start cleaning and found the paintings.

"Just imagine if Freddie suspected . . . Imagine if someone wanted her out of the way. Someone else. An ordinary someone. A lover, someone who had reason to want her dead."

"Sara, this was a farm murder. I know it's hard to accept, but it is what it is."

"Harry . . . "

"Have you ever heard of the different stages of grief, Sara?"

"What does that have—"

"The first stage is denial. At first you don't want to believe this dreadful thing has happened. It feels unreal. In fact, you refuse to believe it. Then you get angry. Next comes bargaining—"

"What are you trying to say? That I'm *bargaining*? With who?"

"With fate, reality, whatever. It's too hard to accept. Senseless. Fact is, your feelings are completely normal. You're struggling to accept it. Anybody in your position would struggle."

Sara gnawed at a fingernail, then said, "Harry, I swear to God, it's not my imagination, and I guarantee you I'm not in denial. That painting looks exactly . . . And there's other stuff too. Things like . . . " The words dried up. She could hear the scepticism in his silence.

At last he said, "Sara. You yourself know that your sister's paintings were kind of weird. And I'm sure you'll come across more like that. Talk to someone. It's a terrible shock, Sara. Such a violent death. Anyone would clutch at straws—"

"I'm not clutching at straws! And I *am* talking to someone! What do you think I'm doing here with you right now?" Sara swallowed hard, paused. "I'm sorry, Harry. There I go again."

But he wasn't angry, just gave a good-natured laugh.

After he'd rung off she returned some of the calls. Locals

mostly, older folk who had known her parents in days gone by. The reactions ranged from bewilderment to rage.

Everyone wanted to know when the funeral was, whether they could help her with anything.

Yvonne Lambrechts had set the table on the stoep. "You haven't maybe heard anything from Nelmari yet?" Sara asked while they were eating.

She struggled with the food, aware of the trouble the older woman had gone to in making the chicken salad.

"No, my dear, nothing. Perhaps she's gone off again."

"I'll phone, then. Maybe go there tomorrow before I head back to the farm."

"Again?"

"I didn't manage to finish everything today."

"I'm not happy with you being there alone. I'm coming with you tomorrow."

How could she explain to her? This was work she had to do alone. She wanted to wash the place down. Floors, walls, everything. Get the smell out. Let the hot sun and the wind into the house, let it blow away all the damp shadows. And then she wanted to clear everything, pack it all up. Freddie's things. Pick up each brush, mulling over its history, its story. Fold up each dress, each shirt herself. The entire substance of her sister's life in this place.

She would pick up the thread that had slipped from her hand. Or *was* it simply clutching at straws?

"It's maybe better for me to go by myself, Tannie Yvonne. I just want to, really . . . " she didn't need to finish, as Tannie Yvonne clearly understood.

After supper, Sara called Nelmari, but there was no answer on any of her numbers. She left messages.

What now?

She fetched her laptop and took it out to the stoep. The 3G connection worked fine. There were eighty emails. A bunch of them from Dawid, the night editor at the newspaper who had seduced her at an office party, stringing her along for months, until, despite his assurances, she found out he hadn't left his wife after all. For a split second she felt like writing back, "The very next message you send I'll forward to your lovely wife!" But it all seemed so unimportant now. She deleted the emails without reading them. There were several from Maria Bosch. She read the last one:

Hi Sara,

I'm so sorry for your loss, truly.

And I feel like a real bitch for being on your case like this. Sorry, hey. Hope you understand my boss is the real arsehole.

How are you?

Don't know if you're getting email over there, but I thought I'd warn you: We're going huge with your sister's story tomorrow. Sunday paper de luxe. Photos, the works. Her friend in town spoke to us—"she was much loved, beautiful, a philanthropist. The Madonna of the Kalahari," and more. That last bit will be the title.

The boss wants to make a real feature. We'll run other articles with it—white farmers in uproar (sidebars on farm attacks, murder statistics in the country, etc.), landless blacks threatening illegal occupation, the fiasco surrounding land reform, the whole caboodle.

Just thought you should know, okay?

Thinking of you. Let me know when you're back in Cape Town.

MB

Sara closed the email. Madonna of the Kalahari!
Dear God. It sounded like a soap opera. And Nelmari

Viljoen . . . Too busy to speak to her, but happy to peddle melodrama to the Sunday papers.

One or two emails from Harry caught her eye. She skimmed them—news about a march against violence in Cape Town. She wrote a quick reply. Then she went to make a mug of tea, sat down at the kitchen table with the computer and typed the words "Farm Attacks South Africa" into the Google search bar.

There were tens of thousands of entries. Freddie's name jumped out at her in a couple of headings. She moved along swiftly. Involuntarily clicked one lower down on the list: gruesome photos bloomed across the screen. Dead bodies. Mostly head wounds. There was one of a middle-aged woman in a floral dress on a double bed. Her hands were bound with neckties, her legs spread apart. Face blue, tongue dangling grotesquely. Her corpse had been raped repeatedly, the caption claimed. Another picture showed a man with his abdomen sliced open, he'd been hanged from the hot-water tank in his bathroom. An image of a baby with angular marks on its tiny dead body, evidently a hot clothes iron. The child's hands had been chopped off.

There were more pictures, but she didn't open them. In the text alongside the pictures:

"Genocide: More than 40,000 farm attacks since 1991 in S.A. Nearly 3,000 dead." And in a smaller font:

> Victims tortured, eyelids cut off, genitals mutilated, babies' bodies set alight with petrol. This is a human rights issue! Why is the South African government silent? The world watches as men, women and children are slaughtered.

She closed the page quickly. What in God's name was she doing? It was madness to be cruising these chambers of horror. But still, she *had* to know. She wanted to know exactly what had happened to Freddie. And how much of her own unease was her imagination, how much was real.

She clicked on an Afrikaans website—an agricultural union, she saw. It was considerably more restrained, estimating the murder rate at closer to 2,500, the number of attacks at 35,000.

It said one had the "impression" that farming and all farming people were totally irrelevant to the government of this country—despite agriculture being a cornerstone of the economy and one of the biggest employers. But whenever a white farmer stepped over the line, it received major attention in parliament. At mass rallies, politicians encourage people to sing "Kill the Boer, Kill the Farmer." But nobody says a word about thousands of farmers, wives, children and labourers alike who are killed and maimed in the most gruesome of ways.

Sara closed the page. That wasn't what she was after either. But maybe that's all she'd find on the Internet. Figures, divergent statistics, emotions running high.

She went out to the stoep with her cellphone, tried Nelmari again. This time she answered.

"Sara! Hi, oh, sorry, we keep missing each other. I'm in Kimberley."

"I hear you spoke to the Sunday papers, Nelmari."

A brief silence, then, "Where did you hear that?"

"Oh, a colleague. Forget about it. That's not why I'm calling. I just wanted to speak to you about Freddie. About a specific painting of hers."

"Sara, I definitely didn't speak to any newspapers."

"It's okay, Nelmari."

"You know, I can imagine you must be very upset, but I promise you I never spoke to anybody. I've been working since early this morning. One crisis after another."

"Don't worry about it. That's not why I'm calling."

"But I don't like being accused of things I haven't done!"

"I'm not. Listen, I just want to speak to you about a painting. Hello? Hello?" But the line had gone dead.

Sara stared at the phone in her hand. What was going on with these people?

26

Beeslaar sat down on a rock in the veld some way out of the town. He was trying to find whatever it was that had been pricking him through his socks. Itching like the devil. His socks looked like hedgehogs with all the spiky little blackjacks. He began the tedious task of pulling them off one by one.

It was still early, barely six o'clock on Sunday morning. Though the sun was long up and the veld was already vibrating with insect calls, sounding like a junior-school percussion band. Swarms of weaver birds and other little brown jobs swooped noisily through the air.

He'd been lying awake since shortly after midnight. Picking over the previous morning's call. All day it had worried him, refusing to yield. And all through the night too.

What did she want to tell him? Because it *was* her. He could sense it. He'd been so sure, he'd even stored the number on his phone under her name.

Gerda.

So he could call her back? He didn't think so. Let sleeping dogs lie, his mother would have said. There was too much chaos between them. Those were *her* words. "And too much pain, Albertus."

Her children—both of them. And he, Beeslaar, *he* was to blame.

He got up and started walking again. Just leave those sleeping dogs be.

Concentrate on this case.

Ja, sure, what case? He had nothing. There were the trucks that had been seen on Tuesday night on the Huilwater road. But that was sweet fuck-all, it could just as well have been the man on the moon. No evidence of any value.

And De Kok. Those trucks certainly weren't hidden on Huilwater, there was no trace of anything of the sort. But the man did have a heavy-duty licence.

And he had money. Did that mean he had accomplices? Were the trucks being stashed somewhere else? And what was a man like De Kok doing managing a piss-poor farm like that? Was it a ruse to cover up something else? With his Code 14 licence. Not every Tom, Dick and Harry could boast of hauling twenty-six wheels. Said he'd obtained the licence before heading for Dubai. So he could drive long-haul trucks if the falconry business didn't work out. And the facts checked out. The licence had been issued before he left, eight years ago. Still.

As a legitimate farm manager, he could in any case come and go as he pleased in the district. Knew the roads like the back of his hand, knew the farmers, their labourers, the movement of stock. And then there was the gaping hole in his Wednesday afternoon. Why had nobody noticed him? He alleged he'd been sitting in his truck, in plain sight, under a tree right in front of the bank. For an hour! Fucking well impossible in this heat.

He looked like a shrewd fellow. With all his books. Christ, poetry!

And motive? That's where it got tricky.

He was on first-name terms with the deceased. She had trusted him. And then what? She caught him doing something? Money? Stock theft? Was there an argument?

Few people liked De Kok. Pretorius found him arrogant. And Nelmari Viljoen had said something else. She had begun to feel more and more excluded by Freddie. So? Maybe he'd had some kind of hold on Freddie Swarts?

What kind of hold could a farm manager have on his employer? Though he'd alleged it was more of a partnership than some subservient yes-ma'am-no-ma'am thing.

And speaking of her: a naïve do-gooder, trying to help the Griqua with their land claim. That must have raised blood pressure in the district. The children—the child with the watch tattoo mentioned by Nelmari Viljoen.

Beeslaar got up and walked on until the heat began to get to him. He glanced at his watch. Almost seven o'clock. If he turned around now, it would be forty minutes' walk back. And anyway, the early-morning magic of the veld had already passed. And the blackjacks in his socks were driving him crazy. He sat down on an old anthill and took off his socks, stuffed them into his pocket. This was probably the reason De Kok went around sockless.

He walked back with long strides, mulling over the case. As he approached town, he heard voices. They were coming from the direction of a rusty old shed on the outskirts of town. He walked closer, his curiosity piqued.

The shed was Sarel Venter's workshop, where he repaired all types of engines, and cut semi-precious stones from the area. It was surrounded by a motley collection of lawnmowers, fridges, old engine parts, piles of scrap metal.

To one side stood a stone-polishing drum. He'd heard that Venter had an army of people collecting tiger's eye and rose quartz, which he cut up and polished. And sold by the bucketload.

A number of cars were parked around the shed. Voices floated from the open windows. A church service, Beeslaar was astonished to realise. He was just about to leave when he heard a voice booming. Shouting about the white blood that would soon flow.

Beeslaar approached cautiously. The windows of the little building were wide open. It must be hellish hot inside under that bare corrugated-iron roof. And there wasn't even a hint of a breeze. He peered in through one of the windows.

"To carry the *torch* of white Christianity in this land," a man with a wild red beard and a barrel belly uttered reverently. He was praying in front of several rows of people sitting on plastic chairs, their heads bowed.

"Amen," they said.

There was a loud braying Beeslaar couldn't fathom, until he saw someone blowing a twisted kudu horn. An attempt, he realised with amusement, to imitate the biblical ram's horn. He'd thought these right-wing churches had died out after 1994, when the AWB and other splinter organisations on the far right had collapsed.

Inside, the preacher had started his sermon, his voice rising and falling theatrically. "A man stands by the graveside with his head bowed . . . "

Who was this preacher? Beeslaar had never seen him in the district before.

"With hunched shoulders, he stands," the voice was mournful, "his hands clasped in prayer. A Boer warrior of old . . . " He took a sip of water and carefully wiped his mouth with a handkerchief. The silence was heavy with expectation.

"Broken by grief!" he exploded. "Crushed by an enemy that robbed him of his beloved land!"

The man looked heavenwards, his eyes feverish. Then his eyelids closed and he dropped his head. "And today, dear brothers and sisters, today he is standing by that graveside once again. The grave of his daughters who have been brutally raped! Whose throats were slit like animals, their bodies slashed open, a sacrifice to Satan! The land of our fathers, which God promised and gave to the Christian Afrikaner. As we stand here today, we are facing our biggest crisis!" He paused, picked up a book whose pages fell open easily, and began to read. "Our people are exposed to the dangers of a black barbarian threat that has destroyed numerous nations." He paused. "We must heed these words of one of the great sons of our nation—Dr D. F. Malan!"

He looked out over the audience. "We're seeing it happen. First Zimbabwe. And now South Africa. Heed the prophetic words of Dr Malan: 'A nation that has lost its racial purity cannot continue to exist as a nation . . . We have the divine right to be Afrikaners. No power in the world can thwart our nationhood, because God created our nation!'"

As he closed the book, Beeslaar glimpsed the picture on the cover: a bald man with round black spectacles, the first premier of the apartheid government, forerunner of H. F. Verwoerd.

"Dearly beloved in the Lord," the preacher boomed after a pregnant pause, "rise up!" And then he hissed, "Before it is too late."

A hypnotic silence hung over the crowd.

The kudu horn was held aloft. It was Polla Pieterse, emerging from his rapture: with ecstatic abandon he blew, breaking the spell.

27

G ood morning! I've just baked some bread."
It was Dam, calling from the row of trees between the two houses. He was standing with a dishcloth over his shoulder and a pipe in his hand.

Sara looked up. She had been hauling packaging from the boot of the car—black plastic bags and folded cardboard boxes. Walking over, she smiled back at him. Happy to see him. Happy about the warmth in his voice. Happy that the long, infernal night had come to an end.

He had set a table on the back stoep. Bright white table-cloth, blue serviettes. In the centre stood a small copper vase holding a single rose.

"I fell in love with roses during the time I spent in Oman."

"Roses in Oman! I thought it was all desert."

"It is. And apparently also the birthplace of the rose."

He pulled up a chair and gestured to her to sit down.

"The Arabs of today are still crazy about roses. It's a passion, the same way it is for the English."

"Makes sense, I guess," Sara said. "I mean, that it would be a desert flower. Roses and cannas and zinnias and African marigolds—stinkafrikaners, as my mother called them—are just about all you ever see in the gardens around here. My mother used to have a rose garden in front of the house. Before she got sick. Freddie and I would catch beetles for her. Those black-and-yellow ones that eat roses. Twenty cents a beetle."

Oom Sak stepped out with a pan of eggs that he set down

while Dam went to fetch bread from the oven. Fragrant steam rose from the slices he laid on each plate. For a while they ate in silence.

"It's a flower of trust," Dam said, resting his knife and fork on the plate. "In Persia, many years ago, they used to leave a wild rose at the door of a room before an important meeting. And in the Middle Ages people would hang a rose over the dining table as a sign that guests were safe there. That everything that was said during the meal would be regarded as confidential."

She cut her bread into little blocks, picked one up and popped it in her mouth. The bread was sweet and lightly flavoured, maybe with aniseed. The butter had melted, tasting like caramel. Slightly salty too. Comforting. But still she struggled to keep up her enthusiasm. A moment ago she was starving, but now everything stuck in her throat.

"Have you ever noticed the round pattern in the middle of the ceilings of old houses?" Dam asked. "If you look carefully, you'll see it's a rose design. To show that the people in the room could trust each other. Later the meaning was lost, and the design was purely decorative. But we still use the expression—sub rosa."

He reached out to the rose. A tiny spider, barely visible, crawled onto his finger. He shook it gently to the ground.

"I'm sorry about my outburst yesterday, Dam," Sara said. She guessed that was, after all, what he was alluding to with his rose stories.

"No, Sara. It's me. I was being rude. Beeslaar had been giving me a rather hard time."

"Yes, but—"

He held up his hand. "A day like yesterday, Sara," he said softly, his eyes gleaming, "most people would have buckled." Then he smiled. "You're probably good at your job. As a newspaper journalist, I mean. There probably aren't too many people who'd mess with you?"

"It's more a case of having a short fuse. Gets me into trouble more often than not. It was one of the main differences between Freddie and me. My father always said I was the goddess of thunder. And Freddie, well, she was the queen of frost. She could stay angry for days. Just like my mother."

A shadow moved over his face. "But she was soft. Too soft. Unlike—" he hesitated.

"Me. Unlike me, I know," she said, completing his sentence.

"That's not what I was trying to say."

"It's okay. I've always been this way. And when I get stressed out, or frightened . . . I can't help it, I get completely beside myself. And it's worse now."

"We've all been through an awful thing this week. None of us are behaving normally. Everyone is scared. And also angry. Off balance. You even more so, I'm sure."

"I didn't mean what I said, Dam. I always talk before I think."

"That's okay, Sara. I understand."

No, he doesn't understand, she wanted to throw back at him. He didn't know. The anxiety, the paralysing guilt, the feeling that it should have been *her* instead. Not a soft-hearted lamb like Freddie. He had no idea how bewildered she felt. The painting, everything. Why didn't he say something about the painting? Was he ignoring the subject on purpose?

She looked across at the birds.

"How are your birds?" she said in an effort to return to neutral terrain. "Are you going to set them free again someday, or what?"

He smiled faintly, but said nothing.

"It's the first time I've seen them up close. They're magnificent creatures," she continued. "Are they the kind you use for hunting?"

"The eagle I'm just helping along until his wing heals. But

the little goshawk. I wanted to keep her, but now . . . I had started teaching her, with the dog. But they killed my dog too. My hunting dog. So. I'll let her go. But first she must learn to hunt. On her own. She's still very young. And they're stupid when they're young. In the wild, many of them die as young adults because they can't hunt well enough yet."

"But how do you teach them?"

"With lots of patience. That's all."

He poured himself some more tea, with milk from a cup-shaped silver jug.

"Have a little more bread, and I'll tell you more," he said. "It's a long process," he began. "First I must gain the bird's trust. It needs to learn it's safe to get onto my hand. So I have to spend at least two hours a day with it. Every day. If I'm away for longer than a day, it turns wild again. This happens very quickly. Then you lose six weeks' work. So, ja. I teach it to associate me with food. And once it's clicked, I let it get hungry."

"How do you know when a bird is hungry? Does it bite?"

"Well, it bites anyway."

"Does it hurt? How do you teach it to stop?"

"You teach it by showing you don't bite back. If you show any hint of aggression, you've lost that creature for good. Birds of prey have excellent memories. Hurt them once, and it's over."

"And then?"

"You weigh them. A bird like that one—the goshawk—weighs about six hundred and fifty grams. With its crop full. But when they're hungry, they weigh less. So that's how I know. You can see it too in the way they become restless. But it's actually their weight."

"And an eagle?"

"The same."

Sara was on the point of asking another question, but Dam raised his hand again, palm flat.

"Now I've got a few questions for *you*. I can see you're working in the big house. But Oom Sak and I have to get to town today. And I don't want to leave you here by yourself. So I was thinking: if we help you, you'll finish sooner and then we can all leave for town later this morning. What do you say?"

Sara pushed her plate aside. "I was actually planning to stay all day," she said. "I haven't even started with the bedrooms. In any case, I'd like to clear it all up myself."

"I already have," he said.

"Was it *you* who cleaned up? I thought it was Outanna and—"

"The problem is, Sara, it's not safe. When Oom Sak and I leave, there'll be no one here."

"Well, I'll keep the doors locked."

"There aren't even dogs here. This is ridiculous."

That word. Ridiculous. The sort of word that cancels out all debate. That made her see red. It was a Freddie word, "But Sara, it's ridiculous to send Pa for an op if he doesn't want it. And he *doesn't* want it. It'll only prolong the suffering. He wants to come here—to Huilwater—to die. It's *ridiculous* to leave him in hospital."

Sara took a deep breath, and said, "Give me till lunchtime, okay?"

28

There was an uproar at the station when Beeslaar arrived later that morning. The charge office was full of people. A rowdy, angry crowd. The two constables behind the counter were trying to make themselves heard above the clamour.

Beeslaar pushed his way through the mob. "What's going on here?" he called out to one of the constables. The man gestured over his shoulder at a young boy in handcuffs standing in a corner behind the counter, his head covered in blood. The boy cowered back, shaking, as if trying to take up as little space as possible.

"They want the child," shouted Shoes Morotse, the young constable with girlfriend trouble. "He stole washing from their clotheslines. The patrol vehicle rescued him. People were beating him with sticks."

Beeslaar looked at the shivering boy. A flap of skin hung loose above his left ear, and blood was dripping down his neck onto a ragged T-shirt. One eye was already swollen shut, and his lip was cut.

Beeslaar raised himself to his full height and clapped his hands together. "Quiet!" he roared.

The commotion stopped instantly.

"Is there anyone here who would like to lay a charge?" he asked.

Silence. Then the racket started up afresh. "A thief . . . Stole our clothes!" was all he could make out, the rest of the cries were in Tswana.

Beeslaar roared again.

In the silence that followed, he spoke firmly, "The child is going nowhere! *Only* those looking to lay a charge against him may stay. The rest of you must get out!" There were mutterings, but Beeslaar ignored them. "I'm giving you one minute— and then I start taking down the names of those who assaulted him like this! Understand?"

Some people began moving to the door, complaining as they went. Beeslaar told Shoes to lock the boy in a cell for his own safety, and to fetch the nurse from the clinic to clean him up. His colleague could take care of any statements.

Then he fled to the sanctuary of his office. He wondered where his two colleagues were that morning. They had agreed to rendezvous in the office around lunchtime. He knew Sergeant Pyl was active in his church, a deacon—singing in the choir, teaching Sunday school. He didn't know quite as much about Ghaap's Sunday routine.

Beeslaar had brought along his portable CD player. He set it down on the windowsill next to a struggling fern, and paged through his CD caddy. Bach, he decided. Music for thinking. Had a positive effect, apparently, on the brain's alpha rhythms, or something like that. He'd read it somewhere. But that wasn't why he was playing it. He'd always been more of a rock 'n'roll man. Kind of. In reality, he'd never been too clued up on any music. But then he'd discovered the Mozart CD.

It had been in that terrible time after Grovétjie died. During one of his midnight ramblings through his house in Fordsburg.

He'd been stumbling about, scratching through long-neglected cupboards. Searching. For what? Nothing, really. Just for the sake of digging around. Maybe for something from his past that might make sense to him, might anchor him. But the things he'd found were worthless. A fountain pen he'd won for composition in primary school. An old, misshapen rugby ball, the leather cracked with age and disuse. It was one of the only gifts he ever got from his father, that rugby ball.

He had stuffed it back into the cupboard, laid his hand on an armless Batman figure next, then an army medal, the bell off his first bicycle. All kinds of things which he'd tossed back into the cupboard again.

But the Mozart CD. He hadn't put that back.

It was a horn concerto, he must have got it as a gift from someone, or won it in one of those bizarre charity raffles. French horn, to be precise. The first time he'd ever noticed the existence of such an instrument. And the sound! He had listened to it night after night, finding a strange kind of solace in it. Even now. It was the only music that had any chance of lulling him to sleep.

The discovery had sparked something. He started exploring the classics by himself. Bought himself more Mozart, discovering the wealth of his works for violin. Then Beethoven: he fell in love with his music for piano. The overwhelming simplicity of the Fourteenth Piano Sonata. Especially the Adagio, the *Moonlight Sonata*.

Now, in his office, he turned on the CD player, volume low, only just audible. He looked over the list he and his two colleagues had drawn up the previous evening: a to-do list as long as his arm. Starting with everything that had to be done in Upington the following day.

He took his cellphone from his shirt pocket. Set it aside on the desk. Gerda . . . Was it really her? His hand hesitated over the phone. But he decided against calling. *There's too much chaos between us . . .*

He had never been lucky in love. His first girlfriend's mother banned her from seeing him, and he still wasn't sure why. Maybe because he was from the wrong side of the tracks.

There had been others. Like Renée, when he'd been a trainee constable. Pretty. Tall, full-figured. Hair cropped short like a boy's. Left him without giving any reason. *That* hurt like hell. She simply didn't want him. Full stop. There were others like that after her. Girlfriends as well as disappointments. They came and they went.

Until Gerda. She was pregnant the first time he saw her. He couldn't stop looking at her. Her slim arms, the large belly. The way her breasts filled out her top. He dreamt of those breasts: her pale skin, the sprinkling of freckles, and, on hot days, the soft blue pulsing of a vein.

The phone on his desk shook him out of his reverie.

It was Sergeant Ghaap, he was on his way to the office.

Beeslaar had hardly put the phone down when it rang again. A journalist, someone called Harry Van Zyl. He was on his way from Cape Town and wanted to know if he could come and talk to the inspector. He was investigating safety issues in agriculture and needed information—the commissioner himself had referred him to Beeslaar, he added.

"I'll hardly be in my office this week," he warned.

"That doesn't matter," Van Zyl pressed on. "I'll be in the area for a while, and can wait for a more convenient time."

"Listen, you might be waiting in vain. My advice is to interview Superintendent Leonard Mogale in Upington. He's the man in charge of this whole area, and he'll be the best person to help you."

A pause. Then, "Inspector, I don't want to be difficult. This is not about the murders out on that farm. I'm working more broadly, just need an informal chat. I'm doing plenty of research, talking to a lot of people and so on. But it's important I talk to someone like you, just to check my facts. And the commissioner says you're the man I need to talk to."

Fact checking, his arse. He'd heard that tune before. "Call me when you're here," he said. "We'll see what we can do."

Half an hour later, Sergeant Pyl walked in. He was wearing his Sunday suit, and perspiration glistened on his forehead, Beeslaar saw with some satisfaction.

He placed a plastic bag on Beeslaar's desk. "From my ma," he said with a smile. "Roosterkoek with curried mince. She made extra, for you."

Beeslaar opened the bag. Inside was an ice-cream tub containing three enormous fragrant rolls, crusts crispy from the embers, branded in big black Xs from the grill. His mouth watered. "Well, thank your mother for me. We'll just wait for Ghaap. I'll take care of the coffee. You go fetch your notebooks and stuff so long."

Once Pyl had left, Beeslaar took his wallet and walked to the café across the road. He bought a meat pie and a big Coke. Back at the station he found a plastic cup, poured in some Coke and walked to the cells.

The boy sat on the floor in a corner of the cell, his head bandaged. Beeslaar offered him the pie and Coke. The boy regarded him with suspicion. Beeslaar put the food down in front of him, stepped away, and leaned with his back against the cool cell wall. The child grabbed the food, wolfing it down, barely chewing before he swallowed. Then he drank the Coke, belched, and wiped his mouth with his hands. He didn't look up. Kept his eyes on the cement floor ahead of him.

Beeslaar crouched down on his haunches.

"What's your name?" he asked.

The boy swallowed and mumbled something. He was still shaking, Beeslaar noticed. He was lucky the patrol vehicle had been around when the crowd had caught him that morning. Otherwise he might have lost more than his voice. Street justice turned violent quickly. Petty thieves like these could pay with their lives—just another of the harsh realities of a society sinking into an ocean of criminality. And a worn-out, over-stretched police force that was simply no match for it all.

"I can't hear, son. Come again."

"Bulelani," whispered the boy.

"Did you steal the people's washing from their lines, Bulelani?"

The boy dropped his head.

"Where are your own people, Bulelani? Your mother and father?"

The boy was skinny, wearing a pair of running shoes, one of which was almost entirely missing a sole.

Where did all the homeless children come from? What happened in the life of a child like this? At what moment did he find he no longer had a home? Was it after his mother had lost the battle with AIDS? Or after his father had laid into him with a sjambok yet again? Or when the lure of his glue-sniffing mates became stronger than home ties? Were these the kind of questions that persuaded a young woman like Freddie Swarts to foster homeless kids?

He didn't know. All he knew was that for this child, the future was grim.

"Where do you live?"

The boy's eyes were fixed on the floor.

"Bulelani?" The child raised his head with a fearful look.

Beeslaar reached for the boy's left arm. There, at his wrist, a watch tattoo.

The detective stood up without a word. At the cell door, he looked around one last time. The boy was already lying on his side, his hands cushioning his head on the floor. Beeslaar pulled the cell door shut and walked away. He walked up to Shoes Morotse, who was on duty at the front desk.

"For God's sake, get that child a blanket and mattress in the cell," he said irritably.

"But there aren't any."

"What do you mean there aren't any? Aren't any what?"

"Blankets. They're . . . " He made a walking gesture with two fingers, indicating they had grown legs.

Beeslaar glared at the man. Then he stormed out through the front door, heading for home.

Twenty minutes later Beeslaar was back with two blankets, a pillow, a bar of soap and a towel. He slammed it all down on the service counter, gave the constable a withering look and stomped off to his office.

He slid a photograph of Freddie Swarts from his file, went back to Morotse, and ordered him to accompany him to the cells so he could translate Beeslaar's questions to the child.

But Bulelani's communication skills were no better in Tswana. After a few minutes it became clear that either he was struck dumb with fear or he had no idea who the woman in the photograph was. Or a combination of the two.

One thing was for sure, this ragged boy couldn't possibly be the Huilwater murderer. That sinister scene was far too staged, too studied.

29

N ow, you go play there by Auntie Donsie's place," Johanna Beesvel said to the five children in the door-way. Her voice was raw, harsh. As if she'd already spent the best part of the day scolding.

Beeslaar looked at the little group emerging from the bed-room. He wondered whose children they were. He knew the old woman didn't have any of her own. And her sister, to whom the house belonged, was elderly herself. Grandchildren, he decided. Where did they all sleep? The house had three rooms, at most—the little lounge they were sitting in, a kitchen and a bedroom. The toilet would be outside, behind the house.

The children peeped at him inquisitively as they passed. One pointed to the pistol on his hip, and giggled. A toddler began crying in the doorway, her frizzy hair forming a halo around her head. "Drikkie," the old woman shrieked, "come take the child!" A skinny girl swept the toddler up and took her away.

Beeslaar sat down and signalled to Ghaap. He'd be the spokesperson for the afternoon, but Beeslaar wanted to be there too.

"We won't be long," Ghaap began.

Mrs. Beesvel sat down wearily on a straight-backed chair at the door to the murky kitchen, hands hidden under her apron. At first her head was bowed. Then she looked up, peering at Beeslaar from beneath her white headscarf. "I haven't got tea, Meneer," she said. "We're only getting on Tuesday again."

Pension day, he realised. Third Tuesday of the month, when people lined up for government grants. Towns filled up with stalls and vendors, braziers where bits of cheap meat and boerewors lay sizzling. There were loan sharks and debt collectors too, street preachers, drunkards, beggars and drifters.

"Didn't Auntie bring anything along from the farm?" Ghaap cautiously probed.

She looked down at her restless hands. "My mind wasn't working too nicely. When old Lammer said there was a place on the donkey cart, I just took my bedding and climbed on. Left everything, just like that. I thought maybe Dam can help me out—and the pension's coming next week." She glanced in Beeslaar's direction. "Then there'll be tea again."

"Why did Auntie just leave the farm like that?" asked Ghaap.

"I *didn't* run away, Johannes. I didn't do anything!"

She looked at Beeslaar, fear in her eyes. "I raised those two children with these two hands—like my own." The apron lifted slightly. "I looked after their mother right up till when she died. Why would I go and murder my very own children? For what? That place is the only home I had!" A hand emerged from under the apron, and she wiped at her eyes.

"Outanna," said Ghaap, "we have to ask. It's important. We have to ask everything. Even if it's hard." He shifted in the deep, uncomfortable sofa, then started again, "Last Tuesday evening, the night before the murder. What happened that evening?"

"What you mean now?" Her face quivered with suspicion and distress as she narrowed her eyes, which disappeared in a nest of wrinkles.

"I just want to know if anything unusual happened—anything different, you know?"

She shrugged, the hand back under the apron again.

"Everyone was at home?" Ghaap prodded. "Nobody away?

There wasn't a visitor, maybe? Outanna didn't hear a car drive off late in the night?"

She looked up. "No, my child. I don't remember anything like that, no."

"And Dam? Was he home the whole evening?"

Her eyes glittered. "Dam didn't do anything. It wasn't him. Wasn't one of our people, you hear? Lammer and Dawid and them, they got good pay. And they're allowed to have their own sheep on Huilwater. Freddie gave me some too, last Christmas, extra pension, she said. Dawid and Lammer look after them for me. They don't have any meanness in them. They work together nicely. Dam too. No, this is another kind of evilness . . . "

"What sort of evil, Outanna?"

She glanced at Beeslaar. "Death. It's death walking around there . . . " Her eyes glistened with tears.

"Wednesday morning, before you went to town with De Kok, Outanna. Was there anyone else on the farm, maybe? Strangers? Did anyone phone? Or did Miss Swarts maybe say she was expecting someone?"

"No, she would have told me. Then I wouldn't have gone to town."

"And did the phone ring?"

"No. No, I don't remember our ring that day. But I don't know any more. I don't know anything. Nothing. That day. It's gone, out of my mind. I'm empty now."

"And the foster children of Miss Swarts, when last did Outanna see them?"

"No," she said after a pause. "Those children went away long ago."

"Didn't any of them come back again?"

She shook her head vigorously.

"Does Outanna remember Bulelani? He was one of them. He didn't maybe come past the farm in the last while?"

"Softie?"

"No, Bulelani."

"Yes, but people call him that. Because he's soft. In the head, you know. Porridgehead, they teased him. Somebody brought him there, but he ran away. Long ago already. What about him?"

"We have to ask everything, Outanna. We're looking for the people who killed Miss Swarts."

"It's the wrong questions! It wasn't the children. And it wasn't our people. It's a *different* evilness. I felt it a long time now, bad things happening, something worse coming."

Her face clouded over.

"What do you mean, Outanna?"

"But are you stupid, Johannes Ghaap?" she asked through her tears. "Look what happened to Frederika, man. And I," she squeezed her eyes shut, "I *knew*. I could *feel* it. I see things, I hear things. But ai, I was too weak. Nothing, I could do nothing. My strength, it wasn't strong enough."

"Outanna?"

"All of us, all of us. We were too late. Herklaas, me, and the sangoma. I was too late, too late," she wept.

Ghaap reached his hand out to her. She grasped it and held it tight in her lap.

"I *know*, you see. That evil thing," she looked at Beeslaar pleadingly, "it's looking for me. Looking-looking-looking. I can *feel* it. My strength is too weak for it. Too weak, weak, weak. But I'm not worried about myself. I know already. It's coming to get me. I can see it—it's already taken my spirit!"

Ghaap looked at Beeslaar, eyes wide, and Beeslaar gave a slow shake of his head.

They waited for the old woman to calm down.

"Who's Herklaas?" Ghaap asked, carefully withdrawing his hand.

It glistened with the old woman's tears, Beeslaar saw.

"That place, it's been bewitched. There's evil everywhere. Herklaas came to tell me. I prayed and I prayed but I was still afraid, for Freddie, for myself, the little one, so I wanted to go get the sangoma again. In Kimberley. To come break up that spell. But I was too late, I could do too little. Next thing we saw, it was too late!"

"Who bewitched the farm, Outanna? Was it De Kok?"

"No, man! It's the witch doctor. He comes to get you. At night!"

"But why, Auntie?"

"Because I was fighting them. *Me!*"

"And Dam?"

"No, Dam doesn't believe anything like that. And he doesn't want to listen, man, he's hard-headed, like a rock. You can talk and talk, but no one believes you. Who listens to the dreams of an old woman like me? And look now—look now. My children . . . " She rocked back and forth, her arms now clasping her frail body.

Beeslaar put his notebook back in his pocket and slowly raised his bulk from the sagging sofa. They wouldn't get any more out of her today, he knew. Besides, he was starting to feel anxious—from the cramped little room, the old woman's arcane fears. And his back was aching from the couch. He looked out the door. Outside, a scrawny dog was pacing back and forth. The piece of rope around his neck was loosely tethered to a length of wire anchored to the ground, making a rhythmic, scraping sound as the dog moved up and down, up and down, like a leopard in a cage.

And so we all have our chains, thought Beeslaar. It's just the length of the rope that differs. He caught Ghaap's eye and gestured towards the door with his head.

When they stepped out, the dog barked furiously and rushed at them, but the rope around his neck jerked him back. The animal yelped.

They walked to the front gate. "Haven't you sent the nurse to her yet?" Beeslaar asked. "I thought you were going to organise that—last Friday already."

Ghaap stopped in his tracks.

"That's not my job," he said irritably.

Beeslaar stopped too and turned to Ghaap. "There's something you don't understand, Sergeant Ghaap. This *is* our job. It's important for this investigation that Mrs. Beesvel gets her marbles back. And quickly, too. Are you with me?"

Ghaap kicked at a stone, murmured assent.

"And while you're at it," said Beeslaar, "find out if there's milk and bread in that house." He saw Ghaap's mouth open in protest, but he ignored it. Walked on.

At the car, a hen was roosting on the bonnet.

"Bugger off," said Ghaap, taking a swipe at the bird. Unperturbed, the fowl clucked back, casting an impassive red eye at the sergeant's tall figure. Ghaap growled something, then grabbed the hen with both hands and lifted her off the car. She stayed sitting on the ground where he'd placed her. But as soon as he walked to the passenger side, she hurried after him. "Voertsek!" he shouted, but the hen just clucked back.

Beeslaar stood watching the comical scene and couldn't help thinking of Gerda. She'd have had just the right words to describe this little tableau of chicken love-at-first-sight.

30

Monday started off scorching, sweltering. Beeslaar was sitting in the hall of the co-op, where he was attending an emergency farmers' union meeting. Outside, a storm was brewing. Or was it perhaps inside, Beeslaar wondered, as he observed the mood of the farmers around him.

He studied the rows of khaki-clad shoulders in front of him. The leathery sun-beaten necks, the close-shaven heads. In just a few minutes he had to address the whole gathering.

Making a speech in front of a bunch of belligerent farmers was not exactly what he'd have scheduled for his ideal Monday. But then the man from the Agricultural Union had called late last night. Jan Steenkamp. A man who had opened many doors for Beeslaar in the district. A man who gets things done. Who was, in his quiet way, pouring an enormous amount of energy into the farm-watch debate.

"We're having an emergency meeting in town early tomorrow morning," he'd said. "It would be good if you could be there. Nine o'clock. But I have to warn you. Come wearing your thick skin. The guys are pretty worked up." He'd mentioned the level of anger, the number of calls he'd received over the weekend. "There are going to be lots of people. Good time for you to speak to everyone."

Beeslaar had his doubts. In an atmosphere like this, reason was the first thing to fly out the window. A frightened man is unlikely to think and plan. He's after one thing only: action. Preferably drastic action. To ease the fear and tension.

There'd been more farm murders that weekend. A couple outside Bloemfontein, the woman tied up, forced to watch her husband being beaten to death with a spade. In North-West province, a farmer had been strangled with his own belt and hanged. And so on.

Beeslaar took out his notes. He had no idea when it might be his turn. Or whether they'd even give him a chance. At best, he could exploit the charged atmosphere, spur people on to cooperate on a new private security system. The response had been poor so far: there were plenty of obstacles—money, the vast distances between farms. But fortunately he had men like Jan Steenkamp on his side.

Beeslaar had done his homework thoroughly before leaving for the job in the platteland. Checked out areas where farm-related crimes had dropped, where farmers were using professional security companies or reservist units on twenty-four-hour patrol.

It was the only way, really. It was fucking impossible to expect that he, Ghaap and Pyl could secure an entire district like this. All by themselves. And the old commandos didn't work either. They depended on volunteers, were prone to political differences and personality clashes. Altogether too erratic. Jan Steenkamp had warned him: it'll take time and money, especially given the persistence of political sentiment.

Today, this fractious bunch of farmers were only one of his problems. Back in Upington, Superintendent Leonard Mogale was still waiting.

But first things first . . .

Right at the front of the little hall he saw Buks Hanekom. And his sidekick, Polla Pieterse. They were part of a small group that kept raising their voices above the general hubbub. Polla wanted the meeting to start with the singing of "Die Stem." But Jan Steenkamp nipped this attempt in the bud.

This was not a political meeting, he warned, it was an information session led by the Agricultural Union.

The hall was filled to bursting. Beeslaar had either met most of the people present or knew them by sight. The rest were strangers, possibly from neighbouring districts. Here and there a brown face or two—farm labourers, no doubt. Emerging farmers were few and far between in this district.

Someone read from the Bible and said a short prayer. Then a fellow with a bushy moustache and a shaven head was introduced. The Agricultural Union's full-time crime consultant: Andries du Pisanie, from Pretoria.

"South Africa's farmers," he boomed, "find themselves in the world's most dangerous profession. More than two thousand men, women, workers and children have lost their lives since '91. How far must this go before we start doing something about it?"

The audience reacted enthusiastically. "It's genocide! Bring back the death penalty!"

Du Pisanie held up his hand, quelling the cries.

"Threats and complaints about a useless police force, a weak government, this gets us nowhere—"

He was drowned out by the Hanekom group. "We will fight back, we will fight back!" They stomped the floor, ignoring the speaker's raised hand.

Then Jan Steenkamp stood up and took the stand.

The chanting subsided.

"Please," he pleaded. "We must give people the chance to speak. Farm attacks are brutal. They happen suddenly. Unexpectedly. But the fact is, no attack, no victim is random. They're chosen with care. Why? Because they're vulnerable. So there's just one question: How do we make ourselves less vulnerable?"

He turned on a projector, activated his laptop.

"What does a farm attack look like?" he asked. The enormous

image of a woman's face, distorted in pain, appeared on the screen behind him. "There is no typical profile. But the most common motive is robbery."

There was low grumbling. "Nonsense!" shouted one. "It's a free-for-all, it's open season on white farmers, and no one will protect us!"

Du Pisanie persisted. "Research shows that most of these criminals are young. That they're black, single and unemployed, with very little education. They are not afraid of being arrested. They've got nothing to lose."

He paused, allowing his words to hit home. Then he carried on. "Also, more than half of you don't even take the most basic security precautions. It's astonishing, but look around you. What do your fences look like? Are the watchdogs trained? So I'm pleading with you: become proactive. Remote-controlled gates, electric fences. That's your first line of defence."

Beeslaar heard more muttering. He knew why: money. Many of them couldn't afford this.

Du Pisanie elaborated, "Security gates inside the house, a metal gate separating utility areas from sleeping quarters, bolts on bedroom doors. Turn one room into a fort—the bathroom is a good idea. In case of an emergency, the whole household must head there. And keep a cellphone or radio there. It must always be charged and active, so that you can call for help immediately—neighbours, police, the farm watch." He took a sip of water and looked over his shoulder at a new image on the screen behind him.

"Another thing: do drills. Practise again and again what you'd do if armed men broke through your door. Remember, a person's brain works like a computer. In a panic situation, it falls back on information that's already been stored. A quick response could save your life, your family."

Then it was Beeslaar's turn.

Ignoring the farmers who got up to leave, he pulled his

shoulders back and addressed the weathered faces in front of him. "How many of you sitting here this morning—"

Hanekom and his group started chanting again, but Beeslaar stood silently, reading his notes as he calmly waited. When their protest petered out he carried on. "Yes. We *must* fight back. But we'll do it intelligently. We'll get proactive. So that crime does not gain a foothold here."

"Bullshit!" someone shouted from the back amid growls of assent. "You're doing away with the commandos and taking away our weapons! We are powerless."

"Okay. Let me tell you when you really are powerless: when someone shoves a pistol in your wife's mouth and demands the keys of the safe from you. *That's* when you're powerless. When you know for sure: one wrong move, an accidental glance or eye contact with the man holding the gun. But it *is* possible to prevent that moment. If we look at the facts, it's clear we need each other. You and the police, together. And it works. In areas where the farmers have joined us as police reservists, introduced a farm-watch system, stock theft and farm attacks have just about disappeared. That's why we say: join us. We'll help you with emergency-communication systems. Just join our Rural Security Plan, help us to map farms. That's how you take control, become part of the solution. Thank you."

There was no immediate reaction, and Beeslaar gathered up his notes.

But the Hanekom group burst into battle chants again, and Beeslaar walked out, eager to escape the racket. He could feel a panic attack stirring in his chest.

Behind him, Jan Steenkamp took the microphone. It was up to him now to coax them from their anger.

Outside, Beeslaar paused to breathe, to pacify the beast in his chest.

Someone tapped him on the shoulder. It was the young Swarts woman.

"I have to speak to you, Inspector."

"I've got to go to Upington right now. Will it be okay if I drop by when I'm back? Were you at the meeting?"

"Ja, I was there," she said.

Brave girl, he thought. She stood very straight, a little soldier. Her slim brown legs were firmly planted in a pair of brown boots. But despite the apparent bravado, there was turbulence in her eyes. "And I saw Buks and his troops giving you a hard time."

"You know him?"

"He's been to the farm, ja. Saying things. But . . . What the man said about torture . . . Do you think that happened to Freddie too?"

"Definitely not, Miss Swarts. Remember, she was drugged heavily. She wasn't aware of what was happening to her, okay?

She bit her lip. "Actually I wanted to ask about Outanna. She's scared of something on the farm, keeps going on about witchcraft . . . She says things were going wrong, Freddie crying all the time, Dam short tempered. That sort of thing."

"I'm not sure how stable Mrs. Beesvel is," Beeslaar said. "We tried to get her to the clinic. But I suspect she needs more help than that."

"I've already made an appointment with a doctor in Upington for tomorrow . . . "

He could see she had more to say, but there was no time right then. Anxiously, he shifted his weight from one foot to the other.

"Inspector, I listened carefully to the man from the agri union, but I wonder . . . Don't you think Freddie and Klara's murder was different?"

"What do you mean?"

She exhaled. "I just mean . . . There's a painting. One of Freddie's. I'd like you to take a look at it."

"Her paintings?"

"Just one. I suspect my sister knew she was going to be murdered. And now Outanna says she herself knew. That she had tried to prevent it—I'm not sure I really get what she's trying to say. But if you look at that painting, and you listen to Outanna, plus the sangoma stuff on our front door—you begin to wonder, don't you?"

"Look, personally I think Mrs. Beesvel is confused, she's still suffering from shock. Try to help her, by all means, but I wouldn't worry too much about the things she's saying. I don't think your sister would have just sat around waiting to be killed. Try not to dwell on it—try instead to remember her the way you knew her. Anyway, those who are left behind often berate themselves for not seeing the signs beforehand. They feel guilty, thinking they could have prevented it. But we'll talk about it some more this afternoon. I'm sorry, but I have to go now."

Hurrying off to his car, Beeslaar did a quick check for phone messages. There were two. One was from Jansie Boois, and he called her back.

"It's the superintendent," she said cheerfully, "he wants to know if you can take something along for him."

"What?"

"Dunno. But I could take a guess. You have to pick it up from Miss Millions."

"Nelmari Viljoen?" Beeslaar smiled at Jansie's nickname for her as he opened the car door to get in.

"And what else?"

"Oh, well," said Jansie, "I just told him I hope he's hungry."

"You what?"

She giggled. "He's going to eat you for breakfast, right?"

31

S ara felt the shadow fall across her back before she heard the greeting. She turned around and a big man offered her his hand. His curly hair was the colour of beer.

"Boet Pretorius," he said.

She took the hand. It was dry and calloused.

"My sympathies," he said. "Freddie was so special." His shoulders drooped in a khaki shirt that looked as if he had slept in it.

He shuffled uncomfortably. Then it hit her. This was the neighbour, the man who had found Freddie.

"Thanks so much," she said. "I heard you were a good friend of my sister's."

"You were at the meeting?" He looked over to the co-op hall.

"I was, yes. Actually I came to talk to Inspector Beeslaar."

"Do they have anything yet?"

"Not as far as I know." She looked towards the hall, where the heckling was still continuing. "Heavens, people's emotions are running high," she said.

"Hmm, yes. This is a fuckup, all right. Actually, it used to be pretty quiet around here, but that's changed, especially over the last few months. Beginning with the stock thefts. And now this. Plus, the guys are fighting among one another—the one lot are completely trigger-happy, while the others are trying to work together. But it's complex. A farm watch costs money. You have to appoint professionals to patrol the roads."

"And where do you stand?"

"I, well, I'm pretty fed up with the politics, actually. I just want to farm." An air of exhaustion clung to Boet Pretorius. He seemed weary of life itself.

"Guys like Buks . . . do you know, he was on the farm the other day, on Friday," Sara said.

"On the *farm*?"

"I went to see how things were going there," she began. Then she saw the fear in his eyes, the horror of his last visit to Huilwater, and she paused.

"I just had to. The animals—our workers had all moved out, you see. But at least the manager is still there, and he has someone helping him."

"Just say the word," he said. "I could bring over one of my workers."

"Buks says the commando's patrolling the area."

"Ag, Buks. It's just him and a handful of diehards, charging around, making trouble."

Sara looked back at the hall, where alternate shouts and applause were drowning the efforts of a speaker.

"Mr. Pretorius," she said, "were you and Freddie—I mean, did you see her often?"

"No." He glanced at her, quickly looked away.

"Before, yes. Before your dad died. He helped me a lot, you know, when I first got here. He was really wise."

Wise? Hell, she wouldn't know. He'd seldom spoken to her. He could talk to Freddie, but there had always been a distance with her. Even in the weeks before he died. Especially then . . . Sara remembered the last time they spoke. In hospital. She'd been sitting next to his bed, barely breathing, telling him about her conversation with the doctor. She'd wanted to take his hands in hers. There was hope, she had wanted to say. The doctor had said so himself. Surgery, chemo. Things that could help him. More than Outanna's herbal concoctions, the buchu, the dagga tea. He just had to stay in hospital a while longer, just hold on a little. Then he could walk out of there, instead of being carried out to go die on the farm.

He'd said nothing the whole time. Had lain there with his eyes closed, as if she hadn't been there. She'd been halfway through a sentence when he said, "My child, you understand nothing. You never have. You'd better go now. I'm very tired."

She never saw him again. She'd been in Botswana when he died, and afterwards she'd tossed away all those letters from the lawyer. She hadn't been interested in her father's estate. She had left Huilwater long ago.

"Are you going to sell now?" Boet asked, as if he had read her thoughts.

"Er, yes. I mean, I haven't thought that far yet. For now I'm just trying to find my feet. I've started cleaning up the house."

He grimaced and turned away.

"And I have to take care of the labourers and so on. How well do you know Dam?"

"De Kok? He's a bit of a closed book. But probably a good manager. I don't think Freddie would have been able to do it all alone. There are lots of things that require a man's strength—fixing windmills, servicing machinery, that kind of thing. And she . . . " He looked up, at the big white storm clouds gathering. "Her hands were made for other things. Beautiful things."

"You loved her?"

"I did, yes. As far as it was possible, with De Kok there."

"You mean Dam tried to keep you away?"

He paused a moment. Then, "That man's too big for his boots." Reading her expression he said, "Look, forget I said that. Just don't let him talk you into anything."

"Like what?"

Boet shoved his hands in his pockets, shoulders hunched. "Selling, for instance. Don't let him influence you about who you should sell to, or the price. Discuss it with an independent party. Someone who won't benefit from the sale. Discuss it with me, if you want."

He looked down at her, something hard in his eyes. Then Boet Pretorius put out his hand, gave her a firm handshake and said goodbye.

Sara drove out to Chicken Vale to find Outanna.

"She walked over to the pastor's," said Outanna's sister, Sanna van Wyk. "But Outanna, she isn't so good now. All, all night long, Sarretjie. She's just sitting there, crying. Praying to the Lord. Too terrible. The whole night. Me and the little ones, not a wink of sleep. Early morning, she's burning the herbs, the buchu. Walking through the house, making smoke. And praying to the Lord. All the time, all the time . . . "

As Sara walked back to the car she thought of her own experience the previous night. Outanna had been completely beside herself, kept going on about the farm being bewitched, that evil had managed to "get inside everyone's head." Freddie kept walking around "crying, crying," and that Dam was irritable the whole time. "Dawid and Lammer and the women, they all just wanted to run away when we brought the sangoma, but really he was there to help us," she'd said to Sara.

"No, girlie, no. I'm not crazy," she'd said. "It's my heart. It's cried itself rotten here inside me."

Shocked at her distress, Sara had let slip her discovery of the chicken feet on the front door the day before. She bit her tongue at the old woman's reaction: "O, dear Lord, he was there. He came. You must leave that place, Sarretjie! That's the devil that took Frederika and Klaartjie. He's here!"

"It's all right, Outanna. You're safe here, this is your sister's house."

"But the devil. Lord, he's here too. Now it's my turn. My time's run out," she'd cried.

*

At the pastor's house, he told her Outanna had left already. Then he fervently assured her that he and his wife and his entire congregation were praying for her.

She thanked him, suddenly vulnerable in the presence of such compassion. He saw her off at the gate, his jacket flapping up in a sudden gust of wind.

"Big rain coming," he said and pointed up to the billowing clouds sailing in from all sides.

The first drops were fat and heavy, exploding in big puffs of dust. Sara set off for Huilwater. She wanted to get to the farm before the heavens really opened up: it was hell on these dirt roads once they were wet.

32

B eeslaar took his foot off the accelerator. He wanted to take the bends at a safe speed. It took his full concentration to negotiate all the ruts and potholes. A car could end up on its roof if a driver didn't show due respect for the tricks of a dirt road. And these roads had quite a few tricks. Sandy one moment—and just as you got used to the surfing and swerving, they became corrugated hard-pack, and then, before you knew it, spattery gravel.

Today he was being extra careful. He was driving his own car—because of the air conditioning.

Bottles clinked on the back seat. Wine from the Cape, for Superintendent Mogale. Two cases, which Beeslaar had picked up from Nelmari Viljoen's office. What was she getting in return for the wine, he wondered.

His thoughts swung back to the murder case. There were still more questions than answers. The Great White Hope of Johannesburg on his way to meet Oom Big Black Elephant in Upington, and all he had to show was a handful of shit.

He thought of what Sara Swarts had told him, the possibility that the murders were premeditated, that there was perhaps a more sinister motive behind it all.

Maybe he'd make sense of it if he asked the questions differently—why, for instance, pump her full of roofies before you kill her? It wasn't a sex crime. There was no sign of that. But it had been important to the murderer that she was sufficiently conscious to experience her own death—without being able to move a muscle.

Why?

Beeslaar blew out his breath in frustration. Farm murders were usually solved quickly. Most often, the perpetrators were identified and apprehended within twenty-four hours. But so far he had bugger-all.

The landscape was a tapestry of colour and texture. A pale shiny carpet of what the locals called Bushman's grass interrupted by dark-green thornbush, with patches of red sand showing through, and here and there a solitary camel thorn tree.

Mercifully, he had left the thunderstorm behind.

A signboard loomed. Waterval. It made him smile. A waterfall, really? Funny how many place names in this arid region had water as a theme. Like Huilwater. Weeping waters. Water of a different kind—tears. Whose, he wondered. Had this once been Griqua land? And before that?

He gnawed at the inside of his cheek, thought of the conversation he'd had with Nelmari Viljoen just an hour before.

He'd had to wait while the short-skirted assistant went to fetch the wine. Viljoen was there herself, but her greeting was chilly. He asked her again about Freddie Swarts's failed attempt to assist the Griqua with their land claim, and the community's reaction to that.

She gave him a long, measured look. "Look," she'd said, her voice low, as if afraid someone might hear. "If you want to know how many people harboured resentment against Freddie, I'd probably have to name half the farmers in the district."

"On Friday you left me with the impression that there wasn't much fallout."

"Did I? I meant that nothing came of the claims. But there was definitely emotion, and threats . . . "

"What kind of threats?"

"Freddie only mentioned it once. Someone called her, on the phone, to threaten her, and there was also an anonymous letter. And that was it."

He arrived in Upington just after lunch. It was an astonishing place. An oasis. Long avenues of date palms quivering in the sun, the arid veld with great swathes of emerald-green vineyards. The broad Gariep quietly flowing through the town. Great River, it meant—the name changed back from Orange River, the name he'd grown up with.

He searched for shade and parked the car. The heat hit him like a brick wall when he got out. Hell, could it possibly get hotter than this? It felt as if rivers of sweat were flowing from every pore in his body. He wouldn't be surprised if it was forty-six degrees—in the shade.

Superintendent Leonard Mogale's office was on the second floor of the police district headquarters. The lift was still out of order—it hadn't worked at all in his two months in the area.

Staggering into his superior's office with the wine boxes, an even sweatier Beeslaar remarked, "I come bearing refreshments."

The big man didn't greet him, just used the gold pen in his hand to point towards a chair against the wall.

It was cool inside the office. Must be the chilly reception, Beeslaar mused as he put down the boxes. But there was an air conditioner after all, which rattled at the window.

"How did the farmers' meeting go this morning?" asked Mogale. He sat with his elbows propped on the desk, twirling the pen in his hands. Well-manicured hands, Beeslaar noticed, the nails flat and square. Mogale looked cool and fresh in his crisp white shirt and tie. Gold cuff links bore the South African coat of arms.

"I didn't stay till the end, Superintendent. But as far as I could see, the meeting went fine. Under the circumstances."

Mogale's eyes were devoid of expression as he inclined his

head. Big eyes, protruding slightly from the broad planes of his face, shiny cheeks as plump as a baby's. "Any right-wing presence?" he asked.

"If by right-wing you mean people with neo-Nazi flags, then no. If you mean people who are fed up, there were plenty."

Mogale's eyelids flickered. "I hear there was war talk."

"Look, there's a small group of people—they're trying to get a commando system started again, to run so-called patrols around the district. But so far they're not doing anything illegal. At least, nobody has made a formal complaint. And yes, there has been some aggressive language. But I think that's where it'll stay—just talk."

"That isn't what I've been hearing." His gaze was hard.

Beeslaar returned the look, tried not to blink, lost the contest. "So what is it that you've heard, Superintendent?"

"I hear there are people stockpiling arms."

Where would he have heard that, Beeslaar wondered. Or was this just a way of keeping him in his place, making him realise he didn't know what was going on in his own backyard?

"I know nothing about that," he replied. He thought back to yesterday's church service. The guy with the long beard—Tjoek Visser, he'd since established. A travelling preacher attached to the Verbondsvolk van Afrika ministries, a right-wing church with branches as far as Namibia. Popular with the AWB, Wit Wolwe and other right-wing nutcases in the last days of apartheid.

Beeslaar decided to say nothing for the time being. First, he wanted to find out more.

"I want you to investigate it, Inspector."

"As in formally?"

"As in formally. Now, as far as the murders are concerned . . . " He put his pen down, leaned back in his chair.

Beeslaar picked up the file and began his report.

Mogale listened, asked a question now and then. When Beeslaar had finished talking, he said, "Can you manage it, or do you need reinforcements? I can hand the case to Inpector Lobatse. But then *he* runs it. From here."

"No," Beeslaar quickly replied. "I'm doing fine. We could do with another vehicle, with better equipment. Another computer, perhaps. But the two sergeants are learning quickly." Mogale didn't push too hard. He had made his point; one wrong step, and you lose your case. And your authority. And your only second chance.

Five minutes later, Beeslaar was on his way down the stairs to pick up the fingerprint results. Halfway down, struggling for air, he stopped. Took a deep breath, exhaled slowly. And again. Until he felt calmer.

And he was calmer, at last. Especially with the good news waiting for him about the new prints he'd taken from the front door at Huilwater on Saturday.

He phoned Ghaap.

"Those witchcraft things we found at Huilwater on Saturday—we have a name. One Herklaas Windvogel. He has a record for poaching."

Ghaap didn't answer right away.

"The jackal man," he offered eventually. "He's an old Bushman, still living wild. He walks all over the area, from one farm to the next. Hunts jackal and wildcats and other vermin for farmers—but only when he needs some cash."

"And sheep?"

"No, not at all. The farmers would have sorted him out long ago."

"You'll have to go find him, boetman."

There was a stifled sound. Beeslaar wasn't sure whether it was laughter or not.

"That man doesn't just get *found*, you know. He'd never let you. And he's scared of the police—like a cat is scared of water. Ever since he caught the wolf."

"What?"

"A hyena. Must have wandered out of the Kgalagadi into one of the jackal man's traps. There was *big* trouble then."

"Whatever," said Beeslaar, "just find out where he is and fetch him. Scared or not. And bring De Kok in too. I think I'm beginning to understand what old Mrs. Beesvel's been on about."

33

The phone was ringing, a thin peal above the din of the storm.

The wind blasted and roared around the house. Sara was sorting the blank canvases from the finished paintings in the studio when the sound finally got through to her. Two short rings followed by one long one, that was the ring for Huilwater! She jumped up and rushed to answer.

"Huilwater 202, hello?"

"I'm putting you through," she heard the operator's voice. Then, "Missy!" a voice calling over the hum of the farm line.

"Hello?" Sara whacked the receiver against the palm of her hand. The line was always crackly, even more so when there was a storm. "Hello! Speak louder, please, the line is very bad. Hello!"

There was a buzzing and a fizzing, then an anxious cry, "Miss Saartjie! You must come right away!"

Her blood turned to ice. It was Sanna, Outanna's sister. Hysterical.

"What's going on, Sanna? Sanna!" There was more humming and buzzing and it sounded as if the line might cut out completely. "Sanna! What is it?"

"They're burning down the house. You must come, Outanna's inside!"

"Phone the police immediately, Sanna! You hear me?" The line crackled. "Sanna! Did you hear me?"

"Everything's on fire! Outanna—"

The line went dead.

Sara slapped the receiver, but it remained silent. Then she banged it down, and wound the crank. Bloody old-fucking-fangled phones, she cursed as she willed the operator to pick up. "Come on, answer!" When she finally heard a voice, she shrieked, "Ma'am, please get the police, tell them there's a fire in Chicken Vale! Hello? Can you hear me? This is Sara Swarts calling from Huilwater. Please—please can you help?"

She was pretty hysterical herself now, she realised. "It's in Block B in Chicken Vale, Number 440!"

The operator said she'd phone, and Sara hung up.

What now? She thought of the Marnet radio in the hallway. But who would she call? She dismissed that idea and grabbed her bag. She'd get hold of Beeslaar while she was driving, as soon as she had reception again.

As she opened the back door, the wind plucked it from her grasp. A cloud of sand gusted over her, into the house. Outside, everything was veiled in red dust, the trees and out-buildings ghastly apparitions in the haze.

By the time Sara could see the lights of town, the rain was coming down with brutal force. The windscreen wipers danced at top speed, but were impotent against the cascade. The car made a deafening racket: the wipers' rubbery grating, air con on its highest setting, and the hammering of the rain on the metal roof.

She turned off into Chicken Vale. A police vehicle with spinning blue lights flashed past her in a watery blur. She headed for Number 440, peering through the downpour.

The house was in ruins. Sheets of metal were missing from the roof, as if there had been an explosion, and the windows were smashed. There was nothing but a black hole where the front door had been.

In her horror, she stalled the car. Just then, the rain subsided, stopped abruptly—as if someone had thrown a switch. Now, the silence was thunderous. Sara sat transfixed, expecting the house to burst into flames again any second.

The passenger door flew open and Sanna, drenched, jumped in. "They've taken her to the clinic," she cried. "The police came and took her away, Miss Saartjie. They couldn't find Papsak, the ambulance man—he must be drunk again. Come, the clinic," she urged, jutting her chin in the direction of town.

Sara shook herself into action, started the car.

"It's tsotsis," said Sanna, wiping her face with her apron. "Those Bantus were shouting. Just screaming all kinds of things, I don't know what."

Sara tried to control the car as it splashed and skidded along the road.

"I kept calling, help me please! But the other people, they just ran away, each and every one of them. Our people, Sarretjie! Nobody helped. I knocked, knocked, looking for a phone, but no one opened up."

Bunching up her apron, she buried her face in it and wept.

Outside the clinic at last, Sara turned to Sanna and asked, "Was she badly hurt?"

"I don't know. She looks terrible. She's got burnt badly." Sanna started crying again, her voice a high-pitched wail. "What's going on, Sarretjie?" she asked between sobs.

Sara saw the police van, its doors open and lights flashing. She flew out of the car and broke into a run.

Inside the clinic, about a dozen people were sitting along the walls. Two policemen were at the reception desk. One of them was Beeslaar.

"Is she all right?" Sara wanted to know.

"She was badly hurt, Miss Swarts. And there's no doctor here today, but Sister January is with her inside. We're trying the ambulance now."

Sara pushed past him to the door marked SURGERY. She opened it without knocking.

A nurse was by a bed, a cellphone to her ear.

Then Sara saw the body. And knew it was too late.

The nurse came towards her, touched her arm. "I'm sorry," she said. "There was nothing we could do."

34

Beeslaar felt his chest constrict. Tried to ignore it. But he couldn't get the key into the ignition. His hands were shaking. A dizziness, then everything around him blanked to white. Dark spots began to bob in the brightness.

It's the child. The dead eyes of the child. "You stole my eyes," the child told him. "You, Big Oom Polisieman, you. I'll be coming to take my eyes back."

He squeezed his eyes tight shut.

But the child's eyes wouldn't let him go. Sparkling, they danced in front of him. Eyes that had been shattered by the force of the bullet. Grovétjie's child.

He felt his elbow give way. It was Ghaap, opening the door. "Inspector! Are you okay?"

Beeslaar tried to push him away, but his body wouldn't obey.

"Take me home," he wheezed. "My pills."

Ghaap helped him out of the car and into his house. Beeslaar staggered to his bathroom, yanked open the cabinet and grabbed his pills. But his hands were shaking too much to open the bottle. Ghaap took it from him and shook one out. They were powerful anticonvulsants, prescribed for seizures and acute panic attacks.

Beeslaar placed it under his tongue, then sank to the cool tiled floor. Ghaap stood in the doorway, watching him anxiously.

He stood there a long time, until Beeslaar's breathing was even again. Then he helped him up and to the bedroom.

Beeslaar heard him scurrying around the kitchen. He swung his legs off the bed, sat up. He felt weary, as if his limbs were filled with lead. He could sleep for a week. Then Ghaap appeared in the doorway, coffee mug in hand. He placed it on the bedside table without saying a word.

"You don't have to make such a bloody fuss, man, it's just asthma."

Ghaap was clearly unconvinced.

"Did you find that old jackal guy?" He didn't wait for a reply. "We have to get back to Chicken Vale, make sure the scene is secured. Have you heard anything from the forensics guys?"

"Hans Deetlefs is coming—and we have two constables who are guarding the scene."

"And Windvogel?"

"But what's he got to do with—"

"Just bloody well find him, Ghaap. He and the old lady knew each other. If it was murder, we need to find out as much as we can, speak to everyone she knew. And where's Pyl?"

"He's gone out to Huilwater. To get De Kok. But first you must drink up. It'll make you feel better. Then you need to rest."

"I don't have to fucking rest. I told you, it's just asthma. Forgot to take my medicine this morning."

Ghaap walked to the door. "Right. I'll wait outside," he said without looking back.

35

S ara poked at the slice of toast on her sideplate. The smell made her nauseous. One of the little dogs was lying on her lap. She stroked its fluffy head.

"Try to eat something, my dear," said Yvonne Lambrechts from across the kitchen table. "You can't keep going if you don't eat. You didn't touch the sandwiches I made for you to take along to the farm yesterday."

Sara wanted to say something, to apologise, but simply couldn't manage. She stirred her tea. Another sleepless night behind her. How many had there been? She was too tired to count.

Tannie Yvonne had helped to find shelter for Sanna and the little ones after last night's fire. Pastor Poolman had offered to put them up—there was an outside room standing empty, big enough for Sanna and the five children. Yvonne rounded up some bedding, clothes and toiletries, and delivered them to the pastor.

When they'd finally got home again, Sara phoned Beeslaar. He had no news: nobody knew what had happened that afternoon. Nobody was prepared to say anything about the tsotsis who'd set the house on fire. But he promised they would pursue every avenue.

"She warned us all," Sara had told him. "But no one listened." She couldn't help the accusation in her tone.

The dog leapt off her lap at the sound of a knock at the door, joining the other two as they rushed noisily towards it. Yvonne got up and followed.

Over the barking, Sara could hear her talking to someone. Minutes later, she was back in the kitchen, a black tin in her hand.

Sara immediately recognised Outanna's tin. Handmade, it was smaller than a shoe box, with a sliding lid.

"The nurse brought this from the clinic," said Yvonne. "Evidently Outanna had it with her when they brought her in last night."

Sara pushed her toast aside and picked up the tin.

"Oh, yes, I think she kept her precious things in here."

The lid was stuck, but after a few taps with the handle of the bread knife, it slid open.

Inside were papers, brittle and yellowed. Heat damage, Sara realised. As she carefully lifted them out, scorched scraps fell onto the table. Right at the bottom were a few photographs. One of Outanna and Sanna, taken when both were considerably younger. Both wearing white headscarves, they were standing in front of Outanna's house on the farm. Must have been right after the house was built. There was one with Outanna on a garden chair in front of the farmhouse, Freddie and Sara flanking her. Sara in her usual shorts and Freddie in a pinafore, Ma hovering on the periphery, cut off, as if she hadn't stepped away quickly enough when the shutter clicked. The most recent picture had been damaged the most: its edges were curled and there were brown marks on the barely recognisable faces of Outanna, Freddie and little Klara.

Sara put the photos aside. Then she picked up a folded piece of paper. It was a letter from Freddie, officially naming Outanna as Klara's godmother.

Sara put it down. If things had been different, Freddie would have sent the letter to *her*. She took a deep breath to stem the tide of emotion welling up inside her. She couldn't stand being close to the miserable letter. She had to get away, she realised. Get busy, do something physical, otherwise she wouldn't make it through this day. She bundled the papers back into the tin, shoved the lid back in place. She would look through everything later when she was calmer. Then she got up to take a shower.

Half an hour later she was on her way to Chicken Vale, to Sanna.

"I was awake all night, Sarretjie," Sanna said in the pastor's kitchen as she poured her guest some tea. They were all worn out from the distress of the day, the lengthy police-questioning. "Those tsotsis, why they want to burn *my* house? What did I ever do to them?"

"Last night you said the people had shouted something. Did you understand what they were saying? Would you recognise the people if you saw them again?"

"That man from the police, he asked me that too. But it was chaos. They screamed something, I don't know what—witches, or something like that."

Declining a second cup, Sara set off to find Dawid and Lammer, who had fled Huilwater with their families. She got hold of Dawid Tieties and his wife Babetjie first. They were living in a tin shanty behind a house that belonged to an uncle of Dawid's. Babetjie started crying when she saw Sara, and Dawid greeted her apprehensively.

They sent a child to fetch Lammer and his wife.

The couple soon arrived, and all five adults headed towards the patchy shade of a thorn tree in the yard. Sara was given the seat of honour—an upturned beer crate. The others sat on the ground.

They talked for a bit about the events of the previous day, then Sara asked, "Why did nobody go to see Outanna after you all moved to town last week?"

Pulling her skirt over her knees, Babetjie said she'd gone there, but Outanna hadn't wanted to see anyone.

"What do you mean, she didn't want to see anyone?"

"No, it's like this. She didn't want to come outside the house. She chased me away."

"Are you sure, Babetjie? Because when I got there on Sunday evening, there was no food in the house. And I know you had some food."

"We don't really understand, Sarretjie. But Outanna, she didn't want me there by her. So then I left again."

"Outanna spoke about a witch doctor," Sara said. "Do you know what she was talking about?"

For a moment, Babetjie looked away, then blurted, "Oh, Sarretjie. Things weren't happy with Outanna. And not there by Huilwater either. It's the Bantus stealing sheep, and the way they cut up those two old men there by Vaalputs. All the people, Sarretjie, scared of those Bantus. Outanna too, just carrying on about that witch doctor. She told Dam he must go fetch the sangoma, that time."

"When?"

"Some other time. Long ago. Close to Christmas, I think. First, Dam didn't want to. But then Freddie took Outanna to Kim'ley herself. So she could go fetch that witch doctor man herself."

She thought for a moment, then started again. "That man. We were all very, very scared of that man. He walked all over the yard, just shouting and swearing, shouting and swearing. We didn't understand what he was saying—it was a Bantu language, see? Tswana or Sotho, one of those. Oh, Sarretjie, we were very, very scared! Then he took a hen, chopped its head off, walked around shaking it, the blood, it was everywhere. We all ran away, far away, ai, we were scared! When we got back, the man was gone. But all his things, it was still there."

"What things?"

"Witchcraft goeters," Lammer's wife, Betta, chipped in.

"Yes, but what was it?"

"I don't know," she said. "Outanna said the farm was safe now. But there were chicken feet all over, there at the gate. Oh, Jesus!" She clapped her hands to her mouth, her eyes squeezed shut.

Sara told them about the paraphernalia she had discovered on Saturday. The women shuddered and the men looked grim. Who would have put it there, she asked, but the four of them were unresponsive, their faces frozen in fear.

"And last week? Didn't you see anything last Wednesday morning?"

Babetjie looked distraught, said nothing.

"Dawid?"

He didn't look at her.

"It wasn't us," Lammer blurted.

His yellow face was rigid, his eyes flicking about nervously.

"I know, Lammer, I know." Then she stood up and asked, "Are you getting along okay here in town?"

The men got up too. "Dam was here on Sunday, at least," Dawid said. "He slaughtered a sheep, brought us meat. And gave us our pay, he paid us for next week too, Saartjie. We're okay. We . . . we . . . "

He was trying to explain their leaving the farm so unceremoniously, she suspected. Ignoring his attemps, she said, "Well, Dawid, then I'll say goodbye for now." She started walking away, but turned around. "I'm staying with Mrs. Lambrechts here in town, if you need me. And I suppose Dam will come by regularly too. And during the day I'm on the farm, mostly."

Sara walked over to the car, turned to them and said, "I'll let you know about the funeral. Freddie's—and Outanna's too."

Beeslaar took a sip of his coffee. He absentmindedly tugged at his shirt collar—an old habit—then realised there was no need.

He was wearing a new short-sleeved shirt with an open collar. Surrendering eventually to the heat, he had bought it at the co-op. Pro: the shirt was nice and roomy in the neck and sleeves, made from light cotton. Con: he looked just like all the farmers from the area—or his top half did. They all wore the same type of shirt—pale blue or green, with front pockets a shade or two darker. He hadn't succumbed to the khaki shorts—not yet, at least.

He put the coffee mug down and looked at the man sitting opposite him, whose mug remained untouched. Dam de Kok had barely moved in the last ten minutes, let alone reached for his coffee. He stared straight ahead of him, answering Beeslaar's questions with just a yes or a no. Or met them with silence.

Worst of all, thought Beeslaar with a touch of resentment, there was no perceptible trace of the fact that De Kok had hardly slept at all the previous night. Or that he'd been sitting here in precisely the same position since six o'clock this morning.

This was Beeslaar's new interrogation room. It was the office the super used when he came visiting, which Beeslaar had "temporarily" equipped with a table and some straight-backed chairs.

"Where were you last night, Mr. De Kok?" Beeslaar asked.

He'd lost track of how many times he'd asked this question today.

No answer.

"Might I hazard a guess? Could it be that you were in the same place as you were last Tuesday night, the night before the double murder of your employer and her daughter?"

Silence.

"Things aren't looking too rosy for you. If I were you, I wouldn't be too harde-gat about it."

Beeslaar rolled his shoulders and leaned forward. He wished he felt more awake this morning. It was those pills. Knocked him for a six every time. And yesterday evening's panic attack, that was an ugly one. The worst in a long time. On top of that, he'd spent long hours with Deetlefs at the scene of the burnt-out house, trying to get an idea of what exactly had happened there. Clear case of arson, Deetlefs eventually declared, his eyes red-rimmed behind his lenses. There was still smoke rising from the gutted house. When Deetlefs had gone, Beeslaar and Ghaap started questioning the deceased's sister, for what it was worth. The woman could hardly speak, she was weeping so much.

Beeslaar took another sip of coffee, glanced over at Sergeant Pyl, whose chair was tilted precariously against the wall.

He wasn't looking too great this morning, either. He'd left immediately after the Chicken Vale fire to bring De Kok in for questioning. But De Kok was missing in action. He wasn't on the farm when Pyl arrived. The old man who lived with De Kok had no idea of what might have happened to him. His bakkie was still there, but he was gone.

Poor Pyl had spent the entire night waiting in the police van, where De Kok had surprised him shortly after five with a mug of morning coffee!

Beeslaar caught Pyl's eye and held out his own mug.

"You can take Mr. De Kok's away, Sergeant. Looks like he had enough of the wake-up muti last night. You have to be wide awake in his line of business, see."

De Kok didn't react.

"But you can bring me some more," he said as Pyl took his mug, "otherwise I'll fall asleep before I've even had the chance to inform Mr. De Kok of his rights."

The door closed and Beeslaar swung round to the man in front of him.

"You're in trouble, Mr. De Kok. Your fingerprints are all over the house on Huilwater."

De Kok looked up. "Are you going to charge me?"

Beeslaar didn't answer.

"I was in that house often." His voice was calm, measured. "Miss Swarts and I discussed business almost daily. Sometimes I had to go to her studio. She usually painted while we spoke. So I wasn't only in the kitchen or the office."

Beeslaar picked up the file in front of him. He opened it at the fingerprint report he had been given in Upington.

"These 'business talks,'" he said, sliding his finger along the edge of the file, "did they sometimes take place in the bedroom as well?"

De Kok was silent, impassive.

"What's that you say?"

"I painted that room, with Dawid and Lammer. We also helped now and again when Miss Swarts wanted to rearrange furniture."

"Ah. That explains everything, because your fingerprints are all over the house, almost as if you lived there."

Pyl came in with a fresh mug of coffee for Beeslaar, then took a seat in his chair next to the wall again.

"How big is Huilwater?"

De Kok looked up. "What's that got to do with anything?"

"Just answer the question, man."

"It's a small farm. The old man sold part of the land some time ago. And there isn't much livestock. He started selling off before he died."

"But is it big enough to warrant a manager?"

"I didn't get a salary. We had an agreement that I would work for free and sort of learn the ropes until I was ready to buy my own place."

"Handy, isn't it, if all the neighbours suddenly start putting their places on the market."

"What are you talking about?"

"Oh, just all the people who want to pack it in after all the stock theft. I hear your neighbour Roger Heidenrich is now keen to sell Vaalputs. He's lost over a hundred head of cattle. And I'm not even talking about his two workers who had their throats cut. What can you tell me about that, Mr. De Kok?"

"You're talking nonsense. I'm not interested in land around here. I'm looking for something further into the Kalahari. That's where I want to buy."

"And you made all this money catching pigeons in Dubai? Come on, De Kok, do you think I was hatched yesterday!"

"I earned in dollars. And invested all my money. I've got enough for a deposit, at least."

"And where were you last night?"

"I told you already. I was in the veld. Walking. At night I check the perimeter fences when I can't sleep—precisely because of the stock theft. So, if you don't mind, I'm really not going to sit here listening to this rubbish any longer."

"Mr. De Kok, your story is as weak as fly piss. Where's your friend the jackal man?"

A jaw muscle twitched—De Kok's only reply.

"Is he your recce?"

"He's nothing to do with me." Frustration in his tone.

"Let me give you some advice, De Kok: don't lie to me. You knew it was the jackal-catcher who planted all that black-magic stuff we found at Huilwater. But you kept your mouth shut. Because he's your accomplice? And was it your accomplices who killed Miss Swarts while you hung around town to give yourself an alibi?"

De Kok got up. "You need to charge me—or I leave."

"Oh, I'm going to charge you. Maybe not today. But I will," said Beeslaar, also rising to his feet. He stopped at the door. "Were you the one who brought the witch doctor to the farm?"

De Kok didn't answer, but his irritation was clearly visible as he brushed past Beeslaar and left.

The inspector walked back to his office. There was a fax waiting on his desk: from Dubai.

It had an eagle as logo and consisted of a short typed note from one J. Steele, confirming that Adam de Kok had been in the employ of Desert Falconeering for five years, that he was a valued employee, reliable, et cetera.

Beeslaar wondered whether he'd hear anything from the eminent man in Oman. He would call again, turn up the heat under their superior Middle Eastern arses.

He sat down, examined the file in front of him.

If De Kok had killed his employer, what was his motive? That was the one missing piece in the puzzle.

He picked up the telephone and asked Jansie to get Willie Prinsloo, the district surgeon in Postmasburg, on the line.

Moments later, his phone rang and he said, "Thanks for holding, Doc."

"Ja-ja, as if I have nothing else to do."

"Well, you can't say your life is boring."

"On the contrary, man. Haven't you realised we take our time here in the sticks? You mustn't come mess with our tempo now!" He gave a snort. "Listen, I won't manage to get around to your burn victim before this afternoon."

"What time?"

"As soon as I'm through with the last of the weekend's eight stabbings, Inspector."

Beeslaar whistled. "Eight! New record?"

Prinsloo gave a rasping laugh. "No, my friend. The record is fifteen in one weekend. January, all the booze, remember. You better go back to Joburg if you want a quiet life."

From the frying pan into the fire: Beeslaar was all too aware that this area had the highest per-capita murder rate in the country—and every New Year, people's rage erupted.

"But before we get too chatty, Inspector, how does three o'clock sound to you?"

"You're on," Beeslaar said with a smile. "See you then."

37

S ara came out of the café holding a can of Coke. She drank it thirstily, her eyes narrowed against the glare of the sun. There was a familiar figure on the opposite side of the street.

"Dam!" she called out.

He was walking briskly, apparently oblivious. Walking right out of town. She called again, louder this time.

One of the ragged characters next to the police station decided to help. "Da-a-a-m!" she squawked.

Dam glanced back at the motley lot, but didn't stop. He walked in long, energetic strides, his back straight as an arrow.

Sara debated whether to follow him in her car. Why was he in town without a vehicle?

Moments later, she was sitting behind the wheel. Dam was already passing the last houses, past the Chicken Vale turn-off, and had broken into a light jog. Lord, where was he off to?

She turned on the engine, made a U-turn and drove up to him.

"Dam!"

As he stopped, Sara pulled up the brake and got out. His face was like thunder. "What's going on?" she asked. "Did you hear about Outanna?"

"I heard, yes. I've just come from the police station."

"What, er . . . What's happened to your bakkie?"

"It's a long story."

"Can I take you to the farm?"

"No, thanks. I'm okay."

At first she didn't know what to say. Then she lost patience. "Man, get in the car, I'll take you where you need to go."

"I want to go to the farm. And I'd rather be alone, if you don't mind."

"That's more than forty k, man!"

"I know," he said, as he turned away to set off again.

"Dam, I haven't even told you everything about Outanna. Don't you want to know?"

"I know enough already," he said. "Good day!" He set off at a comfortable jog.

Sara stared after him. Before long he was nothing but a speck on the dusty road.

38

Beeslaar thought of the chained dog as he pulled up in front of the burnt-out shell of Sanna van Wyk's house. What had happened to the poor creature?

The place was deserted, police tape flapping forlornly on the gateposts. He got out and stepped carefully over bits of rubble and debris that lay strewn on the ground in front of the house. What exactly was it that had happened here?

Outanna's body had been found on the couch in the lounge. As if she'd been tied up there. But Deetlefs found no sign of anything like that. Suppose it *had* been arson, as Deetlefs believed—she'd have fought back, surely, despite her age. She'd have been somewhere else, desperate to get out: at the front door, by a window.

Beeslaar looked about him, then walked around the house to the back. Right behind the house stood an outhouse. The smell of it hit him: the old bucket system, he concluded. Against an exterior wall, a basin with a cold water tap—clearly, this was the bathroom. He was just about to walk on when another smell ambushed him: the smell of a dead thing. He stepped closer.

Then he saw the origin of the stench: blood seeping from under the toilet door.

Warily, he approached. The door was slightly ajar. He took a pen from his shirt pocket and used it to push the door open.

What he saw made him reel back, heaving.

It was the dog. Its feet had been bound with wire and its

throat slit. The poor animal must have lain there bleeding like a slaughtered sheep.

He walked back to his car, shaking his head, wishing he had a cigarette to expel the smell from his mouth and nose.

He felt shaken. And pissed off, dammit. What kind of perverted fuck did something like that? The kind of animal who would burn a vulnerable old woman alive? He looked up and down the road angrily, as if searching for someone to confront. But the street was quiet.

On the corner, sitting under a syringa tree, he saw a woman selling vegetables.

Beeslaar walked up to her. As he approached, she got up and carefully turned over the tomatoes and onions, which were displayed in brightly coloured plastic bowls.

"Afternoon, Mma," he greeted.

The woman greeted him back.

"Are you here every day?"

"Every day, ja. I come from the township next door. But every day I'm here."

"Yesterday afternoon too?"

She looked towards Sanna's house. Clicked her tongue.

"Did you see what happened there, at Number 440?"

She sat down again, flat on the ground, legs outstretched, adjusted one of the blue plastic plates that held four blood-red tomatoes. "Hau!" she said eventually. "I saw it, yes."

Beeslaar crouched down on his haunches.

"Did you see if there were people setting fire to that house?"

She puckered her lips, contemplating her reply as Beeslaar waited.

"There was a bakkie that came," she said at last. "Just before tjaile time. I couldn't see who. That bakkie, it was big. A whitish colour, I think."

"And the people inside, were they white?"

"No. Our people. One, he got out. There were others on the back of the bakkie." She was quiet for a bit, thinking.

"The man who got out, did he go into the house?"

She frowned. "I don't know. I wasn't really looking so nicely. I was busy packing my things up here."

"What time was it? Could you hear anything?"

She looked at the house, then back at him. "No-o-o . . . Yes! Screaming. Screaming at the auntie. All kind of things. But when I'm looking again, that bakkie was going away very quickly. You just see dust, stones jumping. About five o'clock. My time to go home."

"Could you hear what they were screaming?"

She shook her head.

"And the dog?"

"Askies?" She looked at him uncomprehendingly.

"When the bakkie stopped. Did the dog bark?"

"That dog, he's barking always, ja."

"And when the bakkie left, what happened next?"

"Hayi. I couldn't say." She shook her head again. "But," she scratched under her headscarf, "the children, they called. And then the smoke. I'm running to look what's wrong there, but that house, it is a *big* fire."

"Could you smell anything?"

"Smell?" she asked doubtfully. Then her face brightened. "Yes! Petrol. Or paraffin. I don't know. Lots and lots of black, black smoke."

Beeslaar got up. "Thank you very much, Mma. May I take your name down? What you just told me, it's very important."

She looked at him suspiciously. "The people, they didn't treat me nice," she said. "They just come, take all my things."

"When, yesterday?"

"Ja. I went running to look there at the auntie's house. But when I look again, all my things, they're gone. Everything!" She looked at him, eyes wide in indignation.

Beeslaar took out his wallet and asked what the tomatoes cost. One rand each, she informed him. He took four. Put a twenty-rand note into her hand and told her to keep the change.

She was still exclaiming gratefully as he walked back to his car.

Beeslaar contemplated the buttons on the phone in his hand. He pressed the menu button, went to Contacts, looked for "G." He fixed his eyes on the name he'd saved there on Saturday.

He was in his study, the coolest room in the house, south-facing with two mesh-covered windows that allowed the evening breeze in while keeping the dreaded bugs out.

It could only have been her phoning on Saturday on his drive back from Huilwater. Who else would phone him from Joburg? He'd cut his ties with Joburg, didn't want any contact. Changed his number, a way of dumping all the old baggage. Former colleagues, his superiors, drinking buddies. Fucking Doctor Nosey, the shrink he was forced to see so he wouldn't get fired. The people he had alienated in the months before he left. He couldn't bear to see the look in their eyes: part sympathy, part disapproval. Sometimes even revulsion. The latter he could still handle, but the sympathy! He gave them all a wide berth.

Beeslaar hit the call button.

"Hello?" Her voice. It wrenched him back to his senses and he cut the call.

What the hell was he thinking?

He got up, put the phone in his pocket and went outside, heading for the veld. But he walked no farther than the bottom of the road. It was too dark to go on.

It must be after ten already, he realised.

As he walked back he remembered the red roman again. Could that thing still be hiding out somewhere in the lounge? He still didn't dare open the door.

Arriving at the gate, he changed his mind again and kept walking. It would do him good. He was still dead tired after the previous evening's panic attack, but his brain was buzzing.

She wasn't going to call back, he decided. Why had he called her? As if he needed any extra crap right now—this was a chapter in his life that he had written off. Not just written off: he'd damn well torn it out, crumpled it up and chucked it into the fire. *That's* how finished he was with it all.

He sped up, lengthening his stride, building in some light cardio work while he cleared his thoughts.

It had hardly been what you would call a first-rate day— starting with Buks Hanekom.

Beeslaar had gone looking for him at Wag-'n-Bietjie, his father's farm. Found him on the front stoep, on his way to town.

He'd gone straight for the jugular: "Did you threaten Freddie Swarts before her death?"

Caught off guard, Hanekom had blurted, "I went to see her after she started messing around with the land claims, along with that foreman of hers. And I warned her she was playing with fire, sympathising with the wrong side. That's all."

"That's all."

"Of course that's all. The victims here—it's us, *we* are the victims here, us white farmers, whose lives and futures are under threat."

"Did you threaten to kill her?"

Hanekom had sighed, irritated, as if Beeslaar was an annoying child. "Our community has just about been brought to its knees, Beeslaar. We supply food to forty-eight million people, but we're treated like dirt, like some piddling irritation from the past. And the general attitude is, let's leave them to the criminals, let *them* sort it out. Same as Zimbabwe. Big, beautiful plans for land reform, but the officials who have to carry them out can hardly read a koeksister recipe, let alone solve a complicated farming issue. So in fifteen years fuck-all has happened—and then the matter is handed over to a bunch of land terrorists to sort out. That's what happened in Zimbabwe, and that's exactly the path we're on right now."

Beeslaar had tried to interrupt him, but there had been no stopping the man. He'd started quoting statistics and talking about the Land Expropriation Act and plenty more besides. Until Beeslaar had exploded, "Spare me the politics, man, for Chrissake! You can leave that for Sundays at that half-baked church of yours."

That had done it. Hanekom had stopped talking. But only for a second.

"I have absolutely nothing to do with Tjoek Visser and his lot," he'd said indignantly.

"Oh? But your best buddy Polla Pieterse, he sits there every week. Plays the musical instruments, even."

"Okay, listen carefully, Inspector: I'm not a racist. I'm a realist, an ordinary man trying to protect myself and my family and my people. I can't give any assurances about the politics or religion of other people who feel the same. But let me tell you one thing: this government of ours doesn't give a damn. We're being fed to the dogs. And we're definitely not going to sit on our hands and watch it happen. That I promise you."

"You're playing with fire, Mr. Hanekom. For your sake I hope the talk doing the rounds, about you and your efforts to arm people, isn't true. Because then we're talking treason."

"Do you know what happens when your neighbour's farm suddenly becomes tribal land? Overnight, you have a squatter camp on your boundary. And before you know it, all the animal diseases and pests you've spent years eradicating—"

"Enough, please! And you have yet to tell me if you ever threatened to kill Freddie Swarts."

"We farmers won't just roll over like that. We're being—"

"I'm talking about Freddie Swarts, the woman who was murdered last week! The woman you threatened to kill! But what I *really* want to know is: Were you there last Wednesday?"

Hanekom had fallen silent. He'd looked past Beeslaar. "Listen. Do you know what it feels like to hold the dead body of a loved one in your arms Do you *know*? With his blood flowing out of him. And that, just for a *cellphone*?"

"Buks, that's exactly—"

"Okay, *I'll* tell you . . . " His moustache quivered with emotion. "You're powerless. You're nothing. Everything about you . . . everything that makes you human. Everything that's good and sacred, everything that made sense in the world—at that moment it's destroyed."

Beeslaar had decided it was best to leave it there, and had driven back to town.

That conversation with Buks had been his first mistake of the day. The second had been when he let Pyl be the driver when they tackled the road to Postmasburg for the autopsy on Mrs. Beesvel.

The man had driven the way he talked: one moment full speed ahead, the next like a chameleon with an identity crisis. Or like a bloody church-organ player—tap dancing between the accelerator and the brake. Now the gas, now the brake . . . With Beeslaar next to him, seething in silence. Until he had blown his top and taken the wheel himself.

And that, of course, was mistake number three. He had wounded Pyl's pride. And to top it all, the poor man would later pass out at the autopsy table.

It *was* bad, though. Deaths by burning were always awful. The smell of scorched flesh, hair, bones . . .

She had definitely died of suffocation, the doc had said. But the question had been, how? There was no evidence that she'd tried to fight back or escape. Maybe it had been fear that paralysed her. And she had been emotionally disturbed, had been expecting something ghastly.

But who had done it? Who'd been in that whitish bakkie? And what might their motive have been?

Beeslaar lengthened his stride. He walked right around the town, first along the outer streets that ran around the old "white" part, then up and down the few cross streets. The main street was dead quiet, even at the hotel bar. As he passed the police station he saw Shoes Morotse on duty behind the counter, gesturing wildly with his hands as he talked into the phone. Beeslaar smiled to himself. The girlfriend again.

He turned towards home and walked past Nelmari's house.

It was less showy than the office. An ordinary town house, Karoo style, with a verandah roof of curved corrugated iron, low stoep walls, right on the street. The house was dark. How many houses did she own? She was often away, she had told him during one of their conversations. Upington, Kimberley, Johannesburg.

He wondered why, indeed, she was here in this town— house, office, the works—when her main business was in Upington and Joburg. Could the friendship with Freddie Swarts have been that important?

He strode on, his shadow stretching and shrinking with each streetlight he passed. And then he was done walking. He turned back home, remembering with a start that he hadn't locked his front door.

Well, there was bugger-all worth stealing inside, he told himself with a wry smile. And he had his very own fearsome red roman in the lounge to guard the television.

40

S ara tossed and turned all night. Every time she closed her eyes she saw flames, felt she couldn't breathe, then she had to open them again to see the room's serene darkness, dispel the horrible images. Outanna. What a gruesome way for such a gentle woman's life to end. What world was this she'd come to? Her hometown, but everything twisted, changed since the news of Freddie. It was best, she decided, to get up, to get out, before first light—go back to the farm and get back to work.

She and Yvonne had eaten supper on the stoep the night before, sitting for a while after they had finished, neither of them really wanting to go in to bed. In the dark, each with a dog on her lap, and the third at their feet between them. Avoiding the awful details, but talking about practicalities, about the additional funeral that had to be arranged for Outanna now, about what was to happen to Huilwater. Sara had undertaken to get hold of Oom Sybrand Nel today. A retired local lawyer, he had handled her father's affairs in the past.

But as she got into the car in the pre-dawn dark, Sara realised she was even wearier today.

Exhausted. Her body ached. It wasn't just the sleeplessness, it was the ache of sadness. But she couldn't cry, let any of it out. It pressed painfully, suffocatingly against her throat, dammed up inside her, unable to break through.

The smell still lingered in the house. She began opening windows. Passing Freddie's door, she forced herself to step into the room to take a look. It was just a dark empty space, she saw to her surprise, the horror she had dreaded was only in her own mind, after all. The bed had been removed—probably by Dam—and the floor was bare, the floorboards bleached.

Leaving the room, she noticed a small painting on the passage wall outside Freddie's door, hanging next to the bookshelf. She couldn't quite make it out in the dim passage.

Carefully she lifted it off the nail and walked to the front door with it. The central figure was a snake—the very same one that featured in the big painting, with Dam riding its back.

What did the snake signify, she wondered. Here, it lay beside a shallow dam. Water streamed from its eyes. It was apparently weeping. In a tree next to the dam hung a dainty little dress—a little girl's perhaps? And a small bright orange fish leapt out of the dam.

Sara hung it back on the wall and went to put the kettle on for coffee. As she waited for it to boil, she realised that the smell in the house seemed different this morning. There was the sad scent of camphor, reminding her of Outanna. Her and Freddie's real mother. Sara squeezed her eyes shut. Outanna had always been here, in this house, for them, kissing scraped knees and elbows better, administering her own remedies. She'd gathered herbs from the veld—making ointments and poultices for many a childhood illness or pain.

And sometimes she burnt buchu leaves.

Buchu, she had always said, was the smell of deep things. Of the great, important things in life, like God and the ancestors. Sara hoped there was comfort for Outanna wherever she was now, ancestors or not.

But camphor . . . camphor cast the shadow of coming death. Like the wild whiff of a hyena, a beast you could smell long before you saw it.

And as if the hyena had suddenly materialised, appalling

shrieks came from somewhere outside. Sara hurried to the back door and looked out. Was it animal or human, this unearthly screaming?.

Then she saw Oom Sak. He was running blindly into the open veld—away from Dam's house. He stumbled and fell, but scrambled up again and ran as though the devil himself was after him.

41

Beeslaar's mouth was full of toothpaste when the phone rang in the lounge. He spat it out and hurried down the passage, banging into the closed lounge door.

"Bloody hell," he mumbled and yanked the door open.

It was Jansie Boois. "Why aren't you answering your cellphone? The station's looking for you," she said. "It's the Huilwater people. They need you very urgently."

"What for?" He could still taste the toothpaste.

"Dunno. But it's urgent."

He thanked Jansie, hung up and immediately turned the crank to get hold of the exchange. The young lady told him to hold, she'd get Huilwater on the line for him.

Beeslaar waited, scanning the corners of the room. If that red roman decided to run up his legs now . . .

"I'm putting you through."

He perched up on the sofa's backrest, feet on the cushions.

"Inspector! Ag, thank God. Something's happened here again." Sara Swarts sounded more weary than distressed.

"Has someone been hurt?"

"No. It's—someone strung up a dead baboon here in the night."

"What?"

"It's . . . " Her voice was fading.

"I'm coming right away. Please don't do anything. Stay inside and keep the doors locked. Is there somebody with you?"

He heard her say something—more of a groan than a yes.

He called Ghaap and Pyl, who were on their way to the office already, thanks to Jansie Boois.

Beeslaar did the driving himself that morning. Pyl sat in the back, still a bit bruised after yesterday's run-in on the way to Postmasburg. Ghaap, as usual, didn't have much to say for himself. Beeslaar used the time to discuss the investigation so far: what progress had been made with finding the jackal man and the owner of the white bakkie seen at Mrs. Beesvel's house that Monday afternoon. Ghaap said he and Shoes Morotse had gone to Chicken Vale to question the vegetable seller again, but they weren't able to get much more out of her.

"How old is the bakkie she saw? Do we know the make?" asked Beeslaar.

Ghaap shook his head.

"Then show the old lady some pictures of bakkies."

"And where will I find those?"

"Use your imagination, man. Newspaper motoring sections. Buy a bloody car magazine if you have to. Do you have a description of the occupants?"

"Just that they were black."

"See if you can get more. Is the bakkie old or new? Registration plates, marks, or anything that makes it stand out. Did it sound like a diesel—stuff like that."

Ghaap gave a nod.

"Anything else?"

Ghaap took his notebook from his pocket, paged through it. "The neighbours, sorry, Inspector, but nobody wants to say a word about the fire."

In his rear-view mirror, Beeslaar could see Pyl, who was sitting tight-lipped and sulky.

They drove the rest of the way in silence.

At the last rise in the road, just before the turn-off, Beeslaar said loudly, "Sergeant Pyl, after your sleepover on Monday night, I expect you know that farmyard like the back of your hand." He looked for some reaction, but Pyl didn't even glance up. "Nou ja, when we get there, you look after the old man. Take him to one side and thrash him with questions. Dammit, he lives in De Kok's house, but claims to know nothing about the man's walkabouts. Question him from here to Christmas. Leave nothing out."

He turned to Ghaap. "You take photos of the scene. And make sure you check out the *whole* scene. We want to know how the dead baboon got there. Look for tyre tracks, blood trails, footprints. Whether De Kok did it. If someone else drove the dead baboon there in the middle of the night, you'll be able to see it. Take a look around the sheds—watch out for signs of slaughter, animal tracks, blood, stuff like that. Okay?"

"Isn't this a bit over the top for a dead baboon?" Ghaap ventured as they stopped at the farmyard.

"Fucking hell, man! We're investigating five murders. *Five!* The Vaalputs workers, the two here at Huilwater, and old Mrs. Beesvel. And besides that, there are millions of rands in stock losses. And quite possibly the same people are behind it all. It could be anyone—some twisted fuck acting alone or an organised crime syndicate or whatever. Or the man who's just had a dead baboon tied to his front gate. He's also a damn suspect in this whole bloody mess. Wake up, Sergeant!"

Ghaap put both hands up in the air in a gesture of surrender.

"Okay, okay," he muttered, hurriedly getting out of the car.

Beeslaar got out and slammed the door.

"Pyl," he said to the other man, "when you're done with the old guy, ask him for a bag or something we can use to load the carcass in the boot.

"Ja, Baas," Pyl mumbled.

Beeslaar felt a red rage welling up in him. *Baas*. He opened his mouth to say something, but then De Kok appeared at the back door of the farmhouse, Sara Swarts just behind him.

Beeslaar walked up to them briskly.

"Show me where the baboon is," he demanded. "Miss Swarts, you stay here, please."

De Kok led them through the avenue of trees to the front of his house, to a small gate in the fence around it.

The gate was open, swung wide under the weight of a fly-ridden hunk of blood and hair. The baboon had been crucified. Its hands were chopped off. Blood and sinew on the chicken wire.

Beeslaar filled his lungs with air, slowly exhaled through tight lips and stepped closer. The upper arms, wrenched wide, were bound to the gate either side of the limp body, high above the head. A piece of wire stretched tight across the forehead kept the head up so that the dead eyes gazed directly at Beeslaar.

Its throat had been slit, he saw. Blood everywhere. All over the body, in black trails and pools around the gate. It had spurted right onto the front stoep.

"Ghaap!" he called, but there was no reply.

He looked around, and saw only De Kok behind him.

"He's feeling a bit sick," De Kok said.

Beeslaar choked back his annoyance and turned around, almost knocking the man out of his way. Around the corner of the house he saw the two sergeants doubled over, retching. "What the hell's going on here!" he bellowed. "Jesus! Have neither of you two old women ever seen a dead baboon?" Ghaap still had the camera in his hand. He held it out to Beeslaar, who grabbed it, hissed a curse.

De Kok was standing in front of the gate to get a closer look at the carcass.

"Get the fuck away from there, man!" he boomed. "This is a crime scene. You're getting footprints all over the damn place!" He walked closer, then said more evenly, "Please go back to the house and stay there until I call you."

De Kok gave him a contemptuous look and turned on his heel.

Beeslaar started taking photos. He took them from a distance, so that he could record the full extent of the blood trails. They lay in a radius of up to two metres from the carcass, he estimated. The dead baboon was female. She must have had her throat slit here, right on this gate. He took a few more pictures, then went up closer. It was then he noticed the animal's head had been shorn, right down to the scalp. He felt his skin crawl.

There were tyre tracks close to the gate. A bakkie, perhaps?

It was when he turned to walk back to the car that he saw the blood on De Kok's front door. TOKOLOSHE COMING, said the childish scrawl.

Pyl and Ghaap reappeared, their faces the colour of old newspaper, their eyes red. Pyl offered to fetch the fingerprint kit from the car.

Handing the camera back to Ghaap, Beeslaar said to him, "You okay now?"

"Sorry, Inspector," he mumbled.

"Albertus," Beeslaar said. "That's my name. Forget the inspector-inspector thing. Please take more photos of the front door and the bloody footprint on the stoep."

Bemused, the sergeant looked up at Beeslaar.

"I'll speak to De Kok so long. Will you help Pyl with the fingerprints? The door *and* the gate."

"Right." Inclining his head to the gate, he said, "What do you think this is?"

"Fuck knows. Whoever and whatever is operating here sure doesn't like animals. You didn't see the dog over at Sanna van Wyk's house?"

"No, why?"

"Same thing as there. Its throat cut. But this one here," he gestured towards the baboon, "this has direct reference to last week's murders. The head's been shaved."

"Do you still think De Kok's behind it all?"

"I'm going to find out. That's for fucking sure."

T ake off your shoes," Beeslaar barked when he got to De Kok's back stoep.

Without a word, De Kok bent over and undid the leather laces of his velskoene.

Beeslaar took the shoes from him. They were covered in stains, possibly dried blood, but the marks looked older. He inspected the soles. "Stay here," he said and walked to the front of the house, shoes in his hand. The bloody tracks at the front door suggested shoes with ridged soles. But De Kok's soles were smooth. And they were far smaller than the footprints, which were at least a size eight. Still, not big for a man. Beeslaar himself wore a twelve.

Out of the corner of his eye he saw his colleagues look up at him. They were on their haunches beside the steps, preparing the brushes and powders from the fingerprint kit. He left them to it.

When he got to the back stoep again, Oom Sak was there too. Beeslaar inspected his shoes as well. Smooth soles too, and also much smaller than the bloody footprints. He took a size six, the old guy told him.

The three of them sat down at the table on the stoep. The old man said he first saw the baboon carcass at six that morning. He was just setting off for the lamb camp, beyond the main house. He'd heard Miss Swarts arriving and didn't want to bother her, so he'd walked around the front. And discovered the dead baboon.

"So you waited for Miss Swarts to get here, then you put on the show."

The old man jumped up. "Meneer, please! It's not us, that thing. Nee, o Jirre, Meneer!" He looked at Beeslaar in terror, his jaw quivering.

"Calm down, Oom Sak, Mr., er . . . "

"Renoster," said De Kok. "His surname," he explained upon noticing Beeslaar's puzzlement. "Saggarias Renoster. Everyone calls him Oom Sak. He's been living here his whole life. Worked for old Mr. Swarts, right up until his seventieth year. He's seventy-three now. And he most certainly has nothing to do with any of this."

"And since when have you been his spokesperson, Mr. De Kok?"

"Since you started intimidating and humiliating him."

"Watch it," Beeslaar growled.

De Kok glared, challenge in his eyes.

"What I want to know, gentlemen, is how you managed to not notice the baboon carcass until six o'clock this morning."

The old man fidgeted with his hat.

"Were you here at all, last night?"

"I was here," said De Kok, a touch of resignation in his voice.

"You sure? Because it's no use asking Mr. Renoster. With the two of you in cahoots it's damn near impossible to figure out who's lying, who's telling the truth."

"I was here," De Kok repeated. "We went to bed early. Got up at five. Started the day."

"If that's true, you must have been damn well dead to the world last night. That front gate is right up against the house."

"I was tired," said De Kok.

"Tired? I get tired too. *And* I'm a city guy, used to noise. But Jesus, if a bakkie pulls up under my window in the middle of the night, and someone takes out a live baboon, ties the thing to the gate ten paces from my bed, slits its throat so that it can bleed to death, blood spurting like a fountain . . . Shit, man! Unless you did it yourself, of course. Or put something a little stronger in that pipe of yours last night . . . "

"I was tired," De Kok said yet again, his voice flat. "You people fetched me away from here yesterday and I had to find my own way back."

"You walked?"

De Kok didn't answer immediately. Then he said, "If you're looking for someone to blame, go ask the people of the so-called commando. People like Hanekom, who keep coming out here to threaten me."

"Theatening what?"

"Telling me that if *you're* too soft to deal with me, *he* will."

"Where's Herklaas Windvogel?" Beeslaar asked next. Faced with silence, he raised his voice, "Mr. Renoster?"

"I wouldn't be able to say for sure," he eventually muttered.

He was lying, Beeslaar knew, but let it pass. "Are there any baboons around here?"

In unison, they said, "No."

"And Monday night, Mr. Renoster? The night Mrs. Johanna Beesvel was murdered. Where was Mr. De Kok?"

"He wasn't even here. He was looking for Oom Vangjan, you see."

"You don't say. And who's *he* when he's at home?" Beeslaar asked.

"He hasn't got a home, he . . . " The old man stopped, biting back his words.

"Oops," said Beeslaar and looked at De Kok, who merely lit his pipe.

"I went looking for the old drifter—the jackal-catcher."

"Herklaas Windvogel."

"Yes. I wanted to find out if he's the one who'd strung up all that stuff here last Friday night. That stuff all started with Outanna. And that damned sangoma."

De Kok took a few puffs, then set the pipe down carefully. He explained how Outanna and Freddie had brought a sangoma to the farm three months before, back in December. They'd gone to Kimberley for the day and he'd come back with them. Why they did this, he didn't know. All he knew was that it was Outanna's idea.

"I think it was because of all the tensions here on the farm. She grew anxious, had all sorts of fancies about evil approaching and so on. Together with the stock thievery all around us. Freddie took pictures of the sangoma—to paint his portrait, she said. Outanna fed him, and then the guy did his tricks with the dead chicken and the muti at the farm gate. He said it was to keep away evil spirits—and Outanna said it would keep away the evil people, the stock thieves too, keep them from her lambs as well. I wanted nothing to do with it. I can't stand superstition. And when those two men next door were killed with their sheep last month, Outanna was really scared and got it in her head that the sangoma should come again, that I should go fetch him. But I put my foot down. No more mumbo-jumbo. End of story. The next time I saw anything to do with that rubbish was last Saturday. And that's that."

"Then why did you lie about it at the start?" Beeslaar asked.

"Because it's all nonsense. And I was sure Outanna had gone and told the old jackal man to play sangoma and to put that bullshit here on the farm, to protect us, even though she and the others had run away to town. I also knew a city cop would never have believed that story. So, come Monday night, I went looking for him—in the veld. But I couldn't find him. And then there was the fire, and, well, you know the rest."

"That's for fucking sure. And *another* thing I know, is that you take me for a fucking idiot!"

He stalked off, inspected De Kok's bakkie. It was dusty and dry—no blood, nothing.

After he was done with De Kok, Beeslaar walked over to the main house. He found Sara Swarts sitting on the steps at the back door.

She invited him in for coffee, and immediately bombarded him with questions. "Inspector, who did it? Do you think it's the same people who left that witch doctor stuff here on Saturday? Why was the baboon left at Dam's? Do you think it's about Freddie? Could it be the sangoma Outanna was talking about?"

Beeslaar noticed a tremor in her hands as she poured the coffee. After a tentative sip of the hot coffee, he asked, "Why were you here so early?"

She gestured vaguely. "Oh, I couldn't sleep any more. And tidying the house keeps me busy. But . . . It's as if the devil's been let loose here." She bit her lip. "I should have paid more attention to Outanna. She tried to warn me, told me things weren't right—hadn't been for some time. But I didn't understand it. I still don't. And I know it might sound odd, but I still can't believe that ordinary criminals, stock thieves, would kill my sister. Not like *that*." She paused. "And there's the painting. It's as if she prophesied her own death."

"Look," he said, "I'm not excluding any possibility at this stage. But the thieves we're dealing with here are definitely not your run-of-the-mill opportunists—some guy who steals a sheep for the pot now and again. This is a sophisticated gang. They're cruel, they maim animals, think nothing of killing the people who get in their way."

She gave him a strange look. "Maybe I should show you that painting."

It was propped up on an easel, Beeslaar saw as he walked into the studio. Sara Swarts stood beside him as they studied the self-portrait with the mantis man. A female figure, drenched in her own blood, sat with her back against a chair. Strangely, there seemed to be a look of bliss on her face.

No suggestion of murder, he thought, though there were disconcerting details: the blood, the chopped-off bits of hair that seemed to drift around her head.

"What does it mean?" he asked.

"I think she's giving her heart to the praying mantis. Freddie's paintings were always a kind of visual diary of her life. And sometimes they were literal depictions of an idiom, or an expression."

She stopped—someone was at the back door, knocking loudly.

"Here, in the bedroom!" Beeslaar called out. "Sorry," he said to Sara, "it's my man, I think."

Pyl walked in, and Beeslaar asked, "Everything go smoothly with the fingerprints?"

"Not too good. Those guys must have been wearing gloves."

"Have you loaded up the carcass?"

"I thought . . . "

"For God's sake, man. What have you been doing all this time? Or must I come and do that too?"

The man glanced at Sara, his eyes hard and shiny. Then he disappeared through the door, his footsteps hammering on the floorboards.

Beeslaar turned his attention back to the painting. "I think the mantis is some kind of god in the San religion." He looked at Sara, but she shrugged. "She's offering her heart—something valuable. The farm, maybe? Her birthright?"

"I don't know. I hadn't thought about it like that. Maybe Nelmari would be able to say. But that's not the important part, I think. The composition is more significant—the fact that her body has been cut open, her hair cut off, the position she's sitting in. The fact that her death imitates this painting."

The telephone rang somewhere in the house.

"It's ours," said Sara. "Two short rings, one long."

43

L ong distance from Cape Town," Sara heard the operator announcing. "You're going through."
There was some hissing, then Harry's voice. "Hello,
neighbour."

He sounded far away, as if he were calling from the moon.
She could hear he was on a cellphone, driving.

"You have to speak up, Harry," she shouted. "The line is
really bad."

"Are you okay?"

She swallowed. Harry's voice sounded so healthy and
bright in the midst of this nightmare. As if it came from
another world where things were normal and cheery. Where
people sat chattering away in coffee shops, or having an after-
work beer at the Waterfront. It felt so far away, she had a hard
time even remembering what he looked like—the brush cut,
trimmed beard, the aquiline nose, deep-set eyes. Brown.
Always that twinkle of interest, amusement.

"Sara?"

"Sorry. Things are a little rough here. Where are you calling
from?"

"I'm not sure. Somewhere around Loeriesfontein."

"What are you doing *there*?"

"I'm heading in your direction. My article, remember?"

By the time they'd done talking, she felt much better.
Perhaps this was what she needed—a good pal, someone who
went through life as cheerily as Harry. Barely any emotional

baggage, never taking things personally. And he seldom lost perspective. Or his sense of humour. Or his healthy cynicism.

When she turned around, she saw Beeslaar in the doorway.

"A friend," she explained, then went back to business. "Just to finish off about the painting. Don't you agree there's something strange going on?"

He took a deep breath. "I'll be straight with you. Right now it's difficult to say what's relevant and what not. But I'm considering everything. In the meantime I don't want to tell you what to do, but I still don't think you should be here alone."

She opened her mouth, but he didn't give her a chance to speak.

"It's not safe. And personally I believe it's not good for you."

"But I'm not alone, Inspector. I keep telling you. Oom Sak is here. And Dam. And besides, I can't just sit around town doing nothing. And . . . " She gave up. Let him think what he wanted.

44

B eeslaar walked across the yard, back to De Kok's house. He was sweating. Sitting in the cool, dim farmhouse, he hadn't realised it had grown so hot.

De Kok was still on his back stoep.

"Have you been sitting here the whole time?" Beeslaar asked, lowering himself onto the stoep wall.

De Kok didn't answer.

"Were you in the army?"

"No. But I can sit still for a long time. I learnt it as a child. You need to be able to wait if you want to be a hunter."

"What do you mean?"

"You wouldn't understand."

"Try me."

De Kok said nothing.

"You grew up in the veld, didn't you?"

"Is that a crime?"

Beeslaar sighed. "I hear you and the deceased used to argue."

"Where did you hear that?"

"Doesn't matter. I hear Miss Swarts was pretty depressed before she died. Crying a lot, and so on. And apparently you were quite moerig yourself. What was that all about?"

Beeslaar waited for a response.

"I don't have all day, De Kok." He didn't bother to conceal his exasperation.

"If it was Outanna who told you I was upset, it's nonsense. She was an old woman. All alone in the world, apart from her sister in town. These were her people. And she was very attached to little Klara. Too attached, you could say. She became more and more protective, and superstitious—she expected a ghost behind every bush. When the two men were killed next door, she was completely beside herself with fear. And me, I was just trying to carry on with my work."

"Clearly. A farm like this. You've said yourself it's a one-man show. Or are you referring to your extramural activities? The things that keep you so busy at night?"

De Kok clicked his tongue contemptuously, said nothing.

"And what about the two other workers—do they also work for you?"

"Beeslaar, I wish you'd stop singing the same tired old tune. God knows, I might be capable of stealing sheep. But maiming the poor creatures? Slicing through the hocks and leaving them like that? You saw what those animals looked like!"

"You're full of shit, De Kok. And you lie far too smoothly for my liking. You've been lying to me right from the start. About everything. And my question is this: What *else* are you lying about?"

He was tired, Beeslaar realised when he finally got back to his desk at the station. It had been one bliksem of a day already. And Christ, it was hot. And he was thirsty. Always. He still hadn't got used to the foul-tasting water.

He pulled the fan closer, but it made little difference. It just blew more hot air over him, set his papers fluttering.

He phoned the district surgeon in Postmasburg. "Do you do animals?" he asked directly.

Willie Prinsloo's rasping laugh came down the line.

"There's a baboon carcass on its way to you." Beeslaar filled him in on the details.

Prinsloo made a weak joke about Beeslaar going ape, but promised to take a look.

"How long before you get the Huilwater tests back?"

The doctor gave his strange laugh again. "You're pulling my chain, right? Since when do you ask a question like that—after only a week? *One* week, for Chrissake, Inspector. You're a real joker!"

"Ag, you know me. Hope springs eternal." Beeslaar had only just put the phone down when it rang again.

"The super's on the line for you, Inspector," Jansie Boois said and put the call through.

"Superintendent," Beeslaar said defensively. "I was just planning to phone you. There's been another develop—"

"That can wait," the man said, his voice sombre. His breath rasped, a grim Darth Vader, thought Beeslaar.

"There's an urgent matter that requires attention first, Inspector."

Beeslaar held his breath. "I'm listening, Superintendent."

"I have received a formal complaint of racism about you."

"*What*? That's ridiculous!"

"Ja. Afraid there's nothing ridiculous about it. It's a formal complaint. It has direct implications regarding your competence to lead a murder investigation. I'll expect you in my office in an hour."

"But . . . "

"In an hour, Inspector," the superintendent said gravely and hung up.

Beeslaar stood with the phone in his hand, dumbfounded. But then the full impact of the call hit him and he slammed the receiver down. He stormed into the next office, and alarm flared in Ghaap's eyes.

"Where's Pyl?" he roared, not caring that Ghaap was still on the phone.

Ghaap muttered something into the phone and put it down. "He's gone home."

"What do you mean he's fucking gone home?"

"Calm down, Inspector."

"Don't tell me to fucking calm down, man! I'll fucking thrash the daylights out of him. Did he phone the super before he left?"

Ghaap fingered the phone nervously.

"*Did* he? Answer me, man!"

"I don't know if he phoned the super. He's—"

"Or was it you?"

"No! No, it wasn't me."

"Right. Then get hold of him. Tell him I'm looking for him. I'm going to ram my fist so far down his throat his teeth'll fly out his arse!"

"Get him yourself," Ghaap said, getting up. "If you have an issue with Pyl, go get him yourself."

A red mist descended on Beeslaar. He took a giant step to Ghaap's desk and tried to grab him by the shirt. Ghaap didn't flinch, but stepped out from behind the desk, fists ready for action.

The two of them stood glaring at each other, breath racing.

Then Beeslaar dropped his fists and stepped back. He opened his mouth to say something, jabbed an index finger at Ghaap.

But he changed his mind, turned on his heel and walked out. In the passage, frightened, inquisitive faces slipped silently away as he strode past, back to his office.

45

As soon as the police had left, Sara walked across the yard to Dam's house. She found him on the stoep, cutting a steak into strips. For the birds, he explained.

She looked at his face, the stress of the past week was clearly taking its toll—the questioning, Outanna, and Freddie, of course. The blood, the killings, the dreadful stuff of this morning . . .

She stepped closer, hesitantly, then asked, "Did they take the baboon away?"

Dam set the meat and the knife aside and pulled up a chair for her. "Come, sit," he said and carried on with his work. "The baboon's gone. Oom Sak and I have just finished cleaning it all up."

Sara sat watching him a while. When he had finished, he put the meat into a Tupperware container, which he took to the kitchen along with the knife and cutting board. He returned with two tall glasses of ginger beer.

He sat down at the table and lit his pipe. "Aren't you hungry?" he asked between puffs.

"No. Thanks, though. Have you two eaten anything yet today?"

"Oh, I can't eat. Inspector Beeslaar has ruined my appetite," he said, clenching his pipe between his teeth. "And I don't think Oom Sak will be hungry in a hurry either. Not after that ugly clean-up."

"Where is he?"

"Oh, probably in the shed. He spends most of his time there, these days."

Sara cupped her hands around the cool glass in her hand, admiring the pale colour of the drink. She took a sip. It was cold, yet it burnt its way down her throat. It felt good.

"What's going on around here, Dam?" she asked.

"I wish I knew. Taking a poor old creature like that baboon and using it for some kind of mumbo-jumbo devil's work. It's evil."

"I really don't understand—who could possibly be so angry, hey?"

"Sara, if I knew that, you and I wouldn't be sitting here right now."

46

He was screwed, totally in his moer. That's what it came down to.

All thanks to Sergeant Gershwin Pyl. Gershwin. Where the hell did the man get a name like that anyway? The thoughts raced through Beeslaar's mind as he sat in Superintendent Leonard Mogale's office in Upington. Waiting to hear whether he still had a career in the South African Police Service.

"Monday," the Moegel's voice broke in. "The panel will consist of myself, the director of human resources from Kimberley and the deputy here. Until then, I'm putting Inspector Lobatse in charge of your office. He'll head up the investigation with the two sergeants—Pyl and Ghaap. You can bring him up to speed later today."

Beeslaar felt the blood drain from his face. "Am I being relieved of my duty?"

"Your behaviour thus far has been dubious, to say the least. A lot of people went out of their way to get you that post. Sacrifices were made, Inspector. But the return, so far, well . . . " His large froglike eyes were devoid of emotion.

"There's a criminal syndicate terrorising the community right under your nose. And you haven't arrested a single person—not one single person yet. Hell, you don't even have a suspect. They're running rings around you. And now people are getting killed—unchecked theft escalating to murder, and the whites are organising a right-wing uprising. Getting the old apartheid commandos going again. That's treason, in case you hadn't realised! But none of this seems to bother you—not even when I personally point it out to you. What am I to make of that, Inspector?"

Beeslaar said nothing, flicked a bit of fluff off his sleeve.

"You avoid me. No. You completely ignore me. I sit here like a damn idiot, knowing nothing about the five murders you're brooding on over there. Do you think you're too smart for us ordinary folk here in the Northern Cape? You and your old mates from the good old Joburg Murder and Robbery Squad! While you flaunt your racism, treating your colleagues like monkeys."

"There *was* no racism. Pyl is confusing things—my impatience with his shoddy work isn't racism!"

"Save it for Monday's discussion, Inspector," Mogale said in his baritone. "I don't need to remind you that you already have a serious warning for violence and racism on your record."

Beeslaar took a deep breath. So, they were raking up old stories now. It wouldn't help to try to explain—or to ask for some understanding of his circumstances back then, that he'd had good reason to lose his temper. And that the man just happened to be black.

"So what do I do in the meantime?"

"You help Inspector Lobatse with the investigation. That's all for now. You may go."

Beeslaar got up. Halfway to the door he turned around. He wanted to add something. But the expression in Mogale's eyes made him change his mind.

47

"We can bury Freddie, Tannie Yvonne." In the cool, dark lounge, Sara sat curled up in one of the deep chairs, a glass of iced tea in her hand. "They—they're done with her. A policeman gave me the message this morning."

Outside, the heat hung motionless. Man and beast alike sought relief in the shade. Even the birds had gone quiet, sheltering from the worst of the heat.

It was just past three. Tannie Yvonne had returned from her soup kitchen work and taken a nap. And Sara had had a refreshing swim in Oom Koos's dam. Suspended in the water, she had briefly forgotten about the mayhem of the world around her.

"And I don't even know where to start with arranging a funeral."

"You don't have to organise a thing, my girl. The funeral directors take care of everything. Now, have you managed to get hold of Sybrand?"

There was not a single law practice left in town, and though Sybrand Nel was retired, he still kept an eye on some old clients' affairs, among them Sara's father's estate. The same estate she hadn't wanted any part of: she'd brusquely told him that, between the two of them, he and Freddie could decide what to do with her share of the farm. Yet another person she owed an apology to.

Sara snapped back to the present. "No, Tannie, apparently

he's still overseas, visiting one of his daughters in Poland. But they're expecting him in a week or so. I really wish he was here. We need to sort out the farm business."

"Oh, it'll take some time, my child. An estate like that usually takes ages. Months, if I'm not mistaken."

"But what do I do about the workers in the meantime? Dawid and Lammer, they're owed wages. And Dam and Oom Sak too, of course. My savings won't cover this. And is Dam supposed to carry on farming? He and the others have to start thinking of their own futures, surely?"

"You don't have to worry yourself over that now, child. After all, it's only been a week, you know."

"Feels like a year to me."

"Come," said the older woman. "Let's take a walk over to the undertakers."

48

Beeslaar drove slowly home from Upington. He stopped under a thorn tree to stretch his legs, and by then the sun was already casting long shadows across the veld.

His cellphone chirped. It was Ghaap, he saw, but he didn't answer. He'd just have to call Lobatse. Until Monday, *he* was in charge.

Monday: he could predict what would happen. The whole horrible Sithole drama would be dredged up again. The real reason behind the incident wouldn't make an iota of difference. Back then, it hadn't either.

He saw it all again: the fake wounded look on Inspector Moss Sithole's face when Beeslaar had confronted him. There had been stories about him for a long time, that he couldn't keep his hands off the women in the cells. Treated them roughly if they resisted. But this time it had been someone Beeslaar had brought in himself.

It had been during the period right after Grovétjie's death. He'd looked like shit: unkempt, his hair unwashed, several days' worth of stubble—more hobo than policeman. He'd been stumbling out of a bar, half drunk, when he bumped into Shireen with her. "Good shit, just two hundred bucks."

She had been barely fourteen. Overweight and high on something, some of her own "good shit"—heroin—he guessed. Sturdy thighs and plump breasts swelling from her boob tube. She'd been wearing a tiny miniskirt, her hair in little plaits all over her head.

Usually he wouldn't have wasted his time with a drunk prostitute. But she was so young. A child. Should have been playing with dolls, still. Plus, he hadn't been exactly sober himself, fancying himself as a big hero who'd protect her, get her off the street for the night. He'd taken her to the station and put her in a cell, meaning to get in touch with Welfare the next day.

But when he'd got to her cell the next morning, her hair was dishevelled, mascara streaked down her face. A black bulge on one cheek, lip split. When he'd seen the torn skirt, he knew: Sithole.

Beeslaar sat waiting for him. Was met at first by wounded innocence. But when Beeslaar wouldn't let go of it, he'd turned sour. "What's your story, Bees? You want her for yourself?"

And so he hit him. When Sithole had toppled over, he picked him up by the scruff of his neck and hit him again. And again. Until someone arrived and pulled him off the man.

Beeslaar was sent home. Shireen too. He never saw her again. Ten to one she had been "sorted out" by her pimp too.

His punishment was light, the commissioner had said back then. The recent death of his partner, Grovétjie, had served as mitigation. But he'd been given an official warning—a permanent black mark on his file. And he had to sit out the two months with the shrink, Doctor Nosey, all part of a new positive approach to the handling of stress-related misconduct in the service. Fucking old Nosey, who thought he could just sit there, his soft little hands piously folded in his lap, and clean up the rot and garbage in policemen's heads. Not a fuck.

For them, there could be no cleansing, no cleaning-up. The horrors that they witnessed daily. The things they—some of them—had done. Back in the bad old days. He'd been a rookie then. But he saw what went on at Brixton Murder and Robbery. And he would be forever haunted. Tainted. No way that stuff could be cleansed. Shrink or no shrink.

It was late by the time Beeslaar drove into town. He drove past the station, but fought the impulse to see if Lobatse's car was there already. Instead, he stopped at the bar. There was nothing to drink in the house. And he didn't think he'd make it through the night without the help of some alcohol. Oom Koeks at his post behind the counter was willing to sell him some booze to take back home.

When he walked back to the car he felt strangely comforted. He was carrying a six-pack of Tafel Lager and a bottle of his favourite brandy, Flight of the Fish Eagle.

49

Tell me about the stars again, Dam."

The three of them were sitting on his back stoep, with mugs of tea and a plate of biscuits. They'd just finished dinner, a fragrant mutton bredie Dam had prepared, flavoured with crushed cumin and rosemary.

She had phoned earlier that afternoon to say she'd be coming out to the farm again. Also, Outanna was "ready" for burial, she'd been told, and they needed to discuss funeral arrangements. Sanna was distraught, and was grateful for the help with the organisation.

At Dam's suggestion that she join him and Oom Sak for a meal, Sara had said, "I must just warn you, my appetite has gone AWOL."

He'd simply laughed, said his and Oom Sak's had vanished too. But they all went ahead and ate with gusto. When Dam opened a box of biscuits for dessert, Sara and Oom Sak eagerly helped themselves.

There was a companionable serenity, as if they shared a meal together every night.

"Do you know the name of that star yet? The one I told you about the other night?" Dam asked Sara.

She looked up at the western horizon, where a faint strip of light still hung. "I reckon it must be the Morning Star. Because it's so bright. And it appears just before daybreak."

"Yes, you call it Venus, the Morning Star, but for us he's the man who married the caracal."

He struck a match, the scrape clear and sharp in the silence. "The caracal was the most beautiful of all the early people. All the other predators were jealous of her. The made-up face, the black mascara around her golden eyes, and her pointy, tufted ears. She was more beautiful than the leopard with his spots and the lion with his coarse old paws. 'Oh, our sister the caracal,' the other animals sang, 'she is the most beautiful of us all. She is the only one good enough for the Heart of Daybreak.'"

"The Heart of Daybreak," Sara said in wonderment. "But there's a catch, isn't there?"

Dam grinned. "The catch," he said, "lay with the hyena. Hyena is a cunning damn thing. And so jealous!"

He took a puff of his pipe, then picked up his tea again. She pushed the biscuits over to him. He studied the contents, chose one wrapped in foil, which he peeled away slowly.

"Well, yes. What kind of a creature is a hyena? It sneaks out of its hole when it's dark, right? And it's strong, with the mightiest jaws in all of the animal kingdom. But it hunts babies, the weak and the sick. Also, it chooses to live off the efforts of another. It's a scavenger, a beggar—living for the crumbs that fall from the lion's table, from the leopard's table."

"Like the wolf in the fairy tales?"

"Ja, maybe, but not quite. It's different to the wolf. It's a lost soul. Have you ever listened closely to the hyena? And have you seen its eyes?"

"I know the sound, yes, that whimpering laugh."

"If you look into the hyena's eyes, you see a look of desolation. The wolf is intelligent and greedy. It looks at you as if it's scheming. But the hyena's eyes are mournful. They're the eyes of an outcast. You can hear the hopelessness in its voice. The darkness is its only refuge . . . "

Sara looked up as his voice died away. She could guess what he was thinking of: the senseless murder that had taken

Freddie from them. Abruptly, he stood up and stretched. "I'll tell you more another time," he muttered. "It's been a long day."

Wrenched from the evening's calm, she said, "Could we maybe have a quick chat about the funeral? I thought we should bury all three of them together, here on the farm. Tannie Yvonne suggested a service in town, for anyone who'd like to come. It's definitely not what Freddie would have wanted. Such a . . . a public spectacle, for inquisitive strangers . . . and political opportunists. But Tannie Yvonne thinks there should be something formal. Afterwards we could have the real ceremony out here on the farm. Just us."

Dam sat down again, his leg resting on the stoep wall. "It's your decision."

"I don't know. I want to hear what you think."

In the ensuing silence, she prompted, "Oom Sak? Dam?"

"You make the arrangements with the undertakers, Sara. We can bury them over there at the spring, at the dam where your father lies."

"Only us? What about Nelmari? I know so little about her and Freddie, their relationship. Outanna—"

"The question, really, is whether she'd come."

"What are you talking about?"

He didn't answer, just said it was time to go, he'd walk her to the car.

Sara choked her frustration back, resisting the impulse to stamp her feet on the ground and scream at him.

Tomorrow was another day.

When she got back home, Tannie Yvonne was in front of the television, the dogs at her feet. Sara went to the kitchen and tried to phone Nelmari again. No answer. She left a message about the funeral.

Her eyes fell on Outanna's tin, up on a shelf. Someone had

taken the time to wash away the soot. Probably Iris, the house-keeper.

The lid slid open with ease this time. Sara removed all the loose items, the beads and photos, the dreaded letter, and picked up an envelope she hadn't noticed before. JOHANNA DEBORAH BEESVEL, it said in Freddie's flamboyant handwriting.

She opened the flap, took out the sheets of paper.

It was a will, Sara saw. She began to read it, with mounting alarm.

50

The warm sound of Mozart's French horns drifted comfortingly into Beeslaar's right ear.

It was some deep hour of the night. He didn't dare turn on the light to check the time. He'd already tried everything. Counting sheep, the works. But his brain wouldn't slow down, not even for a second. As soon as he drifted off, Ghaap's tense face, his angry stance popped back into his mind.

The Horn Concerto was, as always, his last resort. He'd turned down the volume, and the mellow tones swirled soothingly around his head. Light, like a cloud of fluttering butterflies. Hell, when last had he seen a butterfly? It was too goddamn hot around here. Their wings would scorch right up.

He tried visualising a butterfly. And then a sleep trick the shrink had suggested: visualise the rainbow, one colour at a time. Don't move on until you've clearly "seen" the colour you're on. It was a kind of self-hypnosis.

Not tonight. Not tonight, Doctor Nosey.

He was probably too drunk. Three beers and half a bottle of Fish Eagle later.

He'd guzzled it all up, alone on the back step. He didn't want to sit on the front stoep. Afraid someone might see him. Or rather, afraid *he* might see someone—someone he'd have to talk to. So he'd sat there like an idiot, drinking until darkness fell. Spider time.

He'd made an omelette, using three of the eggs Jan Steenkamp's wife had so generously given him last week.

Washed it down with bread and brandy. Telling himself he wasn't going to hunt Pyl down and beat him to a pulp. No, he would take the "responsible" route. Keep himself occupied in a "positive" way until Monday, start a vegetable patch, something like that. Maybe plant a lawn in his backyard. Drive to Kimberley to buy himself some new CDs. Read. Go for walks. Any damn thing other than thinking about this case. Or Pyl or the Moegel. In that order.

But now he had to sleep. Concentrate on the colours. Think of a bright yellow butterfly—fluttering along to the music.

He saw them. The were so real, it felt as if they were flitting around his head. He slowly opened his eyes. Where were the butterflies?

They weren't butterflies, though, he saw to his surprise. They were hands.

Small and black. Dear God, the baboon's chopped-off hands, dancing around his head. He could hear the baboon's far-off screams. Screaming and screaming and screaming. Louder, more urgent by the second.

Then he was wide awake. His cellphone was ringing.

He was about to jump up and fetch it from the kitchen. But the events of the previous day came flooding back. To hell with it.

He lay back down, realised he'd been sleeping after all—and deeply too. For how long? Felt like five minutes, but it must have been longer. Outside, the first birds were chirping. Wondering whether he was still drunk, he considered a walk in the veld.

But he didn't move, and eventually drifted off again.

When he woke, the sun was streaming in through the window. He was lying in a pool of sweat and his head felt as if he'd stuck it in a mixer-mincer-shredder-liquidiser.

He winced when he saw his face in the bathroom mirror—an image to frighten children with. Bloodshot eyes, a red pillow crease across his cheek, and wild, crazy eyebrows. You're getting old, Albertus, he berated his reflection. Growing old man's eyebrows already. Next would be the tufts of hair sprouting from his nostrils and ears.

He swallowed two Panados and took a cool shower.

In the kitchen, he saw that the orange juice was finished. Then he remembered: he'd drunk it just before he got into bed—preempting the great thirst. Hell, what else had he done last night?

The cellphone caught his eye.

Dear God, no. He'd phoned. No, no, no.

Gerda. He'd phoned her. Collapsing onto a kitchen chair, he picked up the phone, pushed buttons. Dialled Numbers: Gerda. Time of call: 22:45.

She'd been in bed already.

"You didn't tell me you were going away, Albertus."

"I didn't think you'd want to know."

"Still. After everything—"

"Gerda. It's *you* who . . . Oh, never mind. How are you?"

"Hanging on."

"Kleinpiet?"

She was quiet a long while. "He's a cheerful little chap."

"Where are you staying now?"

"Closer to my folks. My mom looks after him in the day."

"Are you working?"

"I have to."

"Gerda, why did you call me on Saturday?"

A long exhalation. "Maybe I was also drunk."

He laughed. "Sorry. Dutch courage, eh? I'm glad you called, Gerda. I . . . It's so far, Johannesburg. And I want to see you again, so badly."

"You need to go to bed. Me too, I get up early."

"Don't go, please. Just talk to me some more. It's been so long, Gerda."

"It was a mistake to call you. I'm sorry. Bye, Bert."

Beeslaar held the phone dumbly. *Bye, Bert*. Then he gripped it tightly, suppressing the urge to throw it at the wall.

And who else had he phoned? Right then, he didn't want to know.

He went to open the back door to let in some fresh air. Three empty beer cans stood in a row on the steps. He slammed the door shut.

A few minutes later he walked out the front door, a wide-brimmed hat on his head. This time he was wearing protection against the blackjacks in the form of a pair of lightweight long trousers. The veld was hot already. But here and there, in hollows and ravines, there were still pockets of cooler air.

The veld was full of fresh scents—wild rosemary, cucumber, thyme, the sweet fragrance of buffalo grass. There were more than forty kinds of grass around here, he'd read somewhere. Each with its own name. He only knew buffalo and bushman grass. And spear grass. But he'd heard of thimble grass and gemsbok grass and love grass and a whole lot more. The San had as many names for grass, people said, as the Eskimos had for snow. Although they weren't Eskimos any more either. They were something else now, a new politically correct word. What was it again?

The people around here still talked about Bushmen—not San. The Bushmen called themselves that too, and so did Ghaap and Pyl.

Ghaap and Pyl.

Hell, he'd almost thrashed Ghaap yesterday. Because he was furious at Pyl. And the Moegel. And most probably at himself. Because ever since he'd arrived, he'd achieved absolutely bugger-all. Mogale was right: the stock thieves were running rings around him.

And he was looking at the Huilwater murders from the wrong angle. Maybe he had to forget about gangs of stock thieves. These murders were different.

It was when Gerda ended the call last night—*Bye, Bert*—and he felt his heart contract, that he thought about it. Freddie Swarts had been in love. That's what the painting was saying. She had given her heart to somebody. The mantis. There was only one person who matched that description.

But the question remained: Was it *he* who'd killed her? What would his motive have been?

Shit, if he got fired on Monday, it would be his own fault. He'd had his head so far up his own arse for so long, it wasn't even funny. He turned back, headed home. A second warning was as good as being discharged. And what then? Slink back to Joburg, cap in hand?

He didn't think so.

No, on Monday he'd fight back. And if fighting didn't do it, he'd beg. Come what may.

Because this was his last chance.

He'd have to solve this case, or he'd soon be on the train to Nowhereville.

51

Dam came walking across the yard as Sara parked her car under the blue gum tree.

"You're back," he called out.

"I want to speak to you." She slammed the door and walked towards the house. In the kitchen, she opened the windows and put the kettle on.

He said nothing, just stood with his hip against the table, following her movements warily.

"Sit." It was more of a command than an invitation. He pulled up a chair.

"Freddie's will," she said, taking the papers out of her bag.

Dam sat with his hands clasped.

"It was a bit of a surprise to me, Dam. You knew about this? And you said nothing?"

He sat motionless.

"I found this in Outanna's tin. It says Freddie left the farm to you, with Outanna and Klara granted usufruct. I didn't know you and Freddie were *that* close."

He shifted uncomfortably, but still said nothing.

Sara felt the rage surging up in her face.

"I want you to start talking to me now. And start by telling me what exactly the relationship was between you and Freddie."

"She was my employer—"

"Oh, for Chrissake, Dam!" She slammed the document down on the table. "You're taking me for a fool, man. All of you! No wonder everyone is so anxious for me to get off the farm! You, Outanna, the whole fucking lot of you. When I ask you something, you ignore me, as if I'm some pesky child. I sit here, worrying about what to do with my sister's farm, and how to sort out all this crap. And you say nothing! You! You watch me carrying on, packing and sorting and working away. How I fucking stumble around, looking and looking and looking. Searching for Freddie and searching . . . " She felt her lip begin to quiver.

"Sara, please. Give me a chance."

"You've had every fucking chance under the sun. I've been here a week already—and you haven't breathed a word to me about Freddie. What am I supposed to read into that, huh?"

"Freddie . . . " He took a deep breath, tried again. "We got along really well right from the start. We could talk."

He took the sugar spoon from the pot in front of him, turned it over distractedly. On the handle was a protea with the words CAPE TOWN emblazoned in enamel below it. He put it down again.

"We met by chance at an auction. You know the story. I was looking for land to buy. But I didn't want to rush into anything. Not if the politics around here wasn't right . . . "

"Dam. That story you've told me already. And you're still not answering my question. What the hell has been going on here on Huilwater? I've been looking at her paintings. And as God is my witness, it looks as if a madwoman painted them."

"Sara, there was nothing wrong with Freddie."

"And I wasn't fucking born yesterday! Stop lying to me!"

"I'm not lying. Recently, Freddie began to talk less and to work harder. I thought she was nervous about the exhibition. And I left her to do her thing. I was busy myself . . . "

He pointed at the document in front of them. "I have one of those too. Freddie gave it to us when she asked us to be Klara's guardians—in case something happened to her."

"In case something happened to her? So was she already afraid of something?"

"No, no, and again, no. It was just about Klara. The adoption was a big deal to her. She wanted to be sure Klara would be well taken care of, whatever happened. And . . . " He looked up at her, but quickly averted his eyes. She knew what he wanted to say: she, who'd have been the logical choice as guardian, was, to all intents and purposes, dead to Freddie. The sister who had ceased to exist.

"So, there was no reason for Freddie to fear for her life? What was Outanna talking about, then? About the 'thing' she saw coming? And what about the paintings that showed Freddie—slaughtered?"

Her words visibly jolted him. He straightened his shoulders and began to speak. "Freddie made a fuss when she decided to adopt Klaartjie. She had a christening here—with a minister friend of hers from Pretoria, Johan Steyn. You probably know about him?"

She knew the name, a well-known gay minister from Johannesburg, often featured in newspapers and on radio.

"Johan did a kind of traditional church christening for Klaartjie. And then Outanna did it the Griqua way—sort of. We don't really have a christening ceremony in our traditions. And she was given a Griqua name, which means little fish or stream. Nsitsi."

Sara sat bolt upright: that painting in the passage—of the fish jumping from the water. And the little dress hanging from the tree!

"It was a small gathering—me and Outanna, Johan, Nelmari. Outanna and I were asked to be godparents, and we signed and read out vows that Freddie had written for us." He pulled a face. "To me it was all a bit of a circus. I had to slaughter a goat—in the old way. She wanted the bones to be preserved for Klaartjie's initiation ceremony one day."

"Her *what* ceremony?"

He shifted in his chair. "The cage ritual," he glanced uncomfortably at Sara. "An old custom. There are some people who want to revive it. Stop it from disappearing completely. According to tradition, Ntsaub, the water snake, lies in wait for young girls at his water hole, where he captures them and drags them down into the water, unless they've gone through a particular water ritual. It's usually performed as soon as they grow up—become young women. Ready to have children. You know what I mean . . . "

"Sh-i-i-t," she interrupted him, "the snake. It's the snake in the paintings, right?"

Dam inclined his head.

"Go on."

He explained the power the snake wielded over a young girl and how, with a beautiful headscarf or some beads, he could lure her to the spring where he lived. As soon as she reached out, he would grab hold of her and pull her into the dark depths, where she would remain forever as his bride.

Sara listened closely, her annoyance subsiding. "It's starting to make sense to me. Maybe the snake in her paintings means the old tribes of Africa—those who are starting to reclaim the land. Or no. It's about the old African belief: If you ignore the old customs, you're drawn down into the abyss. You lose your way."

At last. A spark, something making sense, Sara thought. For the first time she felt as if she was getting closer to Freddie, making contact again, penetrating her enigmatic mind.

"I don't think that will is worth the paper it's written on," Dam said. "She was just worried about Klara's future. And she wanted to make sure Outanna was well provided for. It's definitely not what Outanna or I wanted."

Sara sat down. She felt beyond exhausted. No, she felt betrayed.

"We had plenty of arguments about that so-called will. In the first place, your father's will wasn't finalised—you hadn't yet signed away your share. As for me, I wanted nothing to do with Freddie's . . . her rituals and stuff. And especially not with this sham of a will. Outanna neither. Especially not Outanna. She was worried people would find out—our own people *and* the whites. Outanna said a will like that could only bring trouble. And there'd already been trouble about Freddie's activities in the area. If anything happened to Freddie, people would automatically assume I was the one who murdered her."

"And *did* you?"

The words tumbled out before she could stop herself.

Dam stood up abruptly.

"I've got work to do." He strode out of the kitchen door, his back stiff.

52

The sun was like a blowtorch by the time Beeslaar returned from his walk. He noticed a small, dark figure loitering at his gate.

Beeslaar called out. A boy, who glanced up quickly and then dashed away—possibly Bulelani, the laundry thief?

When it became apparent that he was mentally handicapped, he'd been released from questioning. He could say his name, but communicated mostly through gestures. The boy eventually admitted that he recognised Freddie Swarts in a photo, but Beeslaar was certain he lacked the mental capacity to commit such a carefully staged crime.

When Beeslaar reached his front door, the landline was ringing insistently. He'd better answer.

It was Jansie Boois.

"Everyone's looking for you," she said reproachfully.

"They'll just have to talk to Lobatse."

He explained the situation.

"You can't just stay away, Inspector."

"It's not a question of just staying away. It's a kind of temporary suspension. Unofficial. Until the super decides differently."

"But what do I do with the people who don't want to speak to Inspector Lobatse?"

"Look, Lobatse's handling the Huilwater case now. *And* all my other work. They'll just have to talk to him."

"Ja, but . . . "

"Listen, don't you go messing with a tired old oom, Mrs. Boois. People who know me personally, they've got my cell number, right?"

She groaned softly, but left it at that and said goodbye.

Next he checked the cellphone, which was still on the kitchen table. There were messages, he saw, and he phoned his voicemail. "Inspector"—Ghaap in a whisper—"I think I've stumbled on one of the guys who burnt down the old auntie's house on Monday. I'm at Mma Mokoena's shebeen. But I don't have wheels. Can you call me back?"

Beeslaar looked at the time: six o'clock yesterday afternoon.

Ghaap again, louder this time. "The bliksem's gone and run away. I'm following on foot, but I need help, man. Phone when you get back!"

Next up was Dr Prinsloo from Postmasburg. "Hi, Inspector! You owe me—big time! I was in a good mood yesterday. Worked on your hairy cousin until nine. Had the help of a vet, nogal, an old buddy of mine. You owe him too. But anyway, this little sister of yours was tame, an old farmyard baboon. You could see from her teeth—covered in plaque like someone who eats too much white bread. Signs of a collar round the neck. And, listen to this, she was alive when she was slaughtered. But there are no defence wounds. So I reckon she was doped, fortunately for her—I can check that out, but it'll take a bit of time. And your butcher man is right-handed—the cut goes from left to right, same as with your two victims a month ago, those farm workers. But *definitely* different to the woman and child of last week, okay? That's it for now. Oh, ja, and I drink Cape wine, red, thanks. But my pal, he's a savage. Brandy for him!"

Then Ghaap, again. "Where are you, Beeslaar? I need someone, man!" Probably the message that came through late last night.

Beeslaar phoned Jansie Boois.

"Where's Ghaap, Jansie?"

"I thought you were lounging by the pool, Inspector."

"Jans, I'm serious. I think he's in trouble."

"Heavens, no, I haven't seen him yet this morning. Should I go ask?"

"Yes. But don't say I'm the one asking. And by the way— who says I'm not floating in the swimming pool, anyway? With a beautiful blonde next to me and a passionfruit cocktail in my hand. With a cherry and a little umbrella and all."

"Oh, you!" she laughed and hung up.

Beeslaar got up and went outside. Suddenly he couldn't sit still. If something had happened to Ghaap . . . And yes, De Kok was right-handed. Last month, the two workers were killed by a right-handed person. And the baboon now, too.

Fuckit, the baboon. TOKOLOSHE'S COMING, the message in blood.

He shut the kitchen door. Time to pay a visit to Jan Steenkamp. And maybe take another look at the Huilwater paintings.

Taking care not to run into Lobatse along the way.

53

Sara was relieved to hear Harry's car pull up outside Number 3 Driedoring Street just after sunset.

He'd been delayed for a couple of hours, interviewing farmers and policemen in a few Northern Cape dorps along the way, he explained. And Tannie Yvonne had offered him a place to stay. Glad of his company, she'd said.

"Leave your stuff, you can unpack later. I've already got my cozzie on, come cool off in the pool," she urged. He wasn't keen, but she led him across to Oom Koos's dam anyway, laughing as she jumped in. He sat on the cement wall, legs pulled up, sandalled feet firmly planted. City boy.

She swam up to the side, and rested her elbows on the dam wall, her legs dangling in the water. It was dark already, with only a sliver of moon surrounded by thousands of stars.

"The water's lovely, Harry. Get in. Nothing will bite you, I promise."

"Ja, right, till a water scorpion gets hold of me."

Sara smiled and pressed her chin against the cement. It smelt of dust and algae, still warm from the heat of the day. Funny, she thought, how reluctant the heat is to leave. How long did one's body stay warm, before it turned cold forever? Was Freddie still warm when they found her? She shuddered and pushed away from the wall into the cool green of the water.

On the opposite side, she got out and sat on the wall with her feet in the water. "A water scorpion, Harry, is a harmless water bug."

"Still," he said, "I prefer not to swim with bugs. Especially when I can't see them."

They walked back to the house together. Halfway across Tannie Yvonne's lawn, a figure walked over to meet them: Nelmari Viljoen. Sara introduced her to Harry.

"I can't stay long, Sara," Nelmari warned. "I have to go see someone urgently."

"Just stay for five minutes. I've been trying to get hold of you for ages."

Nelmari hesitated, then agreed. She looked tense, thought Sara. Her eyes shone, something anxious in her gaze.

Sara excused herself, put on some dry clothes, then fetched a bottle of chilled wine and took it out to the stoep.

"I'm glad you're here," she said to Nelmari once she'd poured everyone a glass. "I wanted to tell you in person about Saturday's funeral. We've organised it for ten o'clock, the Dutch Reformed Church. Just a short, simple service. Outanna's is afterwards, at her church in Chicken Vale. Afterwards we'll be holding a private ceremony on the farm. At the place where my mom and dad are buried, and my grandparents too. Just us. I thought anyone who wanted to could say a few words, something like that."

Nelmari opened her handbag and took out her cigarettes. With her white sandals, white trousers, and slim-fitting white halterneck top, the pale-blue leather was the only touch of colour. She looked cool and elegant. But her hands shook as she lit the cigarette.

"I feel guilty, Sara," she said. "I promised you I'd help, but I've ended up being no help at all. I thought I'd be able to take some of this off your shoulders, to support you. But it's as if everything's suddenly going wrong at once, the business too . . . "

She gave Harry a wide-eyed gaze, as if appealing for rescue.

Sara waved her apology away. "The most important thing is

for you to be there with us on Saturday. And maybe say something? At the graveside."

Smoke drifted from her nostrils as she murmured assent. For a while, no one said anything. Then Nelmari stubbed out the cigarette and looked at her watch. "I have to get going now."

Sara sat up. "Oh, but you haven't even had a sip of your wine. And I still have to ask you something."

"I've got a better idea. Come have supper at my place tomorrow," Nelmari said, though without much enthusiasm. "Hopefully by then a lot of this work nonsense will be sorted. Then we can talk properly." She rose from her seat.

"Before you go—did you know Freddie had left the farm to Dam? In her will?" Sara tried to keep her voice light.

"Where in God's name did you hear that?" She sat down again, slowly. "Did you see a lawyer?"

"No, I found a copy of the will."

"I doubt it's valid," Harry interjected.

"As far as I know, your father's estate hadn't even been finalised, Sara."

"Still," said Sara, "it's clear what Freddie's last wishes were. And there's something else. Freddie made a painting that looks just like her murder. Do you know anything about that?"

"Has Beeslaar seen it?" Nelmari asked.

"I showed it to him, yes."

"And?"

Sara searched for words. "Nothing, really," she said at last. "But Outanna said things were very wrong just before Freddie died. Apparently you and Freddie were arguing quite a bit."

"Outanna had too much time on her hands, so she filled her days with gossip. And you believe her!"

A cellphone started ringing in Nelmari's bag. She snapped open the clasp and took out the phone.

"Hello," she said, rising irritation on her face as she listened.

Then she exploded, "That'll be the day! You don't have a leg to stand on." She listened again. Then, even louder, "No, certainly not! What is going *on* with you?"

Sara gave Harry a surreptitious glance as he drained his glass.

"No!" said Nelmari. "Wait right there!" Then, very deliberately, she pressed the end-call button.

"I'm sorry, guys," she said, making a visible effort to pull herself together. Then she made a weak attempt at a smile. "So, you see what it's like. This business is definitely not for sissies. The whole day, problems have kept coming at me. If it isn't the banks, it's lousy builders trying to—oh, it's a nightmare! Well then," she said, standing up, "I guess we'll see each other tomorrow evening. Thanks for the wine."

She quickly got up, clutched her handbag to her chest, and gave a little wave. "Don't worry, I'll let myself out," she called and left.

It was already nine when Beeslaar parked the car in front of his house, too lazy to struggle with the rickety garage doors. All he wanted was to get into bed.

The day at Jan Steenkamp's had been pleasant, but long. They'd talked about this and that, and eventually the conversation turned to the Huilwater murders. Beeslaar had asked him about Tjoek Visser and his weird bunch of followers, about people like Buks Hanekom, the possibility of right-wing violence, revolt.

"Look, as you know, I don't exactly see eye to eye with that lot. But one thing you and I know for sure: people are scared. There are disturbing things about farming these days. Government's sat on its arse for years, promising black people land. But nothing's happening. It's a bloody mess, I tell you. And that's exactly where guys like Hanekom might have a point. If you look at Zimbabwe, Mugabe eventually took a shortcut—a nasty one. And look where those farmers are today—people starving in a country that once exported food."

Then he thought for a while, and said, "Now, Freddie Swarts, she started picking at an old scab. That Griqua land-claim issue—she told me she'd been threatened at the time. And I had my suspicions about who might be behind that. But nothing came of it, as you know. "

"And were the threats finally carried out? What about those right-wing fanatics?"

Jan Steenkamp pondered the question. "I can't see that

happening, really. But you never know. My advice to you is, get hold of the thieving bastards, and you'll have your murderers. It's a big responsibility, Beeslaar. You have to show people that the legal system works. That it's worth their while—for people like Hanekom and co—to stay within the law."

Beeslaar roused himself, got out of his car, noticed that the front gate was standing open. Mildly curious, he walked up the steps to his stoep.

"Evening, Inspector," a low voice rose hoarsely from the dark.

Ghaap.

"What the hell are you doing here at this time of night?"

"Waiting for you."

Beeslaar couldn't see him. The light from the street lamp fell just short of the stoep and the curved roof cast a shadow. He unlocked the front door and turned on a light.

Ghaap was sitting with his skinny limbs curled up in one of the cane chairs. One eye was swollen shut, his lip was split, and there were dark stains on his shirt.

"You'd better come in." Beeslaar walked to the kitchen, took a couple of glasses from the cupboard and poured two stiff shots of brandy.

"Drink up," he ordered.

Ghaap grimaced as the brandy stung his lip. He tipped the liquor down his throat and held the glass out for more. Beeslaar topped it up, and studied the young man over the rim of his glass. He hoped to God that Ghaap wouldn't be his usual tongue-tied self. He simply didn't have the energy for it.

"So, who messed you up like this?" he asked eventually.

Ghaap looked blank.

"You were in the shebeen, right? God knows, you smell like one."

Ghaap tried to smile, winced instead. Suddenly, as if a tap had been opened, the words poured out.

"Sjoe, man, it was a bunch of tsotsis. Ran into them in Mma Mokoena's shebeen. You can say we joined the church of brandy together. Yesterday afternoon—while you buggered off to Upington. I phoned you, you know." His good eye fixed Beeslaar with an accusing stare. "They were already plenty drunk by the time I got there. Mma Mokoena wanted to throw them out, but the little one, he was throwing money around. Bought everyone drinks. I could see it was lightning money."

"What?"

"You know, just out of nowhere. One day he's walking around in rags, then all of a sudden he's sharp-sharp. New sunglasses. New tackies."

"What about him?"

"No, well, he was smoking zols, drinking like a fish. Talking kak to the other gents."

"Did you speak to him?"

"I made myself scarce. Mma said she didn't know where he got the money from. But he was boozing her right out of her own shebeen. The whole week already. That's when I went to call you." He gulped down the rest of his drink and pulled a face. "Don't you have any beer? This blerrie stuff's burning holes in me."

Beeslaar grunted, gave a grudging smile. "You're already full of holes, man." He got up and fetched a beer from the fridge.

"So when did that happen?" He pointed at Ghaap's face.

"Well, I went outside to go make that call—to *you*. And when I got back, the whole lot of them were gone. I went down the road, looking for them. Fokkol. So I just went back and drank some more. Dunno how long I was in there— maybe another two beers or so. Then this old guy I know popped in. He's in my ma's church. Never has any money, but a world champion boozer. I bought him a beer. We talked shit for a while—till my money was gone. Fokkof time. Then those skollies came back. Out of their minds, completely motherless. And then the little one shoved me. Said it was no place for pigs."

"And then you hit him!"

"No ways, man! Told him to get lost, nè, or I'd lock him up. Black bugger said it was *his* place. I belonged with the hotnots."

"And that's when you—"

"No, man, wait. He said the hotnot and his boer-baas—that's me and you, by the way—we're not going to lay a finger on *him*. We're too fucking stupid. We'd still be sitting there when *we'd* get torched as well!"

"Little shit. By him and who else?"

"His connections."

"What a joker!"

Ghaap chortled with stiff lips. "Little bugger was so full of his zol, and so full of himself, he just couldn't stop. He only had to say the word, he says, and it would be tickets with me. Him and his buddies took no shit from the boere. The only pigs they leave alone are the pigs on their payroll. Just like that!"

Ghaap described how he'd gone outside and waited for him and his mates. But they had jumped him together, knocked the shit out of him and locked him up in an abandoned shack. Where he'd spent the whole goddamn day until someone freed him after dark earlier this evening.

"And how did you get here?"

"Shoes came to fetch me." He gave Beeslaar a sideways glance. "He told me about Lobatse."

Beeslaar got up and filled his glass with tap water. He knocked it back and wiped his mouth. "Okay, so why are you here?" he asked, his back to Ghaap.

"I lay thinking all day long in that shack. Pyl isn't a bad guy. But the thing is, they say you've got issues. That you assaulted

a black inspector in Johannesburg. And that you almost got fired. Lost your rank. Only reason you weren't sent packing they say, is because of your experience. And that's why you're here."

"Who said this!"

"Everyone's been talking about it."

"Jesus Christ!" Beeslaar put the glass down in the sink. He turned around, picked up his car keys and put them down in front of Ghaap. "Take my car and go home, Ghaap. I need to go to bed now."

Ghaap didn't move.

"Take the fucking keys. Here. You can bring the car back later." He pushed the keys into Ghaap's hand. "And call Lobatse. Tell him about your tsotsi. He must start looking for him now."

Then he walked to the front door, opened it and stepped out onto the stoep, where he waited for Ghaap. Until he heard a kitchen chair scrape across the floor, and footsteps down the passage.

In the doorway, Ghaap said, "I actually came here to tell you . . . "

"Go home. Now."

55

Sara and Harry headed out to the farm early the next morning. She needed more clarity on the will, wanted to search through the papers. The police had already gone through everything, but had said nothing about a will. Freddie's lawyer, Oom Sybrand might have more information, but he'd only be back in South Africa next Friday, she'd been told.

They talked as Harry drove, Sara telling him about her childhood, the real reasons she'd never told him much about Freddie. He was a good listener, it felt easy to talk to him, even about this. He spoke a little about his family too.

But the moment they entered the house, Harry fell silent. She showed him around, trying to keep her voice even. But even so, she could see he was shaken.

They started searching in silence. First Freddie's drawers, her cupboards, and flipping through the contents of the bookcase. Harry was almost himself again when they stopped at the computer. He bent down to check the power plug when it wouldn't start. As he flicked the wall switch, she couldn't help thinking how healthy and *normal* he looked. It was good that he was here. His voice amiable and lively, like a crackling fire in a wet Cape winter. It warmed and animated the dark silences of this house. Chasing out the ghosts, the shadows of fear and sorrow and death.

"How are you feeling this morning, Sara?" he asked as if he could read her mind.

"Better than yesterday, thanks. But at times it still feels as if I've walked into a nightmare."

"Ja," he said, "it's a horrible thing that happened here. But you know, the house is very different, really, to what I'd imagined. I somehow thought that if a successful artist had been living here—"

"You expected it to be more modern? More arty-farty? Luxurious?"

He shrugged.

"We aren't materialistic—us Swartses. The house is exactly the same as when my oupa and ouma lived here. My parents weren't rich. And Huilwater's value lies in the water, its natural springs. For the rest, it's pretty small-scale."

"That's exactly what makes it such a terrible crime. There's nothing here to steal. It's so senseless."

"You can say that again. That's why it feels so nightmarish."

"I can imagine. The guilt, anger, fear, sadness—huge emotions, all at once inside you. And your mind trying to tell you it hasn't happened, delaying the pain."

"You sound like a damned shrink, Harry."

He laughed softly. "I did plenty of homework, you know. For my article. About trauma and stuff."

She sat at the computer, with Harry watching the screen over her shoulder.

"I'm not in the mood for this. I'm sick of it. Gatvol."

"That's how it is, hey. You're going to feel this way for quite a while still. That's PTSD for you."

She turned around and glared. "Don't lecture me! I don't have—"

"Post-traumatic stress disorder? Really? You don't feel you're in a trance, your emotions aren't playing havoc with you?"

Sara gave a skewed smile. "Okay, well, maybe. I've definitely been pissing people off more than usual."

Harry put a hand on her shoulder. "But seriously, there are support groups these days—specially for farm-attack victims. Don't underestimate what happened—" he broke off as a vehicle sped into the farmyard, braking hard outside the door.

56

Beeslaar stepped into the shower and saw it: the enormous red roman, squatting in the corner. He took a big step backwards and firmly shut the shower door.

Fifteen minutes later he was standing in front of a shelf at the co-op. He filled his basket with tins of Doom and other insecticides. The assistant who rang it all up raised an eyebrow and asked what he needed so much poison for. Beeslaar told him about his battle with the spiders. Minutes later, he was walking out of the co-op, bag of insecticides in one hand, and an order for screen doors in his shirt pocket.

He fumbled as his cellphone rang. "Sergeant Ghaap! I hope you're calling to say you've put those thugs behind bars?"

"Where are you?"

"On my way home. To my vegetable patch."

"But Inspector, the only sign of a garden I saw at your place was the patch of empty beer cans you're growing in your backyard. But that's not what I'm calling about. I want to know if I can come round some time."

"Why? Did you forget something at my place last night?"

"I actually want to discuss something with you."

"You're aware of the fact that you're not allowed to discuss anything work-related with me. Does Lobatse know?"

"Well, it's him I want to talk about."

"No, Sergeant. I'm not going to discuss Inspector Lobatse with you. In fact, I don't even want to be having this conversation with you. Okay? You keep yourself occupied with the guys who klapped you around, but leave me alone for now. I have better things—"

"But Lobatse doesn't want to *know* anything about it. He's fucking around in the wrong place. Right now, he's on his way to go arrest the Huilwater workers for murder!"

57

Dam de Kok came running in through the back door, nearly knocking Harry off his feet. Both men stopped dead in their tracks.

"You okay?" he asked as Sara emerged from behind Harry.

"Dam, this is my friend Harry, from Cape Town," she said.

Dam wiped his hands on his shorts. "Sorry about the over-enthusiastic reception. But when I turned in here, I saw this strange car . . . "

"Is it Kok or De Kok? And are you related to the Koks of this region?" Harry said, smiling at the man before him.

"I'm related to the old chief—on my grandmother's side. She was a great-great-granddaughter of the original Kok, Adam Kok." No trace of boasting in his voice, just a matter-of-fact statement.

"Ah, so you have your grandmother's noble surname!"

Dam shot Sara a look before he spoke. She wondered whether he was still angry about what she'd said the previous day. But his expression gave nothing away.

"It's not exactly noble," he answered. "But my grand-mother's people, they decided to name me after their forefa-ther. Maybe they expected things of me. They called him Dam too, the old chief. For some reason, I ended up not being reg-istered Kok, but De Kok."

"Mmm, interesting. And why's that?" The nosy journalist in Harry had been tickled, Sara saw.

"Oh, you know. I suppose it was my parents. They were just

ordinary people, struggling to put food on the table, without much interest in history. In fact, just probably wanted to get away from the Griqua connection. Plenty of Griquas did in those days. To be an ordinary coloured, well that was a step up from being some semi-Bushman-Griqua," he said wryly.

"Jeez, Saartjie, you didn't tell me you were mingling with royalty."

"I didn't know any of this, Dam. You really are a closed book, hey? So, does that also make you a chief or something?"

"No. Just an ordinary Kalahari Bushman. Well, half Griqua, half Bushman—probably depends who you speak to. My grandmother was a Kok, and my grandfather, N!xi"—his tongue clicked as he said the word—"was a Bushman through and through."

"San, I guess you mean," said Harry, but he didn't wait for an answer. "Tell me, though, did you really not inherit a title or anything?"

"Oh, no. There are plenty of Koks around here. And even more Adams. I can trace my own line right back to the original Adam Kok who moved up from Cape Town. But so can many others."

"What do you mean? I thought you've always been here."

"No. My people only arrived here in the early eighteen hundreds."

"But arrived from where? I don't suppose you *also* turned up in three little ships?"

Dam's laugh was a single, sharp bark. "No. Not even in donkey carts. I suppose it was some kind of march—all the way from Cape Town. But my great-great-great-grandfather didn't stay here very long either. He got into a fight with the missionaries and left for Kokstad with a few of his followers. One of his sons stayed behind—he was my great-great-grandfather. Or something like that."

Sara watched Harry and Dam chatting as if they had known

each other for years. Typical Harry, she thought, he could put anyone at ease and get them talking. She realised if she wanted to apologise to Dam for yesterday, now was her chance.

But he waved her apology aside.

"It's nothing. And you were right. I was carrying on like a stupid donkey." He clicked his tongue in annoyance. "And that stupid will of Freddie's. It stirred up trouble right from the start. And the very thing we feared is happening right now: I'm suspect number one."

"Because of the will?" Harry asked, but Sara didn't give Dam a chance to answer.

She had another question—now that Dam seemed amenable. "Why was Freddie so obsessed by the land issue?"

"I think it started with your father's funeral. Freddie was fascinated by the idea that so many different bones were buried in the soil. Her . . . your parents. And *their* parents. The Bushmen who'd roamed the region before everyone else arrived. The Griquas. I think she wanted to uncover the whole history of the land, and—"

"Were you already here, then?" Harry interrupted him.

"No, she told me about it all later. She'd looked into it, and discovered that a section of Huilwater was once the property of a Griqua chief. His land consisted of parts of Huilwater and a bunch of other farms in the area. She said . . . Hell, I can't remember everything she said. But she was really excited."

"Bloody hell, Dam. So, back *then* she'd already been planning to . . . " Sara swallowed the words.

"Give it away? Yes, she wanted to. You must remember that back then she was looking at ways to get rid of the farm. It was shortly after your father died. And she was also worrying—just like you—about what would become of the land. And it wouldn't actually be giving it away. Farmers usually get compensation."

Harry leaned forward in his chair. "And *was* there a claim?" he asked.

"Yes and no. Actually, I don't know much about the whole business. But I think she helped the Griquas to get their application to the Land Claims Commission—Nelmari Viljoen also had something to do with that. But then it turned out the Griquas couldn't claim the land back—they didn't qualify. Only people whose land had been taken away by the 1913 Land Act qualified for claims."

Harry whistled softly. "I can only imagine how delighted your neighbours must have been with Freddie."

"Well, yes. There were threats. But that wasn't the end of the story. Freddie wouldn't let it go. She said it was a tragedy— that the Griquas had virtually no land left. She wanted me to help. To go to Cape Town, to speak on behalf of the Griquas, but I told them to leave me out of it. I just wanted to do my own thing. Farm. But then, a few weeks ago, Freddie got all excited again. They found new evidence to support a land claim. And then . . . " He looked up at Sara. "Then nothing, really. One day everything was just over. Freddie didn't say anything, but Outanna said something, that they'd argued, had words."

Sara sat on her hands, anxiously listening.

"Nelmari stopped coming to the farm. And Freddie started painting, painting, as if she wanted to paint the whole mess away. I saw very little of her. I was busy too. I started looking at a farm that was for sale—still is. But it's far, deeper into the Kalahari. I drove there a few times to take a look, so I was away a lot."

"And the will?"

"We disagreed about it. I was stubborn. I'd buy myself a farm if I wanted one, I said. She was . . . hurt, I think."

"What do you think really happened here, Dam?" Harry asked. "Sara showed me the mantis painting."

"Well. She was busy with it when the big fight with Nelmari started."

"Did they argue often?" Harry wanted to know.

"Ag, Nelmari has a strong personality. She likes everything to be done her way. She thrives on managing and controlling people. I sometimes gave her a hard time myself—Freddie, I mean. Especially when she wanted to put me in a painting."

"The one with the snake and the naked white women," Sara said.

He smiled crookedly. "Frêtjie," he said after a long while, as if he were speaking to himself.

"Come again?"

"The little one, Klara—she called her Frêtjie."

"Frêtjie," Sara echoed. "That's so pretty. It sounds like a dry little tuft of grass rustling in the wind."

They heard a vehicle stop outside.

It was the police. They had come to fetch Dam.

H is cellphone chirped, and Beeslaar put the spade aside.

"What the hell do you think you're doing, Inspector?" The Moegel.

"Who told you you could just go AWOL?"

"I'm not AWOL, Superintendent. I've been temporarily relieved of my duties, remember?"

"Relieved my arse, man. Nobody said you could just go sit at home! I expressly ordered you to assist Inspector Lobatse."

Beeslaar said nothing. The Moegel wanted something, but couldn't ask directly. He had to cover it up with noise and bluster.

"If you aren't back at the station in ten minutes, you'll find a formal complaint waiting for you."

"Superintendent, with respect, if I understand the SAPS disciplinary code correctly, being relieved of duty means you are suspended until found guilty or not g—"

"Man, don't fuck around with me. I have enough problems to deal with as it is. Report for duty, or come to Upington to pick up a final written warning. I'm giving you ten minutes."

"I'm not working under Lobatse, Inspector. This is my case, my turf."

"You'll work under a donnerse Christmas turkey if I say so, man! Get to the office and then we'll talk again."

"But what about Monday?"

"*What* about Monday? Forget about Monday. Right now

there are more urgent matters. Ten minutes!" he roared into Beeslaar's ear before cutting the line.

Beeslaar put the phone into his pocket and looked at the patch of ground he had dug over. It had been rock hard to start with and the sun had burnt the hell out of him, but the exercise had done him good. He had planted carrot seeds, tomatoes and onions. Now just to water the lot, then take a shower.

He had been waiting for the super's call for some time.

In his absence, Jansie'd told him, things had gone completely haywire. Nelmari Viljoen had disappeared—last night, apparently—and today she'd been picked up in the veld close to the rubbish dump, bruises on her throat, left for dead. Rescued several hours after Lobatse had been informed about the assault, and hours before he discovered how well-connected Ms Viljoen was. And then he made the mistake of hitting one of the Huilwater workers in custody, with the result that the newspapers were now breathing down the Moegel's neck.

In the meantime Beeslaar himself had had a pretty fruitful morning. Willie from the co-op had already been to take the measurements for the new screen doors—and he'd also, thank God and all the holy angels, removed the red romans from the bathroom and lounge.

He'd had plenty to say about the vile creatures. "The thing with them, 'spector, is that they're always on the lookout for shade. So when they come across you outside, they're chasing your shadow, not you. Yes, they can bite, damn sure, but they're not poisonous. But they're fast. Faster than an oogpister. And oogpisters can run helluva fast too. Nearly twenty kilo—"

Beeslaar cut his yacking short. Asked him politely to forget the lecture, focus on the doors. And once the handyman was done, Beeslaar himself got to work with the spade.

It was almost lunchtime when Ghaap called again. "I'm not going to talk to you, Sergeant," Beeslaar told him.

But a minute later there was a knock on the door.

Ghaap.

Beeslaar relented and invited him in.

"You didn't give me the chance to finish last night," Ghaap said as they settled in the shade on the back steps. "I actually wanted to come talk to you about the Upington thing."

"That, my friend, is *my* problem. Instead, why don't you tell me if you've managed to track down your suspect."

"The complaint against you is *my* problem *too*. I'd like to be a witness on your behalf. I phoned the Moegel this morning. And I told him."

Beeslaar snorted in disbelief, but Ghaap carried on.

"Here's how I see things: I get why Ballies has got a problem with you—but not enough that I'd make a complaint. And definitely not one of racism. But Ballies, he hates criticism. Can't take it, too larney to learn. And his head's grown too big for his arse. "

"So, what exactly are you trying to say, Ghaap?"

"That you're walking around like a lion with a sore paw. And it's humiliating for us to be shouted at in front of the civvies."

"Where did I—"

"The other day. You crapped on us in front of De Kok. Swore, too. And in front of Miss Swarts as well!"

"Me?"

Ghaap gave him a look. One eyelid, Beeslaar noticed, was still thick and swollen. For a quiet guy he's suddenly very talkative, he thought. Maybe the beating loosened his tongue as well. Beeslaar kept a straight face.

"I know you're old-school. You guys were all raised that way. And that's what I kept thinking about the whole time I lay in that car boot. It was my own fault I was lying there. You wouldn't have let them catch you like that. And then I thought of all Pyl's bragging each time the Moegel phoned him. Pyl isn't a bad oke. And I think he's already realised where brown-nosing gets you: Lobatse—but that's another story.

"What I actually want to say, is I really want to do this job. Nothing else. But if it means licking the Moegel's arse, then I'd rather pack my bags. So that's why I'm going to be your witness." He took a deep breath. "You *can* get colleagues to testify for you. I looked it up—in the SAPS Code of Conduct."

It was quiet in the charge office when Beeslaar arrived. Shoes Morotse was behind the service counter, helping a woman with a baby on her back to fill out a form. Beeslaar asked what had happened to Bulelani, the laundry thief.

"Probably back on the rubbish dumps," the constable quipped.

Beeslaar walked on. The boy would be back here soon, he knew, it was just a matter of time. In handcuffs or in a body bag.

He stepped into his office, where Inspector Malegapuru Lobatse was at Beeslaar's desk, busy tidying up.

"You're back," he said.

Beeslaar's eyes flicked from Lobatse to the mess of papers and dossiers on his desk.

"I, er, there was no other space for me. So I used your desk." He began to collect his things.

Like hell, thought Beeslaar—what about Pyl's office, Ghaap's. But all he said was, "Have you phoned the super?"

Lobatse nodded, then leaned over to pick up his briefcase.

"And did he inform you about the new situation?" When the other man didn't answer, Beeslaar continued calmly, "You can of course stay on if you like. An extra pair of hands is always welcome."

Lobatse didn't look up. He packed some stuff into the

briefcase. In silence. Beeslaar sniffed. He hadn't dreamt it would go *this* smoothly.

"I see you've been busy," he said. Lobatse was putting statements, pictures and reports back into dossiers and closing them one by one. He was a young man, early thirties. A pencil pusher, Beeslaar had heard. Not exactly adventurous or keen to leave the safety of his office.

The past two days must have been hell for him. Pushed him over the edge. Not only had he charged three people without reading them their rights, but he'd broken someone's nose in the process.

Under normal circumstances it might have been dealt with more quietly. But unfortunately for Lobatse this was a high-profile case, and it wasn't long before a Joburg newspaper got stuck into the Moegel.

And that wasn't the first uncomfortable call Lobatse had had to field that day.

Nelmari Viljoen's lawyers had been on his case too, alleging he'd ignored the first reports of a body in the veld, made by a homeless man. Lobatse had simply shrugged the report off—just the ramblings of "a drunken old coloured," he'd said.

"I know you won't agree, Inspector Beeslaar," Lobatse said, clipping his briefcase shut, "but I believe we did make some headway in the short while you were absent." Seeing Beeslaar's expression, he quickly continued, "If I were you, I'd look very closely at relationships among the Huilwater workers." He picked up the file. "I see you've built up a thorough file, but there's no mention of the murdered employer's will."

Beeslaar set his car keys down on the desk, but before he could reply, Lobatse continued, "Apparently she made a new will shortly before she died—with the manager and her housekeeper the main beneficiaries. Interesting, don't you think?" Lobatse looked around the office, saw his suit jacket still draped over a chair and picked it up.

"Okay, then. Got to go. The superintendent needs me in Upington." He paused in the doorway and looked back at Beeslaar. "Goodbye, Inspector," he said and disappeared down the passage.

Beeslaar walked around his desk and sat down. When he looked up, Sergeant Pyl was in the doorway.

Wordlessly, Beeslaar beckoned for him to enter.

S he's in a private room and she isn't taking any calls," said Harry and turned off his cellphone. Nelmari had been admitted to the Mediclinic in Upington.

It was late afternoon, and at last Yvonne Lambrechts's stoep had started to cool down.

"It could be really serious," said Sara. "Maybe her secretary can tell us more." She searched for the number on her phone and called. "I wonder if Nelmari has any family," she said, waiting for someone to pick up. An answerphone kicked in and Sara left a message.

"Now what?" She looked at Harry, who had just drunk the last of his peach juice.

"I want to go to the information bureau. It's not quite five yet, they might still be open. Want to come along?" he asked.

Sara looked across the sun-scorched lawn. "It's coming closer," she said, "the evil."

Harry looked at her from under his brows.

"I mean, whatever it is—first Freddie and Klara. Then Outanna. And now Nelmari."

He swung his legs off the stoep wall and put down his glass. "I'm not sure all these incidents are connected, Sara." His voice was gentle, as if he were trying to soothe a frightened animal.

"Listen, I know it sounds irrational. But Sunday night, the last time I saw Outanna, she spoke about an approaching evil. And the next day she was dead."

"Even so, Sara. People like Nelmari often make enemies. Seems to me she's got that sort of personality. And it's the nature of her work. She said as much herself. I don't see how it connects with your sister's death. People are getting killed for cellphones. Could well be that she surprised an intruder after we saw her last night."

"Someone phoned her before she left, remember? She seemed so furious, really upset."

He looked sceptical.

"*And* she was found in the veld this morning. That's not the work of an ordinary robber. The same is true of Freddie and Klara. There were three dogs, and Babetjie and Betta were at home, a hundred metres from the farmhouse, and heard nothing. And Outanna, murdered in her own house in broad daylight. And then the baboon over at Dam's. And now Nelmari. *And* there's that oaf of a policeman who came to arrest Dam and then assaulted Lammer. It's like something out of a horror movie. Makes you feel so helpless, no one to turn to. Where's the justice if the police behave like crooks?"

He got up, pulled her up from her chair and held her close.

"It's this country, Harry," she said into the folds of his shirt. "We've all been abandoned. There's nobody who can help . . . "

She felt his stubble on her hair, then his lips against her forehead.

"Once the funeral is over, you're coming with me for a few days," he said, holding her tighter.

She pulled away and looked up at him. "It isn't safe anywhere. Don't you realise? Not here, not in Cape Town. Nowhere. Sometimes I almost think those right-wing farmers have a point, people like that Buks Hanekom guy."

"Who?"

She sat down again, legs tucked up and her chin resting on her knees. "He's a local farmer. Looks like one of the Village

People—big moustache, khaki outfit. Struts around with a pistol on his hip, threatening armed resistance, stuff like that."

"Really? Does he have an organisation or something?"

"Oh, I don't know. I heard him carrying on at a farmers' meeting on Monday. You know, the old story: farm murders are a form of undercover land reform, a covert dirty-tricks campaign of the government's, à la Mugabe."

"That's idiocy," he said and sat down on the wall again. "That's just fear talking. Seems to me people react in one of two ways: Come, let's shoot the buggers, or Let's flee into the arms of the Lord."

"As if that would make farm murders any less cruel," Sara said sceptically.

"Ja. The farmers have a raw deal, really. Always been a career with political baggage—in this country, at least. Carries the name of all the old evildoers of apartheid. No wonder the number one hit at a political rally is still 'Kill the Boer, Kill the Farmer.'"

The landline rang, and Iris's voice floated in. A moment later she emerged, saying, "Miss Nelmari, Sarretjie. On the phone."

Sara got up, but Iris stopped her. "No, she's gone, she just wanted me to tell Sarretjie she's all right and you mustn't wait for her to start the funeral."

"Is that all?"

"That's all, Sarretjie. I asked. She didn't want to talk."

"Thanks, Iris." Sara exhaled hard. "Oh, well, at least she's okay." Then she got up and said, "Come, let's get out of here. I'll drive myself crazy, sitting here talking in circles like this."

In front of the café they came across Sanna. She was on her way back from the undertakers.

"They did her up nice," said Sanna. "In a dress she made herself a long time ago already. If people could just see her. But the people . . . Hai, Sarretjie."

"What is it with the people?"

"There's going to be no one, tomorrow. All the stories running round now. After the fire. That she . . . "

Sara and Harry looked at each other.

"The pastor, he's talking to them. He's talking *very* nice. Outanna wasn't a witch, no, he says. But their heads, they're all twisted. I think it's because of the old water-striking custom."

"What's that?"

Sanna pursed her lips, a despairing look on her face. "It's a thing from the old people, the women who did the water striking. Our mother was one of them. In our young days, the young girls all still got the cage. Me, I was in the cage too. Outanna. All of us. That custom was part of it."

She screwed her eyes up against the sun and said, "And these are things today's people don't know any more, the old ways."

Sara was reminded of the story of the water snake—Ntsaub—that Dam had told her.

"When a girl grows up now, see. And she's getting ready to bear children," Sanna gave Harry a quick glance, "she's put there, on her own. We call it 'she goes into the cage.' Then one day the water woman comes. She slaughters a goat. And she mixes together blood and stuff from the goat's stomach. Now the girl, they bathe her and they rub the mixture onto her skin, and then they take her to the water. The water where Ntsaub has his little house. The old woman, she strikes the water. For Ntsaub to hear. She sprinkles buchu on the water. If the buchu sinks, the snake is happy. Then the girl is safe. He won't pull her down with him into the water. But if the buchu doesn't sink, then that girl, she's never safe by the water. He'll grab her. You watch, he'll come. Sometime, someday, he'll come."

"And Outanna was one of those water women?"

"Yes. Our ma was, and Ouma too. Now the people are

saying Outanna's death was the Bantus, they've come to burn all the diviners and witches."

"Oh, but that's nonsense, Sanna. They're skollies. I'm sure they tried to rob Outanna. And when they saw there was nothing to steal, they burnt the house down. It's shocking that people now believe all this witch nonsense."

"I know, Sarretjie, I know. But the people, they're just stupid, stupid. And now, now everyone's running around with this story of a ghost."

"A ghost?" said Harry.

"Meneer, it's the children that started it. They said they saw . . . " Sanna glanced at Sara. "You mustn't get cross now, Sarretjie. But the people are saying it's Frêtjie in her blue dress."

"Freddie!" She wanted to laugh. "Oh, now that's really nonsense. And if Freddie really wanted to go haunting, it probably wouldn't be in Chicken Vale!"

"Ja, there. You said it, Sarretjie, you said it. I think it's one of those people who live on the rubbish dump. There by the place where they burn things. They turn white, those people, from living in the ash."

60

I've withdrawn the charges, Inspector," Sergeant Pyl stated, with as much dignity as he could muster.

Beeslaar sat looking at him, arms crossed. He felt like making the little bugger sweat. But then he relented. "Come take a seat, Ballies."

Pyl approached warily, as if forced to kiss a mamba.

"The two of us, my friend, we don't know each other too well," Beeslaar began as Pyl sat down. "But there's one thing about me you'll soon realise. My work always, *always* comes first. And I don't have patience with whining old women. If you work with me, you give it your all. We're a small team, but we're good at what we do. The best. We don't need the Upington guys sticking their noses in our business. Okay?"

Pyl nodded sheepishly.

Strike while the iron's hot, Beeslaar decided, and pressed his message home. "And you know what, this isn't about us." He pointed at himself and then at Pyl. "It's about other people. Those people you and I declared ourselves willing to protect. *Especially* those people who can't speak for themselves any more. Like that little girl at Huilwater who got her throat slit last week. *That's* what this job is about. You with me?"

Pyl looked down at his hands, gave a nod.

"I can't sleep at night when a little girl gets murdered and her killers are running free. Because *we've* failed her, people like you and me. It's ordinary guys like us who stand between that little girl and the criminals of this country. Just us. We can't afford this other crap. You and Ghaap are still green, but in time you'll see—*this* is what the job's about. Just this. I'll teach you everything I know. But then we work together as a team. And if something's bothering you, come and sort it out with *us*. You don't go running to the outside guys, okay? Thus endeth the lesson."

Pyl looked up, his old smile breaking through.

"So let's carry on," said Beeslaar. "In half an hour you and Ghaap get in here and we throw everything we have on the table and divide up the work. In the meantime, you can give me an update on everything I've missed. I hear things have been crazy here."

Beeslaar immediately regretted his question, as Pyl leapt upon the opportunity with alacrity. Lobatse, he explained, had arrived with orders to make an arrest within twenty-four hours. He took one look at the murder file and concluded that the three Huilwater employees—Dawid Tieties, Lammer van der Merwe and Dam De Kok—had the weakest alibis. And proceeded to pounce on them. "We're going for just one thing," he'd said, "and that's a full, voluntary confession." His motivation: the three men's fingerprints in the victim's bedroom and studio.

"But didn't you tell him we'd already moved long past that?"

"I did, Inspector, I did! But he said we're working this case from scratch again. The fact remains, he said, it was a coloured labourer in a white woman's bedroom. On top of that, neither Lammer nor Dawid had a solid alibi. And De Kok, well, De Kok is the—"

"But our statements are all in the file! And you were there, on the afternoon of the murder, when we went to fetch the two men working on fences in the veld."

"I did tell him, Inspector. All of it. But he said they could easily have walked home, killed the white woman, and then gone back again to wait for us. That's what he said, and that's what he wanted to hear from those two men."

"No, man," said Beeslaar, "you knew that's bullshit."

Pyl persisted. "I'm telling you, he said he wanted a signed confession from all three of them. Sommer there and then. The men begged, they said he must go ask De Kok, they couldn't have left their fencing, because by the time they were fetched they'd used up a whole new roll of wire. But then Inspector Lobatse told them it was De Kok who'd squealed, so they must sommer confess straight away. And that's when they started going on about the fighting and stuff on the farm just before the murders. And about the will."

"What did De Kok have to say about the will?"

"No, he said it's damn worthless because—I think he said because it wasn't the woman's property to begin with. It was still in her father's name, or something like that."

"And when did the hitting start?"

"Lammer van der Merwe, he started crying. He said he wouldn't sign, he wanted a lawyer, this was police harassment. So the inspector smacked him. And then he was squawking about laying charges against him, and then he hit—"

"All right, I get the picture. When were they released?"

"Shortly after the Moegel phoned."

"And the estate agent woman? Just keep it short, Ballies."

"Ja, well, no. We were still busy with those two guys, see? Then there was a message that someone from the rubbish dump came with a story that someone was hurt, or something like that."

"Who brought the message?"

"The jackal-catcher—old Windvogel—he sent one of those guys who scratch around the rubbish dumps to come and tell us." Pyl stopped, took a breath, started again, "Inspector Lobatse, he—"

"Yes, I know. He couldn't be bothered. Does anyone know how long she was lying there?"

"No, Inspector."

"Was she conscious when you got to her?"

"Yes, the jackal-catcher must have helped her. She already had a bandage around her neck and also her head. It had some kind of muti on it. My ma says Oom Vangjan knows lots of medicines from—"

"All right. So she was able to talk. And then she told you what had happened, how long she'd been there?"

"Ja. No, that's what I'm trying to say, Inspector. She didn't want to speak."

"She couldn't or she wouldn't?"

"Look, she was weak and her voice was gone because of the strangling. She said she couldn't really remember anything. But you could see she was lying there a long time already, probably unconscious. Her skin was red from the sun. And the old rubbish-dump guy said he already told someone early this morning."

"Who did he tell?"

"I can't say myself. But he told us that when nothing happened after the first time, he came back again. But he didn't want to come inside the station, see. Because this guy, he was picked up before—he killed a sheep belonging to one of the councillors, it happened in the municipal—"

"So, what time did he come in?"

"Around nine. Told the constables, who came to tell us, and when Inspector Lobatse said they must bring the man in, he ran away."

"Jesus, Pyl. So when did you guys eventually decide to go and look?"

Pyl dropped his head.

"Who were the constables on duty early this morning?" asked Beeslaar, but he didn't wait for an answer. "I want a statement from each of them—before the end of the day—about everything. And you do the same."

"But it was Inspector Lobatse—"

"Don't you worry about him. He'll get plenty of time to explain himself, because I can guarantee you *one* thing— Nelmari Viljoen is going to take him to the cleaners!"

Beeslaar's phone rang: Sara Swarts. Before she could say anything, he asked her about the will.

"Ja," she said sharply. "I have the impression your people have already knocked the so-called truth out of the Huilwater staff, Inspector. And I'm sure Dam told you it's highly likely to be worthless, and that he would have nothing to do with it."

"All right, Miss Swarts. And I'm sure we've already apologised for this morning's misunderstandings. So, if that's all you're calling about—?"

But that was not the reason for her call. She mentioned a phone call that Nelmari Viljoen had received when she'd seen her last and had a curious tale about a "ghost" at the rubbish dump.

Beeslaar listened with growing excitement. When the call ended, he said to Pyl, "I think we may have found the stolen Huilwater goods. You take one of the guys and drive out to the rubbish dump. Apparently someone's walking around there in Freddie Swarts's clothes. Bring them in and do a thorough search of the dump. And while you're there, find out if the old jackal man is still around. We need to speak to him."

"I think Ghaap—"

"Ghaap is still in the township, he's searching for his own attackers. I'll go find him, and we'll come along afterwards."

But Ghaap was nowhere to be found. In the end, Beeslaar hurried out to the municipal dump on his own.

An hour later he was back at the station, together with a stick-thin woman, a white sheen on her skin from living in the ash, in a long blue dress—which had apparently belonged to Freddie Swarts. He would get her sister to identify it—that and the few items of cheap jewellery that were found in a blackened backpack the woman was clutching. None of the special items, no ring or chain, Beeslaar noted. Sara Swarts would be disappointed. As for Herklaas Windvogel, there was no trace of him. And as Beeslaar had expected, there was no Huilwater killer to be found among the ragged lot who sheltered under plastic sheeting at the dump. Those scavengers lived like lepers from biblical times—pariahs.

The bedraggled woman in the blue dress wouldn't say much, apart from the fact that she had "saved" the backpack from the smouldering part of the dump. Beeslaar told Pyl to give her something to eat, take her statement and get the items identified.

He had things to do, places to go. On his way out, he asked the constable on duty to be on the lookout for young Bulelani.

"If you see him, tell him he must drop by the station. Tell him Beeslaar said so. Tell him I have a job for him." He ignored the strange look he got and left.

Outside, it was as if a dragon's breath enveloped him. He braved the scorching air to buy a cold Coke from the café farther down the street, then set off for Nelmari Viljoen's house. He thought of his phone conversation with Sara Swarts earlier. She and that Van Zyl guy might have been the last people to see Nelmari before she was attacked, when they'd overheard her arranging to meet someone.

He knocked on her neighbour's door. An elderly woman opened. She and her husband had been watching television last night, she told him, but she thought she'd seen a bakkie parked in front of the house. Boet Pretorius's. She hadn't seen him in the bakkie. Didn't know what time he'd left. Quite late, probably. The seven-thirty weather forecast was over and it was already dark. Viljoen's car wasn't there. But she thought she'd heard it pulling in later, not sure though. The TV . . .

Beeslaar thanked her and said goodbye.

At Viljoen's office he found the secretary at her desk, in a fluster. She was fielding two calls at once—talking on the cell-phone, while holding the landline receiver pressed to her chest.

He waited for her to finish.

"Sorry, Inspector," she said and patted her hair self-consciously. "All hell's broken loose here. Everyone's looking for Nelmari. They just don't get that the poor woman was almost at death's door. Have you caught anyone?"

"No, but have *you* heard from her yet?"

"Oh my word, she phoned a minute ago. She must be in a lot of pain." Meaning, thought Beeslaar, that she had given the poor girl grief.

"Did she say anything about the attack?"

The young woman shook her head. "She doesn't want to talk about it, Inspector. I think she's still in shock. But this thing, it's come at a bad time for us. We're just about to start building in Upington. Everything's up in the air—the bank, the municipality, everything. We're falling behind schedule. It could cost us millions."

"Do you know if Boet Pretorius is one of her clients?"

She looked at him anxiously. "I really shouldn't be talking about her business, Inspector. Nelmari wouldn't be happy. She always says it could—"

"Listen here, your boss was nearly killed. If you want to help her, you'd better just talk to me, Miss, er . . . "

"Charné Jefta."

"Miss Jefta, I'd like to know about everyone who came looking for your boss yesterday, who she had appointments with and everywhere she went. Please."

The girl reached for the diary. The telephone rang again, but she let it go to answerphone. She flipped some pages and named a few businesses in Kimberley, and an estate agency in Upington. "She wants to rent a bigger office. We're moving," she explained.

"Oh? Since when?"

"I don't know. Nelmari told me a week ago to organise phone lines for new premises. And to start packing up here so long. She wants to be in Upington before the end of the month. She's giving up her house here too."

"Don't you have other interests here?"

"All our business is really in Upington. She's also starting some other place . . . And I guess it's all got a bit crazy round here. I'm sorry, you'll have to ask her yourself."

Which I certainly will, he thought.

"Boet Pretorius," he said, to remind her of his original question.

"He wasn't here."

"Did he phone?"

"I don't really know. The people who get through to me, they're not always very polite." She rolled her eyes. "If they hear Nelmari's out, they just slam the phone down. Without saying who they are."

"And were there any such calls yesterday?"

"Yes, definitely. And when I arrived at work this morning, there were about three more like that on the machine."

The phone rang again and the girl grabbed for it. Beeslaar left her to it. He stood there, hands on his hips, allowing his eyes to wander over the fancy reception area. He paused at a single strelitzia in a weird green vase. Meant to be modern and elegant, he suspected. But the pointy orange petals—a bristling abstraction—reminded him of something: the razor wire, he suddenly realised, on Boet Pretorius's boundary fences.

He turned and walked out, deep in thought.

61

The town museum was right next to the police station, Sara and Harry discovered as they walked into the building. Very old, they could tell, dating back perhaps to colonial times. Sturdy walls of rough-hewn stone and cement, thatched roof and a heavy wooden door. Probably a national monument, said Harry, though he couldn't see the bronze plaque usually displayed on historic buildings.

"Stolen," the blonde woman at the counter chirped. "Like a lot of stuff that used to be in here. Our baptismal font, the communion cups, and the old Dutch Bible. Heaven alone knows what they wanted with *that*." She was actually closing up, she said, but invited them in all the same. Short and dumpy, she had fat cheeks and bright blue eyes. A red rosebud mouth fought for attention in the great moon of her face.

She introduced herself as Vicky Voges, curator. The museum—or what was left of it—was a hobby, she explained. It was municipal property, but the funds had dried up years before. Now it survived on donations, mainly from an Afrikaans cultural organisation. And also on Vicky's enthusiasm.

Harry introduced himself. And Sara. But Vicky had already recognised her, and offered her condolences.

"You're welcome to take a look around," she said, gesturing at glass shelves filled with historical objects, an old pulpit decked with an embroidered pulpit cloth, antique firearms and spear and arrowheads on the wall, and other historical paraphernalia. "I'm in no hurry. We also have a good collection of literature about the history of the town and the area. Few people know it, but this region has quite possibly the most interesting history of any part of the country. It was a real Wild West in days gone by."

"We'd love to, but maybe another time, Vicky," said Harry with professional amiability. "Today my quest is for information. My magazine, of course, would be prepared to make a donation for your trouble."

"Then how can I help?" Her cheeks dimpled when she smiled, Sara noticed.

"Do you have any information about the Griquas? Their history and so on?"

Vicky gave a satisfied nod. "My archives are the very best on that subject. I even have people from universities coming here to do research. Freddie and I . . . "

She looked at Sara and suddenly went quiet.

"Wait, I'll go get it. You and Miss Swarts can take a seat over there so long." She pointed towards a reading table with a display of newspapers and magazines in a corner of the room.

"Are you the only one here?" Harry asked when she returned.

"Yes. Me and history. I taught before, you know. History. It's in my blood."

"Here in town?"

"Yes." She took a box file off a shelf. "But I had to leave."

"You had to leave? I thought there weren't enough teachers."

"It's a long story. But my husband and I—he's a land surveyor, but we farm too—we decided to send our kids to Kimberley, to good schools. And then I, er, sort of lost the post. Oh well." She shrugged.

"Sorry to hear that," said Harry.

"It's sort of a race issue, really. After '94, many parents feared that standards might drop, and so they sent their kids away. Then the good teachers began to leave. And white teachers who'd sent their kids to city schools were pushed out. I can understand the thinking: if our local school's not good enough for your kids, you shouldn't be teaching here. But it's okay. I get great pleasure from the museum, and I still get to see kids who come in here for school projects and so on. *And* I get to meet interesting people. Like you."

She opened the box file and took out a stack of books and papers. "This is the best I have about changes in land ownership over the past hundred years. I presume you'd like to look at the situation before the Native Land Act of 1913 too, land that was still in non-white hands then? With a view to land claims?" Her eyes gleamed inquisitively.

Harry gave her an affirmative smile. Then he began to pick items from the pile.

For a while they worked in silence.

"Harry, what are we actually looking for?" Sara asked at one point. She realised she was spending more time staring than reading. She just couldn't focus.

"We're trying to find out what exactly it was that fascinated your sister."

Despondently, Sara realised that though she was keen to find out, she somehow couldn't muster the energy. At least not in the way Harry could.

She picked up a page, a neatly typed summary of the history of the Griquas.

It went back three centuries, she saw. To the early 1700s—to a farm at Piketberg just north of Cape Town. The farm had been awarded to the first Adam Kok, a freed slave. His father was white—possibly a cook on one of the Dutch East India Company merchant ships—hence the name Kok. His mother was a Khoi slave.

Sara put the page down. Normally, the information would appeal to the journalist in her—as it had apparently prompted

Freddie's need to understand the world she lived in. And the tragedy of the history of this land would, normally, have moved her. But since Freddie's death . . . Sara simply felt stunned. Paralysed, somehow, by the cruelty.

"Just say if I can help," said Vicky, carrying a tray over to the table.

"What's the shortest version you can give us of the history of the area?" Harry said with a winning smile.

"Well, yes," she said and eagerly pulled up a chair, "if you ask me to go right back to the beginning, it's a long story."

"We're happy to get the short version. Journalists. Short attention spans."

"Don't worry, I'll give you the bored-teenager version, which I do for school groups," she laughed. "Well, at the beginning everything around here was no-man's-land, really. There were the nomadic San, but no permanent residents. Until the Griquas arrived."

Sara lifted the sheet she'd been reading, summoned up her energy and said, "But this document says they had land in the Cape."

"That's right. That's by Professor Nel, University of Pretoria. But what he also says is that they weren't a true tribe. More of a motley crew—freed slaves, Khoi, Namas, Goringhaiquas. And a group called the Oorlams. It's a rather odd name, means cunning—or crafty. It referred to Khoi people who'd grown up on farms and adopted the white way of life."

She smiled impishly. "Very un-PC in today's terms, all the old names."

Sara noticed Harry's encouraging nod. She was suddenly irritated by all this cosy friendliness. Then she realised, with surprise, that what she was feeling was jealousy.

"But," the curator continued, "the authorities at the old Cape decided to round the whole lot up under one leader. Someone they could negotiate with. Well, that was Adam

Kok. They appointed him chief of all the little tribes in the area and gave him a farm close to where Piketberg is today, as well as an official baton to show that he was leader. Then he became 'Captain' Adam Kok, chief of 'the Basters'—another lovely name for the PC police. Can you imagine calling a group Bastards today!" She snorted, then continued, "You know there's still a tribe in Namibia that call themselves Basters?"

"They speak Afrikaans, don't they? And I'm told they're proud of their name," said Harry.

"Absolutely right, but where was I? Ja, for some reason the Captain decided to move away from Piketberg, and trekked north. About halfway to Namibia, around where Kamieskroon is today, they stopped. They lived off hunting, trading ivory and hides, and so on. And became quite rich. Remember, in those days the annual migration was massive—literally millions of springbok and other antelope. The Serengeti today would pale in comparison."

She offered them biscuits from the tea tray, took one herself and dipped it in her tea, her pinkie daintily held aloft.

"But there was plenty of competition with white hunters, and of course before long the missionaries arrived too."

Sara looked meaningfully over her cup at Harry. With some satisfaction, she noticed that his attention was focused on a fly crawling across his wrist, his other hand held aloft, ready to strike.

"Now," Vicky Voges declared, "the *British* missionaries. I could keep you busy for hours with that lot. Oh, the damage they did to this continent! They didn't just come bearing the Bible, they believed they were bringing *civilisation*. Believed people should stop their 'wild' nomadic lives, settle in towns, go to school—become good little Calvinists along the way." She gave a derisive guffaw. "So they convinced the next chief, old Adam Kok's son, Cornelius, to go somewhere they could do just that. And that place was here, this side of the Great Gariep."

She paused briefly, then said, "Sorry, I'm boring you. I've been a history teacher far too long."

"No, no, not at all," Harry said.

Sara wanted to kick him under the table. She'd expected to take a quick look at some old maps, and that would be that. End of story.

But it wasn't, of course.

God knows who had killed Freddie. Perhaps it was the very people Freddie was trying to help. Maybe she shouldn't have been playing the rescuing white madame, like some modern-day missionary.

And maybe she herself just needed to be left alone. To think. Get some perspective, sort out her emotions. Maybe she should leave. But she knew Harry wouldn't.

"They were pretty smart, those Griquas," Vicky continued. "They had guns and wagons and stuff, owned thousands of cattle and sheep. Made their own gunpowder. You can see all that in our little exhibition right here. They were fearsome fighters, shooting on horseback—a formidable bunch. They cleaned up this area pretty damn quickly. Drove out the Bushmen—the San, you know—and other nomadic tribes."

"Drove out, as in killed, you mean?" said Harry.

"More chased off, I'd say. And ja, probably killed too, I suppose. There were clashes all the time. In those days, they saw Bushmen as an aggravation to everyone, see. Their hunting grounds dwindled, so they had to steal livestock. Often ambushed and killed people, too. People were scared of them, even more so than of lions. And because the Bushmen knew the veld so well, you wouldn't see or hear them, not until you felt the poison arrow. Ja, white and black alike detested them. Thought they were sub-human. So they were hunted down like animals."

Sara opened a big hardback book and paged through it, looking at the pictures, only half listening to the woman. One of the photographs reminded her of a Freddie painting, a portrait of a Griqua chief and his wife. In the photo the man wore a black top hat and tails, and the woman had a Voortrekker bonnet on her head. In Freddie's painting the two of them were sitting at a dinner table, knives and forks in their hands. The tablecloth was a landscape of thorn trees.

"Did my sister come here often?" she interrupted the curator's performance.

"At one point. She was such a gentle person. Shy, really." Vicky's eyes clouded over. "I'm so sorry about this horrible thing."

Sara closed the book. She didn't quite know what to say. She just wanted to go. Get away from this history lesson, from this woman's preening in front of Harry.

"Actually, she was really brave, your sister. Helping with a land claim the way she did. And were people upset! I tell you. My own husband . . . I wanted him to help me with the old maps, him being a land surveyor and all. But that almost ended in divorce. In the end, Freddie and I muddled along on our own. And the history of that period was so messy—the discovery of diamonds and the British annexation, and then a small-scale Anglo–Griqua war and large tracts of land changing hands. Was quite a task to establish what belonged to whom—and when. But Freddie managed, eventually. And the land she identified, well, a whole bunch of today's white-owned farms straddle it. Part of my husband's land too, mind you, which he's certainly not happy about. Goodness knows why he was suddenly so in love with it. He'd been wanting to sell for years. But oh, well . . . " she said with a shrug.

Sara wondered if this woman was genuinely so accepting of the whole affair. But she dared not ask. No, she just wanted to get away.

"But it was all for nothing, in the end?" asked Harry.

"Ja. Nothing came of it."

Sara started stacking up the books in front of her. She couldn't listen to one more word about the Griquas or her sister. She had to get out of this place.

"You can borrow it if you like—the pictures are especially interesting."

Sara was about to say no, but Harry picked up the book and promised to take good care of it.

"I hear the funeral is tomorrow," said the curator, putting the cups back onto the tray. When she was done, she looked into Sara's eyes. "I just want to say, try not to take any notice of what people say. There are people around here . . . They're spreading poison."

"What poison?" Harry was oblivious to Sara's murderous glare.

"Nasty things . . . "

In the silence that followed, Sara capitulated. "It's okay. You can tell me. Might be better for me to hear it."

"The worst is probably . . . people saying she shouldn't have a church funeral. They're gossiping about satanism and moonlight animal slaughter and baboon riders . . . "

"*What*?"

"It's what they call black witch doctors. And she slept with the foreman, they say. Forgive me, I feel so ashamed of these people. They can be so . . . backward."

Sara was at a loss for words. Then she found her voice again. "It's all right. People used to slander my mother too. The same hard-hearted people who fill the church pews every Sunday. Pretending to be such great Christians, so great they wouldn't notice a good person if they fell over her. A person without a scrap of hatred in her . . . " She stopped, suddenly tired. She was fulminating against the wrong person in any case. "But thanks for warning me," she said wanly.

Harry put his hand on her shoulder. For the umpteenth time she was glad of his presence, a shield against this harsh and horrible reality.

Then Harry said goodbye to their host, and gently steered Sara out into the late-afternoon light.

62

H er name was Debora," Pyl said breathlessly. He looked as if he had literally come running to deliver the news.

Beeslaar threw down his pen. He was busy sorting out the Huilwater notes and statements, getting them back into meaningful shape.

"The baboon," Pyl beamed ecstatically, as if he had seen the Messiah himself. "I'm almost positive it's her, Inspector. My cousin, she lives at Kalkfontein, see, Hannes Botha's farm. Apparently the baboon was theirs."

"Nice work, man. And what's your cousin doing with a baboon?"

"No, it isn't *her* baboon. She's too young, still. Her parents have been on the farm for years, and the baboon too. She lived there by the house, like she was one of the dogs. They were all here this morning."

"The animals?"

"No, Inspector, my cousin. My *cousin* was here. It's Friday, see."

Beeslaar waited. He knew Pyl would eventually get somewhere with his long-winded story.

"These days the farmers bring the workers to town on Fridays for shopping and banks and other stuff, see—instead of Saturdays, like they used to. You know, the towns are busy and most people are drunk on Saturdays. Well, Hannes Botha brought his people in this morning, all of them, on the lorry.

My cousin too. And then she went to see my ma, at home. You see, *her* ma and *mine* are distant cousins. They had the same grandfather, but not the same mother, because my grandfather was married twice, see. And my ma is from his first wife and—"

Beeslaar chuckled. "It's okay, Ballies, I get the picture." God knows, the last thing he wanted was a full exposition of the Pyl family tree. "The baboon—your cousin says it was Hannes Botha's . . . "

"Yes. No. Actually Auntie Debora's. Debora."

"Sergeant, you're losing me. Which Debora are you talking about?"

"The baboon!"

Beeslaar grinned, but Pyl didn't see the joke.

"The baboon also has that name. Vytjie says—"

"And who's Vytjie?" Beeslaar couldn't stop himself.

"My cousin, Inspector! My cousin. My ma's half-sister's child. Okay?"

"Okay, I get it," Beeslaar said wryly.

"Now, Vytjie says they could never have children, see. The Bothas, I mean. So then Oom Hannes caught his wife the baboon. Didn't even catch it, really. It was the baby of a baboon he'd shot. The baboons gave him a hard time at his feeding troughs, see, and so he—"

"Do you know if Hannes Botha is still in town?"

"I think so, Inspector. Must I go see?"

"Please, man. Ask him to come in. We don't know yet if it's really his baboon. See if you can find him at the co-op."

"Aikona," said Pyl, shaking his head. "He'll be drinking at the Red Dune—that old guy likes his dop."

Beeslaar looked at his watch. Nearly five o'clock. He got up.

"Well, what are we waiting for?"

The bar was buzzing with voices.

Pyl pointed at a corner table where Hannes Botha was sitting by himself.

"You go get us each a cold one from Oom Koeks over there. He knows what I like," said Beeslaar, taking a fifty-rand note from his wallet and pressing it into Pyl's hand.

Botha looked up in surprise as Beeslaar leaned down at his table.

"May I take a seat, Mister Botha?" he asked.

"Sit, sit, Inspector. Can I get you something?"

"Thank you," Beeslaar said and pointed towards Pyl at the bar counter. "Well, I'm glad I found you here today, Oom. I wanted to ask a few questions about that tame baboon of yours."

He noticed a look in the older man's eyes, somewhere between fear and wistfulness.

"Old Debora. You know, it's like a death in the family. Now I really hope you're not going to lock me up about the poor creature. I know we didn't have a permit and everything. But she was honestly like a child to my wife."

"It's okay, Oom, I was just wondering if it was your baboon that ended up at Huilwater earlier this week."

"God, Inspector. It's a bad, bad story. The one day she was still there, and next thing we saw, she was gone. Chain and all."

Pyl put a beer and a Coke on the table. When Beeslaar introduced him, Botha said, "Didn't you come sing at our church last Christmas?"

"Ja, I did." Noticing Beeslaar's puzzled look, he explained, "Our church choir. We went to sing at the white people's church. Seeing that they don't have a choir of their own any more."

"You sang a solo too, if I'm not mistaken?" said Botha.

Pyl's laugh rang with pride as well as bashfulness. "'Silent Night'—it's my favourite! I sing it at our church every year. My ma—"

Beeslaar slapped his hand on Pyl's skinny shoulders.

"There's plenty of hidden talent in the police force, as you can see!" he joked. "But if I may return to your baboon. When did she go missing?"

"Tuesday night. She sleeps in a cage outside, next to the back door. Best watchdog you can think of, believe me. My wife doesn't like it when I talk about the baboon like that, but really, strangers run a mile when they discover a baboon at your door. Anyway. Wednesday morning she was just gone. Poor old thing. Loved sweeties, especially Smarties. She got a few before bedtime every evening. Loved the red ones . . . " He looked away, trying to hide the tears in his eyes.

Beeslaar gave him a moment to compose himself. "She wouldn't have run away, maybe?"

"Oh, no. No. She was like a child in the house. We often let her off her chain, and she never ran away. Once a wild troop came by, but oh, she was so scared of *that* lot. No. Baboons are cruel to strangers—other baboons, I mean. They'd have torn her apart, that's for sure."

"Do you have any idea who might have stolen her?"

Botha pursed his mouth. "No, my friend. No idea."

"And if someone had come to get her in the night, a stranger, she would probably have screamed?"

"She would have, yes. She could *really* scream—like a pig. But we heard nothing. And that's what's so strange. Her chain was cut with a bolt cutter. We just couldn't understand it. All those years with the old baboon there. And then suddenly someone comes and steals her. Then we heard about the thing at Huilwater. Hell, my wife's been crying all week long. I hear they cut the poor thing's throat."

"Among other things, yes. Both her hands . . . "

"Good God. Blacks?" He looked from Beeslaar to Pyl, who sat primly sipping his Coke from a straw, deliberately ignoring the question. He was clearly not at home, didn't approve of bars—and probably not shebeens either.

"Well," Beeslaar said, "could be anyone. Anyone clever enough to drug her. Who knew they could lure her away with a handful of Smarties. Maybe she was fed the pills along with the Smarties. Because she was alive when they cut her throat, which they did right there. At Huilwater. We suspect they used her as some kind of warning."

"For what, though? There are no people left at Huilwater!"

"But there are," said Pyl. He was sitting upright, very much the alert young law enforcer. "The manager is still there. It was at his place, in fact, that the baboon was crucified."

The old man took a gulp from his glass. Brandy and Coke, Beeslaar guessed. And not his first, either, judging by the man's drooping eyelids.

"I tell you, it's those bloody blacks," he whispered conspiratorially. "They want to terrorise us off our farms. And they're the only ones who'd want baboon hands. For their witch doctor muti, of course."

Beeslaar raised a sceptical eyebrow, but before he could speak Pyl broke in: "Still, I think you'd better just ask around, sir, speak to your workers. Ask if they heard or saw anything. You can just call me," he finished crisply, taking a card from his pocket and placing it next to Botha's drink.

Beeslaar was stunned. Someone had stolen old motor-mouth country bumpkin Pyl and replaced him with Captain Courageous. Beeslaar stood up.

"Do you have a driver, Oom?" he asked.

Botha craned his neck, looking up at Beeslaar. "My foreman. I won't drive myself, Inspector, don't worry."

As they headed for the door, they bumped into Buks Hanekom.

"Afternoon, Inspector. I see you managed to get your job back." He smiled broadly, ignoring Pyl.

"And I see you're back in your office," said Beeslaar, gesturing at the bar counter.

"I was just wondering how your investigation is progressing. Seems to me your black bosses were just beginning to head in the right direction before you got back."

Beeslaar turned to leave, but Hanekom blocked his way.

"You're looking in the wrong places, Inspector. You're allowing a very sly Bushman to pull the wool over your eyes—no offence, Sergeant," he said, inclining his head towards Pyl, "but that's what he is—one who kept the boss lady's bed warm at night, while his sidekicks terrorised the farmers. He's got big plans, that man. He wants to present our forefathers' land on a platter to the political bosses in Pretoria. It's in his direction you should be looking!"

"And is that the message you went out there to give him this week?"

Hanekom made no reply.

"Maybe you should go explain to Oom Hannes's wife what kind of patriot you are, Hanekom," Beeslaar continued. "Maybe *she'd* understand how you and your henchman, Polla Pieterse, could hurt a poor old pet baboon like that—your warped patriotism. Volk en vaderland, nè? Because me and Sergeant Pyl here—we certainly can't comprehend that level of cruelty."

Hanekom said nothing, and Beeslaar knew his hunch had hit home.

63

S ara had no sooner shut the door behind them than Dam called to discuss final details about the next day's funerals. Harry suggested they all have supper on the farm, he'd braai for them.

It was almost dark by the time they arrived, and Harry lit a fire straight away. Sara went for a swim in the dam just beyond the garden fence, its cool water pumped from deep underground by the creaking windmill. Harry, meanwhile, fetched the book they'd borrowed from the museum and took a seat on one of the chairs under the vine while they waited for Dam.

He did not look up as Sara walked past, towelling herself dry. Moments later she had changed, and was in the kitchen, making a salad and putting buttered potatoes in the oven. Harry had already seen to the cutlery and plates. She put a bottle of chilled white wine and three glasses on a tray and took it outside.

"Any the wiser?" she asked, opening the wine.

Harry smiled at her. "You look good," he said.

Sara touched her damp hair, suddenly self-conscious.

"But. The book," he continued, "it's actually damn interesting, you know. The Griquas waged war like it was going out of fashion. And they were the first of all the indigenous tribes in the country to have their own written laws, courts, executions, the works."

"And all this is for your article, is it?" She handed him a

glass and she felt their fingers touch. She quickly withdrew to pick up her own glass. "So," she prodded. "Your article."

"Ja. Maybe in the future, yes. But I'm definitely beginning to get more of an idea of why your sister went so gaga for them. They were rather formidable. Especially this one guy, Adam Kok the Second. An incredibly interesting person. He was leader of the Bergenaars—who, you guessed it—lived in the mountains."

"A tribe, or what?"

"Well, more of a gang, if I understand it all correctly. A bunch of tribeless Bushmen and Korannas who raided and robbed for a living."

"But what did they have to do with the Griquas?"

"Adam Kok the Second. The Griquas asked him to become leader, but the missionaries were having none of it, he was a little too wild for their liking. Then they 'fired' him and got their own man—Andries Waterboer. He's the guy whose great-great-grandson, so the book says, still lives in town today. Waterboer was an educated man—a teacher and lay preacher. Much more their cup of tea."

"And could the missionaries just send a chief packing like that?"

"I guess that's how things were those days, Saartjie. Or is it Sarie, my Sarie Marais?" He leaned over playfully, humming a bar of the old song as he tugged on a wet strand of her hair.

She had to smile. Maybe it wasn't just the water that made her feel good, she thought. Then she raised her glass to him. "No point in waiting for Dam while the wine gets warm." Sara took a sip and said, "Mmm, nice. So, Professor Van Zyl, do continue with the fascinating lecture. You were enlightening us about the arrogant behaviour of the missionaries."

"Actually, it was about Andries Waterboer the First. You should pay better attention. Here, have a look." He held out the book and Sara recognised a picture she'd seen earlier. "He was San, and a fighter of note. The first group he tackled were the Bergenaars. And then he moved on to the Korannas. At one stage he was even giving the mighty Mzilikazi of the Matabele a run for his money. The British colonial rulers loved him—plied him with guns and ammo. In exchange, he took care of the 'troublesome' tribes in the region."

"Oh my God, if it wasn't the missionaries, it was the imperialists. But the Griquas weren't British subjects, surely?"

"No ways." He got up to see to the braai. The coals were ready and he started putting meat on the grid, talking all the while. "But then the whites started arriving on the scene. And of course . . . " Carefully, he positioned the grid on the glowing coals.

"Then what?"

"You know the story about the pawpaw and the fan?" He walked back to his chair.

Sara smiled ruefully. Funny, she thought, how little of this history is known. And how sad, actually. No wonder Freddie had changed her mind about the future of Huilwater. She must have dug up the same truths—the things everyone on the farm had been oblivious to. How excited she'd have been.

"You still with me, Sara?" Harry touched her arm. His eyes were soft, a warm light in them. "Okay, where was I? The whites. Hell, what an unruly bunch it was that washed up here. Many were fleeing the law. A lot of them came for the game— ivory hunters."

"Mmm, ja, ja," Sara said.

She was squinting at Harry through her wine glass, anxiety stirring in her gut. Tomorrow she'd be saying goodbye to Freddie. For the last time. She shivered. The shadows across the yard had deepened and she wondered what was keeping Dam. She had gone to say hello when they'd arrived, but she'd found him on the phone—his face grim. He said he'd join them as soon as he had seen to his birds.

"Helloooo," Harry said, waving a hand in front of her face.

"Ja, ja, Professor!" she said with a smile. "The hunters and the elephants. And ivory. Go on."

He had strapped on his camping headlamp, which cast ghostly shadows on his face. "Things were hopping in these parts back then. Genuine Wild West, this place was, just like Vicky told us. Crawling with fortune seekers, pioneer farmers, natives, rogues and missionaries galore. As far as law and order went, things were staggering along sort of okayish. And then diamonds were discovered—all over Griqua territory. And everything went to hell in a handbasket pretty quickly. The Griquas lost their land—"

"Hi," Sara called out, seeing Dam walking towards them. "You're just in time to save me from a history lesson. The meat's already on the braai. You must be hungry."

He sat down and took the glass of wine she held out to him. Then he put it down and said, "Later, Sara." He smelt of soap, she noticed. He must have showered and changed before coming over.

But he looked tired, tense and uncomfortable, and Sara felt her stomach knotting. It was going to be another difficult evening. She wished he'd just drink his wine and relax, but he sat staring at his shoes. "Please carry on," he said, "the smell will soon sharpen up my appetite. So, what's the lesson about?"

"The history of the Griquas. Sara and I were at the museum this afternoon."

Dam gave a tight smile.

"Actually I'm curious about the land claims Sara's sister was looking at."

"Oh," Dam said flatly, but it didn't curb Harry's enthusiasm.

"I'd got as far as the British Crown Colony, hey Sara?"

"And the diamonds."

"I suppose you know all about it, Dam. At the time of annexation, the British gave a mere hundred and fifty-six farms to the Griquas. And that, you could say, was the beginning of the end for the Griquas."

Dam didn't react at all.

"So," Harry said, getting up again to attend to the meat. The fat had started spattering, the sound and smell filling the twilight air. "The Griquas rose up against the Empire—and were well and truly fucked forever." He went on about old Queen Victoria who became their baas. And rebels being sent to prison in Cape Town en masse. Their wives and children were rounded up and divided among the white farmers as labourers. They became serfs overnight. "There was nothing left of their people. Nothing. Even history has forgotten them." He turned the grid and looked back at Sara, his head-lamp blinding her for a moment. "And that, Saartjie, is what I believe stirred your sister so."

She glanced at Dam, his face scarcely visible in the darkness, which had fallen swiftly.

"Dam?" she said hesitantly.

"I told you already I wanted nothing to do with the whole business. Freddie just went ahead on her own. She and a few political guys from some cultural society or whatever. I just told them to leave me out of it all."

Sara got up to fetch the rest of the food. Dam went with her, poked around in a drawer for serving spoons and took out some trays. He had brought along herbs from his garden, which he chopped up with a big kitchen knife before sprinkling it all onto the salad.

He was completely at home in this kitchen, Sara thought as she stood watching him. Hell, why hadn't she noticed this before?

64

The sun had gone down by the time Beeslaar drove out to Karrikamma to see Boet Pretorius.

He was startled by the man's appearance when he came out to meet Beeslaar on the steps. His lips were tightly pursed, and his tall frame seemed hunched, his skin almost grey.

"To what do I owe this honour, Inspector?" He didn't invite the policeman inside.

"Nelmari Viljoen. She was attacked last night, most probably at her home, and assaulted."

"Ja, I've heard. Is she . . . ?"

"She'll live, but she was badly hurt."

"And you've come all this way to tell me what exactly?"

"Your bakkie was spotted in front of her house."

"Well, she wasn't there."

"But *you* were there. What were you doing there for such a long time if she wasn't there? Waiting, perhaps?"

Pretorius's mouth moved slightly as he chewed the inside of his cheek. "I didn't do anything. I knocked and waited on her stoep for a while, and when there was no answer, I left."

"Why were you there?"

"Business. I was in town, at the co-op, then I decided to go round to her place."

"But the co-op had been closed for ages by then. Your bakkie was only seen there after eight in the evening, maybe even later."

"What is this, Beeslaar? Lots of people wanted to wring

that woman's—wanted to hurt her. I just happened to be around, by coincidence, and I thought I'd quickly drop by. That's all."

"Have you had any contact with her since she was admitted to hospital?"

"God, no. Of course not. We weren't such great friends."

"Oh? Then how do you know someone tried to strangle her?"

Pretorius looked at him as if he were stupid. "It's fucking all over the district, already. And anyway, why would *I* want to harm someone like Nelmari Viljoen? It makes no sense, man."

"You still haven't said what kind of business you had with each other. Or was it something more personal?"

Pretorius looked past Beeslaar. "Just business. I don't think I have to discuss it with you. I know my rights."

"All right. If that's how you want to play it. Just remember, I have rights too. And one of them is the right to know you're lying to me. You were looking for Miss Viljoen yesterday. I know, because you called her a couple of times. And the co-op closes at five-thirty. So you waited damn long to go and pay your impromptu visit. Sorry, but I don't buy it."

"You're being ridiculous, man. I was in the Red Dune. And on my way home, I wanted to stop by at Nelmari's. That's all."

"The same way you wanted to stop by at Freddie Swarts's place last week?"

"You're full of shit, Beeslaar, you know that?" A strange smile wavered on his face.

Beeslaar pressed on. "Look, you haven't exactly told me why you were there that day. At Huilwater. I was led to believe that the two of you were no longer seeing each other, and that you didn't really visit there any more, but on *that* day, that *one* day, you suddenly 'popped in.' I find that rather remarkable."

"I think you'd better go, Beeslaar."

"Oh. Just like that, without an answer?"

Pretorius moved up a step. "I'm not obliged to tell you anything, but if you must know, it was jealousy, plain and simple. I'd heard that very day that Freddie was having a relationship with that foreman of hers. And now you really need to go."

"Who told you?"

"Hanekom, who else? Hanekom and his hooligans. They've had it in for Freddie for so long. Bullied and threatened her with anonymous calls and all kinds of things."

"How do you know it was him?"

"Oh, God. He's so bloody transparent. He and his big pal Polla go around everywhere saying the white uprising is going to start here." He gave a hoarse laugh. "The white uprising! I told her back then she should lay charges against the little shit. But nothing came of it." He exhaled loudly. "Just like nothing came of the fucking land claims, for what they're worth."

"Why not?"

"Ag, I don't know, man. Go ask Nelmari Viljoen."

Beeslaar turned to leave, but changed his mind. "How well did you know Freddie Swarts's work, her paintings?"

"From the little I saw . . . " Pretorius pulled a face. "Let me put it this way: it certainly wasn't her painting that attracted me to her."

Then he turned on his heel and went inside.

It was properly dark by the time Beeslaar drove back to town. At Huilwater he saw lights burning in the main house. He thought of his phone conversation earlier that evening with De Kok, who had called him out of the blue, wanting to offer the proverbial olive branch. Turns out he'd found the old jackal-catcher after all that night Pyl slept in his car out at Huilwater. And the old bugger had apparently agreed to show De Kok the stock thieves' spoor.

But De Kok wanted to make a deal with him: he'd lead him to the stock thieves—but only if Beeslaar left the old man in peace so he could attend the old lady's funeral the next day.

He'd agreed. And was already regretting it.

65

S he was a steenbok," Dam said pensively.
The three of them were sitting around the fire. Dam had revived it after dinner and the flames played across his face, highlighting the planes of his prominent cheekbones.

"My ancestors had a place for each animal, see. And the steenbok . . . she was the special child of the veld." Wistfully, he went on, "She's wise and she's good, they used to say. She looks at you like so-o-o . . . and she sees your everything. Not like the duiker, who runs away, ducking and dodging. She's wide awake, all pert and poised. On tippy-toes in her little black shoes. And she checks you out, from far away."

Harry and Sara sat motionless as they listened to his soft narration. "The ancestors believed that all people were animals once. The eland, the gemsbok, the hyena and the jackal. But of all the antelope, the steenbok was the one with magical powers." His eyes narrowed, as if he were retrieving a thought from the furthest recesses of his mind.

"Freddie had that kind of magic. She could make you believe again. And she could *see*. Totally see you. Not only the things you wanted to show, but also the stuff you hid behind your back."

"What do you mean, Dam?" Sara said, wary of disturbing the intimacy of the moment.

"My whole life, I tried running away from the veld, Sara. Little by little I ran away. I had dreams of becoming a doctor. Or a professor. Something civilised and Western. In high school I was one of those ridiculous nerds. Just read and read. And studied. Did my homework as if my life depended on it. Took part in all the cultural activities. Sang in the choir. I didn't care that the other kids teased me. They teased me anyway. But I was on a mission." His cheek lifted in a half smile. "And then, later, when I went to Dubai, I went to the other extreme. I learnt the language. Hell, I was more Arab than the Arabs themselves."

He gave a sharp, sudden laugh.

"She called me the Lord Bushman. I wanted to be anything other than what I was, an ordinary old veld gogga."

"The mantis," said Sara. "That's the painting, right, Dam? She gave her heart to that veld gogga?"

At first, he made no reply. Then he spoke again. "The mantis is a rascal, a sort of trickster. He dreamt us, that we know. All the animals of the veld. We were dreamt up by him. And he played with us."

He got up and put more logs on the fire. The dry wood crackled, shooting sparks up into the blackness of the night.

"Here at Huilwater," he said as he sat down again, "with Freddie, I became my own man again. I started remembering the old stories. Those my father's father, Oupa N!xi, had taught me." He smiled as he heard Sara quietly mimicking the click to herself. "I was already ten when I started school. I couldn't read or write, had never even seen a TV. Lived in the veld with my grandfather. I was raw, a wild Bushman. I didn't wear any clothes. You can imagine how out of place I was, how rough my feet were. And on top of that, I was small. Fu-u-uckit . . . "

He laughed quietly to himself, his shoulders heaving in the flickering light.

"So, this Bushman had to shake the dust and grass off his feet. So shy, you can imagine. But once I got *here*, only then did I realise how privileged I'd been—to have had a childhood like that. My grandfather taught me. By the age of ten you could have left me on my own in the veld. I would have survived. I knew the veld and the stars and the seasons the way today's kids know a cellphone. I could read it all, hear it, play it and predict it. I was part of the veld. And until I came here, to Huilwater, I was blind to the wonder of it. But *here* . . . " He swung his arm out. "Here I began to accept the fact that I am who I am: a Bushman from the veld. A rare thing, in fact."

For a moment he stopped, staring into the fire.

"And that's why I say: Freddie possessed the magic of the steenbok. She let me see myself through *her* eyes, helped me to cast off my false skin."

"You loved her, didn't you?"

Dam turned away.

"You know the stories that are going around, don't you? About the two of you."

"At first I thought it was Boet Pretorius. I thought he was a kind of boyfriend or something." Dam's eyes glittered in the firelight. "Talk about a wolf in sheep's clothing," he mumbled.

"But he was in love with her. Tannie Yvonne thought they'd make a handsome couple, she says everyone thought they'd get married, combine the farms."

"Ag," Dam grunted, "Freddie chased him away."

"Why?"

"I'm not sure that's a story you want to hear, Sara."

"Come on, Dam, we're way past that."

"Well, she said he'd become too forward, that kind of thing. Tried to force his attentions on her. I think he went too far. That he might have—oh, I don't know. She was suddenly different, changed somehow. Prickly, moody. Thinking back now, I realise she was actually not well at all."

"When was that?"

"Now, just recently. A few weeks ago. And things between us were, ja, tricky. We'd had our argument about the will. I thought she was upset about that. But Outanna told me it was Boet. And by then Freddie didn't want to discuss it any more."

A jackal howled in the distance, and Dam cocked his head to listen.

Harry gave a loud yawn, then asked, "The Griqua story, Dam. It's a helluva tragedy. No wonder Freddie found it so compelling."

"Well, she tried to do the impossible. How do you restore a people's dignity, anyway? And land alone isn't enough to bring it back. That's something I've learnt here. I came here thinking that I was going to show these people something. But look where that has got me. I've got nothing."

He leaned forward, held his hands to the fire. "Ja, never mind the Griquas—where are the Bushmen today? After all, they were the first owners of this land. Well, maybe not owners. Occupants, more. Now all they're left with is a few pockets of the Kalahari. From Botswana-side the diamond miners are pushing them out, and from the south it's the developers— modern-day fortune seekers in their fancy BMWs. So. The spoor of the veld people, the old ways, are being erased, everywhere. Of all the people in this country, they've probably had the worst deal. Still today."

"But doesn't it make you furious, all the injustices of the past?" Sara asked.

"Yes and no. It's an old, sad story. Freddie was the one who got emotional. As for me, ag, I suppose I was more resigned, maybe I shut it out on purpose. One day she read me something from a book—the diary of some settler, a field cornet in the Eastern Cape in the seventeen hundreds. It was his job, apparently, to sort out the stock thieves—the Bushmen, of course. Hunted them down, killed the men and brought the women and children back for slave labour. On one such commando they killed two hundred Bushmen. He recorded it in his diary so matter-of-factly. The guy was a well-respected,

God-fearing man protecting his own people. And they in turn were trying to survive. Those were violent times, with violent measures. The world had a different morality then. That's why I say this land is soaked in blood. We all have blood on our hands."

"True," Sara said, "and the slaughter continues. Tomorrow we're laying a steenbok to rest."

Dam stood up. "I think I must go to bed now. Tomorrow's going to be a long day." And then he left, his slight figure swiftly swallowed by the dark.

66

He sat moodily scratching at a scab on his arm.

"I want smokes," said the boy, squinting at Sergeant Ghaap.

"You want a snotklap, that's what you want. That's all you'll get till you talk."

The boy pulled a face, clicked his tongue and started picking at the scab again.

It was Saturday morning and Ghaap was slumped in his chair, arms crossed, legs stretched out in front of him, eyes half closed. He looked like someone talking in his sleep. The bruises on his face were healing nicely, but the dent in his ego, thought Beeslaar, would take a bit longer to fix.

"Go on, tell the inspector what you told me the other evening."

The boy gave Beeslaar a silent, surly glance.

Beeslaar was also silent. This was Ghaap's show. The three of them were in one of the police station's two holding cells. It was bare and very basic, no bunks or chairs—apart from the two Ghaap had brought in.

The boy was sitting on the floor, his back against the wall. It was quiet and surprisingly cool inside the cell. The only sound was a fly droning at the window. And the sound of Thabang Motlogeloa's fidgeting.

Beeslaar looked at his nails. He'd have to buy a nail brush. The vegetable patch in his backyard was done. And soon he might even have a lawn, which he would water every evening.

Along with his vegetables. Thanks to his new gardener: Bulelani, the laundry thief.

He wasn't sure yet whether he was doing the right thing. Earlier that morning he'd shoved a spade into his hands and then left him in the garden. It had been the quickest solution he could find when the boy suddenly turned up at his door, bedraggled and hungry.

Just the weekend before he was hiding in these very same cells to escape an angry mob. The same Bulelani who had, Beeslaar suspected, been standing at his gate earlier in the week, fleeing, when he'd come walking home from the veld.

He'd go and talk it over with Yvonne Lambrechts in the next day or so. The boy must have lost his parents at a young age. He could barely speak, apparently just scuttled around the rubbish dumps and the township in search of food, and was certainly mentally handicapped. So school was out of the question, and for the rest, Yvonne would have to help: there was no official refuge for kids like him around here. For the time being Bulelani would clean up the yard and earn a plate of food for it.

"Where are your people, Mr. Motlogeloa?" Ghaap's low drawl brought Beeslaar back from his predicament.

"I don't have people," came the answer.

"Well then, where do you live? You must live somewhere." Ghaap waited.

"Everywhere," the boy said eventually.

"Where do you live most of the time?"

"Auntie Beauty."

"Thabang, are you going to start talking properly now, or do you want a klap?"

"I know my rights. I want a lawyer."

"You'll get your arse kicked, *that's* all you'll get. Which Auntie Beauty, and where does she live?"

He scowled at Ghaap, said he didn't know her surname, that he lived in a shack in her backyard.

"So who's this big man who pays you so much money for all those little odd jobs you do? The man you were bragging about the other night? With all the connections and the so-called 'pigs' working for him? Hey, Thabang? That sharp dude, the one you'll just say the word to, then it's curtains with me and Inspector Beeslaar here? Hey? Tell me. The man you helped to burn down the old auntie's house in Chicken Vale—what's his name, hey?"

No reply.

"You know that auntie's dead, nè? And you know you're going to sit in jail all by yourself if you don't tell me? Do you want to go to jail all alone, Thabang?"

The boy clicked his tongue loudly.

"Talk to us, Thabang, tell Inspector Beeslaar here how you assaulted a policeman. And how a rubbish like you is suddenly rolling in cash."

Beeslaar straightened up in his chair, put his fists on his knees. Barely perceptibly, the boy shrank away, making himself smaller as he faced the big man.

"I didn't burn that auntie's house," he mumbled hastily. "And I don't know who it was who did it!"

"Oh, really? That's not what you tuned me on Tuesday night! You were windgat, boasting about all your connections, remember?"

The boy contemplated his bare feet, rubbed at the film of dust on the roughened skin.

"You can sit here in this cell till you talk. You hear me, Mr. Motlogeloa? And afterwards you're going to sit in jail in Kimberley—for the rest of your life—for the murder of Mrs. Johanna Beesvel! You hear?"

Thabang's eyes narrowed as he shot him a venomous look.

Ghaap slowly straightened up. "Let's leave it there for the moment, Inspector, because I can see you're itching to show this little shit what we do to people who assault policemen.

He's been stubborn like this the whole time, this little fucker, ever since I found him over at Mma Mokoena's last night, flat broke again, trying to sell his brand new Nikes to the gents in there!"

Back in his office, Beeslaar placed a call to Wag-'n-Bietjie, Buks Hanekom's farm—or rather, his father's farm.

No, Buksie wasn't home, he was off on important business. Beeslaar asked for details, but the old man said he wasn't sure. There was an air of despondency to his voice.

67

The sun seemed to melt away in an intense glow of heat and dust. It had been a long day—people, preachers, and heightened emotion. Tears, hushed voices, the hesitant notes of an organ and the mournful singing of woeful hymns.

Sara was sitting on Dam's back stoep, together with Dam and Harry, each with an ice-cold glass of Dam's ginger beer. They didn't speak much, having just walked back from the small farm cemetery in the veld. It was a quiet spot next to a spring in the shelter of a koppie, just a few hundred metres from the farmhouses. The rest of the mourners had left earlier—Dawid and Lammer and their wives, all the people from the undertakers, who'd looked oddly out of place in their black suits and shiny shoes.

"Now Freddie is at rest too," Sara said, breaking the silence. "Strange, it seems like yesterday, the two of us, little girls running around here, full of beans at this time of the day." Her eyes swept the yard and the workers' houses beyond the shed, as if she were searching for memories. "Just yesterday."

There was no response from the others, each wrapped up in his own thoughts.

She looked back at her old family home visible through the cluster of trees. "I should go water the lawn over there. It's looking so brown."

But she made no sign of moving.

Three funerals in one day. First Freddie and Klara's in the

white church in town, then Outanna's in a hellishly hot corrugated-iron church in Chicken Vale. And the afternoon's short ceremony at the spring.

The official funeral for Freddie and the child was exactly the way she'd thought it would be. Sombre. And flat: a muddled sermon, lacklustre singing, an old lady fumbling at the church organ. The congregation hadn't had a full-time organist for years. Afterwards, the tea, organised for all the local farmers and their wives. Buks Hanekom was there, along with a bunch of farmers in their commando clothes. And Boet Pretorius.

She was glad she hadn't invited him out to the farm as she'd originally planned. Especially not after what she now knew about him and Freddie. All those disturbing revelations—and the conflict here on Huilwater, the tension and turmoil. It was probably best, too, that Nelmari couldn't make it today.

In the end, the service on the farm had been intimate, meaningful.

"Thank you for your poem this afternoon, Dam. Freddie would be happy with her funeral—wherever she is now."

"Oh, she's around here," Dam said quietly.

"Like the birds?"

"Yes, like the birds. In their own dimension."

"Why today?"

"They were ready. I wanted to release them earlier in the week, but I thought I'd rather wait for Freddie and Klara to be there too."

"Was it difficult?" asked Harry.

"They were never mine."

"Do you think they'll come back? Maybe they'll be back here with you tomorrow. For food."

"No. You see, I was just a branch they rested on for a moment. To catch their breath a while. They've long forgotten me."

344 · KARIN BRYNARD

"The tree you planted by her grave," said Harry, "what is it?"

"Camel thorn. It's the old man of the Kalahari. The wise man. Did you know, they can live for up to three hundred years?"

"It's a lovely gesture," Sara said and took their empty glasses inside.

In the cool, dim kitchen she filled a glass with water and downed it in one go. She wiped her chin and throat and filled it up again. She hadn't realised she was this thirsty. Must be all the emotion. There at Freddie's graveside. She hadn't prepared anything—unlike Dam with the poem and the tree and the birds he'd set free.

But it had happened then, when he'd set the eagle free. When the giant colossus of feathers and claws and power had risen weightlessly from Dam's hand, eclipsing the angry eye of the sun for a second and soaring heavenwards in a thunderous rush of wind. It had been at that moment that Sara had felt the shift.

A sudden, irresistible urge to break the silence of the past two years. It had caught her unawares, overwhelmed her. She must have spoken out loud, said Freddie's name. Whether the others had heard her, she still didn't know. Because it had been just her and Freddie there. Like it used to be. She wanted to thank Freddie. For helping her understand. Ever since she was a child. All the times she'd sat crying at night in front of Ma's closed bedroom door. Or beaten her head against the wall of Pa's impatience.

Freddie would explain, she would soothe by drawing pictures: Pa—bent double, dragging his broken heart behind him on a big, heavy chain. Or Ma—a swooning angel beside a butcher's block.

I know now, Sara had said to Freddie somewhere out there in the veld, I know what I must have looked like to you. A wounded cub snapping and snarling at everyone around her. I understand that now.

And I'm so sorry, Freddie, she'd added. And Freddie had smiled down on her. Sara had felt it in her bones, on her skin, all over her body.

For a good long while she'd stood there, eyes closed, in the blissful peace of reconciliation, redemption. She only became aware of the sun and the veld again when she'd heard the whoosh of the falcon's wings as Dam set her free too.

Sara rinsed the glass and turned it upside down on the drying rack.

Outside, Dam was explaining where he had gone to fetch the camel thorn.

"We'll have to keep it watered, I suppose," said Sara as she joined them again.

"It doesn't need rain. It's a desert tree. Its roots will find water forty metres deep. It can see, that tree. Very far. Into the future. And into the past. It knows everything—even before it happens—so it makes provision. The old people say it has second sight, because it predicts the drought. So," he lowered his voice, as if divulging a secret, "early in summer, if the tree produces extra pods, you know that a drought is on the way. Animals eat them, those pods. That's why it makes more than usual. And it's excellent food-value—more than a third protein."

"Jislaaik," said Harry, impressed. "But then we should be getting whole plantations going!"

"Ja, but a wild thing like that won't allow itself to be tamed into neat little rows."

"That's a little stupid—from a survival point of view, don't you think?"

"No. The old man is what he is. Mother, father, medicine man too. My ancestors could doctor anything by using the camel thorn tree—from fever to headaches and nosebleeds, diarrhoea. Anything." He tapped his pipe against his sole.

"She had a thing about those trees. Always said she wanted

to come back as a camel thorn. And now she's going to. That old man will soon go pick her up out of the ground, make her part of himself. That's how a person becomes a tree, I think."

Harry got up. "I think it's time for a glass of wine. Are you coming?"

"I'm just going to sit here a bit longer. It's been a long day."

Sara was about to leave too, but stopped. "Sad that Nelmari couldn't make it. Poor woman, must have been terrifying, the attack."

Dam took the pipe from his mouth. "You know, I wonder if she'd have come anyway, even if she could."

68

Beeslaar poured himself a drink and went to his back door for the umpteenth time to take a look at his garden.

Bulelani had cleaned it all up and seemed overwhelmed at the money Beeslaar pressed into his hand. But he wouldn't cooperate about going to see Yvonne Lambrechts, who had organised a place for him in the AIDS orphans' shelter in the township.

"It's only temporary, Inspector," she'd sighed. "The place is overcrowded as it is. We'll have to make another plan with your Bulelani."

But Bulelani wasn't having any of it. And he suddenly mustered quite a vocabulary to say so. He insisted on sleeping in Beeslaar's garage, even though Beeslaar had offered him a bath, food and a bed—in that order. The boy wouldn't budge.

He feared water and soap. He flatly refused to go near either. And he reeked—mostly of his rubbish-dump home. So Beeslaar gave up and hauled a foam mattress and an old sleeping bag from the house. Bulelani was happy then to promise, come tomorrow, he would go along to the lady from the soup kitchen. Beeslaar fed him and said goodnight, but had a strong feeling that the boy would be gone by first light.

He went back to his desk, where the Huilwater file lay open. He paged through it slowly, sipping his brandy.

De Kok had called earlier that evening to thank him for not collaring the jackal-catcher at the old lady's funeral. And to confirm that he was meeting the old man that night—hopefully he'd have information about the stock thieves by the next morning. The old guy evidently had plenty of information about the gang and their movements. He'd been keeping an eye on them for some time, and might just know where to sniff them out.

As Beeslaar slammed the file shut, he hoped to God he had his money on the right horse. Because otherwise he'd be well and truly in the shit.

A knock at the back door interrupted his train of thought, and he shuffled down the passage, drink in hand. It could be only one person.

And it was: Bulelani. Standing in the doorway with tears streaking his cheeks and blood on his mouth. Someone had attacked him at the café and taken his money.

ara was taking a cool bath when she heard the vehicle come to a halt.

She ducked her head under the water. When she surfaced, she heard men speaking. Harry and someone else, their voices trailing off to the front garden.

She sank down again. The water was blissful, a perfect temperature. The lapping as she stirred her limbs echoed sharply in the empty room. She had cleared it earlier in the week—an awful task. The shelves, the bathroom cupboard, the mirrored cabinet over the basin. She could hardly bear to touch Freddie's face creams. So personal, intimate, the thought of Freddie's fingers dipping and dabbing, the daily rituals. It had been as though she could suddenly smell Freddie again in that ghoulish house, amidst the oppressive silence and horrid atmosphere.

There had been the odd lipstick, though Freddie never really wore make-up. Still, she could see her pressing her lips together, the way their mother did after applying one of the flame reds she preferred.

And Klara's bath toys. She imagined the small brown body in the bath, butterfly hands splashing about with sponges, bright plastic playthings and a bubble-bath bottle. A hairbrush, the tangle of downy, golden frizz and Freddie's longer, lighter strands still stuck in it.

In the end she couldn't go through with it, just raked everything off shelves, windowsill, the edge of the bath, piling it all into cardboard boxes and carrying it out to the shed.

The front of the house she still kept shut. They only used the kitchen and the toilet. Tonight was a first for the bathroom—Sara was desperate to wash away the heat and dust and emotion of the day.

She took a sip of the wine Harry had poured her. He'd brought meat along, to braai after the funeral. But she had no appetite. Hopefully the wine would help.

Her thoughts wandered back to the sapling at Freddie's graveside. Today was the first time she'd visited Pa's grave. She hadn't had the courage. Or the inclination. A kind of punishment, perhaps. Yet who and what she'd wanted to punish no longer mattered.

It was over, all the bitterness, the rage.

She'd smiled as she looked at the spot where her father lay. Freddie's touch was there. A simple wooden cross that would weather and eventually disappear. In a hundred years, there'd be only Ouma and Oupa and Ma's cement headstones left. And Freddie's tree.

By the time she got out of the bath, the vehicle she'd heard was pulling away.

"That was Buks Hanekom," Harry said when she joined him. "Says he and his men are on patrol tonight. They'll be coming by here, we mustn't be concerned."

"What is it with those guys and their commando uniforms?"

Harry moved the grid over the flames to burn away the soot. "All I know is, that's one angry man. He gave me a long political tirade. Then told me how his best friend and the man's son were shot dead in a hijacking last year, right in front of him. Apparently the guy bled to death in his arms."

"Fuck, that's shocking."

"Yep, it's the kind of thing that drives some people over the edge. Anyway, he told me about their rally on Monday. Invited me along too."

"He's got a nerve. Especially if it's his lot that went around slandering Freddie because she took pity on the Griquas."

Dam came walking over with a dog on a leash. He wouldn't be joining them for supper, he said, explaining that the dog was Lammer's. He'd left him in the shed after the funeral— some sort of gesture, Dam supposed, to make up for having left, or because the other dogs had all been killed. Dam hoped they would look after him. He just wanted to be alone.

"What's his name?" Sara asked, tickling him under the jaw. Yellow eyes looked up appealingly as his crooked tail wagged stiffly, like an old windscreen wiper.

"Ag, his name is just Hond. He's an old dog, but he's a good dog," Dam said, then took his leave and disappeared into the night. Hond flopped down at Sara's feet.

They ate their meal, surrounded by the night-time sounds of the farm. They'd no sooner finished when the dog pricked up his ears and started barking. Only then did they see the headlights bouncing along the road, and hear the car rattling over the cattle grid before idling down the dip and turning into the yard.

Sara got up, the dog at her heels, wagging his crooked tail.

It was Boet Pretorius. He looked even worse than he had at the funeral service. His eyes were sunken, his cheeks hollow and dark with stubble.

He greeted them awkwardly, apologising for arriving so late and unannounced.

"I saw the lights," he said, slurring slightly.

Sara introduced him to Harry, then went to fetch the brandy and ice he requested when she'd offered him a drink.

When she got back, Harry was saying that he planned more articles—covering the Free State, Mpumalanga, KwaZulu-Natal and the Eastern Cape.

Boet sat fiddling with something, turning it over in his hand. When he put it down on the table to take his cigarettes from his pocket, Sara picked it up. It was a smooth river pebble.

"Freddie," said Boet. "She made it for me. Long time ago."

She shone a torch onto the pebble. The surface was covered with tiny outlines of animals—antelope with curved horns, giraffes, the angular heads of blue wildebeest. The lines were like skeins of a spider's silk. "Incredible," she said, "the most beautiful thing of Freddie's I've seen recently." Harry looked at the stone too, then Boet took it back and slipped it into his shirt pocket.

Sara looked at him uncomfortably. A wolf in sheep's clothing, Dam had called him. If it was true what he'd said about Boet's behaviour, she hoped he'd be on his way soon.

"Where's that foreman?" Boet demanded.

"Gone off to bed," Harry answered.

Boet muttered something, put his empty glass down.

Did he know about Dam and Freddie? It would have wounded him deeply—that she would choose a farm manager over someone like him. Enough to . . . ? She shivered.

"Is he going to stay on now, or what?"

"I don't know," Sara said.

"And you? You going to sell?"

"I'm not sure about that either."

"God," he groaned softly, "it's such a waste. She was such a unique person, you know? But of course you know. You grew up with her." Then he swung round to Harry. "Did *you* know her?"

The fire had died down, making Harry almost invisible as he answered no.

"If you could only see the way she took care of your father," said Boet. "So gentle. And he was difficult, hey. In the last days. The pain must have driven him crazy."

He paused, crunched on a piece of ice he'd taken from his glass. Sara couldn't quite make out his face in the dark. She could only see the blur of his big rugby player's knees.

"But that changed. She changed. At first she wanted to get

rid of everything. Asked me to start selling it all. Animals, tractors, the works. Next day, suddenly—no, she wasn't selling
after all. Started talking about theft and stuff."

"Ja? What theft?"

"The land, she was talking about the past, how people were
cheated of their land."

He crunched on another piece of ice.

"Well, whatever. But way back, when your dad was still
alive, I already told him I wanted to buy the land. And
Freddie, I didn't want to put pressure on her. You don't want
to pressurise someone when their father's so ill. So, I told her,
just take your time."

He went so quiet that Sara wondered whether he had fallen
asleep. Then she heard his chair creak.

"I would have paid her well. Water. That's what Huilwater's
got. Jissus, lots of it! Two, three fucking springs. That's the
fuckup with this area. I've got lots of land, five farms, but the
water, it's buried too deep. Like fucking gold reefs . . . " His
voice faded away again.

"Boet, listen, it's late." She really wanted him to go.

"Yes. I gave her a year to decide, but then she gave me—
what do you call it again?"

"Let's talk about this tomorrow, okay?" Sara said, but again
he interrupted her.

"First option, ja. But the next thing I knew, she changed her
mind. Just like that." He repeated this, slowly enunciating each
word, "Just like fucking that."

He picked up his glass, swirled an ice cube around in it.
"She said Klara needs to know her ancestors were respected
people—and not just a useless bunch of alkies. I told her. I
warned her. She must be careful. After all, she was an
Afrikaner woman! Whiter than Freddie, there's no one, I tell
you. And . . . " He fumbled for a cigarette, lit up and inhaled,
searching for the thread of his story. "And then when the new

manager got here, things were suddenly different. Before that we still," he hiccupped loudly. "Pardon." After a pause, he went on, "Freddie and I used to see each other quite a bit. And old Nelmari would also be around. Before things changed."

He suddenly stubbed out his cigarette, which crumpled in a white zigzag heap.

"Bitch!" he spat out the word. "She's poison, that woman. Poisonous bitch. She orders everyone around, tries to organise everyone's lives. Thinks she owns everything and everyone, can just come in here and take over everything—"

Sara held her breath. She had to get him to leave.

"She's the biggest control freak I've ever . . . Fucking freak. Full stop."

"Boet, it's late. We'll take you home."

"Giving the farm away to a hotnot," he mumbled. "That's what they're saying."

"Harry, are you awake?" she said to the darkness.

She heard him stir, and he switched on a torch.

"Bedtime, Boet," Harry said.

"Hey? Jissus, people, I'm drunk as a skunk, I think. Sorry, hey. Sorry."

He tried getting to his feet, but couldn't quite make it, tumbled onto his knees instead, landed on all fours, his head hanging down from his shoulders. He looked as if he was about to throw up.

"Sorry," he said again and hiccupped, his body sagging dangerously. Sara took a step towards him, trying to stop him from falling over.

"It was ter-ri-ble." He pronounced each syllable, and leaned against her. "Ter-ri-ble. That day, that day. Seeing her like that. And it's us. *Us*. My fault. Oh, God, I'm so sorry. It's my fault. Oh my God, I'm fucked!"

His huge shoulders started shaking.

At first Sara didn't know what to do, but then she crouched

down and put her arms around him. Over his shoulder, she stared at the dark farmhouse. It looked deathly, she thought. Already abandoned and empty and cold in the grey-blue glimmer of the night.

70

D eep in thought, Beeslaar whistled along to Vivaldi's *Four Seasons*—"Spring," he thought—floating in from the kitchen.

His day had started well, with a long walk. Then he checked on Bulelani, who'd left, as he'd expected, sleeping bag and all. But it wouldn't be long before he'd see the boy again, he suspected. He'd checked his new vegetable patch too, hoping to spot some green shoots. He chuckled at his over-optimistic impatience.

He'd just poured milk over his muesli when he heard a car pull up outside. He went to the front door and saw that journalist fellow from Cape Town getting out. Beeslaar went to the garden gate to meet him.

"I hope you don't mind me bothering you on a Sunday, Inspector," said Harry Van Zyl.

Beeslaar crossed his arms and frowned at the man. "Now's not the time for interviews, Mr. Van Zyl."

"Yes, I know. Actually I've come to tell you something."

"Ja, then go ahead."

The man glanced up at the sun, squinting his eyes against the glare. Then he looked at Beeslaar. "It's helluva hot out here."

"Oh, all right then, come in."

In the kitchen, Beeslaar sat down and reached for his bowl of cereal. "And so?" he said, taking a mouthful. The cheerful gambolling of the Vivaldi suddenly irritated him, but he didn't turn it down. He didn't want to give Van Zyl the opportunity to get too comfortable.

"I've just come from the bar."

Beeslaar looked at his watch, but didn't say anything.

The man smiled. "Actually, I wanted a coffee. Not that stuff you get at the Welkom Café—anyway, I've discovered the coffee's even worse at the pub."

"And now you want to lay a charge against the barman?" Beeslaar asked.

Harry laughed. "Actually, I bumped into a certain Mr. Pieterse there. Do you know him?"

Beeslaar's tongue worried at an oat flake that had wedged itself between a molar and his cheek. "Polla. Yes, I know the man. What about him?"

"I've been thinking . . . You know, we could be on the brink of another tragedy."

Beeslaar reached over to turn down the music.

"I know it sounds melodramatic, but since last night I've come across two people who're convinced that Dam De Kok is a murderer. And they're threatening to sort him out themselves, if the police won't."

"Oh yes? And Polla Pieterse is one of those people?"

"Yes, and Buks Hanekom too—last night. He was over at Huilwater—in his commando uniform, on patrol. Normally I wouldn't pay any attention. God knows, in my line of work, I meet a lot of bitter people, crime victims, and so on—I hear enough war talk as it is."

He looked at Beeslaar anxiously. "But these guys, it seems they've found a scapegoat. They might do something to him. I mean, after that baboon was killed at his house. And then the message on his front door—"

"So, did they say anything specific?"

"No, nothing you could really put your finger on. Both throwing around phrases like 'take action' and 'sort the thing out ourselves,' and stuff. But then they go on to actually state that De Kok is the mastermind behind the stock theft. And therefore behind the murders at Huilwater. You see? And I understand they've organised a rally for tomorrow, on Pieterse's farm."

Beeslaar got up to put his bowl in the sink, then turned around and crossed his arms.

"Now what exactly do you have in mind, Mr. Van Zyl?"

"Harry, please. I, er . . . Look, besides the fact that I don't think De Kok is a crook or a murderer, I don't want a bunch of bedonnerde farmers to get hold of him and do to him what they did to that baboon. That's really all I came tell you."

Beeslaar switched on the kettle. "Coffee?"

"Something cold, if you have it," he said, wryly explaining, "I don't think I'll be able to stomach coffee for a while."

Beeslaar took two cans of beer from the fridge.

"What makes you think that a bunch of bedonnerde farmers are behind the baboon thing? Something someone said?"

"No. But who else could it be?"

Beeslaar pulled the ring off his can and took a sip.

"I was at the museum on Friday," said Van Zyl. "I went to see which properties would have been eligible for expropriation if the Griquas' land claim had been approved."

"Ja? And why did you want to know that?"

"Journalistic curiosity?" he smiled. "Seriously, I wanted to understand why people were threatening Freddie. There was quite a bit of emotion surrounding the land claim. She'd had threats, and her friendship with Nelmari Viljoen—well, I suppose you wouldn't say it was actually *destroyed*. But clearly they'd had a falling out about something to do with the land claims. And Dam tells me he also had an argument with Freddie. Over the will—another land-related thing."

"Ja, that will," Beeslaar gave a snort. "You think it's worth the paper it's written on—that Adam De Kok really is the heir of Huilwater?"

"I think that's what Freddie intended, but I don't think the farm was hers to bequeath yet. Their father's estate hadn't been wound up. Anyway, the lawyer will be back this week, and then we'll know for sure."

Beeslaar's can was empty, but his mistrust of journalists was stronger than his thirst. To his relief, he saw that his visitor was getting up to leave—though not before asking him how many farmers he thought were part of Hanekom's resistance group.

"Enough, probably," said Beeslaar, "but still a minority in the district. Most of the people around here are pretty calm. Everyone's wary, frustrated by the situation, but not everyone thinks that Buks and his cronies are the solution."

71

Hond sat panting on the back seat of the car. The scrawny mutt was hardly a guard dog, but he did have heart. Already, he followed Sara everywhere, his crooked tail wagging every time she looked at him.

Sara made mental notes about the admin she needed to check before Oom Sybrand arrived. But she was also looking for an excuse to spend some time alone on the farm. Hoping to feel Freddie's presence, too, perhaps.

She thought she'd begin by washing the dishes from last night's dinner. It had been such a difficult day, especially ending as it did with Boet's drunken visit. Ignoring the lassitude that suddenly overcame her, Sara walked across to the pantry to find a new bottle of washing-up liquid.

Her eyes fell on a brightly painted wooden box. It was sitting in a dark corner of a shelf, almost hidden from view. For children's toys, perhaps, with those bright yellow fishes and red seaweed. She took it down, found it locked. She looked around, upended a row of empty flower pots beside it. She wasn't surprised when she heard a clink. A key. Inside the box was a square cake tin, a picture of a swan on the lid. Sara recognised it immediately: Freddie's old crayon tin. How had she missed all this stuff? She carried the box to the kitchen and sat down at the table.

A spiral-bound notebook lay on top of a pile of papers inside the tin. She took it out carefully, as though it might bite her if it were disturbed. She didn't open it. Later. It looked like a diary.

Underneath this were sheets of paper, envelopes, old birth-day cards, the invitation to Freddie's exhibition in Johannesburg, the first little signet ring Pa had bought her. She recognised the handwriting on one of the envelopes—her own.

It was *that* letter.

Cape Town, 24 July
Freddie,
Don't contact me when Pa dies. And he will die before his time if you deprive him of proper care. Let that be on your conscience.

It doesn't concern me any more—as you so clearly pointed out to me. You think you know what you're doing and I don't want any part of it, all your rituals and potions. This is the 21st century and you and Outanna are behaving like two medieval witches, do you realise that?

Sara

She folded the letter and put it back into the envelope. Two medieval witches. God, how cruel. And childish. How blinded by her own fear she had been, cutting herself off from the peo-ple she loved. Sorry, Outanna, for callling you a witch too.

Is that why Freddie painted herself with her hair chopped off? Isn't that what they did to witches in the Middle Ages? The Inquisition. Cut off their hair and paraded the poor women through the streets?

Sara felt an ache rising in her chest so fierce it took her breath away. If she could just cry properly for once. But it was as if her body was refusing to surrender, fearful of the grief that would overwhelm her.

She put the letter aside and looked through the rest of the papers. A small pencil sketch—a study of Klara's face. And a bundle of envelopes, bound with a rubber band. The envelopes were addressed to Freddie at Huilwater in small, tight handwriting. Inside each there was a single postcard—the Johannesburg skyline at sunset, rowers on Emmarentia Dam in the morning, the Rissik Street fountain with its leaping impalas.

The messages on the back were short and intense, signed with an "M."

> My little dove
> I'm dying without you. When are you coming back?
>
> M

The postmark on the envelope was July, two years ago, a month after Freddie had come to the farm. Who could "M" be?

She looked at the other postcards. "Went to G's exhibition. Excellent. But soulless. What do you dream about?" Several of them had just a single sentence: "You're forgetting me" or "Miserable without you" and "I'm coming, my lamb" and "You're playing hide-and-seek, hey?" Sara skimmed the messages. The last postcard in the pack showed a street lined with jacarandas. "Don't think you can just throw me away like this."

Whoever he was, the poor bugger was in a total state. Enough reason for Freddie to never want to go back.

Could it have been an infatuated teenager, from the last school where Freddie had taught? Or the guy from the bank, the one from way back? But that relationship was surely long over—even before Pa's illness. And this last while, when Freddie was staying with Nelmari? She couldn't remember her speaking of a boyfriend then. Maybe this was some kind of stalker.

Strange that Freddie had never mentioned it, and strange too that the postcards suddenly stopped after last February. Had her admirer suddenly lost interest? Found someone else to stalk? Or had Freddie just chucked out any further correspondence?

Inside a large brown envelope were a few pamphlets. She opened one and her heart lurched. "GENOCIDE!" it said.

White Farmer! Save yourself!

Commandos—last nail in the coffin of the White Farmer!

The White Farmer has become the main target of the Communist-inspired ANC government. "Kill the Boer, Kill the Farmer!" is the war cry of its campaign.

We're being disarmed, our security systems are being taken away!

2,800 Farmers have been killed already!

Wake up, White nation! We are being slaughtered as the world watches, no one is doing a thing to stop it!

We're being chased off our land by land claims and expropriation!

Come! Join us! We will defend ourselves!

Underneath the printed text, someone had written, "Traitors get shot!" And on another pamphlet, two handwritten Bible verses and a warning:

Rev. 22:15: Outside are the dogs, and sorcerers, and whoremongers, and murderers, and idolaters.

Rev. 20:9: And fire came down from God out of heaven, and devoured them.

You are next!

Sara flung the pamphlets onto the table. The vitriol seemed to scorch her fingers.

Poor, poor Freddie. How had these things reached her? Were they delivered here, to the house? Or posted? And by whom? Buks Hanekom and his cronies?

She'd have to go to Beeslaar, take all this stuff in to town.

But first she'd find Dam, show it to him. She left everything on the table and walked over to the house behind the trees, Hond trotting behind her.

Sara knocked, called out. She tried the door. It was unlocked, and she walked through the kitchen to the living room. Called out again.

She peered into his bedroom: the bed was made. She had the feeling that he hadn't slept in it at all. On a bedside table lay a small stack of books. The spine of one said *Livestock Farming*. On top were two slimmer volumes. She picked one up. *Heuning uit die swarthaak* by Donald W. Riekert. There was a slip of paper sticking out. She opened it.

It was the poem Dam had read at Freddie's graveside yesterday:

The Source

> The green water snake's tongue
> laps, for many years
> at the pale-grey dolomite
> till a shard of light
> shines into the cave
> and with the great rain
> a rivulet washes
> over rock and stone
>
> dousing the bushman's primal fire
> to smoke and ash
> the bushmen astounded
> by this water that is stronger
> than holy fire.

She slammed the book shut, suddenly aware that she was invading the man's privacy.

The dog was barking, she realised. And was she imagining it, or was there a car engine too? She walked back to the kitchen, stood still to listen. All was quiet, except for Hond's barking, growing louder, more frantic. Then she heard a car door slam shut, an engine starting up. She ran out the back door, over to the big house, but she was too late. A dust cloud hung over the yard. Whoever it was had left in a hurry. She glimpsed a bakkie turning onto the main road. Buks? Why would he run away like that?

She called after the dog, who had made a valiant attempt at racing after the vehicle. "Hond!"

What a ridiculous name.

When she got back to the kitchen, Freddie's tin was gone. Contents and all.

72

Cinnamon. A pale shade of cinnamon.

He couldn't make out the figure, but saw the colour. Then the head turned, looked directly at him. He saw a pair of eyes—slanted, wide-set. They were looking directly at him—a confident, inquisitive gaze.

It made him nervous. What was he supposed to do?

The eyes became dull, like dry mud. Then burst, fissures cracking open in them. They were the eyes of the child. The Huilwater child. "But I don't even know you," he wanted to say to her.

"You're too late again, Oom Polisieman," she whispered to him.

Beeslaar jerked awake. He had fallen asleep in a chair in his lounge. His neck had a crick in it and his shirt front was wet.

Ag, shit, man, he must have been drooling. He wiped his mouth, then yawned and stretched. His notebook tumbled from his lap. He'd been making notes after the journalist's visit. He phoned De Kok, but the bugger wasn't answering. He was supposed to phone today with information about the stock thieves.

Beeslaar went back to his notes, but in the end he just sat there doodling, his thoughts not focused on work at all.

They were focused on Gerda instead.

She had phoned him again.

"Is it also so hot over there?" she asked matter-of-factly, as if she were chatting to someone at the bus stop. But her voice sounded tired.

"Er, yes. It's hot, yes. Very hot." He hadn't known what else to say. Too afraid she'd put the phone down on him.

"It's hot here too. And noisy. I've moved, did I tell you?"

"Yes, you did. East Rand."

"I wanted to get closer to my parents."

"You said so, yes. Are you well?"

"There are so many hadedas here. At the dam. I live close to the Germiston Dam. They fly off early in the morning, right here over my flat, towards Joburg." She'd given a strained laugh. "I always wonder where they're going. I'm already awake by then. I'll be feeding the little one, and he always gets a fright at the racket they make. I think they're probably flying off to Zoo Lake. Or maybe fleeing. I wouldn't want to live round here either. Too ugly. God, Albertus, it's ugly around here, these days. The dam is full of litter, so dirty. Why is everything so dirty nowadays?"

"I don't know, Gerda. But tell me about yourself. Are you well?"

"I'm alive, Albertus." But she didn't sound entirely convinced.

"Are you seeing someone?"

"I . . . yes, there is someone."

It had given him a sudden jolt, the pain. *That* wasn't what he had meant. He'd just wanted to know whether she was seeing a psychologist.

"Its actually nothing serious. Just another lonely person. Nothing will come of it."

"That's good, Gerda. It helps one to move on." He tried not to sound like Dr. Phil.

"And are *you* moving on yet?"

More like to hell and gone, he'd wanted to say. But he'd just laughed and said, "No, hell, there isn't much company around here. It's a very small little place, this. My house is the only one in my street, to give you an example. And there are only about six streets. And I'm working pretty hard too."

A baby cried in the background. "Little piggy says it's feeding time," she said, her attempt at ending on a lighter note not wholly successful.

Afterwards he had kept thinking about her, wondering if it was just the Highveld heat, or whether she'd really become this weary, this dispirited.

The old Gerda was gone for good, that he could tell. That zest, her lust for life. He could sense the hopelessness. Kleinpiet didn't know it, but he had to keep a grown-up woman going, one little baby—all by himself.

Beeslaar leaned over to pick up his book, then noticed the movement.

Eight legs rushing at him at a furious pace.

He leapt from the chair and sprinted for the door.

He slammed it shut behind him and stood wheezing in the passage. God, he felt like a wimp. He shuddered, then locked the door. Just to be sure.

Suddenly, he missed the city litter, all those noisy hadedas.

73

First thing Monday morning, Beeslaar walked briskly to the co-op. It had just gone seven-thirty and the door was already open.

He still hadn't heard from De Kok, and he was beginning to have a bad feeling. But there were more pressing matters.

"Sjoe, but the inspector is up and about early!" Willie greeted him.

Willie and an assistant were standing in one of the aisles, packing nails and screws into brown-paper packets and sticking on prices.

"When will my doors be ready, Willie?"

"I worked all weekend, Inspector. All I still need to do is paint them."

"Painting can wait, Willie. When can you come hang them?"

"Lunchtime?"

"The sooner, the better." Beeslaar's cellphone chirped. He waved at Willie and walked out.

It was Jansie Boois. "I think you'd better come in. The whole world is looking for you."

"Oh, ja? Who?"

"The Moegel, for starters. And I think there was more stock theft last night. Ghaap is speaking to the man right now."

Jesus, just what he was waiting for. That bloody De Kok.

Beeslaar parked his car under the shade netting erected for the exclusive use of the superintendent. Everyone was under strict orders that the bay had to remain vacant for his visits. Bugger that, Beeslaar thought. For the first time in months his car was spick and span, inside and out. Thanks to Bulelani.

The boy had reappeared at the back door in the late afternoon yesterday, silent as a ghost. All eyes. Beeslaar had fried some eggs and heated two whole wheat rolls in the oven. A feast fit for a king.

But Bulelani had pulled the rolls out from under the eggs and handed them back to Beeslaar. "White bread."

Not a wish, but a command. As if Beeslaar was his personal chef who had forgotten, in a moment of senility, that Bulelani didn't eat bread made with pips and seeds. He had to swallow his urge to grab the plate back from Bulelani and send him packing, off back to—wherever.

Beeslaar strode down to his office, glared at a young constable who came trotting down the passage. The man jumped when he noticed Beeslaar, then slowed down to mumble a greeting.

What's this about, Beeslaar wondered, then hurried to answer the phone that was ringing in his office.

It was Harry Van Zyl, phoning from Huilwater.

"Dam De Kok is missing, Inspector."

"You sure?" Beeslaar felt white-hot annoyance washing over him. What a damn fool he'd been! Doing deals with bloody idiots he didn't even trust. "How long has he been gone?" said Beeslaar.

"Since Saturday night, we suspect. We last saw him just after the funeral out here on the farm."

"And you've looked everywhere?"

"He's not in town. But his bakkie is still here, keys and all. And none of the doors to his house are locked. I'm worried he might have been abducted, Inspector. And there was a theft here yesterday. A small thing, a tin full of bits and pieces, though I think some of it could be important—there were threatening letters."

Beeslaar noticed Ghaap hovering at the door. He beckoned to him to come in, and told Harry to wait on the farm. He would drive out there in the course of the morning.

"Where did they hit this time, the stock thieves?" he asked Ghaap before he could open his mouth.

"Yzerfontein, Peet Venter. He says his fence was cut at the koppie next to the road. About ten k from the entrance to Huilwater. They didn't take everything. He thinks the thieves were interrupted. The sheep are all over the show, so no easy tracks. But one of his men found blood next to the fence. And one of the workers says he heard shots in the night."

"Where's Pyl?"

"Er, he's here. He's busy doing stuff for the Moegel."

"What stuff?"

"Stuff he has to take through to Upington. Something the super told him to fetch from Nelmari Viljoen's office."

Beeslaar banged his desk as he leaned forward and hissed, "And we're in the middle of a *multiple* murder investigation here." He pulled the telephone towards him, asked Jansie to put him through to Upington, and told the Moegel's secretary he had to speak to the man urgently.

"Mogale," the deep voice oozed down the line and Beeslaar's stomach tightened.

"Superintendent, we definitely won't be able to drive to Upington for you today. We simply don't have the spare manpower."

"Ah, Inspector Beeslaar. I see you're back to dishing out orders to the darkies. But allow me to remind you—*I'm* not working for *you*. These days, it's the other way around."

"With respect, Superintendent, we have a suspect under arrest for a murder in the township last week, we had a stock theft incident last night which we've only just been informed of, one of our main witnesses in the farm murder has just disappeared, *and* we have a right-wing revolt brewing. It would be really difficult—I mean, we don't have a single man to spare."

"Inspector, last week you turned down any help from my side. I'm sure you'll get by. But what is this about a right-wing revolt?"

"It's a rally, on a farm."

"Who told you this?"

Beeslaar could hear the Moegel breathing down the line. He could probably smell the promotion already—the leather seats of his official BMW, COMMISSIONER MOGALE in gold lettering on his office door.

"Reliable source." He decided not to breathe a word about the fact that Van Zyl, a bloody *journalist*, was his source. "And I absolutely *have* to see Miss Viljoen. There's certain information pertaining to the murders on the farm twelve days ago that only she can help me with."

"You just leave Miss Viljoen in my hands for now."

"I simply have to speak to her, Superintendent."

"Listen, man, I'm busy with her. And that's why Sergeant Pyl is bringing me stuff. Don't you worry, I'm taking good care of her. And as you know, I'm a man of my word."

A pause—probably to give Beeslaar the opportunity to agree.

But Beeslaar kept stubbornly quiet.

"Well, then, don't let me keep you from your work any longer, Inspector!"

Beeslaar slammed the phone down.

"You know he's having a new house built at that fancy place of Ms Viljoen's?" asked Ghaap.

That explained a lot. But the big question was: What did Nelmari Viljoen expect to get out of all this?

"Come, we'll drive out to Yzerfontein without Pyl then. But

you'd better take a separate car, I want to swing by Huilwater
as well as Hanekom's farm afterwards. De Kok's gone AWOL."

"There's no extra car. Pyl's got the Golf," said Ghaap.

"Jesus, man! You'll just have to get the patrol bakkie from
the guys at the front desk. They can use bicycles in the meantime."

He got up, lifted a file as he looked around for his notebook. "Your Mister Motlogeloa found his tongue yet?"

"No, but I don't know how long I can keep him," said
Ghaap.

"You just keep him till his hair's gone white and he needs a
fucking Zimmerframe. Now, where the hell is my book?"

"Look in your drawer."

"It's *not* in my drawer. I specifically put it here," he said,
patting the files and papers on his desk.

"Look in your drawer. Maybe you just forgot."

Beeslaar went over to a steel cabinet and took out a new
notebook.

"It's a white BMW, I think," Ghaap said, "that we're looking for. Can't believe I haven't seen it yet—it's the kind of car
you can't miss."

"What are you talking about, man?" Beelaar picked up his
holster.

"The stranger, remember? The one I was talking about earlier, there at Mma Mokoena's shebeen? Yesterday I ran into the
old guy again, the one I had drinks with there. He's in my ma's
church, remember?"

Beeslaar felt like shaking the man. Not just to get to the
point, but because he dragged out . . . every . . . word . . . so
. . . slowly.

"Okay, so Mma Mokoena's boyfriend drives a white BMW.
Model? Registration number? Or am I expecting some kind of
miracle here?"

"Okay, what I *do* know is the boyfriend sounds really larney.

Ostrich-leather shoes and gold chains. Pays in rolls of notes, like a drug lord. Literally chucks the money on the floor when he pays. The old guy says he buys his beer by the crate and that little snot-nosed Motlogeloa helps him load it up."

"Jesus, Ghaap. And you've only *now* got this information? When you fucking suip at that bar night after night!"

He stopped when he saw Ghaap's face. Lowered his voice, continued in a monotone, "When we're done at Yzerfontein, you head for the township and find people who'll give a description and a registration number. Turn that auntie's she-been inside out—tell her she'd better talk to you, or get her fat arse arrested as an accomplice to murder. And get something on that car, anything we can use to identify it—soccer balls dangling from the rear-view mirror, a dent, a scrape, whatever the hell you can think of. Tinted windows, any damn thing. Then you call a colleague from Karos or Christiana, any of those dorpies, ask if they have anything on a car like that. See if you can find pictures—maybe youngsters who have taken selfies of themselves next to the car. You know the kind of thing. And if that guy is our link to the stock thieves, I'll personally give you a medal."

Ghaap's reaction was a single slow-motion blink.

"Right," said Beeslaar, "let's go—you grab the bakkie."

An emaciated yellow dog launched itself at Beeslaar, barking rabidly when he stopped under the blue gum and got out of his car.

"Voertsek!" he snapped and the dog skulked away, its twisted tail tucked between its legs.

Sara Swarts emerged from a door, shielding her eyes against the glare. Her face was pale under her dark hair.

"Come in," she called, "get out of this heat!"

"You here alone?"

"No, Harry came with me. He's trying to get my dad's old

bakkie going. It hasn't been switched on for a while, so the battery must be flat."

She looked as if her own battery was pretty flat too, he thought.

Sara held out a glass of cold water.

"Still no sign of De Kok?" He took a tentative sip of the water. Windmill champagne, my arse, he thought.

"No," she said, her eyes troubled. "I don't know what's going on."

"Whose dog is this?"

"Lammer's. He left him here for Dam—on Saturday, after the funeral." She looked at the dog, who was now sitting beside the fridge as if he were guarding some treasure.

"And the old guy? Where's he?"

"Oom Sak? In town. He's visiting family. I think he got a dreadful fright, from the baboon thing. Inspector, do you think something happened to Dam? Do you think it could be Buks and his guys?"

"I'm planning to find out, Miss Swarts. Now, can you tell me about those threatening letters?"

She filled him in on the pamphlets with the Bible verses.

"And there were just two?"

"No, I think there were more. I only read two of them."

"And you say it's a white bakkie you saw afterwards, a Toyota Hilux, like the one Hanekom drives?"

"I think so. He's been dropping by all the time. He says it's to check if everything's all right and that he's just patrolling. He must have done so yesterday too. Just his luck I wasn't in the house when he arrived. He was probably looking for those very things when I caught him in the kitchen last time."

Beeslaar thought for a moment, then said, "Your sister's paintings—may I take another look?"

She got up and he followed her to the studio where several paintings were propped against the walls. The mantis painting was still on the easel. He studied it closely, then walked around to look at the others. There was a painting of an elderly couple at a dinner table, knives and forks in their hands. He recognised the two, an old Griqua chief and his wife. The tablecloth showed a landscape of thorn trees, tufts of grass and sand.

There were also a number of self-portraits—one of Freddie with a plant growing from her stomach. Another of her naked, being smothered by a rambling rose with sharp thorns. In another she was a bride, standing beside a church in a long bridal veil. The bride was as tall as the church tower itself, a flock of white doves hovering around her head. At her feet, a number of tiny soldiers were shooting at the doves. Blood had spattered the bride's gown.

Sara turned around anxiously as Harry rushed into the room.

"There's been another stock theft, and some shooting too."

Sara blanched, said breathlessly, "Inspector, you have to tell us—is it locals helping the thieves?"

"Without a doubt. They know exactly where to hit. But you'll have to excuse me. I have to go."

In the kitchen, Sara flopped down at the table and the dog put his head on her lap. She stroked his ears, scratched the underside of his chin, and his crooked tail gave a contented wag.

Harry walked Beeslaar out. "De Kok—did he say anything when you saw him on Saturday night?"

"It was a tough day for everyone. But especially for him, I think. It was only when we buried her that I realised how attached he'd been to Freddie, how deep their relationship went. He didn't want to eat with us, said he was tired, wanted to go to bed. Do you think something's happened to him?"

Beeslaar considered his answer. In truth, the possibilities were grim. If De Kok had tricked him this weekend, he might just as well pack his bags, clear his desk, and make way for

Lobatse. But if Van Zyl was right, and that bunch of ridiculous right-wingers had come to get De Kok, things would get messy. That's for bloody sure.

But aloud, he simply said, "Let me know the moment you hear anything from him."

He was just about to get into the car when Sara came running out.

"Inspector," she called, "You're needed in town, urgently. There's been *another* murder!"

74

A crowd had already gathered in Winnie Mandela Street when Beeslaar arrived at Mma Mokoena's shebeen.

They opened up to let him pass to where a bewildered Ghaap stood surrounded by a cluster of people, all talking and gesturing at the same time. He broke away when he saw Beeslaar.

A little way off, just outside the door to the shebeen, a body lay under a blanket, a dark stain seeping from it. People watched wide-eyed, while skinny dogs sniffed around. One that came too close was chased off with a kick.

"Jissus, I was just too late," said Ghaap. "She was still alive just before I got here. People say it's that little kak Thabang Motlogeloa's bossman who did the job. They saw him speeding away in his BMW."

"Come, Ghaap." Beeslaar touched his shoulder. "Let's get all the people away from here. Everyone! Go make them stand behind the fence. This is a murder scene now. And find out if anyone got a registration number. We have to start looking for that BMW immediately."

Beeslaar crouched next to the body and lifted the blanket. She was lying on her back, a towel and what looked like dishcloths at her throat. He took out his pen, tried to lift the cloths. They were heavy with blood, but he could glimpse the gaping wound beneath. Her throat had been cut. He heard Ghaap telling the people to remain calm, to leave Mma Mokoena's yard and wait behind the fence. He spoke to them in formal Afrikaans, his voice hoarse.

Beeslaar got up and walked over to Ghaap. The man had aged ten years in one morning, he thought as he got closer. Mma Mokoena's was pretty much his second home.

"There's nothing you could have done, okay? But we *can* find the fucker who killed her. So, get hold of Constable Kgomotse so long and tell her to get everyone on the job. And she needs to phone the other stations and tell them to be on the lookout for that car—tell them the man is a suspect in various murder cases and must be apprehended immediately."

Ghaap raised his head, took out his cellphone and started calling.

Beeslaar returned to Mma Mokoena's body and surveyed the scene. Her murderer had either been desperate or incredibly arrogant—slitting her throat in broad daylight like this, and just about on the street too. Her blood lay pooled in a wide arc on the neatly raked earth.

When Beeslaar looked up Ghaap was talking to an old fellow by the fence. He walked over to them.

"This is my ma's friend from church," Ghaap said, "the one I've been telling you about. He lives nearby, he was one of the first people on the scene. And he's confirmed it was the man in the BMW. He saw the car speeding away and then heard the screams coming from the shebeen. When he got here, Mma Mokoena was already lying on the ground."

"Could you see a registration plate on the BMW, Meneer?" said Beeslaar.

"Well, I wasn't really looking at that. But it's a dangerous guy, that one. Always carrying a knife."

"Ja? How's that, Meneer?"

"See, he's always coming here, nè, ordering whole cases of beer. And not cans either, had to be quarts—those long bottles, nè. Six cases at a time. This time the auntie said, no ways, he should go buy in town, she didn't have enough. Then he pulled out the knife and said he didn't buy from mlungu dogs—askiestog, Inspector," the man said apologetically, "that's not my words."

"How many times did you see him here, Meneer?"

"Just a few times. Two, maybe three."

"When was that?"

"Oh, long ago. First time was probably, where are we now? Maybe November of last year? And the other time now, two weeks ago, or so."

"Please try to remember exactly."

"No, how can I say, now. Monday, no . . . Or yes. Last Monday. He had that little skollie with him, the one that don-nered Ghaap. That time, he called the Mma over and ordered her to bring the boy some meat. She brought out a plate of pap en vleis, but the man smacked it out of her hands. Then he told her to pick it up again—and when she was bending over to do that, he stuck the blade right under her eye and said he asked for *meat*, not this dog food. Just like that!" He pushed his index finger underneath one eye, nearly popping his eyeball out of its socket.

Beeslaar clenched his teeth: damn Ghaap! Here he is, drinking with the old guy, but the whole time he's sitting on his damned ears.

"What time was he here last Monday?"

"Ag, around five or so. They weren't here long, they then left together. In a bakkie that time, the one the man used to load up the drink."

"What kind of bakkie, and did you see number plates?"

"No, I think an Isuzu, North-West plates. The BMW is from Gauteng. But don't ask me numbers."

Beeslaar thanked him, told him not to leave: Ghaap would come and get a description of the man with the knife. Then he walked over to the shebeen, past Mma Mokoena's body, to where Shoes Morotse was waiting for him. Together, they walked inside.

The whole structure was made of corrugated iron, neatly cobbled together. The windows had wooden frames—one in each of the four walls of the big bar area. White plastic tables and chairs dotted the room, and rows of upside-down beer crates lined the walls as extra seating. In one corner a large TV set was suspended from a metal arm. It was flashing infomercials, the reception snowy and the sound turned low.

A middle-aged woman sat at one of the tables, an empty coffee mug in one hand and a scrunched-up handkerchief in the other. Shoes introduced her as Mma Lerathu Ramahole, the cleaner, and explained she'd been there at the time of the murder.

"I was here—inside," she confirmed, "then I hear that man, he's outside. He calls Antie Dollie out, he says he's looking for that boy. Then she says, no, he is too late. The police came, took him away. Then, that man, he got very very angry. He shouted she's a—a—moerskont. Lots of very very bad things, he says to her. She says he must voertsek, she doesn't want any more tsotsis here. And then . . . "

She put the handkerchief to her nose, gave a sob and blew loudly.

"The man, he said Antie Dollie must bring beer and medicine things."

"Medicine?" Beeslaar's heart pounded—the blood at the Yzerfontein fence?

"Plasters and medicine stuff. Antie Dollie said he must just voertsek. I went to the window to look. Oh, God, baas. That man. He's messed up, blood on his head. Everywhere. On his shirt, everything. And he's sitting in the front there, in the yard. He had the knife out. But Antie Dollie, she wasn't scared of him. She said he . . . " her voice faltered, "he must just fokkof, if the police find him here, they lock him up. Thabang, he's already there, he's been sitting with them since Thursday. But the man won't go. He wants to know what Antie Dollie said to the police about him. But she just laughed, she said she told the police everything. That his ma, she's a hoer. Antie Dollie, she was very angry, but she wasn't scared."

Mma Ramahole cleared her throat, continued, "He said she's lying, there's nothing she can tell the boere. Then he said he's not a whore's child. He's—I don't know, because then I just saw blood, and that man running away and, and . . . Antie Dollie lying on the ground!"

75

S ara stopped at the entrance to Boet Pretorius's farm. It looked more like a prison than a luxury game lodge, she thought, as she leaned out of the window to buzz the intercom.

Harry had managed to get the Huilwater bakkie going, and she'd taken it for a drive to charge the battery, though she wanted to speak to the neighbours anyway, find out whether they'd heard or seen anything of Dam. She'd already dropped in at Roger Heidenrich's and the Matthees'. On her way back she drove past Karrikamma again. This time she decided to stop after all. Wouldn't hurt to ask, though she couldn't help feeling nervous, especially after Boet's antics on Saturday night.

"Ja? Can I help you?" a voice came over the intercom.

"Boet, good morning. Can I ask you something? I won't be long."

"Sara? Right, come in!"

The big gate swung open and she drove through jerkily as her foot struggled to reach the clutch pedal.

The farmhouse was some distance from the main road, nearly five kilometres. It was surprisingly beautiful. Had it always been here? She certainly didn't remember it from her childhood.

In front of the wide fanned steps that led up to the stoep, a fish pond with a fountain welcomed the visitor. But no water sprayed from the fountain, and the pool, she saw, needed a good cleaning. She walked up the polished red steps, and stopped when Boet Pretorius appeared in the dark rectangle of the doorway.

"Jeez, Boet, are you ill?"

His eyes looked vacant and bloodshot, like those of an old dagga smoker. He was wearing a crumpled T-shirt and boxer shorts. His hair was lank and oily, and he hadn't yet shaved.

"Just a bit hungover," he mumbled apologetically. "Come take a seat so long, I'll just get changed quickly."

Sara sat down on a cane chair and looked around the verandah. A side table stood to her left, its legs fashioned from gemsbok horns. On it was an ashtray of thick, heavy glass. Next to this lay Freddie's pebble. She picked it up. In daylight the decoration was even more lovely.

"Sorry to keep you waiting," Boet said as he walked out of the house.

He came over and stood leaning against a pillar in front of her.

"So, to what do I owe this honour?" He'd made an attempt at combing his hair, she saw, and was wearing a crisp shirt and khaki shorts. But he didn't look any better for it.

"I . . . well I was wondering if Dam had maybe come by."

"You mean *here*?"

"He's not at home, he's just vanished. We're worried about him. It's not like him."

"Ja, that's quite a problem. I assume there's nobody now to take care of things?"

"Exactly."

"Well, I could send someone over. My foreman. He knows his way around your place. He's been there with me a few times. His name is Piet September."

"That's kind of you—I could just wait for him?"

"I'll get someone to call him," he said and disappeared back into the house.

She heard talking inside, and moments later he was back.

"Piet and another man are on their way." He remained standing, his hip against the pillar.

"Did you hear about the stock theft last night?" she asked.

"No. What happened?"

She filled him in on the details. "The police came over this morning, they'll probably be paying you a visit too."

"I bet they will. But you know, we never really had stock theft around here—not on this scale. Not until De Kok arrived." His voice was agitated. "He's the only person who'd be able to move around among the farm workers in the district without anyone asking questions, you know?"

"You mean at Huilwater? Like you said the other night?"

He scratched at the stubble on his chin. "Listen, I can't remember all the things I said the other night. I was drunk. Sorry."

It was a rather half-hearted apology, but Sara didn't say anything. Instead she got up. "Do you think Piet's on his way yet? I could maybe come back this afternoon."

Brusquely, he gestured to her to wait and walked inside again. He called out sharply from the back door.

Sara was annoyed with herself for coming out here after all. All she wanted now was to leave. Hearing his footsteps on the floorboards, she moved towards the steps.

Just then a young man in dark-blue overalls came around the corner of the house. Piet September, Sara guessed. He glanced to where the farmer was standing on the stoep, then took off his hat and greeted Sara. But he barely looked at her, as his eyes flicked back to his employer.

"Where's Sipho?" Pretorius demanded.

"He can't come, Meneer." He shuffled his feet and said, "Miss, excuse me, Miss, but I just need to talk to Meneer Boet."

Pretorius leapt over the stoep wall and landed halfway down the steps. The young man lurched back, fear on his face.

"Are you going to get on the back of that bakkie yourself, or must I help you?" His hands were clenched into fists.

"Sorry, Meneer," September said, taking a step back. "But—"

"Sara, you go start the bakkie so long. He'll be there in a moment." Then he sprang down the remaining steps and grabbed at the young man, who jerked free and took a couple of long paces backwards.

"Please, Meneer. There's police at that place!"

"Shut your fucking mouth!" Pretorius screamed, lunging at him.

"Boet!" Sara rushed forward.

"Go get into the bakkie!" he yelled, then turned back to face the young man. "And *you*!"

"Please, Baas Boet!" he pleaded. "The police are there all day long, I—"

Pretorius hit him in the face. Someone shrieked from the front door—a middle-aged woman wearing an apron, who rushed out towards them. She grabbed hold of the burly farmer and pulled him away. Pretorius let go and stepped back, panting.

Sara walked briskly to the bakkie. Behind her she heard more shouting, the woman yelling at Boet, screaming at the young man to go to the kitchen.

She turned the ignition, and the bakkie kicked into life. She stepped on the accelerator, hard, desperate to get the hell out of there.

76

Beeslaar put Ghaap in charge of the Mokoena case. It would do him good. Give him the opportunity to make up for his shoddy detective work so far. In the meantime, he himself would take care of Buks Hanekom and his brave bunch of boere today.

Beeslaar slowed the car when he saw the Wag-'n-Bietjie sign, and turned off. There was no gate, just a cattle grid. He shook his head—and yet they're all so worked up about security.

He drove some distance before spotting the farmhouse—a simple brick home with a weatherbeaten roof of red corrugated iron, blue gum trees, outbuildings, windmills.

He stopped under a thorn tree and got out. A geriatric Labrador lumbered towards him, giving a lazy wag of its tail and a couple of compulsory woofs.

Beeslaar patted the dog's head, looked around for signs of life. But the house was quiet. Behind a screen door, the front door stood open. Potted ferns were scattered on the stoep, together with an assortment of sagging chairs. It was a picture of old-time rural idyll, peace, innocence.

Were these the kinds of people who'd stockpile automatic rifles and send death threats to a naïve do-gooder like Freddie Swarts?

A grey-haired man appeared from round the back of the house. He had a greasy cloth in his hands, and was rubbing something vigorously with it.

"Afternoon, Oom!"

"My goodness, Inspector! Welcome, welcome."

Bossie Hanekom wiped his hand on his trousers before offering it to Beeslaar.

"I'm actually looking for Buks, Oom."

"Oh, Inspector. The guy's like the wind, nè. He's so busy these days, I just about have to make an appointment to see him." The old man's smile revealed a too-perfect row of false teeth.

"Oom, can I sit down? I'm here in my official capacity."

Oom Bossie hesitated a moment, then gestured towards the stoep.

He'd been tinkering with a broken pump, he explained, holding a metal part up for Beeslaar to see.

"Right. Oom Bossie, I'm really worried about Buks's—well, his political activities."

"But what on earth are you talking about, Inspector?"

"Oom, I'm afraid Buks and his commando are getting mixed up with dangerous things."

"But belonging to a group of concerned farmers surely isn't against the law now, is it, Inspector?"

"Oom, Freddie Swarts, who was murdered at Huilwater last week. She received death threats from Buks and his friends. Shortly before she was killed."

The older man removed his spectacles and wiped his eyes. Then he replaced them carefully and studied Beeslaar closely. His eyes were a faded blue, but there was still fight in them. "That's a serious allegation, Inspector."

"Issuing death threats against someone *is* serious, Mr. Hanekom. And it wasn't just Freddie Swarts who was threatened. I have reason to believe her farm manager was threatened too. She and her daughter were killed, and now her manager has disappeared. These are serious matters."

"And what proof do you have?" There was an edge to his tone.

"I'm not at liberty to discuss that. But what I can say, is: I have a witness to connect Buks to housebreaking and theft— and also with plans for people to take the law into their own hands. Possibly having done so already. Are you aware of any of this?"

The old man's jaw moved from side to side as he ground his teeth.

"I'd like an answer, please."

"Look, I don't know what he does all day and every day. He came back here to take over the farming business. I'm getting too old. We have our differences about how things should be done, and I'd believe a lot of things about Buks. But *murder*?"

"Did he put the farm on the market with Nelmari Viljoen?"

"What? Where did you hear that?"

"It doesn't matter, Oom. Is it true?"

"This farm isn't for sale, Inspector. It's all I have to pass on to my son. Buks is our only . . . But Freddie . . . " his look of dismay had hardened into something fiercer, his jaw jutting stubbornly. "She really upset people, the way she carried on."

"Would you also have been affected by a land claim?"

"No. That land, it's over on that side." He pointed with an oil-smeared finger. "But the thing is, nobody really wants that kind of squatting right next door. Everyone knows where things then start heading, no?" He gazed at Beeslaar, seeking agreement. When none came, he continued, "Just look at the bunch of Bushmen around here, the lot from Namibia who got given land after the Bush War. Look at the squalor they're sitting in over there! I don't stick my nose into politics. I've had enough of it, politicians trying to screw us over. The old lot as well as this new bunch. But as God is my witness, at least the old lot robbed us more subtly."

"And that's reason enough for your son and his sidekicks to send death threats to a defenceless woman?"

"Look, Inspector. My son would never do something like

that. And God knows, he's got reason enough to be angry. His best friend was killed in a hijacking. Died in Buks's arms. His little boy, too."

"That's bad, really bad. But still."

"He's never been the same since, Inspector. That's the reason he came back to the farm. He just wasn't coping, his work was suffering. And he's never really recovered from it, even now."

"What job did he do?"

"Admin for a security company up there. He and his friend had worked there together."

"Does he still have ties with the company?"

"Why would you want to know that?"

"I want to know who supplies him with his weapons. What is the name of the company?"

"You're treading on thin ice, Inspector. I'd believe many things about my son. But murder? And illegal weapons? No, man."

"And pamphlets calling on people to take up arms? Freddie Swarts was threatened with pamphlets like that—with quotations from the Bible about the destruction of whores, that kind of thing. And soon afterwards, she and her four-year-old daughter were slaughtered like animals."

The old man gave Beeslaar a shocked look.

"Inspector, we're decent people. Really. I raised that boy well. The things you've described . . . Lord, never!"

"Where was Buks last Tuesday night, Oom? Did he spend the night here? And yesterday morning between ten and eleven o'clock?"

The old man's skin was grey. "I don't know," he mumbled.

"He wasn't on the farm?"

"I can't remember last Tuesday. He's often—well, sometimes he stays out all night. Stays over with a friend. And yesterday, my wife and I were at church in town. The NG church.

He wasn't with us. We came back around twelve, half past twelve. But why do you want to know this?"

"Those pamphlets, with the threats—they were stolen from Freddie Swarts's house yesterday. Her sister saw your son driving away. And Tuesday night your son went and stole Oom Hannes and Tannie Debora Botha's old pet baboon. He hacked off its hands and tied the creature to De Kok's gate, where he slit its throat and then wrote a warning on the front door in blood. If you'd like to help Buks, we have to stop him before he harms any more people."

The old man sat there, defeated. Then he got up.

"Come, I'll go show you his office," he said as he shuffled off.

77

Sara floored the accelerator, but the old bakkie just chugged along. Cresting the rise before the Huilwater turn-off, she glimpsed another bakkie at the gate. It was Dam's. He must have returned while she was over at that crazy Pretorius bastard's place.

She stopped at the gate, climbed out.

"Dam?" She stepped closer. Someone was in the passenger side of the cab, apparently asleep against the window. It was Dam. She ran up to the door, then stopped. She stifled an urge to scream as she turned the handle and Dam's body slumped sideways, limp and almost naked. She grabbed at his torso, trying to prevent him from falling to the ground. He was heavy. Too heavy for her. She tried to wedge herself underneath him, cradling his head and shoulders as they flopped into her lap, his legs still half inside the bakkie.

"Dam!" He didn't answer. His hair was covered in dust, matted with tiny acacia leaves and twigs, cuts and scratches all over his body. He looked as if he'd been dragged through a haak-en-steekbos. A bloodied bandage was wrapped around his chest.

"Dam! Jesus, man." She patted his cheeks, but he didn't react. She put her ear to his nostrils, heard a light rattle from his chest. "For God's sake, Dam," she whispered as she dragged his legs out of the bakkie and settled him on the ground.

She turned him on his side. Panic rose in her throat as the

bandage shifted, revealing an ugly wound and a steady trickle of blood. He gave a loud moan as she repositioned the bandage.

Sara jumped up and shouted for help, remembered there was no one left on the farm, and took her cellphone from her pocket.

No reception. She'd have to run—to Huilwater, to get to the landline, or along the main road till she got a signal on a rise.

But she didn't dare leave Dam like this. She leaned over him, holding her hands over his face to shield him from the sun.

"Dam!" she said as he moaned again. "Can you hear me?"

"Go, go away." His breath was shallow as the words seemed to surface through his delirium. "Leave . . . farm, go away, go."

"Dam, I'm going to get help. I'll be back."

"No," he wheezed, eyelids fluttering.

"Dam?" Why were his eyes so dull? And his skin was so clammy, his face covered in scrapes and bruises. She had to get him to a hospital in Upington—and fast.

She wedged her arms under his torso, and with a rush of adrenaline propped him up against the side of the bakkie. Then she squeezed herself behind him and took him by the waist, heaved and lifted and collapsed onto the seat under him. He was halfway in, his legs still hanging outside.

He howled as she wriggled out from under him and slid across to the driver's seat from where she pulled him further inside. There was so much blood on the seat that she could literally slide him in until his legs were inside the cab. She tried to fix the bandage, making sure that the poultice covering the wound was in position.

She turned the key in the ignition, and had driven some distance before she came to her senses. Her cellphone still showed no signal. She looked at the body on the seat beside her.

"You'd better pray, Dam," she yelled over the noise of the

engine, "for God's sake, don't just fucking lie there bleeding. Pray!"

Sara gripped the steering wheel as she tried to avoid the worst of the corrugations, slowing down only when she reached the stormwater humps that ran diagonally across the road. Children's graves, she grimly remembered, that's what they used to call them.

Thoughts jolted through her head: was Dam somehow caught up in last night's robbery, how did he get so hurt? The shooting Harry had mentioned. Had Dam come back to fetch his bakkie—but when? It had been there yesterday morning, keys in the ignition—she'd seen it, she and Harry both.

And why the hell was he wearing a leather loincloth over his underpants?

The black line of the tar road became visible. A signal at last. She dialled Harry's number. It didn't ring, just beeped. No network.

Where the fuck was he? Who else could she call? Beeslaar? And get Dam arrested? No way. She'd get him to a hospital first, then decide what to do. She couldn't think any more, but she knew she had to drive, and fast. She hit the accelerator the moment she was on the tar—but the bakkie was as unresponsive as ever.

Dammit, Dam, what have you got us into?

78

It had been a hasty affair, the search of Buks Hanekom's back-room office, but Beeslaar nevertheless made some useful finds. One of which had been the cake tin containing Freddie Swarts's letters and papers. And the other a laptop, which Beeslaar had carried out to his car. Old Mr. Hanekom offered half-hearted resistance, with Beeslaar realising he was on thin ice—no search warrant, and all. But there was much at stake and no time to bugger around waiting for a signature.

The older man had watched in silence throughout the search, holding his wife's hand as they stood to one side. With a dishcloth in her other hand, Buks's mother had gazed around the room as if she were seeing it for the first time, her eyes frightened and unsure. The walls were covered in slogans and posters of Boer heroes, and there was one of a khaki-clad Bok van Blerk no doubt belting out "De la Rey," rousing the spirit of the old general.

Before he'd left, Beeslaar phoned the office. There had still been no registration number for the BMW, but Ghaap swore he'd wangle it out of Motlogeloa, if it was the last thing he did. And Beeslaar had told him they needed to sort out the warrants—he was on his way to Polla Pieterse's farm, in search of De Kok.

"Did you find anything at Hanekom's place?" Ghaap had wanted to know.

"More than enough. I'll tell you later. But you better tell your ma you won't be coming home tonight!"

Oom Bossie had been waiting outside on the porch.

"Inspector, is our Buks in a lot of trouble?"

"I think he might be, Oom."

Then the old man wouldn't stop talking. Nothing left of his earlier defiance. "God knows, we didn't raise that child to threaten defenceless women. We knew Freddie's father very well. He was a good man. I don't know what's got into that child of ours. But it's like I said, he changed in Joburg, after what happened to his friend."

Beeslaar watched as the two defeated figures receded in his rear-view mirror. The old woman with her untidy bun and faded floral dress and the old man in his overalls and velskoene. Together they stood in front of the house, watching as a police officer drove off with their son's shame in the boot of his car. They must surely have long been uneasy about that son of theirs, and what he was up to, thought Beeslaar. More than uneasy. Otherwise they'd have been far firmer in defence of him today.

It took him nearly half an hour to find the road to Pieterse's farm. What a hell of a deserted corner of the world this was. In the past half an hour he had passed just one other vehicle—a donkey cart. How then, was it possible to miss a couple of big trucks carrying sheep? Or a white BMW with a black guy behind the wheel?

But he did at least have a hunch about where they'd all disappeared to so mysteriously. A hunch that De Kok would hopefully be able to confirm—if they found him alive.

Some distance on, he saw the antique plough that marked the entrance to Pieterse's farm, Volop. There was another car, Beeslaar saw, parked outside the farm gate. Harry Van Zyl was standing with the passenger door open, leaning his elbows on the roof. He looked around when Beeslaar pulled up behind him.

The gate was shut, and an old Ford bakkie was parked inside. A pudgy sunburnt boy sat on the bonnet, a gun resting across his knees. He slid forward and stood up, his feet planted on the bull bar mounted on the front of the vehicle. "Afternoon, Oom," he called. "Does Oom know the password?"

Beeslaar squinted into the sun, cocked his head by way of reply.

The boy hopped off the bakkie and walked closer to the gate, rifle slung over his shoulder.

"Is that thing loaded, boet?" asked Beeslaar.

"Oom, I can't let anyone in without the password."

Van Zyl interjected, "Well, *I've* been invited."

The boy's jaw set and his brow creased, but his attempt at fierceness failed. He seemed barely sixteen and wore rubber flip-flops, with a sun-bleached shirt tucked into a pair of rugby shorts. Farm boy. Brown curly hair sticking out from under a baseball cap, with a downy beard glinting on his pimply chin.

A pup, thought Beeslaar, but a nervous pup with a shotgun in his hand, all the same.

"Police," Beeslaar said sternly. "Drop your weapon and move your vehicle out of the way."

The boy's mouth gaped. He licked his lips nervously, but didn't move. "This is private land, Oom. And there's a private meeting going on. Sorry, Oom."

With the back of his hand, Beeslaar wiped away the sweat on his forehead. "I'm going to tell you just one more time to drop that rifle, and then I'm coming in to get you *and* that gun of yours. You understand me?"

"Ja, Oom, but my dad said no one can go through without the password."

Beeslaar looked at Van Zyl, who was observing the confrontation with interest. "Get inside your car," he told him. "You could get hurt this afternoon."

Beeslaar walked purposefully towards the gate. This is ridiculous, he thought. He felt like Clint Eastwood in a Bugs Bunny cartoon.

With each step Beeslaar took, the boy took a step backwards, his eyes trained on the advancing man, his cheeks reddening. The moment Beeslaar touched the gate, he jerked the rifle up and took aim.

"*Drop* that thing, man!"

The boy stood his ground, gun trained on Beeslaar.

"I'm going to count to three, and then you drop it, okay?" said Beeslaar as he lifted the chain from its hook.

"No!" the boy shouted, and fired a deafening shot.

When Beeslaar opened his eyes he saw the boy lying on the ground. He must have fired a shot into the air, with the recoil jerking him off-balance. Beeslaar flung open the gate, rushed over to him and tugged the rifle from his hands. He threw it aside, then patted the boy down for other weapons.

The boy moaned.

Beeslaar noticed the bruised collarbone, probing it lightly. Nothing broken, it seemed, and helped him up. When he squawked again, Beeslaar said, "Ag, stop that, man." He'd nearly had a heart attack himself. "If you'd listened to me in the first place, you wouldn't be in this shit now!"

He led the boy back to his car, picking up the shotgun on the way. The boy waddled along, whimpering.

Back at the car Beeslaar took out his handcuffs. He gave the collarbone another swift inspection. Definitely just a bruise, he decided, then cuffed the boy's hands in front of him and helped him into the back seat.

"Please, Oom. My shoulder—"

"Shut up, boytjie! I don't want to hear another peep out of you."

Beeslaar took out his cellphone, and was relieved to see the signal strength was three bars. He called Ghaap, who said he was on his way.

Well then, he'd have to wait. He certainly wouldn't be going onto the farm without backup. He sat with one butt cheek on the bonnet and watched as a cloud of dust approached from the direction of the Pieterse farmhouse.

Van Zyl sauntered over and peered at the boy, who was bravely gritting his teeth but unable to suppress his tears. They left furrows in the dust on his cheeks.

"Is the child okay?" he asked.

"Ja. He'll live."

"Are you going to charge him?"

"For sure, man! He pointed a firearm, for starters. At a policeman. *And* he fired it." Beeslaar kept looking at the approaching brown cloud. It would take quite a convoy to kick up that much dust.

"Listen, Inspector, I was actually looking for you earlier. To tell you about a conversation I had with someone at the telephone exchange."

By now the dust cloud looked really ominous and Beeslaar said, "Later, Mr. Van Zyl." Then he pointed and said, "See that? You'd better get going. This is no place for a civilian." Or a nosy news monkey, he wanted to add. "We'll talk back in town, when this thing's settled down."

But Van Zyl didn't budge. He came to stand next to him.

"These guys," he said. "They want to make a political statement, a big noise. If you ask me, Freddie's murder played right into their hands. They needed something dramatic to happen, and it did. It's almost as if one of them were behind it—for their cause, I mean."

"Look, some of them might just be crazy enough. But it's definitely not one of *these* guys."

"So you think it was the stock thieves?"

"No, that's not what I'm saying either, and no, I no longer think—"

Without finishing his sentence, Beeslaar rose from the bonnet as a bunch of bakkies roared to a halt at the gate.

A burly man swung himself out of the front bakkie. He held a rifle in his right hand and a pistol was holstered at his hip. "What the hell's going on here? Where's Kleinboel?"

Grootboel Pieterse, Beeslaar decided: with that big woolly head and those fat red-veined cheeks, he had to be the sire of the chubby boy and Polla Pieterse. Boela senior had wet, fleshy lips. Across his belly stretched a stained short-sleeved shirt, tucked into shorts. Khaki socks hugged his huge calves.

"Your son is under arrest," said Beeslaar. He was standing with his arms crossed. "And you'll be next if you don't put away that gun."

Grootboel shifted the rifle to his other hand, looked past the policeman, at Harry van Zyl, and then over to where his son was sitting in the back of Beeslaar's car, calling out to him.

The man's face reddened. "What's wrong, why's he crying? Did you assault him?"

Beeslaar grimaced. "He assaulted himself—with his own rifle, bashed his collarbone. It's okay, nothing's broken."

"You let my child go immediately, or—"

"Or what, Mr. Pieterse? You'll shoot me? Or will you do the same as you did to Freddie Swarts?"

Pieterse's cheeks purpled. "*What*?"

"You heard me."

"You've lost your fucking mind, man!" He looked over his shoulder at the other farmers, who by now were all out of their vehicles.

"You and your friends threatened to kill Freddie Swarts!"

"You're off your head, man. Where did you hear rubbish like that?"

"I'm talking about the pamphlets you sent Freddie Swarts. And I'm talking about the threats you made against her manager last week. And now she's dead and he's missing."

"You're bloody crazy. And how are you going to prove it, huh? Where are these *pamphlets*? God, Beeslaar. We should be working together, man. You and us. But it seems to me we're the only people who want to make this district safe. Trying to prevent our people from being wiped out and our land taken from us. While people like you and our so-called upholders of the law sit around on your arses waiting for promotion. We're the ones driving around here, doing your job for you. Nobody else!"

Beeslaar leaned against the bonnet of his car. He let the man vent while quietly praying for Ghaap to arrive.

"Who searched this district with a fine-tooth comb after the Huilwater murders? We did! And what do we get, hey? Just a slap in the face! And now our innocent children are being locked up!"

His voice broke, and he caught his breath.

"Mr. Pieterse, if you're doing such a good job of patrolling the district, how come you've missed the thieves again and again? I think either you're not patrolling as carefully as you claim, or you have some reason to turn a blind eye. Because it suits you just fine, all this thieving, doesn't it? Grist for your political mill, no?"

Grootboel stepped forward, but a farmer grabbed his shoulder.

"And as for your son—he pointed a firearm at a policeman and fired it. That's attempted murder. I'm going to lock him up for that. But you needn't worry—I'll see he gets a medical check." Beeslaar rested his palm on the bonnet, but withdrew it from the hot metal. "Meanwhile I'm looking for Buks Hanekom. Where is he? Or is he hiding now?"

Pieterse looked towards the boy in the car. "That child needs to get to a doctor."

"He will, as soon as I've charged him. But tell me: where's your main man, Buks Hanekom?"

Grootboel looked over his shoulder at the men standing behind him. Beeslaar recognised a good number of them.

"Interesting," he said. "Today's your big rally, but your leader is missing."

"He isn't missing, Beeslaar. He's on his way!"

The growl of a vehicle grew louder and everyone turned to look. A police van. Beeslaar stood up, and the men at the gate closed ranks.

Ghaap stepped out of the police van, with Morotse at his side. Together they walked up to Beeslaar. "Sorry, we haven't been able to get a warrant yet," Ghaap whispered in his ear.

"Bugger. Where's Pyl?"

"He's coming, he's not far behind us. He was trying one more time to organise something from Upington."

"Ja, well. Shoes," Beeslaar gestured, "you can take the boy into the station so long. Ghaap and I will wait for Hanekom. And hopefully Pyl will be here soon, waving a warrant."

Ghaap looked over Beeslaar's shoulder at the crew of khaki-clad farmers huddled at the gate.

"And you think just you and me's going to make all those bebliksemde boere open that gate for us?"

Another vehicle pulled up: It was Pyl. "Yes, Sergeant Ghaap. I have the fullest confidence we will—warrant or no warrant."

Then he walked back to his car.

An hour later Beeslaar flopped like a sack of mielies onto the chair behind his desk. He was tired. He was gatvol. He was sunburnt. And he was hot. God, he was hot. But most of all, he'd had it with driving these distances.

But at least his new best buddy, Sergeant Gershwin Pyl, had come to his rescue with two warrants. He'd had the presence of mind to involve the super. And he'd delivered the goods, all right. Chop-chop, he'd got both a state prosecutor and a magistrate to sign the warrants.

He could have kissed old Gershwin!

And there had been an added bonus, in the form of Hanekom. No sooner had he turned up at the Volop gate than he was summarily arrested.

But one big problem remained: De Kok. After their search, it had been clear that he wasn't hidden anywhere on Volop after all. Which could mean just one thing: he had made a fool of Beeslaar, who was now well and truly fucked. He'd see his arse, all because he'd broken every rule in the book by trusting the word of a man who was *already* a goddamn suspect in the whole damn thing. He was so pissed off, so furious, he could bite the head off a live mamba.

But where to start looking for the sly bastard now? It was clear Hanekom and his lot didn't have the faintest clue about De Kok. Grootboel's disbelief when Beeslaar had confronted him about it a couple of hours ago was simply too credible. And there was also nothing to be learnt from that arrogant shit Hanekom.

He reached for the telephone, but didn't call. He was hungry and thirsty. He hadn't eaten since breakfast. And you can't think straight on an empty stomach. He'd stroll across to see whether Oom Koeks was serving anything. And the Red Dune would be far more agreeable without the likes of Hanekom around.

Just then Jansie walked in with a tray and Beeslaar's mood lifted instantly. "You're psychic, you know that, Ms. Boois?"

She put down the tray, passed him a mug of coffee and

offered him a plate of buttermilk rusks. He took one, recon-sidered, then took another. She laughed and placed the whole plate in front of him.

"Can you get the super on the line for me quickly?"

She spun round, throwing him a smile at the door.

Beeslaar dunked a rusk in the sugary coffee, sucked at the glutinous mess, then licked his fingers clean as the phone rang. It was the Moegel.

Beeslaar thanked him for the warrants and informed him of the day's events—starting with the murder of Mma Mokoena. When he was done, he asked about Nelmari Viljoen. "I need to speak to her urgently, Superintendent."

"What for? Do you have any information about her assault yet?"

"That's exactly why I have to speak to her. I've got infor-mation that she arranged to meet someone on the evening of the attack. And I have a hunch who that person might be, but I need her to confirm."

"I'll see what I can do. Send the information through to me," he commanded before ending the call.

Beeslaar looked at the mug in his hand. The coffee was cold now, with blobs of rusk floating in it like dead larvae. He banged the mug down, and a mushy bit landed on his desk.

He had to get to the Viljoen woman. And he had to find De Kok.

So much depended on this—his career included.

80

There had been no signs for the hospital as Sara drove into Upington. As she pulled in at a petrol station to ask directions, the pump attendant's eyes widened at the sight of the half-naked, blood-soaked man on the seat beside her. Sara'd pulled away before he'd finished his convoluted description—at least she knew she was heading in the right direction.

At the hospital Dam had been admitted and whisked off to theatre. And then the long wait started.

She kept her eyes on the wall clock, but all time seemed to have stopped. Questions churned through her mind, and the mantis painting haunted her: Was Dam involved with the stock thieves, with Freddie's murder? Or was it simple jealousy— had "M" reappeared? No. Dam was different. The way he'd planted that tree on Freddie's grave, the way he'd talked about it all. But how well had she known him? And the will—how sincere were his claims? And the land. The bloody land. Everything came back to it. Boet Pretorius—his mad jealousy. Isn't that exactly what the whole murder scene was saying? Freddie Swarts, this is your punishment for giving your heart to the wrong man.

The sheer cruelty of it all. Even the poor dogs—oh Jesus, Hond! The dog was still on the farm.

Someone touched her shoulder, startling her. For a moment she had forgotten where she was. It was the doctor—still wearing his theatre cap.

"Miss Swarts?"

Sara jumped up. "Is he okay?"

The doctor gave a reassuring smile. "Fortunately he's pretty tough. But he was hurt really badly. We'll have to take good care of him."

"But how serious are his injuries, Doctor?"

"He's still weak. The bullet damaged his ribs and grazed a lung, but the damage is contained. Whoever bandaged him up did a pretty reasonable job. Was it you?"

"No. No, it wasn't me."

"Well, he'll be in a good deal of pain for a while, more from the ribs than anything else, but it will heal."

"Thank you. Thank you so much."

"You look as if you could do with a dose of meds yourself. Come, let's go find you a cup of tea or something." He led her down the passage. "But perhaps you should go wash your face first. There's a bathroom just around the corner."

She was shocked by her reflection in the mirror. There was blood on her face, her clothes, her arms. Even her legs, she saw when she looked down.

Once she'd rinsed herself off, she felt much better. She found the doctor in a cafeteria down the hall, waiting for her at a small table, with two white cups and saucers in front of him.

The tea was good. It made her feel a bit more human again. More in control, less of an unwilling actor in a horror film.

And Dam would pull through, after all.

Somehow, good things still happened.

81

Ja?" Beeslaar barked. Bloody cellphones!

"Inspector, it's Willie."

"Willie, man, listen, you've caught me at a bad time."

"But don't you want those doors? I worked on them all weekend, remember?"

"No, of course I want the doors. I've just been a little busy today. Could you maybe store them in my garage so long? I can't get away from work yet, okay?"

Willie didn't sound so okay with it, but he left it at that.

Beeslaar rang off and strode down the corridor.

He found Ghaap and Thabang Motlogeloa in the Moegel's office, their makeshift questioning room. Ghaap was lounging in the Moegel's chair in his customary position—virtually supine—while Motlogeloa seemed less surly than before.

Beeslaar studied the boy: *another* life wrecked, he thought. There was little hope for orphaned kids like this. Yvonne Lambrechts's overcrowded shelter was their only refuge. They blew about like dust on the wind, survived on their scrapings, and invariably ended up here for petty theft.

Like Bulelani, who'd drifted back to his place early that morning again. Bulelani, with his rotten teeth, who ate only white bread. He looked at Motlogeloa's mouth. Two front teeth missing, several gaps along the bottom. His face was still turned towards Ghaap, but he flicked his eyes warily at Beeslaar. The big white man looming so close to him clearly unnerved him.

"Our Thabang doesn't want to play along so nicely, Inspector," Ghaap said in a bored tone. "He keeps saying he doesn't know the man in the white BMW. But we know better, don't we?"

Beeslaar leaned his bulk towards the boy, who shrank back.

"Thabang only wants one thing, and that's a lawyer," said Ghaap through a long, gaping yawn. "But I keep explaining to him, Inspector. I talk nice. I tell him there aren't any lawyers here. And I tell him we can take him to Kimberley. There are plenty of lawyers there. There he'll find lawyers for Africa. Pick 'n' choose. They're all over the place, one behind every bush. And while he does his picking and choosing and all, he can go check in at Sing Sing so long, over there with the big guys, the ones that like pretty young boys, like him. But Thabang won't listen, Inspector. He won't tell me who that tjommie of his is."

Ghaap dropped his chin to his chest, apparently exhausted by this speech.

"He isn't my tjommie!" the boy shouted.

Ghaap glanced at Beeslaar, mischief in his eyes. Then he said, "Did we tell you what your great tjommie did to Mma Mokoena this morning, Thabang?"

The boy's eyes flicked nervously between the two policemen.

"Hey, Thabang? I'm talking to you, man."

"What did she say about me?" He looked suspiciously at his two tormentors.

He was old before his time, Beeslaar thought, fifteen going on fifty. The whites of his eyes were yellowed, and a scar slashed across an eyebrow. His face so gaunt that his chin and cheekbones threatened to pierce the mottled skin.

"She just gives me something. When I'm hungry," he muttered.

"So, she gives you food. Was it there you met the man with

the BMW?" Thabang's mouth was twisted into an obstinate knot.

Ghaap tried again, "Did you know Mma Mokoena is dead?"

The boy's head dropped, his chin digging into his scrawny chest.

"Mma Mokoena was murdered this morning," said Ghaap, clearly, deliberately.

The boy's head snapped back up. He watched as Ghaap slid an index finger across his throat.

"And guess who killed her, Thabang. Slit her throat. Like a dog!"

"Hayi, wena!" the boy cried out. "You mustn't joke about that antie. Not with cutting the throat." He frowned angrily at Ghaap, then at Beeslaar, as if *he* should tell Ghaap off. But Beeslaar remained impassive.

"Guess who knifed her, Thabang? It was your friend, man!"

Thabang slowly moved his head from side to side. His mouth hung open.

"Yes! He grabbed her and pulled out that knife of his and he cut her throat. And you know his name, but you don't want to tell us. So you'll be going to jail for this murder too, you hear?"

The boy shook his head again, but his eyes glistened with anxiety.

He ducked as Beeslaar walked past him to the door. He wasn't needed here any more. Thabang would be talking soon.

He walked over to the charge office. There were two other prisoners in need of his attention.

"Hey, Shoes, you still here?"

"What can I say, Inspector? Captain Crime Stop, at your service!" He flashed a perfect row of white teeth.

"Won't you please go get Buks Hanekom and bring him to me? See that he's cuffed, we don't want him running away. Has anyone been around to bail him out?"

"Nope. His mother doesn't love him any more," the constable grinned.

Beeslaar turned back to his office. The constable didn't know it, but he might well have touched on a big, sad truth in Buks Hanekom's life right now.

His cellphone rang again. Willie.

"Yes, Willie. Everything okay with the doors?"

"Hell, Inspector, I thought I was going to have a heart attack. There was an intruder in your garage!"

"Did you catch him?"

"No, Jissus. I got the fright of my life, and he ran away."

"Relax, Willie. It's just Bulelani. He sleeps in my garage at night."

"So, what's he run away like that for? He nearly scared my balls off!"

"Sorry, man. But we'll talk tomorrow, okay? I have to run."

He put the phone down just as Shoes stepped into his office with Hanekom.

"Go get us some coffee, Shoes, and fetch Sergeant Pyl," Beeslaar said as he sat down behind his desk.

Hanekom's hair was unkempt. He struggled to walk in his laceless shoes. The constable had also removed his belt, watch and a gold chain when he locked him up.

"I have nothing to say to you, Beeslaar." Hanekom's rage had simmered down somewhat after his initial incredulity—and his fierce, cursing fury at being bundled into the back of the police van at the Volop gate.

"Hell, Buks. I haven't even asked you anything yet. Are you sure you're not in the mood for a chat?"

"I don't have to tell you anything without my lawyer present."

"Well then, that leaves us with a bit of a problem. Because I don't see any lawyers here."

"That's because you haven't let me phone him!"

"What?" Beeslaar smiled wryly. "Ag, that Shoes. He must have forgotten. All of a sudden we're so busy around here, as you can see. And it's naughty guys like you keeping us so busy. Keeping us from our jobs, really. We have a murderer and a crime syndicate on our hands, and in the middle of it all you come buggering around with things like a dead baboon you've stolen from a friend of yours. Have you heard how Tannie Debora's been crying over that baboon? They say it was like a child to her."

Beeslaar sighed theatrically, waited for a response.

"But why would something like that bother you, after all? You're a tough guy, aren't you? Chopping the hands off a poor old pet baboon. And then crucifying her alive and slitting her throat. Shame on you, man."

"I don't have to listen to this, you hear, Beeslaar? Either you let me phone my lawyer, or you let me go."

"And where do you plan to go? Your cell, maybe? Because you're not just walking out of here. You've had your chips, my friend. Threatening women. Mutilating animals. A proper bully!"

"You're talking rubbish, Beeslaar."

"Where's Dam De Kok?"

"What?"

"You heard me. Where is he?"

"I don't know what you're talking about, man. And you'd better let me go. You're arresting the wrong damn people. I want to phone my father and my lawyer immediately. Now! You can't just keep me here!"

"I know you've got him, Hanekom. And for your sake I hope he's still alive. Because if you've done to him what you did to Tannie Debora's baboon, they'll lock you up for much, much longer. You're already a suspect in the Huilwater murders. And I'm not even talking about treason and all the other crimes yet."

"You're mad, Beeslaar." He squared his shoulders and gave his interrogator a challenging stare. "I'm trying to *prevent* genocide! Against me and the persecuted Afrikaner people! The victims of a cunning plan to wipe out the Boer nation, drive us from our land." Red blotches had broken out on his cheeks.

"Spare me the political diatribe, Hanekom. Where's De Kok?"

"I don't *know* where De Kok is. Why are you asking *me*? Why don't you do your job and catch the stock thieves? De Kok is with *them*. Then you'll have him and the murderers in one go. And now I'm not saying one more word without legal representation. You're accusing me of all sorts of shocking things and I'm not going to sit here and let myself be caught in your stupid traps."

He was sitting bolt upright in the chair, his fingers woven together tightly, the knuckles white.

Shoes came in with two mugs of coffee and put them on the desk in front of Beeslaar. He'd put milk in both, Beeslaar was sorry to see.

"Thank you, Constable. I hear Mr. Hanekom here is complaining that he hasn't been able to call his lawyer yet. Won't you please tell him we'll do it with pleasure? As soon as he's told us where he's keeping De Kok."

Nonplussed, Shoes looked from Beeslaar to Hanekom then took a seat next to the farmer.

Just then, Ghaap swung into the doorway. "Got it!" he shouted at Beeslaar. "The plates!"

"Great, man! Phone them through to the national network. Ten to one they're fake, but who knows—and tell the guys in Upington. Shoes, you go help with the phoning around."

The constable scuttled out after his colleague.

"Oh dear, Mr. Hanekom. There goes your opportunity to make that call, again."

"Beeslaar, you're trying to make a fool of me! I swear, I won't hesitate to lay a charge against you!"

"Yes, you don't hesitate about much. Death threats to women and children. Kidnapping, animal abuse, theft, breaking and entering. Never mind treason and conspiring to overthrow the state! In the old days you'd have been swinging before you could even say 'boo!', my friend."

"I'm *not* your friend."

"Your parents were pretty disappointed when they found out about your shenanigans, you know?"

"You leave my parents out of this!"

"I'm quite prepared to leave them out of it. But it was you who dragged them in, Hanekom. Your father almost wept when he heard you'd offered his farm to Nelmari Viljoen to sell."

The man was red-faced and wild-eyed. Beeslaar had evidently touched a raw nerve.

"You're out of your fucking mind, you know? I didn't offer her that farm!"

"That's not what I heard."

"If she's the one who told you that, she's lying. And you're lying too. You know nothing about my parents."

"Ai, Buks. You should have seen your father's face when he discovered those letters, all those death threats, in your office."

"I told you—leave my parents out of this. They've done nothing to you."

"No, but what have *you* done to them? Sold the farm from under them?"

"I haven't! How many times must I tell you that? That's another business altogether."

With both elbows on the desk, Beeslaar leaned forward. "What business is that?"

Hanekom closed his eyes. For a while they sat in silence.

"It's just . . . business," he sighed at last. "My father would never sell that blerrie farm of his."

"Okay, then. So what business is this?"

His eyes weary, Hanekom hung his head in silence.

"Don't worry," Beeslaar said, "we'll find it all on your computer."

Hanekom looked up at Beeslaar in disbelief. Then he laughed mirthlessly.

"You really think I'd keep all my private stuff on that computer?"

"I guess I'll just have to go and find out, won't I? Meanwhile I'm going to take you back to your cell and let you make a phone call to your lawyer, and even to your father—if you still have the guts to talk to him. Maybe they're not even wondering where you are any more. They don't dare wonder, if you ask me."

Hanekom stood up and followed Beeslaar back to his cell. He shuffled down the corridor in his laceless shoes, like a weary old man about to retire for the night.

82

Y ou look as if *you're* the one on the brink of major surgery," said Harry as he laid his hand on Sara's head. "Come here." He pulled her closer and folded his arms around her. "Poor old Saartjie," he said into her hair.

Sara leaned against him with her eyes closed, her face burrowed into his shirt. It smelt of spicy soap. She could stand like this forever. She felt him touch his lips to her hair before lifting her chin and kissing her softly on both eyes, his palms pressed to her cheeks. She raised her mouth, seeking his lips.

"Let me take you home," he whispered into her ear.

She felt so grateful to Harry. He'd arrived just in time to help her out of her predicament with the doctor, who'd wanted to know how Dam had ended up with a gunshot wound. The hospital needed to report it, inform the local police—unless she'd already done so? Right then, Harry had stepped in: Inspector Beeslaar knew already, he'd told the doctor. Then went on to say that it seemed to be a hush-hush case, what with the suspicion of a far-right uprising, Dam being a victim and all.

But still, Sara had to give her details—for a regulation report, the doctor said.

Afterwards they were allowed a visit. She hardly recognised Dam, almost dwarfed in his pale-blue hospital gown. His skin was a waxy yellow as he lay in a deep sleep, not reacting at all when she leaned over and said his name. An oxygen mask covered his nose and mouth, tubes were attached to his arms, and a monitor beeped above his bed.

Sara's chest contracted. The thought that he too could have died. Could have disappeared—gone from the veld and the birds. Taking the stories with him, the stories of the morning star and the hyena and the wise old trees of the veld.

"You didn't *really* tell Beeslaar?" she said to Harry as they walked to his car.

"No, of course not. But we have to let him know, Sara. We could get into trouble. When I left, the police were still under the impression that that right-wing lot was holding him hostage. At least it seems Dam's no longer the only and chief suspect in your sister's case. But I'm not so sure he's off the hook with the stock theft. Personally, I just can't see a man like him being involved in it. Any of it. No way. How about you?"

"You know, I'm not sure of anything any more."

83

More hunger pangs eventually propelled Beeslaar out of his chair, where he'd been hunched over his desk in the gloom. He walked down the corridor, found Ghaap and Pyl on their phones. He raised an imaginary glass to his mouth, nodded in the direction of the Red Dune across the road and gave a cheery wave.

Twilight had brought with it a cool breeze. He filled his lungs and stretched his arms wide, then crossed the road, knees stiff from so long at the desk.

The Red Dune was empty. Beeslaar didn't head for his usual table, but took a seat at the bar counter.

"Beer, Inspector?" said Oom Koeks. The cigarette pasted to his lip bobbed as he spoke.

"The coldest you have," said Beeslaar, perching on a stool.

"Blue Monday?" the barman asked, eyes narrowed against the smoke curling from his cigarette. Then he opened a bottle of Tafel Lager and poured it into a chilled glass.

"Just the Wild West, Oom," he laughed. The beer was so icy it seemed to burn a hole through him. "Is there anything to eat?"

"Oh, the usual. Mixed grill or a hamburger and chips."

"Give me a plate of chips so long. I'm waiting for my colleagues, then we can order."

The barman stubbed out his cigarette, shouted an order and said, "So, the De Kok guy from Huilwater got badly hurt, I hear."

Beeslaar sat up. "Where'd you hear that?"

"I thought you knew."

"I don't know anything. Where did you hear this?"

"Listen, my daughter's going to kill me," he said, avoiding Beeslaar's eyes.

The young woman from the telephone exchange, Beeslaar realised. She was Oom Koeks's daughter! And hadn't Van Zyl made mention of her earlier today? "Tell her she needn't worry, Oom. I'm sure she doesn't broadcast her news. She only tells you."

The barman laughed soundlessly, beer belly jiggling. "She'd disown me if she found out I told the *police*—of all people. It's not that she's an eavesdropper, don't get me wrong. But sometimes she hears what the people say while they're waiting to be put through. Some people phone her and tell her things. Ja, well. I thought you already knew the man was in hospital in Upington. Found in the veld, apparently, left for dead. The girl from the farm took him in this afternoon. She let Yvonne know."

"Thanks, Oom Koeks. She was probably planning to tell me in any case."

The plate of chips arrived, brought in by a woman in a crisp white apron. Beeslaar's mouth watered. It smelt just the way real slap chips should—the tang of the vinegar mingled with hot oil and salt. He picked up three chips at once, blew at them and popped them in his mouth. He took a gulp of cold beer to cool his tongue. Needed more salt, though. He sprinkled some over them while Oom Koeks topped up his beer.

"Been in this business long?" Beeslaar asked, between bites.

"Retirement job. I sold the farm. Living in town now, with the daughter I mentioned."

"Why did you sell?"

"Ai, man. Round here it's only really the big guys who make

money. The rest of us get by through God's grace and by the skin of our teeth."

"How's that?"

"Take a guy like Pretorius, for instance," he said. "Boet Pretorius."

Beeslaar prompted him. "Yes?"

"Guys like that, they make a good living. If that man doesn't turn into a multi-millionaire in the next few years, I'll eat my hat."

"Oh?"

"Buying up farms! Where he gets the money, heaven only knows. Okay, sure, he got his first farm for a song, at an auction—a bankruptcy."

"He must have started off with money, though? After all, he sold a big business before coming here."

"Rubbish. That business of his wasn't that big at all. What he's got *now* is a big business. Bought four farms already. And he stocks them all with game. I hear sometimes it's like an auction's being held there, the number of animals that are offloaded at his place."

Beeslaar put down his beer and listened attentively.

"I tried the farming game myself," Oom Koeks continued, squinting at Beeslaar. "I know what it costs, you know."

"Right, right." Beeslaar nodded.

"You struggle like hell in this area if you don't have water. The drought ruined me. It happened over and over. At one point I even sold all my livestock, worked for peanuts at a petrol station in Upington. We barely scraped by every month. My wife went to work in town too. Ja, well, I carried on like that a few years. And the rain just stayed away, stayed away, stayed away . . . "

The memory clearly pained him. Then he coughed and continued, "But then came '95, and it rained. I could look the world in the eye again, buy some animals. Get back to farming.

My wife kept on working in Upington, and I looked after our daughter. In the evenings when my wife got home, she always asked what the child had eaten. Then I'd say biltong. And what veg, she'd ask. Then I'd say raisins."

Oom Koeks's belly shook again; this memory at least amused him.

"But how come you stopped farming, then?"

"For me, the last nail in the coffin was the fire. You see, after a drought, for the next two seasons, there's no grass for the animals to eat. No farm can take these beatings, again and again. So I folded."

"And what caused the fire?"

"Lightning, probably, who knows? Septembers are bad here. The grass is dry after the winter. Burns like petrol. And that's also when we get the first summer thunderstorms."

"So, who did you sell to?"

"Who do you think?"

Beeslaar turned around as a second plate of chips arrived. "Some more for you," Oom Koeks winked, "while you wait." The woman gave a polite smile and Beeslaar thanked her, though he had enough now.

"For peanuts," said Oom Koeks. "Sweet blue bugger-all!"

Beeslaar sprinkled some salt on the chips, but didn't eat any.

The phone rang. It was mounted on the wall, next to a row of brandy bottles. Oom Koeks reached up to answer it. As he spoke, Beeslaar mulled over what the old man had just told him.

Then Oom Koeks hung up, faced Beeslaar and continued his tale. He spoke about drought, and the carrying capacity of the land. "One head of cattle per hectare, but in Botswana and in the deep Kalahari it's just one animal per thirty-six hectares, almost zero carrying capacity. When it rains, though, those animals are the fattest anywhere, with all the seeds just beneath the surface of the sand. First bit of rain, and within forty-eight hours it's all green. A miracle—but then the Kalahari wind comes, it kills everything. Overnight—"

"Oom Koeks," Beeslaar interrupted him, "did Pretorius buy only your farm at first?"

"Yes. Just mine. It's only recently that he bought the others too. And I think he's very sharp. Look, this part of the world, it isn't really made for sheep and cattle. It's game country. Always has been. And it's good business. Kudu, for instance. Just take your best commercial horn—about 1.2 metres. You don't shoot that for under ten, twelve thousand, you know! And the farmers near the Kgalagadi—the advantage over there is the game from the reserve. When the farmers drop their fences, gemsbok and a whole lot of other game just wander in. They're perfectly adapted to graze around here, but they need to roam, otherwise you have to feed them. Most antelope are roamers, actually. Eland, for instance. It's better not to fence them in. They like to move around. Same thing with kudu."

"So Pretorius's farms stretch all the way up to the Botswana border?"

"Yes. He's in the pound seats, if you ask me. He can supply meat and hunting trophies on both sides of the border. Kudu for horns and trophies, maybe other things too. I hear he's talking lions and rhinos now. But a kudu doesn't deliver on meat. They look so big, but on average they only give you about a hundred and twenty kilograms each. But eland, now that's another story. He delivers his three hundred. But he eats fences, man. You've got to fix fences till you're blue in the face. There's not a fence that can keep him in." He suddenly interrupted himself. "Are you going to eat those chips, or should I send them back?"

"Sorry, Oom, I wasn't expecting this, and I'm full," said Beeslaar sheepishly.

"Anyway, if Huilwater comes on the market again," Oom

Koeks continued, bending over to reach for a beer in the fridge below the counter, "then old Boet will have everything he wants. It's the only farm in this whole district that has so much water. It has three, four springs, you know. A man like Pretorius wants to go into tourism, so he needs his water!"

Beeslaar got up. "Sorry, Oom, but you're going to have to excuse me. I'll skip that cold one. I've got to skedaddle." He slipped a couple of notes from his wallet and put them on the counter. "That should cover it, the food too. Got to push off now, I'm afraid, but my colleagues should be along any minute," he said and turned to leave.

"What about your change?" Oom Koeks shouted after him.

"For your soup kitchen tin," Beeslaar said as he strode out of the door.

A second later he popped his head through the door again. Oom Koeks was putting the money into the cash register, his eyes still screwed up against the cigarette smoke.

"I forgot to ask—what's your daughter's name?"

Oom Koeks glowered as he looked up. "You're not going to tell her!"

"No, no. I owe her flowers."

"Riet. Short for Rita, her mother's—"

But Beeslaar was already out the door.

84

S ara slid slowly into the cool, dark water. She tucked her knees into her chest, and dipped her head underwater too. For a moment she hung there suspended below the surface, her hair spread out like seaweed. Eyes closed, surrounded by the underwater silence. Then she kicked off against the dam wall and swam to the other side in long, lazy strokes.

On their way back from Upington, she and Harry had made a short detour and stopped off at Huilwater to pick up Hond. She wouldn't be going back there again after the attack on Dam. The echoes in the dim uninhabited farmhouse had seemed hostile, and she'd jumped at every sound, every shadow, anxiously listening for footsteps, each creak of a floorboard.

As they'd driven away, dusk was falling. Sara had looked back at the house from the main road one last time. Dark and deserted. And lonely, it had seemed to her, as if it knew it was being abandoned for good. It had made her feel guilty and sad and she felt she was leaving Freddie there all alone again.

When Sara came up for air at the other side of the dam, she saw to her surprise that Harry had also jumped in. Feeling bolder today. He swam straight up to her and pulled her towards him. His eyes shone darkly and water droplets clung to his eyelashes, glistened in his closely trimmed hair.

She slid a finger over the arch of his nose and he pulled her closer, his lips on her forehead. He traced the curve of her hips, cupping her buttocks, and she swung her legs around him, lifting herself effortlessly in the water. They were enveloped in a velvety blackness, while above, the stars seemed alive. His breath was warm against her skin as he slipped the straps off her shoulders.

For a moment his hand was caught in a tangle of hair and straps. "Oaf," she breathed, and they laughed softly into each other's mouth as she wriggled free of her costume. She felt delight at how naturally their bodies found each other's rhythm. Because she had forgotten the tenderness of intimacy, this sense of completeness. And this man's body fitted so perfectly into hers, as if he belonged there.

The night had grown quiet by the time they swam apart, feeling for bathing costumes gone astray in the water. He helped her out, put his lips to her neck, then towelled her hair. She laughed as he tied his shoelaces—he still refused to go barefoot. "Kalahari cool? Forget it," he said before taking her in his arms again.

Back at the house, Tannie Yvonne had prepared some sandwiches and cold meat, which they ate on the stoep. Sara met Harry's eyes as he poured her wine, a slow secret smile passing between them. But the conversation soon brought reality flooding back.

"But what will happen on Huilwater?" asked Tannie Yvonne, shocked when Sara had told her how Boet Pretorius had roughed up his worker.

"I phoned the neighbour over on the other side, Oom Roger Heidenrich. He's got a man who knows the farm pretty well, he says—helped Dam out a few times with dipping sheep or fencing or whatever. He promised he'd bring him over tomorrow. So, I'm hoping."

They finished eating, and Tannie Yvonne excused herself to watch her TV programme, the fluffy little dogs scurrying after her. They'd been anything but pleased at the arrival of Hond. They utterly ignored this farm mutt, so far beneath their dignity.

The despised mutt trotted after Harry and Sara when they went off to wash the dishes. But the going was slow and hilarious, Sara slapping Harry with a dishcloth each time he made a grab for her, his hands dripping with soap suds.

He was rinsing the last plate when the dogs began barking and raced to the front door. Harry dried his hands and went to see who was there. He returned with Inspector Beeslaar. The big cop looked irate, out of breath, sunburnt and sweaty.

"What's happened?" Sara asked, her voice sounding strangled.

Beeslaar's bulky frame stooped at the kitchen door, as if the ceiling were too low. "I understand your foreman was found, after all." The dogs were still sniffing and growling around his ankles.

"He's not a foreman, he's the farm manager," Sara corrected him. "And what of it? He got really badly hurt and is in intensive care."

"And you were planning to inform me . . . when?" He looked from Sara to Harry, a frown notched between his brows.

"We were, yes," Harry said quickly. "We've just come from the hospital and only just finished supper."

"May I sit down?" he asked, placing his hand on a kitchen chair.

"Let's go outside." Harry stepped out to the stoep, with Sara and Beeslaar following after.

"So?" Beeslaar said after he had taken a seat.

As Harry told him what had happened, the policeman looked from the one to the other, his eyes sharp and searching.

"Dam is no stock thief, Inspector," said Sara.

He ignored her protest. "How does he get on with Boet Pretorius?"

"I don't think Dam likes him," Sara said quickly. "He calls him a wolf in sheep's clothing."

"And what about Nelmari Viljoen?" he asked.

Sara was surprised. "Why do you ask that?"

He waited for her reply to his question.

"Dam says she's terribly controlling. The cause, I believe, of the quarrel before Freddie's death."

"Quarrel about what?"

"It was about the land claims," Harry interjected. "Nelmari was going to help, I don't know how, but in the end the land claims fell through. And the two of them had a fight and never spoke to each other again."

"How long ago was this?"

"Recently, it seems. Just before Freddie died. You'd have to ask Dam. He wanted nothing to do with it."

"So De Kok never got involved with the land claims?"

"Absolutely not," said Harry.

"So what was the argument about?"

"I have my own theory, that it has to do with the will of a former Griqua chief and a theft from the Cape archive. And so on."

"Where do you *get* all this stuff, Harry?" Sara asked. "Is it from Vicky?"

"Who's Vicky?" Beeslaar wanted to know.

"Your neighbour," Harry smiled. "She runs the museum, it's right there next to your police station. I saw her this morning."

"Oh, ja," he said sheepishly. "But what does *she* know about the fight?"

"What she knows is why the land claims eventually fell through."

"And?" Beeslaar asked impatiently.

"She said it goes back to the discovery of diamonds."

"Just get to the point, Mr. Van Zyl."

"Okay, okay. The long and the short of it is that there was a will—expressing the last wishes of a certain chief, Nicolaas Waterboer. He owned land that the British had not annexed, about sixteen farms in all. In his will a later chief bequeathed this land to his Griqua descendants. But by then white settlers were already sort of occupying the land. I'm talking about 1896, when the old chief died."

"The same land that's the issue now?"

"Yes. Eleven of the farms were sold—this was before the 1913 Land Act was passed. And the rest was given to whites after 1913, it was their land now."

Harry paused to let this sink in. But neither Beeslaar nor Sara looked impressed.

"Ja, and so?" Beeslaar prompted. "So there are five farms that the Griquas can claim back now. So?"

"So, they need proof that they have rightful claim to the land. And Miss Swarts's sister found that proof, namely the will in the archive in Cape Town!"

"Then what?"

"Then the pawpaw hit the fan. The will suddenly disappeared. Stolen from the archive. Bam! Bye-bye, land claim."

"Who stole it?"

"That's as much as I could uncover," Harry said, shrugging. "And for the rest we just know what Dam told us—that Freddie and Nelmari had this falling out."

Beeslaar got up. "Do you know which land it is, this so-called land-claim land?"

"I can show you. I have a book here, with maps."

"Later," said Beeslaar, "I have to go now. You can just tell me."

"A section of Huilwater. A big part, actually. And several other pieces, including a farm west of Boet Pretorius's Karrikamma—I think the name is Mokaneng. It borders on the Kgalagadi reserve."

Beeslaar raised his eyebrows and for the first time, Sara saw him smile. "You know, you're quite a mine of information, Mr. Van Zyl."

"Just call me Mr. Wikipedia. But I hope you see what I see, namely that there are plenty of people who would benefit from Freddie's death. Far more than just De Kok, right?"

Beeslaar didn't answer. He walked over to the kitchen door. "I have a man posted at his bedside," he said. "We'll speak to De Kok as soon as we can."

85

Beeslaar walked briskly back to the police station, relieved that the heat was dissipating in the gathering darkness.

In his mind a picture was forming. It was still vague, though, and there were still many more questions than answers. Starting with Freddie Swarts—and all the drama that had unfolded around her in the last weeks of her life.

She had drawn up a new will, in which she gave the family farm to her foreman. She found new proof which would see five farms—of which one was her own—fall back into Griqua hands. She had received death threats for her trouble. She declined the attentions of her über neighbour. And she and her best friend had the mother of all arguments. So bad that they never spoke to each other again.

Why did she leave the farm to her foreman? To make doubly sure it wouldn't end up in Pretorius's hands?

Why not leave the farm to her champion and so-called surrogate sister, Nelmari Viljoen? What would make the otherwise gentle Freddie Swarts angry enough to chase away her bosom friend and never speak to her again?

Question upon question upon question. And the biggest question of all: Was it relevant to the murder? If Boet Pretorius had been watching his future plans for Huilwater disappear down the plughole, with Freddie rejecting his advances while at the same time also targeting the area around him for a land claim, would he have killed her?

Yet he was the one who had discovered the bodies. And if he had been putting on an act that day, he was a man who'd missed his calling. It was a performance worthy of an Oscar. He'd puked as hard as Pyl and Ghaap put together.

And Nelmari Viljoen? He'd put his head on a block that Boet Pretorius was the one who put her in hospital. He wanted her dead, that's for sure. But why? And what business did she have with Buks Hanekom?

And the man who murdered Mma Mokoena and the old Huilwater lady—the man from Gauteng, in the white BMW? Injured himself. Perhaps during last night's theft at Yzerfontein? Could De Kok be his partner? Or did De Kok want to stop him from whatever he was up to? He had come looking for the boy, Thabang Motlogeloa, at Mma Mokoena's that morning. What did he want with the boy? And what did he have against poor old Mrs. Beesvel?

There was something about the murder of Mma Mokoena that bothered Beeslaar, but he couldn't put his finger on it. It had been bugging him ever since he'd lifted the blanket that morning and looked at the woman's face.

Beeslaar suspected, though, that the answers to some of these questions were both lying in Upington's Mediclinic, one with her throat bruised black and blue and the other with a gunshot wound to his lung.

He needed to speak to his two young colleagues. But Ghaap and Pyl were still both on the phone. There was expectation in the air, like at a rugby match when your team suddenly wakes up and starts to score.

Pyl gestured to him to stay, and pressed the phone to his chest. "We have a name, Bees, we have a name! Masilela, first name, Vuyo. We're issuing it right now."

"Get onto the media guys at HQ right away. Do we have a pic?"

Pyl nodded excitedly, the phone at his ear again.

Bees? Did Pyl just call him "Bees"? The last guy to do that was still missing two front teeth. But this time the old beast wouldn't be charging at anyone, he smiled to himself as he ambled back to his office.

He called the Red Dune and ordered three hamburgers. Extra large. With chips. And lots of Coke. To go.

Oom Koeks had made it clear that he didn't usually do takeaways, but this time he'd make an exception, he said. He understood that it was a crisis. When Beeslaar asked whether his daughter was still on duty, Oom Koeks gave a cautious yes. But first he made Beeslaar swear again that he wouldn't rat on him. "Jissie man, she'll—"

"I know, Oom Koeks. She'll disown you. But don't you worry, there's a little corner for you in my garage, for when she kicks you out. But you'll have to hurry, the place is filling up. Meanwhile, ask her to let me know as soon as she's off duty. Doesn't matter what time it is." He ended the call, suspecting she'd already got the message.

The clock on the wall said nine. Had Pyl informed the Moegel yet? He called to check, and found the superintendent in the middle of his evening meal.

"It's late, Inspector," said the Moegel, his mouth obviously full of food. "But I suppose you have your reasons."

He heard the man slurping at something—the wine Nelmari Viljoen had given him, Beeslaar thought sourly. "I assume Sergeant Pyl has let you know we have a name for our man here."

"So I've heard, yes," the Moegel answered, sucking at his teeth. "And you're calling to say you've got him?"

Beeslaar laughed dutifully. "Give us twenty-four hours, Superintendent. But that's not why I'm calling. I want to hear if you can help us again. We're urgently looking for authorisation to enter certain premises."

"At this time of night? What's going on, is this where the suspect is?"

"We believe so, Superintendent. It's on a farm I suspect is at the centre of the stock theft operation."

"*Suspect* . . . Listen, I'm not going to call on a magistrate at this time of night on suspicions alone. And certainly not after your 'suspicions' this morning, concerning Mr., er . . . "

"Pieterse," Beeslaar said dully.

"Yes, Pieterse's farm, which ended in a big fat zero, and a waste of police time!"

"I'm pretty certain this time, Superintendent."

"And what makes you so pretty certain? Do you have evidence?"

Beeslaar felt his confidence falter. "No . . . But it's the only logical place where the stock thefts could have been orchestrated from. And the owner is a man with too much to gain if all the farmers around him go bankrupt as a result of stock losses. A man who desperately needed Freddie Swarts's land—and especially her water—to survive."

"Oh, for heaven's sake man, no, that's too flimsy. I'm not going to jump through hoops for such vague conjecture. Go find decent evidence and then we'll try again, okay? And now I'm going to finish my dinner. Goodnight, Inspector."

Beeslaar sat back in his chair and closed his eyes. He'd have to think it all through again, right from the start. Write everything down, one thing after the next, and work it out step by step.

As he reached into his top drawer there was a fierce sting to his finger. He cried out and jerked his hand away. What the hell? Something had bitten him!

He jumped up and shouted as a grotesque, hairy thing flew through the air. A red roman. And it had barely touched the ground when it started running, its multiple legs working furiously. Beeslaar leapt onto the desk, tucking his knees up to his chest. He barely registered that Jansie's flask and a water jug had toppled to the floor.

The floor was awash, his finger hurt like hell and his heart was hammering at his throat. He heard running down the corridor, voices calling to him.

He slid off the desk quickly. Then Ghaap and Pyl were in his doorway, panting.

"What's going on?" asked Pyl. He even had his pistol out.

"Nothing," said Beeslaar coolly. But he could see they didn't believe him.

Then Ghaap started laughing, and Beeslaar understood: so *that's* why Ghaap had carried on about searching for his notebook in his drawer.

"You bliksem," he said. "It's *you*!"

"What's going on?" Pyl asked again. His eyes darted anxiously from giggling Ghaap to Beeslaar.

"I'll wring your fuck—" He felt something brush against his leg and he jumped again. "Eee-uw!" He kicked out wildly, but saw nothing. Then he walked smartly to the door, as quickly as he could without actually running. Past Ghaap, who by now was weak with laughter. Past Pyl, who still wasn't sure if he was meant to laugh or shoot at something. Beeslaar walked the length of the passage and then bent over, hands on his knees, trying to catch his breath.

His finger ached as if a black mamba had bitten him, but it was nothing compared to the murderous thoughts swirling in his head.

When he looked up, he saw the wide-eyed constable asking from the other end of the corridor whether everything was all right.

"Get back to your desk!" Beeslaar bellowed.

Then he went to the bathroom and held his throbbing finger under a cold tap. When he looked in the mirror, he saw that the water had splashed onto his trousers. It looked as if he'd pissed himself.

He pulled his shirt out, let it hang down over the wet spots. Then he left the building, and in the street outside, he heard Oom Koeks calling after him.

Probably about the hamburgers.

But he didn't stop. He was far too likely to thump anyone who came near him now.

He'd only just fetched a beer from the fridge when he heard a knock at the door. It was Ghaap, a takeaway box in either hand. "I come in peace, brother Beeslaar," he intoned, though his dark eyes twinkled.

Beeslaar grabbed the burger, turned on his heel and stalked off.

"That white BMW is gone, by the way," Ghaap called after him. "Not a trace of it. But its owner, this Vuyo Masilela, he's got the connections that Thabang kid spoke about. *Big* connections. He escaped from detention in Joburg a few years ago."

Beeslaar stopped and turned around, glared at his colleague and gestured to him to come inside. In the kitchen Beeslaar took out two plates, some salt, a bottle of tomato sauce. The chips were cold, so he zapped them in the microwave. Ghaap didn't wait, and tucked in to his hamburger. In between bites he carried on with his story, how Masilela was connected to a syndicate specialising in hijackings, robbery, drugs, arms. He'd also been arrested in connection with a cash-in-transit heist, but escaped before the case came to court.

"Ballies phoned Jan Steenkamp too," he said, elbows splayed on the table, his mouth full of burger. "So that he can contact everyone in the district by radio, tell them to keep their eyes peeled. And now we just have to wait, right?"

"We have to drive out to Boet Pretorius's first thing tomorrow."

"What for?"

"I want to go see what he keeps in those great big sheds of his. The more I think about it, the more I know we're looking for the thieves in the wrong places. We thought they raced straight off to Kimberley or Gauteng. But what if they simply go hide out right around the corner first, then take off a day or so later? Nobody expects them to still be around so long after the crime. And what if they're driving around in trucks everyone knows anyway, trucks with the Karrikamma logo."

"Shi-i-it!" Ghaap's eyes bulged as he swallowed a chunk of burger. "Jissus, and you've seen the locks on those fancy farm gates. Have you got a warrant?"

Beeslaar looked at him from under his brows and shook his head. His burger was finished, but he was still hungry. And the chips were inedible. Gone soggy in the microwave.

"Um, about that spider . . . " Ghaap began.

"Ag, leave it." He looked at his finger. It was still swollen.

"I didn't know you were going to get *such* a big fright."

"Let it go, Ghaap! Want something more to eat?"

The younger man shook his head. "I have to sleep." He got up to leave, but his cellphone rang.

It was a short conversation. He listened intently then said, "Yes, I'll tell him."

He sat down. "It was Pyl," he stated soberly. "The Moegel just called. Miss Viljoen is missing."

"What do you mean *missing*?"

"Missing, as in gone. She wasn't discharged, nothing. Just gone from her hospital bed."

Beeslaar cursed.

"And, oh ja," said Ghaap, "Oom Koeks sent a message—his daughter is ready for you." He looked at Beeslaar with a sly grin.

"What?"

"Ready for you. You know . . . " Ghaap wiggled his eyebrows cheekily.

"Ag, you're being stupid, man. I don't even know the woman." He thought for a moment. "Maybe you should come along."

Ghaap chuckled and shook his head. "No, I'm going to bed. Fifth wheel and third fiddle—no, man, that's not for me."

"I think that woman knows a lot of stuff."

"Not just a *lot*, Beeslaar—*everything*. You city guys don't know the first thing about the 'nommer-asseblief' tannies at the exchange."

Beeslaar got up. "I should have thought of it ages ago, you know. All those places without cellphone reception, they all have to go through her. All the farms—Boet Pretorius, Huilwater, the Hanekoms."

"But you don't have authorisation," Ghaap said, following him to the front door. "She won't speak to you without official authorisation. She's a tough antie—that way, she's really strict."

With his hand on the doorknob, Beeslaar turned to Ghaap. "Watch and learn," he said. "Watch and learn."

It was nearly eleven o'clock when Beeslaar got back home. He poured himself a brandy and went to sit on the kitchen steps. The garage was dark. If Bulelani had returned after giving Willie such a fright, he must be hungry. Something to eat would probably go down well. It was too dark to make out details, but the yard looked neat enough. Good job, Bulelani. With a groan, glass in hand, he got up and poked a finger into the soil. It felt dry. Not such a good job, after all, Bulelani.

He went to fetch the hosepipe coiled up at the tap against the back wall. The sprinkler was already attached, and he carried it all to the far corner of the vegetable patch. He opened the tap, and soon heard a gurgling, the refreshing sound of gushing water. It felt good out there in the cool of the night, alongside his onions and beetroot and carrots, all growing invisibly. Maybe he should build himself a dam too, big enough to take a dip in. Later, maybe, once this case was behind him. He sat listening to the gentle shushing of the sprinkler, thinking over the day's developments.

His visit to Oom Koeks's daughter had been interesting. Initially Riet was cautious, but after the necessary official reassurances she began to open up.

She'd said two crucial things: firstly, that Nelmari Viljoen had been the last person to phone Huilwater on the morning of the Freddie Swarts murder. And secondly, no conversation had taken place. Viljoen had called a few times—from a cellphone—but hung up as soon as the call went through. Or else the cellphone reception had cut out.

Beeslaar had promised her a huge box of chocolates, but she hadn't looked overly excited at the prospect. She'd made him promise again that he'd bring the necessary paperwork to authorise their conversation. Tough antie, indeed.

After leaving Riet's house, he'd headed back to the office.

Pyl had still been there, tinkering with Hanekom's computer. But his email hadn't revealed much. It seemed that Hanekom had deleted messages permanently once he was done with them. A number of right-wing websites were listed under his Internet browser favourites.

"We might have to send the computer away so that the IT guys can take a look," Beeslaar had decided. "Turn it off, Ballies. And go home. You've done more than your share today."

Beeslaar was ready to go home himself. But first he emailed the Moegel a short report. Then fetched Freddie Swarts's diary from the safe, and left.

He moved the sprinkler and went back to the kitchen. Last little nightcap. But first he cut four slices of bread—white bread—and buttered them, took out four pink vienna sausages, put it all in a Tupperware container and took it to the garage with a mug of sweet tea. Bulelani was half asleep already, but one sniff of the food and he was wide awake. He sat up and tucked in immediately, taking big slugs of tea as he did so. Beeslaar left him to it and went back to the house.

His last drink was a little stronger. And he had it on the rocks.

By the time the glass was empty, his entire vegetable patch had been watered, so he got up and turned in for the night.

Freddie Swarts's diary went with him. Bedtime story.

86

Beeslaar woke with a splitting headache. Had he had that much to drink? Just one beer and a brandy or two, after all. Or was it three?

Maybe four, even. Because he hadn't been able to sleep. And Gerda had phoned.

After midnight. She couldn't sleep either.

"I've been thinking about you," she'd breathed into the phone sleepily, her voice muffled, sounding far away.

"I've been thinking about you, too."

"I wonder if it's time."

"What do you mean, time?"

"To, well, to see each other."

His heart lurched. Joy. And fear.

"You mean, as in—for me to come to you. To come see you?"

She didn't respond.

"Gerda? Is that what you mean?"

"I don't know what I mean. I want to stop thinking about you. It makes me remember. And I don't want to." She sobbed quietly.

He'd felt the old dread settling over him. He used to be able to make her laugh. But that had changed, that day. Forever. And now he could only make her cry.

He'd wanted to say something, to comfort her, but she hadn't given him the chance. She'd whispered goodbye and the line had gone dead.

That had been his last chance of getting any sleep, for sure. Beeslaar had felt around for the diary, even though it was hardly bedtime reading. He had a hell of a time deciphering the hieroglyphics of her handwriting. He just couldn't concentrate. So, diary under his arm, he'd got up and—well, why not?—went to the kitchen to pour himself another brandy. The woman's talent had definitely not been a literary one. The notes were cryptic and often incomprehensible:

Painted Lottie-Lamb's little shoes red. Little red Cinderella shoes. Rosy shoes. Ring-a-ring-a-rosy, we all fall down. Oh, we laughed and laughed, split our sides laughing. But I wonder: how do you actually laugh like that? What is it that splits? And what comes spilling out?

Another passage: "Wonder what's up with Maria. Always cross and huffy and puffed up, but she stays thin as a rake." Weird recordings of dreams, perhaps:

Three wheels and an ox. We ride the dunes. A fox keeps following us. Look at its head, how it dangles, all askew. Says D: Mad dog. She's rabid. She's coming. We quickly kill the fire and pack up our things. Old Mad Dog Skew-head follows: comes closer, closer, closer. I look back and see it's nothing, really. Just an old towel someone has tossed in. Ha-ha.

Some pages had been dated, though she'd written nothing. Then, an odd and disturbing entry a few weeks ago, in mid-January:

The eyes of men. All eyes, all hands, no heart. All cruel cock. Poison penis, poison pen. He dips his pen, scorches his mark on me. Spears me with his assegai. I burn, from the inside out. He spews his poison, screams his ecstasy.

Greed spewed, power sated. But me, I shrivel to ash, float free. My body claimed and staked. My blood in the sand. But my soul is mine . . .

One of the last entries, written a week before her death, even more disjointed, dark:

> Friendly Freddie's Friend is done.
> Kaput. Finis.
> Dried-up. Empty. Out.
> Heartsore, but relieved.
> Amen. Amen.
> But bleeding, sore—my flesh is ripped and torn asunder. I keep plucking, tugging, picking. One by one, the thorns of Sleeping Beauty's jail, I flee the nest in the haak-en-steekbos.
> M the wicked fairy. Black heart.
> Green-eyed monster. A thieving crow.
> Stealing the land of the chief's poor people. It's her. I know it. She and that brute with his poison cock! Robbers and thieves. Scavengers.
> I see everything now. Through the glass, darkly.
> She knows I know. She will come back, haunt us.
> But I'll take up my ashes. Drift away.

He must have been pretty far gone, but one thing he remembered now was the growing sense of anticipation, that old flame he thought had died down after the dramas of Joburg. This jumbled diary, he realised, was the key to what had happened to Freddie—she had given it to him herself, from the grave. In her own crazy language she pointed her finger at two people, without naming them. But the mysterious M could only be one person: Nelmari Viljoen. And the "brute" with the "assegai," the rapist: Boet Pretorius. All he needed to do now was to go get them. Both. Find the evidence and put them away for good.

By this time he was thoroughly exhausted, but too hyped up to sleep. So he poured another . . .

Beeslaar glanced at his bedside alarm clock. Hell, five o'clock already. He tossed the sheet aside and stumbled to the bathroom. Panado. Two now, and two for later. He brushed his teeth and looked at himself in the mirror: bags under the eyes, a deep crease between his eyebrows. He smacked down the toothbrush and stepped into the shower. There was work to be done and the dawn had already broken.

Warrant or no warrant, he had to get to the Pretorius farm. And to Upington. Even if De Kok was still a bundle of bandages, he was going to talk today. Him and the Viljoen woman, he'd make damn sure of that. He dressed, grabbed a bottle of water from the fridge and ran for his car.

Ghaap was already waiting for him when he pulled up in front of the police station. He got into the car without a word, a cigarette dangling from the corner of his mouth.

They drove in silence, Ghaap nodding off now and then—though as usual it was hard to tell whether he was awake or asleep.

Beeslaar mulled over the details of the gamble he was about to take. Boet Pretorius was hardly likely to throw his doors open in welcome, that's for bloody sure. So, what was he hoping for? That a surprise visit would catch him off guard? Fat chance. This Vuyo Masilela, was he one of the workers Pretorius had been so mysterious about? And Ghaap, damned fool, had allowed big white bossman Boet Pretorius to intimidate him, hadn't interviewed all his labourers. A hand-picked bunch, no friends or acquaintances among the locals. A convenient isolation for workers moonlighting as stock thieves.

And the stolen animals—moved to the Botswana border across his land, the trucks disappearing quickly, unnoticed?

And Nelmari Viljoen—where did she fit into all this? The "crow" and the "brute," Freddie Swarts called her and Pretorius in her diary. The two comrades seemed to have fallen out. And Pretorius had been looking for her urgently last Thursday—his new friend Riet had confirmed this. The night she was left for dead near the dump.

Now all of a sudden she was missing. Had Pretorius kidnapped her from the hospital?

Beeslaar glanced out of his window as they passed Huilwater. It looked desolate, the white walls of the house glowing eerily in the early-morning sun. The blue gum trees, with their smoky green leaves, had a mournful air.

They approached the gates of Karrikamma and Ghaap snapped out of his slumber. "Do you think he'll let us in?" he asked.

"Why wouldn't he? Unless he has something to hide, no?"

They stopped in front of the gates which, Beeslaar noticed, now had a chain on them. He pressed the intercom, waited, pressed again.

Ghaap got out, then gestured to Beeslaar to come and look.

"There've been a lot of wheels through here." He pointed to tracks in the gravel. "Look here. There are ridges, even. An ordinary bakkie wouldn't leave furrows like this." Then he jerked his thumb at the fence, his eyes gliding appreciatively along its length. "Looks like Bonnox, that—the BMW of fencing."

At least two and a half metres high, Beeslaar estimated, as he waited before the mute intercom.

"Okay, what now?" asked Ghaap, clearly impatient.

"Upington. We've got to get to De Kok—before he disappears too."

The ward sister didn't look at all impressed as the two policemen flashed their IDs. She gave them ten minutes max with the patient.

"He's still very weak, Inspector," she warned.

Beeslaar and Ghaap walked past the policeman stationed outside the ICU and headed towards the heavily bandaged man on the bed.

Dam lay immobile, his skin a corpselike beige, but his eyes flickered open as the two men stopped at his bedside. "Karrikamma," he said, before Beeslaar could even open his mouth to ask.

"And why didn't you let me know, man? The whole world is running around because you damn well refuse to communicate with anyone. Who did this to you? You look like roadkill!"

De Kok struggled to sit upright, but was overcome with a coughing fit. He grimaced and flopped down again. "Oom Vangjan," he said in a weak voice, "the jackal-hunter. He went to show me on Yzerfontein, Saturday night. We waited. The whole night, on a koppie. A white car came. A man, we saw him cut the fence."

"Well, why didn't you phone me then? We'd have caught the fucker, and you wouldn't be halfway dead." He decided against mentioning Mma Mokoena, who might still have been alive.

De Kok blinked. "No. The old man wanted to go show me. Where it was from." He swallowed and slowly went on. "We walked, through farms, lots of fences. To Pretorius's place. Oom Vangjan saw an aardvark hole, we used it to crawl under the fence. He showed me the white car, it was the same one we saw earlier. At the koppie. Parked behind a shed. He said it's the shed where the trucks come from."

"So you decided to be the lone hero."

The nurse came past and told Beeslaar to finish up. He

raised an index finger, signalling he needed one minute more. She frowned and turned on her heel.

"How did you get hurt like this?"

"When I saw that man. In the night. When the trucks came. I just lost it." He squeezed his eyes shut again.

Beeslaar had heard enough and got ready to leave. "You'd bloody well get better, okay?" he told De Kok jokingly, "so I can donner you properly. I refuse to slap corpses about." De Kok acknowledged the attempt at humour with a weak smile.

The two of them were on their way again when Beeslaar called the superintendent. Once again, he was interrupting a meal—breakfast, this time. He informed him about his conversation with De Kok, and the Moegel promised an armed unit, together with a warrant against Pretorius. Beeslaar would hear from him once he had everything organised. As for Viljoen, he shouldn't worry about her. The Moegel himself was on the case.

The drive back was speedy, but mostly silent. When they passed Karrikamma again, they looked out for signs of movement, but saw nothing.

Ghaap of course was slumped down on the seat, hands thrust deep inside his pockets. He somehow managed to be supine wherever he was sitting—on a kitchen chair, behind a desk or in the cramped space of the car. Hell, even on a bar stool. Always catching a nap.

As if on cue, Ghaap raised his head. "Where does Pretorius get all his money? I mean, it's not like he's Mark Shuttleworth. No pumps are going to earn you that much. Big bucks have been spent here."

"I think that's where Nelmari Viljoen comes into the picture," said Beeslaar.

They were approaching Huilwater. Beeslaar slowed down when he noticed a bakkie at the farm gate.

It was the neighbour, Roger Heidenrich. He'd come to drop off a labourer, he explained, as requested by Sara Swarts.

He opened the tailgate and a dog jumped down from the bakkie. It sniffed around dutifully, then sped off after its owner, who was already heading down the road.

"I hear you've arrested Buks Hanekom," the farmer said.

"He was involved in some really nasty stuff."

"I feel sorry for his parents. He's changed. He wasn't always so bitter."

"Guess not," said Beeslaar and got back into his car.

"I hear the Pieterse crowd are organising a march to town," Heidenrich said, bending down to his window.

"Where did you hear that?"

"Jan Steenkamp. He's just called to tell us we'd better stay out of town today. It could be chaos. Apparently they're going to march in with horses and tractors and wagons and anything they can get hold of. You didn't know this?"

Beeslaar turned on the engine, revved it and slammed the car into reverse.

Then he headed out on the road and floored it all the way back to town.

87

Even though it was early, Sara showered and dressed, grabbing a cotton top and a short skirt. Her plan was to drive to Upington, be there when Dam came to—before one of Beeslaar's guys decided to arrest him.

Harry was at the kitchen table, staring at his computer screen. She went over to him, kissed the top of his head. He put his arm around her legs, rested a palm on her thigh.

"Here, take a look at this, Sara," he said.

She put a hand on his shoulder, leaned forward, her cheek touching his. It was a web page for *Die Volksblad*, with a picture of a black man and detailed report alongside: he was being sought in connection with the "much talked-about farm killing" of "the beautiful artist."

Sara sat down heavily beside Harry.

"They say he killed someone else yesterday. Here in town. A shebeen owner," he said.

"And he hasn't been caught yet?" Sara chewed a fingernail.

"No, they're still looking for him. Vuyo Masilela. Sounds like a really dangerous guy. Hijacker, cash-in-transit robber, stock thief, you name it."

Sara stared. The man's face—like something out of a horror movie. The dead eyes, utterly expressionless. Was that the last face Freddie had looked at, those empty eyes?

"Sara?" she heard Harry saying. "Sara." She felt his hand touch her cheek. He brushed her hair back, lifted her chin with his thumb. But she jerked away and walked out the back door.

Tears burnt at her throat, her eyes. God, how was something like this possible? A man like that! And doing it to Freddie . . . What was happening to this society, why this excessive rage? And not a single expression of disgust from the rulers of the country. Like Dam's hyenas in the darkness, all of us, she thought. Lurking in the shadows.

Harry found her and put an arm around her shoulder. And mercifully said nothing.

They stood there, the morning sun no comfort.

"I'm going to Upington," Sara eventually said.

He pressed her closer, kissed her hair.

"Not on your own, Sara."

"Yes, Harry, on my own."

"Let me come . . . "

"Please, I need some space," she said, turning to him.

He let it go. Then said, "Okay. I'll hang around here, then. Maybe later on I'll get to meet the man from the Griqua cultural society."

88

G haap kept an eye on his phone until he saw he had a signal, then waved at Beeslaar to stop. Beeslaar pulled over, and Ghaap said to the exchange, "Give me the police station, please. It's urgent. Stay on the line till they pick up."

Ghaap waited. And waited, and waited.

"Bliksems," he cursed. "They're in the stock room at the back, sleeping again. Or drinking tea, like a bunch of old tannies."

Beeslaar pulled out his own cellphone and speed-dialled Pyl.

"Inspector!" he wheezed.

"Where are you, huffing and puffing like that?"

"I'm out jogging!"

"You're *what*?" Pyl surprised him more with each passing day. "Listen, Ballies, you need to get to the station. The farmers are staging a march to the office. You need to get Hanekom and that Pieterse boy out of there immediately, someone must take them to Upington. And get hold of as many people as possible to come in to the station so long. We're going to need all hands on deck. Ghaap and I are still out in the district—about twenty minutes from town."

He heard Pyl panting into the phone.

"Did you *hear* me, Ballies?"

"I did, yes, but there's a problem. You might get to town long before me. I'm too far out."

"What are you running so fucking far for, Pyl? Which road are you on?"

Next to him, Ghaap had begun to talk loudly into his phone. Beeslaar couldn't hear what Pyl was saying, shouted at him to hurry back and ended the call. He tapped Ghaap's shoulder. "Tell them someone needs to let the Moegel know, so he can organise reinforcements!"

But Ghaap's phone had given out, flat battery, he said sheepishly.

Beeslaar irritably handed him his phone, pointed to a number on speed-dial, and waited as Ghaap made the call, ready to drive on as soon as the message had been delivered.

"The bakkies are out," Ghaap told him. "And there's just two on duty—Morotse and Kgomotse. You'll have to step on it."

They still got to town too late. The main road was blocked by a big tractor and trailer parked across it. Beeslaar stopped the car and got out.

"Police. Let us through," he called out to the young man perched on the tractor seat.

But he just sat there, and there was no time to argue. Beeslaar got back in the car, reversed, and moments later he'd swung left onto a gravel road running out of town. It crossed a piece of open veld before hitting the shacks on the edge of Chicken Vale. Beeslaar found a rough track that led back to the town, and they shook about as the car bounced over potholes and ditches at high speed.

"When we get there, you need to get those two guys out and hightail it to Upington," Beeslaar shouted.

"Won't it make things worse?"

"I don't give a fuck." Beeslaar's head hit the ceiling hard as he accelerated through a donga in the road. He decided to keep his mouth shut and focus his attention on driving until they were safely parked behind the police-station fence. They would have to use the back entrance, the main road would already be jammed with vehicles.

Shoes Morotse was waiting for them round the back.

"They want to speak to *you*, Inspector," he said over the clamour of agitated voices coming from the charge office.

"And who's they?"

"Pieterse and a whole bunch of white farmers," Morotse explained.

"Could you get hold of Upington?"

"They've just occupied the phone exchange too."

Beeslaar turned to Ghaap. "Use my cell—if you haven't killed my battery as well! Call the Moegel, his number is under 'DM.' Get backup, lots of it."

He took a deep breath and headed for the charge office. As he entered, a hush descended. The place was packed, from the front doors to the service counter.

Beeslaar got himself behind the counter, Constable Kgomotse visibly relieved to see him.

A red-haired giant stepped forward. "My name is Abraham Visser, and I'm speaking on behalf of all the people here." He waved a thick arm. "We come in peace, but we demand the release of our people."

Beeslaar recognised the burly Boer he'd seen in action at the tin church two Sundays ago—the community called him "Tjoek"; he looked and sounded like a locomotive.

This morning he looked even more like a caricature with his full red beard, khaki trousers and khaki shirt, a bandolier slung over a swollen belly, Bible under his arm. Not a man you could ignore. His voice was the deep bass of a church organ. His sheer size and weight commanded attention. He had an electric presence—Rasputin meets Jimmy Swaggart, Beeslaar thought.

"Good morning, Mr. Visser." He concentrated on sounding

calm, and even managed a bit of a smile. "I'm afraid I can't agree to your request. The men to whom you are referring will be able to apply for bail—once a magistrate has granted permission. Unfortunately that can't happen here, because, as you know, there is no magistrate's court in town. We will have to take them through to Upington."

Visser squared his massive shoulders. "We're not here to bandy words about, Inspector," he boomed, "we are demanding the release of our people, one of whom is in need of medical care."

More shouts and raised voices as a scrum of bodies pushed forward. Visser held up his Bible as they started pressing up against him.

The front door was continually opening and closing, as more and more people pushed in. By now there were twenty or so armed men in the room, either with shoulder holsters or guns at their hip.

Beeslaar tried to maintain the appearance, at least, that he was in control. "Mr. Visser! It is illegal to enter a centre of law enforcement armed. The superintendent of this region is on his way here to speak with you. I suggest you wait outside and then we negotiate like civi—"

"We're going nowhere! Not without our men!"

The line had been drawn. Now it was his authority against the big guy's. And he already knew who would win. He felt the blood pulsing in his ears. Then he raised his voice. "I give you, and these people of yours, just ten seconds to evacuate this room. *Right*?"

A heavy odour of sweat and stale cigarettes hung in the silent air. Everyone waiting for the red giant to make mincemeat out of Beeslaar.

Beeslaar held his breath. Twenty pairs of eyes had him in their sights.

Behind Visser stood Grootboel Pieterse, with his other

sons. All clones of their father. Beeslaar kept his eyes on them, but addressed his colleague. "Constable Kgomotse, let's get hold of the army in Postmasburg. Go get Sergeant Ghaap and Constable Morotse. See that they call up all units in the district, and that they inform headquarters in Upington and Kimberley that we're sitting with a riot on our hands here!

"Make way, there!" he boomed at a group of men that had begun to block the counter gate. Outside, in the street in front of the station, he heard the roar of heavy 4×4s and bakkies.

"Look, Mr. Visser," he said. "You need to watch your step. I don't want anyone to get hurt here today. I suggest you leave the station and we meet outside, then you can air your concerns and we can sort out the dispute. Like civilised people."

"There's no dispute! Only injustice!" Visser shouted and turned to his people, who agreed enthusiastically. Then he looked back at Beeslaar. "We are, however, law-abiding people," he said. "We give you ten minutes. Then you let our people go. We'll wait outside."

With that he raised his chin high and walked out of the charge office, his Bible held aloft. The men crowded after him, their voices a low rumble.

Beeslaar watched till the last of them had gone through the door. Outside, Tjoek Visser stood on the steps, his Bible a talisman. Someone handed him a loudhailer.

He doesn't need the thing, thought Beeslaar. With a voice like that you could hear him on the moon.

"Friends!" The word reverberated in the seething street. Somewhere, a baby began to wail.

"We are gathered here together today! In the *darkest* hour! Of our . . ."

Beeslaar swung his frame over the counter and went to bolt

the doors. He was buggered if he was going to stand and listen to that shit like a trapped springhare.

Pyl came in through the back door. He was still in baggy track-suit pants and a T-shirt, a stained sweatband on his head. "The super's nearly here, he's just phoned," he said, peering around the room as if some wild farmer might still be hiding there.

"How far away is he?"

"A few minutes. Did Shoes tell you about the man who was here early this morning?"

"We don't have time for bullshit now, Ballies. What man?"

"The Karrikamma foreman. He came to lay a charge of assault against his boss."

"*What*? And why didn't Shoes call me? Where is he?"

"Here, outside with—"

"Jesus, Pyl, don't act stupid now. The fucking *foreman*!"

"In your office."

Beeslaar squinted at the front doors. Through the glass, he could see that Tjoek had relinquished the loudhailer. But he was still bellowing on, about sixty faces gazing raptly up at him. There were more flags flying and he saw at least four young men on horses, rifles on their shoulders.

"What a bloody mess." He turned to Pyl. "You stay here. Keep the front doors locked. No one comes in here. Nobody, not even the good Lord Jesus Christ himself. And put someone on guard at the cells."

"Ja, baas," he heard Pyl mutter as he walked out.

Beeslaar swung around furiously, walked right up to Pyl and pushed a finger in his face. "Listen here, *Gershwin*, if you start with that racism crap again, you can go home right now. We all have to pull together now, so get on with it!"

"Relax, man, relax."

Beeslaar glowered and pointed at the door. "Look outside, man! Does this look like a time to relax?" Then he spun round and left.

"Can't even take a joke," he heard Pyl mutter. But he walked on.

Morotse and Ghaap came hurrying up to him with the news that an army unit was on its way. Ghaap shrieked, "And they're sending a helicopter!"

89

Constable Kgomotse was waiting for him in his office. With her was a wiry young man in blue overalls. "This is Piet September," she said, a hand planted firmly on the seated man's shoulder. September looked up at Beeslaar nervously, dark bruises on his cheeks.

"He says Pretorius did this to him late last night. He was about to leave the farm with his mother, but Pretorius apparently went berserk, locked him and his mother up, but Mr. September managed to escape during the night and walked to town. His mother is still there and he's afraid Pretorius might harm her. He won't say why."

Beeslaar perched on the end of his desk, looming over September.

"I don't have a lot of time to talk. Just one question: Is Vuyo Masilela still on the farm?"

"Pretorius will kill my mother if he knows I'm here."

"Who's your mother?" asked Beeslaar.

"The housekeeper. I'm the foreman. He hit me yesterday. The first time my mother stopped him. But later he hit me again. Now my mother—"

"Look, I can only help you if you help me. Tell me if Masilela is still there."

September licked a cut on his lip, touched the swelling on his eye hesitantly.

Beeslaar waited, acutely aware of the blood thudding in his ears. He wanted to shake the man, but realised the guy had some big decisions to make. If he ratted on Pretorius, his own involvement would come to light too. But on the other hand he wanted to save his mother's skin.

In the street outside, the air was loud with voices and the rumbling of engines. Beeslaar looked out at the crowd milling around. There were women too, holding placards, though he couldn't make out what was written on them.

He turned back to September, said, "If you want me to drive out there and bring your mother home in one piece, you'd better talk to me, Mr. September. And it will help me a lot if I know I can pick Masilela up at the same time."

"He isn't there any more, sir," came the quiet answer. "He was there till last night—on Karrikamma. But he ran away. They had a big fight. He stabbed Mr. Pretorius with a knife."

"Where'd he run to?"

"I don't know. He just drove away—in the Defender."

"And Pretorius?"

The man looked as if he might cry. "He's gone mad. Last night he said he was going to shoot us all and set the farm on fire. Please, sir, I just want to get my mother out of there, before something happens."

Beeslaar got up. "Constable, get the man something to eat—the rusks and tea in Jansie's office. And make sure he stays in here." Turning to September, he said, "Nothing will happen to your mother, you hear?" He glanced out of his window one last time, his legs jelly, his heart hammering, and then walked to the door.

The whole thing was fast becoming a circus.

90

Sara hurried over to the bed as he opened his eyelids and whispered, "Dam!"

He smiled weakly and tried to lift his head. But his body stiffened with a spasm and he squeezed his eyes shut. His breath rattled in his throat, became a bubbling cough. She turned to look for the nurse, but then the coughing subsided and Dam sank back with a groan, his eyes still closed.

"Oh, bloody hell, Dam," she said and took his hand. There was a yellow tinge to his skin, and he looked old and shrunken.

"Sara." His eyes met hers.

She put a finger to his lips. "Don't speak, Dam. Just rest, get better."

"No, wait. You must keep away from the farm. The murderer is right next door, at Karrikamma."

"What? Did *he* do this to you? But how, were you there?"

In a barely audible voice, he explained it all.

Sara sat back in shock. She'd been to Karrikamma just the day before. Jesus. Right there, with that crazy man. And the way he'd reacted to his worker . . . She had a thousand questions, but asked just one. "Did Boet kill Freddie?"

"No. It's that man."

It didn't make sense to her. Stock thefts being launched from Boet's farm. By his workers—and this Masilela, who was one of them. *They* were the murderers. So Boet must have known. But why had he been so distraught that Saturday night—he was so obviously cut up about Freddie. Her thoughts swirled: stealing from neighbours, the Griqua land claim, the will of the old chief, Waterboer. Maybe Harry was right about it—the final scrap of evidence. It included parts of Huilwater. But what else? Boet's land, maybe?

Dam's hand was wriggling free from her clasp. She hadn't realised she'd gripped it so tight.

"But why didn't you tell us anything, Dam?"

He gave a tired smile. "Ag, just call me a stupid Bushman. On my own mission. That man, I wanted to—I *myself* wanted to . . ."

Sara smiled wanly, she knew what he was trying to say.

"Harry! Man, why aren't you answering!" Sara cried out as she stood in a patch of shade outside the hospital.

Then her phone rang, and there was his voice. "Sorry, I've only just seen your missed call! All hell's broken loose in this little town of yours. Are you all right?"

"I'm okay, but what's going on there?"

"It's hectic! I'm taking pics like crazy. People on horseback carrying placards, burning flags, it's a madhouse."

She tried to tell him what Dam had said, but he shouted something and cut the call.

She slammed the car door shut, counted to ten, then switched on the ignition. Dam needed a toothbrush, toiletries. She'd go and buy some—pyjamas too, maybe.

Thoughts assailed her as she drove. The old chief's will. And Boet: Had *he* given the order to kill Freddie—it was his fault, he'd drunkenly stated that night. And the painting: If he'd seen it, why on earth stage her murder in that grotesque way? Revenge, maybe? And Masilela—might he be the mysterious "M"? *My little dove* . . . No, no, impossible!

91

Outside in the street someone had started singing the anthem of the old Transvaal Boer republic, "Kent gij dat volk vol heldenmoed . . . " Within moments, the crowd had joined in, a mournful choir.

The Moegel had just arrived, the promised armed unit apparently following in his wake. He cocked an ear in the direction of the street.

"What the hell are they singing there?" he asked in his deep Darth Vader voice.

"It's an old Boer version of 'Umshini wami,'" Beeslaar said, fumbling with the velcro of his vest. He didn't know whose Kevlar they'd unearthed from the storeroom for him, but the previous owner seemed unacquainted with deodorant. From the Moegel's expression, his vest smelt rather ripe too.

"Isn't the super going to speak to them?" Pyl asked. He was struggling to fasten the straps around the Moegel's belly.

"Listen, there's nothing I can do without the army."

"But what if they come up here and storm the doors?"

Beeslaar peered through a door pane. "Kent gij dat volk" had started petering out. He guessed people no longer knew all the words. Then Tjoek Visser took charge of the megaphone, exhorting the crowd to sing "Die Lied van Jong Suid-Afrika."

The singing started up again, this time with a little more enthusiasm. "En hoor jy die magtige dreuning? Oor die veld kom dit wyd gesweef . . . "

"Shouldn't we just surrender the two white men to them?" Pyl asked. With the Moegel's Kevlar vest in position, he was now working at adjusting his own. He looked almost comical, with the harness over his clownish tracksuit pants and the sweatband still on his head. The poor man's answer to Luke Skywalker.

The superintendent went to stand next to Beeslaar, and they both looked out over the crowd.

"That's a possibility," he said in answer to Pyl's question. "I don't like the idea, but it is a possibility."

"With respect, Superintendent, we can't give in to these people's demands. But I'll go out and talk to them. For what it's worth. This lot are out to make a point."

"No. *I* will," said Mogale.

Beeslaar was aghast. Was the man utterly oblivious of what he was dealing with? To Tjoek Visser, a black man was the Antichrist incarnate. Especially a black man with rank. But Mogale did have a pleasant surprise for Beeslaar.

"Listen, we need to get this mess sorted quickly, we've got more important things to deal with. I brought you your warrants, plus one for Miss Viljoen's office and her home."

"Yes!" Beeslaar exclaimed.

"We're investigating her for fraud in Upington. That's why I wanted Sergeant Pyl to fetch me some documents from her office yesterday. The secretary handed them over quite happily, but then phoned Viljoen, and she put her lawyers onto me. I think she realised her number's—"

His words were drowned out by the blare of Visser's megaphone. He had turned around, and was now aiming "Die Lied van Jong Suid-Afrika" directly at the police station.

Mogale put his hand on the door, ready to go out.

"Don't," Beeslaar called out. "These people are—"

But he didn't get to finish his sentence: the cheering and shouting reached a crescendo, and as Beeslaar peered out, he saw that the national flag was on fire. The smoking banner was being waved around by a young man Beeslaar recognised from the church meeting. A feverish light burnt in his eyes as he yelled and jabbed the blackened shreds in the air, the once-bright colours gone.

From somewhere, the crack of a gunshot sounded.

"We can't just sit here like a scared bunch of rabbits!" Mogale shouted and reached for the door again.

"No!" Beeslaar bellowed. "You don't *know* these people, sir. The last thing they want to see is a black face right now!" Beeslaar saw the Moegel's eyes harden, but he didn't wait for a reply. He pushed the door open. "*Please* stay here!" he cried before stepping outside and shutting the door behind him.

92

At first no one noticed him on the steps of the charge office—all eyes were on the red-haired colossus leading the singing of old-time anthems, his eyes closed, head flung back.

While Beeslaar waited for them to finish singing, he observed the crowd, which by now was about a hundred strong. Nearly every man and boy carried some kind of gun—most, though, were hunting rifles. But some of the younger men had handguns in holsters too.

Across the street, behind the men on horseback, he saw two young boys high up in the branches of the karee. Usually, the group of homeless people sat under it. Today, though, they were nowhere to be seen.

Right in front of him, just below the steps, women waved placards.

FARM MURDERS = GENOCIDE
PIET DE KLERK—ACHILLES TENDONS SLICED, SHOT IN THE HEAD
BRAAM DU PLOOY—HANGED

There was no way, Beeslaar realised, that he and his small band of colleagues could control this situation. The army was their only hope.

As the song reached its close, Beeslaar felt his heartbeat accelerate. Showtime. To the right of him a camera flashed:

Van Zyl. "Inspector, are you going to give in to their demands?" he called out.

"I'll do nothing of the sort—" And then he felt a heavy hand on his shoulder. He turned, annoyed, and tried to shake free, but the preacher had him in an iron grip. The crowd had grown quiet, its full attention on him and his antagonist.

Tjoek Visser raised the megaphone, barked out a staccato exhortation. "Burghers! We demand this! Release our people! Our call echoes! As far as the United Nations!"

Beeslaar took a step back, as a wave of cacophonous cheering washed over him. That was clearly what the preacher had in mind: whipping his people up in a wave of hysteria and overwhelming this stupid policeman, the Poephol from Prieska.

He steadied himself, knew he'd have to do something—and fast.

93

Dam was asleep again when Sara stepped into the ward. She unpacked her purchases, arranged them in his bedside cabinet. Then she pulled up a chair, sat down and took his hand in hers. She examined it: rough and calloused, the fingernails trimmed short. The skin was grazed and scratched—just like the rest of his body.

With her index finger, she traced the marks on his hands and forearms, thinking of what he'd told her about the night he'd lain in wait for Masilela: how the old jackal-catcher, Windvogel, had sent for him on Saturday night with instructions to leave his clothes at home, to come in just his loincloth, like an old-time hunter, soundless, invisible, a phantom of the veld. He'd found the old man with a young boy, a kid who wandered the veld with him as his helper. The boy was mute, but skilful, the old man had told him. He knew where to dig for water, which bulbs to dig up for food and where to set traps for the springhare they ate. Dam and the old man had sat waiting on Yzerfontein, on a koppie surrounded by swarthaak trees, from where they'd seen Masilela arrive in his BMW, doing a recce of the terrain. Afterwards, he and old Windvogel had slept on the soft, cool sand of a ditch on a neighbouring farm. The glow of their fire had been hidden by the high limestone walls of the ditch—which apparently provided frequent shelter for the two veld folk. As they'd arrived, the boy had dug out karosses of soft sheepskin, kept carefully buried in the river sand, for them to sleep on. And a loaf of bread and butter too—the sand used as a kind of veld fridge. Dam had watched as the boy chewed the toothless old man's food for him first to soften it.

On Sunday morning they'd crossed several farms to show Dam how the thieves' trucks were hidden on Karrikamma. And they'd shown him the back roads where stolen livestock was transported to the Botswana border.

That evening they'd returned to the koppie and had sat waiting for the thieves. Hours under the stars, silent and still, but at ease, like a genet lying in wait for a mouse outside its hole. She remembered Dam's words: "It was as if I was walking with my grandfather N!xi again. Relying on instinct alone." But when Dam had seen Masilela with the trucks that night, a wave of rage washed away all those old instincts. He rushed through the swarthaak like a madman, with only one aim: to use his knobkierie against the thief's head . . .

She felt Dam's hand stir in hers. He opened his eyes, but his eyelids were heavy. "Sara," he whispered.

She smiled at him. His face looked softer, more relaxed now, perhaps from the painkillers.

Her sister had loved him, she realised with a sudden sadness. Loved him so much that she felt her heart would burst, so much she wanted to pluck it from her chest for him.

Frêtjie . . . Where did your love for this man begin? Did you watch him as he worked with his birds, so calmly, so carefully? Or perhaps you saw how gently he picked up the child. Held her on his knee, telling her about the beautiful caracal.

Dam's eyes were brimming. It was as if he were reading her thoughts. Sara reached over, wiped at the tears with her fingertips. Then she took his hand again. He lay there with his eyes closed. But the tears kept coming. She sat with him, her hands folded over his, until eventually she saw he was sleeping again. Then she got up quietly, kissed him on the forehead and left the ward.

*

On the hospital steps, Sara tried to reach Harry again.

"Sara, I can't talk now," he panted. There was one hell of a ruckus in the background.

"Harry! Can you hear—"

"What? Sara, I'm stuck in a crowd. Hang on . . . call you back."

She walked to her car. She had only just put the key in the ignition when he rang back.

"Harry, things okay?"

"Jesus, Saartjie, it's hectic. People are demanding that Hanekom and the Pieterse boy be handed over to them. Looks as if they're ready to charge the police station. And there are more guns here than in Baghdad. Apart from Beeslaar, I can't see any sign of the police. I think they're all sitting trapped in that little building."

She told him about Masilela and what Dam had said.

He whistled through his teeth. "What a cock-up, with the police stuck here, in this mess."

"At least Beeslaar and his guys were with Dam earlier this morning. Maybe they've been out to Boet's already. For all we know, Boet and that man are locked up already!"

"Are you coming back now? Call once you're close to town. I don't know if you'll be able to drive right in. The whole damn place is barricaded."

"I have to go past the farm first. Go see if Roger Heidenrich's man is there."

"No way, Sara. You're not going out there alone!"

"I'll just swing by to see if he's there, Harry. Don't worry."

"No. It's too dangerous. We don't know if Masilela has been caught yet, or where he might be."

"Okay, well. But you know, I still can't believe Masilela killed Freddie. He wouldn't have done it like *that*. Like in the painting . . . "

"You're overcomplicating things, Sara. It's time to stop your damned nonsense about the painting."

"It's not nonsense."

"Wake up, Sara. First you suspected Dam, and now you say it can't be Masilela. Who the hell do you want it to be?"

"Don't talk to me like that. I can't help—"

"Sorry, Sara. Just come back, and stop these ridiculous theories. It was just another farm murder. Look, I'm sorry, but that's all it was. Just like the thousands of others these people are protesting about here this morning."

"I'm not sure, I really don't know. It was so brutal—"

"Sara, for God's sake! Hundreds of farmers have been tortured and killed like that. Just the other day, you remember, that family near Rustenburg—forced to drink coffee laced with rat poison, a slow, agonising death, the mother and daughter raped. This kind of thing happens. All the time. We don't know what goes on in the killers' heads. Just accept it, won't you? Farm murders are brutal, horribly brutal. And your poor sister was caught up in one of those brutal attacks."

"But Harry, the painting—"

"Oh for goodness' sake, Sara! Just come *here*, then, come read these placards, listen to the stories they're telling—friends and family who had their fingers chopped off, bodies burnt with cigarettes and hot irons, their eyelids sliced off. Listen, I don't want to fight with you, Sara. I just don't want you walking around with the idea that Freddie's murder was somehow different. And that *you* can do anything about it. Okay?"

She bit her lip. Curtly, she ended the call, and started the engine.

94

The women at the bottom of the stairs had started up a rhythmic chant. "Let our children go! Let our children go!" It swelled to a rousing war cry, and with every beat the crowd moved closer to the police station.

Beeslaar wondered where they'd all come from. Rounded up from neighbouring districts, he suspected. He put his arms up, called, "Give us a chance to talk!" But his voice was drowned out by the din.

The crowd was already pushing up the stairs, forcing him up against the station doors. He could feel the heat of the rising hysteria as the faces, red with excitement, got closer and closer. The air was thick with dust and sweat; it made his throat close up, suffocating him.

"Call for order, before someone gets hurt!" he shouted at the red-bearded giant next to him, but the man just smiled triumphantly, a fanatical gleam in his eyes.

Beeslaar felt the door behind him open, and a hand tugged at his shirt. He turned around, glimpsed Mogale's eyes.

"Get back," Beeslaar shouted. "And bolt the door. They're going to try to force their way in!"

"I have the two detainees here," Mogale shouted.

"Get back!"

"Open the fucking door—that's an order!"

The crowd was pushing up the steps, closing in on him. Beeslaar could see the wildness, the madness in their eyes. The door behind him was pushed open again and Mogale edged his way out.

"Stand back!" Beeslaar shouted at the crowd, trying to make space for Mogale. But they just kept jostling. He turned to Visser. "Use your megaphone, man, tell them!"

But the clamour was drowned as the faces in front of him suddenly looked up: a loud whump-whump-whump reverberated, and a wind whipped at them all—it was an army helicopter hovering overhead for a second before slowly descending, the noise by now deafening. Then there was a shot. And another, followed by a series of swifter volleys. With an outraged roar, the helicopter rose and disappeared behind the roof of the building.

Beeslaar scanned the crowd. Who had fired the shots? He saw several men with pistols and rifles cocked, aimed at the sky. But around him the crowd had started retreating. He turned to Mogale, shocked to see he had Kleinboel and Buks Hanekom either side of him. Hanekom had his fists held high in a gesture of victory.

Then another shot rang out. Beeslaar heard a sharp crack as the bullet hit the wooden door behind them. "Get down!" he shouted. "Get down!" He grabbed at the superintendent, bringing down a few others who fell in a heap. There was another shot. And another.

Then sudden silence.

Beeslaar lay there, with Hanekom, Mogale and the red beard either side of him. He cautiously raised his head and reached out for his superior, to see if he'd been hurt.

It was then that he saw the blood.

95

S ara slowed down at the turn-off. The farm gate was wide open. She hesitated for a moment, then drove through. Heidenrich's man must be there by now, anyway. Keeping an eyes on things, the farm implements, the house. She'd be fine.

She wanted to fetch the painting. The answers lay *there*, she was sure of it, they could all be found in Freddie's macabre self-portrait. She'd be in and out in no time.

As she approached the house, she saw the beige bakkie of her benevolent neighbour parked near the shed. There wouldn't be much for the worker to do, what with all the animals being gone. Still, it was good that there was someone to keep an eye on things.

She parked in the usual spot under the tree by the back door and killed the engine. Before getting out, she felt in her bag for the house keys. The farmyard was dead quiet. Apart from a few chirruping birds, there were no other sounds.

She must go find Roger's man, thank him for coming. She put the keys in her skirt pocket and set off towards the shed, her sandals crunching across the hot sand.

The shed's sliding doors stood half open. Sara called out into the cool darkness. "Hello? Are you there?" She called out again, but all she heard was a soft sound inside—probably a feral cat. Good, she thought, without any dogs here, the place would soon be overrun with rats.

She stepped inside, tried again. "Hello, are you here?" The man was probably out in the veld, seeing to stock.

It was murky inside. She slowly scanned the interior of the familiar old shed.

It was then that she saw the black drag-marks on the cement floor. She moved closer, leaned over. There was a big patch, a smear. A dark trail ran from it towards a heap of hessian sacks next to a few empty diesel drums against the wall. She stood up, gingerly stepped forward. Then she froze. It was a foot! Someone's foot, under the hessian. A scuffed old boot, immobile in the dark. Beside that, the hind legs of a dog. They were sticking out stiffly from under a sack.

Sara held her breath and pricked up her ears. It was deathly quiet, but she suddenly knew someone was there. The hair on the back of her neck prickled as she felt and smelled the hot breath against her neck.

Before she could move, he grabbed her by her ponytail and jerked her head back roughly. She screamed and dug her elbows into him. But he was too strong, had her head pulled back, exposing her throat.

"You die, white bitch!" His voice was harsh, his breath vile.

Her hands grasped wildly at the air. She tried to scream, but no sound came out. Then, in the corner of her eye, the glint of a blade. With all her strength, she kicked back with the heel of her sandal.

The man yelled and loosened his grip for a second.

But she was off balance, stumbling, and he got hold of her ponytail again, jerked her head back. She screamed.

"Shut up! The car. Where are the keys?"

The car keys! Where were they? She'd had them in her hand, had she dropped them when he'd grabbed her?

"Stand still, bitch! The keys!"

"They fell! They're on the floor. Let me look for them!"

She felt the cold metal under her chin and his voice rasped in her ear again. "You better find them. Or I cut your throat."

"I'll find them! Please, just let me look for them! They're somewhere on the floor. I had them in my hand."

"Then do it! On your knees, now!"

"Please, please, here, they're somewhere here, I had them," she heard herself plead incoherently.

He shoved her down with his knee, until she was on all fours. She started scrabbling around blindly. "Please! Let go of my hair!" she pleaded. "My head, I can't see the floor!" Her head was pulled back so hard she could barely choke the words out. He released his grip a little and she groped around wildly.

"My pocket!" Thank God, she thought. "They're in my pocket!" She struggled upright, feeling inside the pocket of her dress.

"Stay down, stay down!" He kicked at her and she sank back down. He leaned over her and probed with the blade, feeling for the keys. It moved over her hip and her belly, then touched metal with a clink.

"Ja, umlungu bitch!" he spat and shifted his weight as he reached for the key, transferring the knife to the other hand as he did so.

This was her chance! She pushed her toes into the ground, like a sprinter about to leave the starting blocks, propelled herself up from the floor. Her assailant swore loudly as he lost his balance. He let go of her hair and the knife clattered to the cement floor.

"Fuck!" He dived after the knife.

She threw her body forward and headed for the door. But he had her by her hair again. They struggled fiercely, stumbled together against an open toolbox. She reached blindly into the box and lifted a large metal tool. With both hands, she swung it round, heard a dull thud as it connected with his skull. He howled, lunged at her, and she felt a searing pain in her leg. She glanced down at the oozing wound, at him, and for a split second watched in fascination as the blood streamed down her assailant's eyes and over his face as he clutched at his head in agony.

Ignoring the man's enraged shouts, she ran out of the dim shed. Into the light.

96

Kleinboel Pieterse lay slumped against the door of the police station, his eyes staring, lifeless.

There was a hole just above his left eyebrow. A trickle of blood ran into his eye, dribbling into the pale down of his cheek.

Beeslaar looked at him in shock, hardly processing what he was seeing. Then he came to his senses and scrambled over to the boy.

He yanked off his Kevlar vest, pulled off his shirt, and bundled it against the boy's head. With his free hand he felt for a pulse in the neck. No, no, no. Dear God, please let the child live. He pressed his head firmly to the boy's chest.

Maybe he'd got it wrong.

But Beeslaar knew. He knew, of course. He had been here before: the body of a child, limp in his arms. Praying for a pulse. To an oblivious, deaf God.

In the distance he heard someone call for an ambulance. And still farther away was the whump-whump of the army helicopter.

In the quiet street behind him, a woman's muffled scream, the fretful shifting of horses' hooves. But here, here in the little space between him and the child, here it was quiet. Eternally quiet. He listened to the boy's chest. To the silence that had conquered that place.

The policeman looked into the wide blue eyes staring sightlessly up at the scorched heavens.

"Kleinboel," Beeslaar said quietly at the boy's ear. "I'm sorry, my boy." Christ, why did it always have to be kids?

Why? Fucking why?

He closed the boy's eyelids carefully, only then becoming aware of the circle of people watching in stunned silence.

97

The pain in her calf made it impossible to run. She limped, dragging her leg behind her. She had no idea where her attacker was. She could hear nothing.

Sara threw a fleeting glance over her shoulder, was grateful not to see him following her, and limped on. Past the shed, until she rounded the corner, saw her car, began to grope for her car keys.

"Stop! I'll kill you!"

The man had stumbled into the light. He stood there, blood streaming from his head onto his shirt. His knife was pressed against his thigh. She recognised his face from the newspaper. Masilela!

She pressed on against the pain. She was barely ten paces from the car when she saw the the silver 4×4 coming from the gate towards her. She looked back: Masilela was standing outside the shed, holding his hand to his head.

The car came to a smooth halt. "Help!" Sara screamed as she hobbled towards it. "Help me!"

The door opened and Nelmari Viljoen got out.

"Nelmari!" she shouted. "It's him! The man who murdered Freddie! Help me! We have to get away!"

Nelmari didn't respond. She just stood there, a strange expression on her face, the yellowing bruises alarming in the sunlight. She looked at Sara, then at the man behind her.

"Nelmari! It's Masilela! The murderer. We need to—"

"Shut up!" Nelmari shouted.

Incredulous, Sara stopped. "It's *me*! Sara. Freddie's sister! Please help, he nearly killed me!"

"Maria!" the man called out. "I need a car!"

Sara looked back at the man. Who in God's name was he talking to? Who was Maria?

Masilela was moving towards her unsteadily. He was trying to wipe at the blood in his eyes. His jaw and neck glistened in the sunlight. She wished she'd killed him, could kill him now.

"You fucked it up, you bastard! You fucked up everything!" Nelmari was shouting at the man. "And you're going to fix it. Now! I want Preto—"

"Nelmari!" shouted Sara. Had the woman gone completely mad? "Listen, please, it's him! We have to get out of here, he'll kill us both—he's got a knife! He's the one who killed Freddie and the girl, and Outanna, and the woman at the shebeen. And—"

"Shut your fucking mouth, Sara. I can't *think* with you carrying on like that!"

Nelmari had a pistol in her hand, aimed at her. And then at the man.

"It's not me, it's Pretorius!" Masilela called out. Then, swaying, he stepped forward.

"Stay right there!" Nelmari screamed, clutching the pistol in both hands.

The man stopped. "It's Pretorius! It's him, that fucking Boer! He's the one who fucked up," he said. "He's mad! He tried to kill me. And he's locked everyone up, says he's going to the cops. He's going to burn the whole place down. Please, I need a car!"

Sara's heartbeat hammered in her ears. She had to get away. *Now.* While they were fighting it out.

"Maria, I can help you get away," Masilela said. "I know the roads across the border. We can be in Botswana in an hour, in Zimbabwe at the end of the day. We'll be safe, I know people there."

"Shut up. You're going back to Karrikamma and you're going to silence Pretorius for good."

"So you can kill me afterwards?" The man laughed hoarsely. "And you will just walk away, like you are innocent? And what about this bitch here? You going to kill her too? Like her sister?"

"Shut up, I said! Fucking shut up, or I'll shoot you like a dog! You hear me?"

Sara felt her legs go limp as the truth hit her. The painting. "M" for Maria.

"Nelmari . . . ?"

Nelmari swung round, the gun on Sara.

"She's going to kill you, little sister," her attacker taunted. "She's going to do another farm killing, this one. Blame it on the kaffirs." Then his voice became more menacing. "Shoot her, Maria. Just get it over with and let's go!"

"Nelmari—*you*? Poor Freddie . . . "

"Poor Freddie? Like hell she was! So where does this sisterly love come from all of a sudden, hey? Tell me!" She pointed the pistol at Masilela, hissed at Sara as she threw glances at her. "*You* called her a witch. You! Broke her heart. She started painting herself as a witch, in one painting after another. You left her here alone, all by her fucking self with a dying, screwed up old man. All those long cold nights with the old bastard moaning and screaming, shitting in his pants. And with the concoctions that interfering old bitch gave him, which he just spewed up. Freddie dealing with it all alone here. Where were you then, hey, up on your moral high horse?"

Sara saw the hate and insanity in her eyes, the flat, bitter line of her mouth, her sinewy body bent tensely as she held the pistol.

"What did Freddie—"

Sara's voice was powerless against the venom in the other woman's words.

"What did she do to me, hey? Cast me aside like a piece of *trash*, that's what. She feathered her fucking love nest here on the farm—with my money. *My* fucking time and effort and hard work. She used me like an old rag. Looked right past me, her lame ducks and orphans and lost causes, all of them *far* more important than me. I drove out here every fucking weekend, holding her, wiping away her tears, soothing her, helping her get to sleep. And I was the one who put the old man out of his misery in the end. So we could have some *peace* for a change, so that *she* could have some peace and quiet to paint again, to be with me. Not just cleaning up shit."

"You *what*?" Sara went cold. "How? God, what—"

Nelmari gave a dry laugh. "Oh my God, you two are so fucking stupid. So naïve—you make me want to puke! With heroin, dearest little sister. A nice, long, slow boat to hell for old Pa Swarts. And for Freddie there was something different: a tiny little tablet in a good cup of tea. Something to keep her eyes open nice and wide, and her hands out of the way, all the way to dreamland. Nice little farm murder, hey, blame it on the blacks, no one will ever be the wiser. She just sat there looking at me, hey, my little Freddie, as I took off her necklace, her ring even. No way that bloody Bushman was going to get his hands on it. She wanted to give him everything, *everything*. And it was mine. *She* was mine. I *made* her!"

Her voice was shrill. She had a maniacal gleam in her eyes.

"Give her heart to the mantis man. Bah! She didn't think I'd know what those paintings meant, all her little secrets and codes. Too scared to tell me, her own sweet "M"? What happened to that—all those lovely words: darling "M," how can I ever repay you? She owed me, big-time. And I owned her. They were all taking me for a fool. That stupid policeman, too busy bumbling about to see what was right in front of his idiotic nose. And these half-witted farmers, thinking I'm just a pretty face, that they can use me, then chuck me away, when all the time, they've got no fucking clue. I've got much bigger plans than their stupid little wars, and nobody—nobody," her voice rose to a shriek, "will stand in my way!"

She seemed swept up in her tirade. Masilela took a small step forward and she screamed, "Stay the fuck where you are!"

Then, lowering her voice, she growled, "Farm murder! I could see the headlines already, even as I was trashing her room. All her precious things, that silly little girl of hers, and all the time Freddie watching me, *knowing*."

Sara felt her stomach heave, she put a hand to her mouth and discovered her face was wet with tears. She could smell the fear and the blood Nelmari was describing, then realised her own hands were covered in blood. She tried to wipe them on her shirt, then pressed them desperately against her ears, trying to block out the words.

But Nelmari hadn't finished spewing. "So *clever*, all her visionary paintings that everyone loved so much. Well, *I'd* give her a painting. She could be *in it*," she cackled. "Joke was on her, hey, Freddie's long-lost sister? Do you miss her now, hey? Do you? Because *I* don't! I'm glad the spoilt bitch is gone."

Masilela fixed his eyes on the screaming woman who by now seemed oblivious, lost in her own mad narrative, then leapt forward, blade glinting in the sun.

The pistol went off with a loud crack. For Sara, it was as if the earth was rushing towards her.

98

Beeslaar turned around to Tjoek Visser and shoved the loudhailer into his hands. "I hope you're fucking happy now. That child is on *your* conscience, preacher man. And if you want to do *one* decent thing today, just get those people away from here. Your little game is over now. The army has the town surrounded. And if I hear *one* more bloody anthem from that big mouth of yours, I'll take you down myself! Understood?"

The defiant rabble-rouser stood defeated, shoulders slumped, tears slipping down his cheeks into his beard.

"Now!" Beeslaar yelled. Visser slowly raised the megaphone.

"Beeslaar!" Pyl was tapping him on his bare shoulder. "There's one helluva veld fire out on one of the farms."

"Where?" But he knew the answer already. "What's happened to Hanekom?"

"Back in the cells. The Moegel had him locked up again after the shooting. That bullet was meant for the superintendent!"

"I think the shot came from across the road. High up. There were two young chaps in the tree. Get Shoes or someone and start looking."

Mogale stood behind them in the door to the charge office, shouting into his cellphone.

Beeslaar tugged at his arm. "Supe, we need the helicopter. The fire is on the farm that's at the centre of the stock-theft jobs. And our murderer is there too."

Mogale nodded his head furiously and barked orders into the phone.

"Get yourself cleaned up, Beeslaar," he said to Beeslaar when he was done. "The helicopter is on its way."

Beeslaar looked down. His white belly was smeared with blood.

He was just pulling a spare T-shirt he kept in his office over his head when his cellphone rang. "Bloody hell, Van Zyl!" he answered. "I don't have time now."

"Listen, Inspector! I think Masilela is at Huilwater!"

Beeslaar's heart lurched. "How do you know?"

"I'm standing on the rise above the house. I can see Sara's car and a BMW."

"White?"

"Silver, it's a 4×4. And there's a bakkie too, looks like Pretorius's Defender."

"Masilela and Viljoen. Okay. Stay where you are. Don't go in there on your own."

"But Sara and Nelmari—"

"Listen, there's no time for heroics. That man has killed a number of people already."

Van Zyl shouted something, but Beeslaar's ears were ringing, and his heart felt as if it were bursting from his rib cage. He gasped for air, like a drowning man. He pressed the cellphone to his chest as he felt his legs buckle. He shut his eyes. He had to concentrate.

The child's eyes. Buddy, they had called him. Grovétjie and Gerda's eldest . . . The shot had entered behind his ear, diagonally, as he lay on his pillow. His eye had exploded.

The eyes danced furiously in front of him again. It's you, Oom Polisieman, you *pushed our father over the edge. You, sleeping with our mother. You! Look what you've done to us . . .*

His tablets—he had to put a tablet under his tongue.

Beeslaar dropped the phone and struggled over to his desk. God, he was suffocating. Black dots swam in front of his eyes, his breath rasped loudly.

He opened a drawer, scrabbled for the pill bottle. His fingers were clumsy, but eventually he managed to flip the lid off. Tiny tablets scattered over the desk like confetti.

He pressed a shaking forefinger down onto one. It stuck on his skin, and he brought it to his mouth.

He had no sooner tasted the sweetness than he slumped to the floor. He swirled his tongue around to dissolve the tablet, and tried to calm his breathing. Inhale for four counts, hold four, exhale four. He repeated it over and over until his breath came more evenly and the shaking subsided.

Beeslaar opened his eyes. The black dots had gone. His chest was still tight, but at least he could breathe.

He got up slowly, leaning on the desk. God, he was tired, so tired. He stumbled back to the cellphone and picked it up, put it to his ear. "Hello," he said hoarsely, but the line was dead. He cursed, found Van Zyl's number and called him.

Van Zyl answered immediately, panting as he ran. "What's going on, it sounds like someone's throttling you!"

"Nothing. Wait for me!"

"Sara's alone. I have to go!"

"Just wait, I said! A helicopter's on its way."

"I *can't* wait—there's already been shooting!"

Then the signal dropped.

99

S ara was sitting flat on the ground, both arms shielding her head. Her ears were ringing, but she hadn't been hit. Cautiously, she looked up, saw Nelmari with the pistol dangling from her hand, her body flung back against the bakkie by the recoil of the shot, but Masilela was still standing.

Sara tried to move, felt a stab of pain in her bleeding leg. She couldn't possibly get up, let alone make a run for it. She felt nauseous, but knew she had to act. Putting both palms on the ground, she slid herself backwards, inching towards the house behind her.

"Stay where you are!" Nelmari warned.

Sara froze.

"Just shoot her, Maria—let's go." Masilela pointed towards the horizon and shouted, "Look there! Pretorius is burning the fucking place down. We have to get past the fire if we want to drive to the border!"

Sara looked up. There was a brown haze in the direction of Karrikamma. She edged backwards again as they looked at the sky.

"See, Maria? Let's go!"

"Drop the knife, and walk towards me, slowly."

Nelmari's feet were planted wide as she pointed the pistol. "Drop it," she demanded.

"First you kill that woman! Don't be stupid, man!" He started walking towards Nelmari again, holding the knife.

Still sitting, Sara bumped herself backwards. She was close to the door, had the keys in her hand already.

"Fuck," the man called out. "She's getting away. Shoot her!"

Sara scrabbled on all fours like a creature possessed. Nelmari shouted, there was a loud clap, bits of plaster fell from the wall, but Sara kept crawling.

She was at the door. Another shot rang out. This time the window above her shattered.

Sara hauled herself up, jerked open the screen door and reached towards the keyhole. Out of the corner of her eye she saw Masilela make a sudden lunge. Nelmari screamed, and there was another loud crack.

Sara turned the key and shoved the door open, almost falling inside. She slammed it shut and bolted it.

An engine roared, and she could hear tyres spin on the gravel.

Then everything was dead quiet.

For a moment Sara lay on her side, her knees pulled up against her chin, listening for movement. She had to get away from the door, but she was too scared to move. And the pain in her leg was fierce.

Turn the bathroom into a fort—that's what he'd said, the man from the Agricultural Union. Using her elbows, she tried to leopard crawl, aiming for the bathroom—at the other side of the house.

She was concentrating so hard that she did not register when she heard her named being called.

"Sara!"

Footsteps crunched across the gravel and there was hammering at the back door.

"Sara! Are you there?"

"Harry!"

Then the door burst open and he sank to the floor, lifting her up in both arms.

100

After his trip out to Huilwater, Beeslaar set off for Karrikamma, next door.

The once-elegant farmhouse was a charred wreck. The outbuildings, too, were in ruins. And so were the sheds farther off in the veld. Inside these were the burnt-out shells of three cattle trucks. The whole world seemed to be enveloped by a thick black pall. Toxic smoke billowed from buildings where Pretorius must have stored diesel and gas. The entire area looked like a battlefield.

Beeslaar sat down on the open tailgate of Jan Steenkamp's bakkie. He felt weirdly hyped up from all the adrenaline of the day, and gratefully accepted the coffee Jan's wife had brought along. There was milk in it, but mercifully it was sweet.

Even before Pyl had called, Steenkamp had hurried to the fire together with thirteen other farmers from the district. They had forced open the Karrikamma gates and—with no wind to fan the flames—they'd managed to stop the fire from spreading into the veld.

There was no trace of Pretorius's labourers, who seemed to have fled, though the housekeeper, Mrs. September, was found unharmed in an engine room—the one building Pretorius hadn't yet destroyed.

Steenkamp had found Pretorius on the steps of the engine room, not far from the burning farmhouse. He had a shotgun across his knees and was drinking from a half-empty bottle of brandy.

"Dear God, Beeslaar, he looked like a creature from hell. Totally blackened, even his hair scorched by the flames. He didn't say a word. Just kept staring at me." The farmer had shuddered, as if the awful image still danced before his eyes.

His clothes had been soaked in petrol, which he'd also splashed on the walls. He gestured at Steenkamp not to come closer. But it had been clear what his plan was: to strike a match, and then to put the double-barrel in his mouth. Steenkamp had tried to talk him round, to convince him at least to spare the life of the screaming woman inside.

But Pretorius had been beyond talking. It was as if his brain had shut down, done with life. "You know, he looked at me as if I was invisible. I've never seen such dead eyes—like an ox just after you've slaughtered it. Good Lord, not a word. Even when he struck the match. The first one didn't take—even the matches were soaked in petrol. But hell, Beeslaar, that man's eyes—completely dead. I couldn't move, man. Just stood there like a damned pillar of salt."

But Roger Heidenrich had stepped in. He'd seen Pretorius struggle with the match, took a few long strides up behind him and wrestled the gun off him.

It hadn't taken much to overpower Pretorius. He was finished.

101

B eeslaar was sitting behind his desk, the night sky black at his window. There seemed to be no stars at all tonight.

Willie Prinsloo in Postmasburg had just called: he was over-loaded, six dead in yet another taxi accident. They'd have to send Viljoen's body to Upington for the post-mortem.

Beeslaar himself had seen more than enough corpses today.

He recalled the pitiful figure of Nelmari Viljoen lying dead in the farmyard, a deep gash to her throat—though Deetlefs said the chest wound had more likely been the cause of death. A stab wound to the heart. Sara Swarts, however, was alive, and, besides the nasty cut on her calf, was basically unharmed, just mute with shock and fear. She'd kept clinging to Van Zyl's neck like a bushbaby. But between the two of them they'd managed to describe the events that had preceded Viljoen's killing. He'd sent them off immediately to get medical attention in Upington, and then called in a warning with a description of Masilela's escape vehicle—Viljoen's silver BMW 4×4.

The other body he didn't even want to think about: Kleinboel Pieterse. A tragic waste of a young life. The thought of it enraged him, he wanted to beat that arrogant fuckhead Hanekom to a pulp. Fortunately the man had been sent away, along with the preacher man and young Thabang Motlogeloa. Must have made for interesting company—the three of them bundled up together in the back of the police van, all the way to Upington. They'd left shortly after Beeslaar took off for Huilwater and then Karrikamma in the helicopter.

The Moegel, in the end, had been as good as his word. A small army of policemen under the command of a rather subdued Lobatse had helped to quell the farmers' revolt. They'd also identified the young shooter before going off to search Nelmari Viljoen's home as well as her office.

Turned out the Moegel had been investigating Ms. Viljoen for some time—and hadn't found it necessary to inform Beeslaar of the details. He'd been looking into Viljoen's Red Sands operations in Upington, where she evidently had two town councillors and a whole bunch of officials on her payroll. And where, it was suspected, she had been the instigator behind the attempted murder of an opposition party councillor—the very same person who'd come forward about the bribery debacle surrounding the project. Viljoen had even tried to butter up Mogale by offering him a house in the development at a ridiculously low price.

Beeslaar looked at his untidy desk. He could still see a few tablets dotted about. Great timing for a panic attack—but the pills had saved him. He'd pulled himself together during the helicopter ride and said a prayer, too, for September's mother and the Swarts girl.

Fuck it, he had a heap of paperwork ahead of him. He pushed a stack of files to one side, hauled himself up wearily. Time to head for home.

He walked back to his house, where he found Bulelani on the back steps. And the backyard completely drenched. Bulelani had clearly decided there was no way he was going to be ticked off over a dry garden again. Beeslaar didn't say anything, just made him dinner: the remainder of a pack of viennas on four slices of buttered white bread. Pouring a glass of milk for his guest, he thought of the new inmate in the cells back at the station: Boet Pretorius, the stupid piece of shit.

He left Bulelani at the kitchen table and went to rummage around in his cupboard for a clean shirt and trousers, some underwear, a cake of soap and a towel. He needed to get back to the station.

An exhausted Constable Morotse unlocked the cell for him. The whole place stank of petrol. Pretorius lay sleeping in the corner—no surprise after the amount of alcohol he'd drunk and the tranquilliser they'd given him.

His big body was curled up on the floor, on the blankets Beeslaar had brought in for Bulelani. Beeslaar gestured to Shoes to wake him up.

"Go get us a bucket of hot water, Constable," he said when Pretorius stirred. "The man needs to wash." Shoes looked like the walking dead—everyone had been through the wars today, Beeslaar thought.

Pretorius struggled upright, his back to Beeslaar. His broad shoulders sagged. Some of his hair had been singed, and the rest stood up in dirty, oily tufts. He looked like he'd been hit over the back of the head with a spade.

With great effort, he turned to Beeslaar.

Beeslaar was shocked by the emptiness in his eyes. He could see for himself now what Jan Steenkamp had been on about. Pretorius could just as well have been blind: it was as if he wasn't looking at you, but through you. As if he couldn't focus on real objects, but saw things beyond normal human perception.

He mumbled something, and Beeslaar crouched down on his haunches. To his surprise he heard him laugh, a rasping, mirthless sound. "My mother would have enjoyed this, you know," he said, his breath coming in short, weary bursts.

Beeslaar held his breath, unsure whether Pretorius was delirious or still drunk.

"She always said I'd turn out just like my father. A jailbird.

She was the only person who saw me for what I was, saw through all the bullshit and big talk. Saw that underneath it all I was just a drunk and a crook. Ma. And Freddie . . . "

He repeated the name softly, seemed to roll it around in his mouth. "I killed her, do you know that, Beeslaar?"

Beeslaar sat down on the floor, his back against the wall. He rested his elbows on his knees.

"I wasn't holding the knife, but I might as well have been. She trusted me, you know? Like an older brother. When the man she *really* loved . . . " He rolled back his eyes, as if the effort of remembering had cost him his last breath. But then his lips moved again. "De Kok. When he threw her generous gift back in her face, she came to me. Yes, to me! She came to cry on my shoulder, because she thought she could trust me. Like a brother. But I was hungry for her, horny, I just wanted to fuck her. I couldn't stop myself." He looked away as he whispered, "I raped her."

Beeslaar felt the bile rise in him as he struggled to keep his emotions in check—the urge to lash out, yet also pity for the whimpering creature in front of him.

It was a relief when the sound of footsteps and the slap-slap of water broke the silence. Beeslaar gestured at Shoes to just put down the bucket and leave.

Pretorius seemed not to notice the constable on the other side of the bars. He licked his cracked lips and went on. "That day, the Wednesday. I wanted to go beg her. Ask her to forgive me. I wanted to tell her everything. About that Viljoen bitch. How she'd wriggled her way under all our skins. Like a leech. All that blood on her hands. Starting with Freddie's father. She killed him, you know? His drawn-out death didn't suit her. Back then, the old man was almost crazy with pain. But he didn't want to go back to hospital. So she came to me—Nelmari, I mean. Said she had a few million coming in from the sale . . . "
He coughed, asked Beeslaar for a cigarette.

"What? And torch us both? First go wash yourself. I've brought some clothes and stuff."

He left the cell and went out to the front steps, where he gazed at the quiet street. There were still remnants of the day's violence—pieces of burnt cloth, placards, and police tape at the spot where Kleinboel had died. He crossed the street and bought a pack of cigarettes from Oom Koeks.

Back at the cells, Beeslaar encountered a cleaner version of the man he'd just left, though the look in his eyes was unchanged. Shoes took away the bucket and the acrid-smelling clothes as Pretorius took the cigarette Beeslaar handed to him, inhaling gratefully. He breathed the smoke out slowly, seemed to lapse into a reverie.

"When you're ready," Beeslaar prompted.

"Ja, that woman. I fucking wish I'd had the guts to strangle her properly. She'd sold a building in Joburg, said she could help me get hold of two farms closer to the Kgalagadi. Said we'd build a private lodge, better, more expensive than Londolozi or Phinda, even. Aim at the super-rich from around the world." The words were flowing more easily now. As if he couldn't wait to get the story off his chest.

"I was ready, you know? Ready to work hard. And ready to get rich. Ready to take any risk. To sell my fucking soul to the devil, to take a low-down scum of a person like her as my partner." He gave a crooked smile. "And she sure brought the money rolling in. I bought two, three farms. In the first year alone. But then she started reeling me in. Brought in her own people. Masilela, for one. A lazy fucker from Joburg, bank robber or something. A helluva chip on his shoulder. Attitude. By that time there was no stopping the bitch. She bought trucks, built sheds, and every time I opened my mouth, she stuffed it full of money."

He took a last puff, rubbed the stub between his thumb and index finger and held out his hand for another. Beeslaar lit a cigarette and passed it to him.

"And then she came with the story that she needed Huilwater. And Freddie, well, it was so soon after her father died. And she *was* actually ready to sell. But we needed old man Matthee's land too—it was a sort of corridor between me and Huilwater. By now Nelmari was like a machine. On a mission. She wouldn't take no for an answer. Used Masilela to threaten and terrorise if she didn't get her way. I think the poor old housekeeper, Outanna, she must have suspected something, and Nelmari told him first to frighten her, then get rid of her. A vicious man, he likes to hurt people, I think.

"But then De Kok arrived on the scene and everything changed. Freddie was suddenly all dreamy-eyed about the Bushman, the Griquas, wanted to adopt that little girl, started with the land-claim nonsense. And Nelmari herself went and stole the will from the Cape archive to try and stop it—but that was too soft a solution for her in the end. She wouldn't listen to reason, and by that time I was an irritation to her. Maria! Ha! That's her real name, you know? Petronella Maria Magdalena Viljoen. She hated those old-fashioned names, called herself Nelmari. But Masilela and his mates called her M—like she was some kind of Mafia woman boss. I think she liked that," he sneered.

"I wanted to walk away back then already, pull out of the whole thing. But she put me in my place fucking quickly, made it clear who was in the driver's seat. And then she brought even more of her scum in. Masilela's brothers. And the trucks started running at night. Came back full, raced off to Botswana across my land. And I sat there powerless. Trapped. No way round her, no way out. It was one Friday night when I went to shut them up at their boozing when I discovered the arms. AKs and other stuff. For that little shit of a Hanekom. Can you fucking believe it!"

The cigarette was burning down between his fingers, forgotten in the heady rush of this unburdening.

"Ja. Hanekom. Leader of the Great White Uprising. Too stupid to realise she had him on a leash shorter than the length of an AK. An idiot, just like me. Thinking you'll do straight business with a bitch like that. Madame had Masilela do the hand-over, and she recorded it all. Her insurance, you see. Then she could expose the whole lot if she needed to. Controlling, had us all by the short and curlies. Each and every one of us. We're all better off without her."

He killed the glowing stub and sank back against the cell wall. But he still had more to say.

"When the murders started—those two Vaalputs workers—some of my own people began leaving. Just a few stayed on, including the foreman and his mother—I hear she insisted. Typical mother-hen type, she bossed us all around. But I'd reached breaking point. I wanted to come see you back then already, spill the beans. But Nelmari had me by the balls. And it was then—God, Beeslaar. I don't know what got into me. Maybe Freddie was my last hope, you know? The only thing around me that was good and pure. I thought—God, I don't know *what* I was thinking. If she could only *love* me. She could give the land to her Bushman lover if she wanted to. Everything. In fact I was glad she'd got the land claim going, I thought it might stop that bitch. It's just that I so badly wanted her to love me. Freddie—there was no one like her. She was so sad about the land claim mess, and that bastard foreman throwing her gift back in her face. Then she came over to see me."

He dropped his head and his shoulders shook. "And me, what did I do? You know what I did? I tore her apart."

Beeslaar held out the towel he had brought. Pretorius pressed his face into it, and when he looked up again, it was as if a great weight had been lifted off his shoulders.

"When I got to Freddie that day. That Wednesday, Beeslaar. When I found her there like that, I knew. I just knew. Nelmari worshipped her. I don't know if she was a fucking lesbian or what. And I don't know if Freddie ever had a relationship with her. I just know she was always there, always hanging around, treated Freddie like some kind of princess. So jealous too. And she hated De Kok. Then Freddie drew up a new will . . . "

He lay down, rolled on his side and curled up his body, his face to the wall.

Beeslaar still had many questions, but they could wait. He waited until the only sound in the cell was the even rhythm of the man's breathing. Then, wearily, he picked up the damp cake of soap from the floor and went out, locking the cell door behind him.

Three in the morning. It was so damn late it was almost early, Beeslaar thought as he pushed open the gate and walked up the steps to his front door. He struggled with the key in the dark, swearing under his breath, but managed to turn the lock at last.

He walked straight to the kitchen. There were still a few beers in the fridge. He took one out and unscrewed the top, and was just about to take a sip when his cellphone rang.

Van Zyl.

"How's your patient—she okay?" Beeslaar asked, but didn't wait for an answer. Too tired for niceties, he plunged straight in. "I'm coming through later today to take her statement."

"Thank you, Inspector," Van Zyl said, "for allowing me to get Sara away from there so quickly. She's suffering more from shock than anything else, I think. But I'm calling to find out how *you* are. I heard about the shooting. About Kleinboel Pieterse."

"No comment," he muttered, and, ignoring the journalist's protestations, he ended the call.

Beeslaar picked up the beer bottle again, threw his head back and drank. When he put it down, it was nearly empty. He belched loudly as he opened the back door to look out over the watered yard and his new vegetable patch. He was sure he could see the first green sprouts in the dimness.

He turned back into the kitchen, leaving the door open.

Fuck the goggas, he thought, taking a deep breath of cool night air.

He tossed three rashers of bacon into a pan, had second thoughts, added another. The fat hissed and sputtered companionably. He cut two fat slices of his whole wheat bread, and grated some mature cheddar to sprinkle over it all.

He was still busy when he heard a voice at the front door: Ghaap.

"In here!" he called, and listened to the slow footsteps on the floorboards. "There's beer in the fridge," he said, scraping up a heap of cheese.

"How did you know I was coming?" Ghaap asked and came to stand next to him, beer in hand.

"Listen, if you're hungry, you need to tell me now, so I can add some more."

"Ja, I'm hungry, but no cheese, please. Just eggs and two bits of bacon." Ghaap flopped down at the table. "Jissus, what a day. I thought it would never end."

"Where's Pyl?"

"Ag, the poor fucker. He's still in Upington, jumping like a grasshopper when the Moegel clicks his fingers. That'll teach him to go arse-kissing. He phoned just now. But sjoe, the man can moan, hey!"

Beeslaar smiled, flipped the bacon over.

"What a mess. And the dogs—did you hear them howling when Pretorius was crying his heart out in the cells? They were tjanking along, all over town. Spooky, I tell you."

Beeslaar stood with the egg lifter in one hand and the beer bottle in the other. "How do you like your eggs?" he asked.

"Um . . . cupped and lightly fondled by a blonde," he quipped.

Beeslaar grinned dutifully at the tired old joke and cracked six eggs neatly in one pan. Two for Ghaap and the rest for him.

When everything was done, he dished up onto two plates,

sprinkling the cheese over his eggs. He poured himself a brandy and got another beer from the fridge for Ghaap.

They ate in silence. Halfway through, Ghaap put down his fork. "So, how did we screw up like that? The whole time it was that larney woman, hey?"

"Ja," said Beeslaar and sprinkled more salt over his eggs. "The world is full of fucked-up people. Sometimes they're white and sometimes they're black. But they're all equally crazy."

"Jissus, man," Ghaap exclaimed. "She sure got what she was looking for! Some of her own medicine. And Masilela's just vanished into thin air."

Beeslaar stuffed the last piece of bread into his mouth. "At least you didn't puke all over the place again this afternoon."

"Ja, but I think you need to pour me a brandy too. If I don't get motherless right now, I won't get to sleep."

Beeslaar took Ghaap's plate, slid the uneaten egg onto a saucer and saved it in the fridge for Bulelani. Then he poured Ghaap a double and they got up and sat on the kitchen steps.

The first birds were chirping, and as a rose-grey tinged the horizon, things in the backyard began to take shape.

"Just explain one thing to me," said Ghaap. "What the hell d'you plan to do with all those carrots?"

"Eat them."

Ghaap gave a snort. "Do you believe everything Pretorius told you tonight?"

"Money," Beeslaar said after a while. "And power. 'The sounding brass and the clanging cymbal . . . ' How does it go again? 'But the greatest of these is . . . ' Desire, actually. The endless desire for more."

"That sounds really deep, but what do you actually mean?"

"What I'm trying to say is that it's everyone's story. Take us whites, for example. Until just the other day, we had all the power. But not any more. For some, the only game that remains is money. Getting more of it. And more and more. Money can buy anything. Security, health, education—eventually power too. And there are always people who want it all. Just look who's really in charge of this country. The lily-white money moguls who make sure the ANC coffers are filled. *That's* who. The oldest game in the book. And Nelmari Viljoen understood it really well. Poor bastards like me and you, we get drunk on cheap brandy. But those people—they get drunk on desire. For power and money. For more and more of it."

Ghaap took out his cigarettes, offered one to Beeslaar. They lit up, blew plumes of smoke into the grey dawn.

"Take a guy like Pretorius. His whole life he's wanted to be something—not just poor son of a miner. And he wanted it so badly. Boy, did he want it. Then one day he meets the money fairy. Over at his new neighbour's place. She grants him three wishes: money and money and money. The chance to become the Sol Kerzner of the Kalahari."

"The who?"

"Never mind. It's before your time."

"And what does the fairy get out of the game?"

"Power. Her game is people. She wants to own them. Strings them along, then strings them like beads, nice little accessories she wears around her scrawny neck."

"Jissie, Beeslaar, what did you put in that drink of yours? Are you going to talk in tongues the whole time now?"

"Everyone wants to be somebody, Ghaap. Some are just more desperate than others. Their desire is bigger. Greed. Avarice. They'll do anything—persecute people, whatever it takes, just to get their way. They'll even kill if they have to."

"And you think that's what happened to Freddie Swarts? She stood in the way of their greed—Pretorius and Viljoen?"

"That too. But Freddie's real transgression was that she pissed off the golden money fairy. She was the one special pearl on the string who threatened to jump off, see. And that the fairy couldn't allow."

"But do you really think a woman is capable of that kind of killing? Women use poison, maybe even shoot, or pay someone else to do it for them. Isn't that what happened here? She got Masilela to do it."

"No. That's the thing that's been bothering me ever since yesterday morning. It was only when I saw Viljoen's body while she was still clutching the gun that I realised she's a southpaw. Masilela is right-handed. The Vaalputs workers, Mma Mokoena, it was a right-handed killer. But Freddie and the girl were killed by a left-handed person."

"The crooked fairy."

"Yes, with a devil's claw. Obsessed with another woman. A woman who then went off and gave her heart to the mantis man. Nelmari Viljoen was there on the morning of the murder, I'm a hundred per cent sure of that—and if I can get hold of old Windvogel I'm sure he'll confirm it. Of course we'll do the full DNA as well, though there's no one to put in jail now. Justice has been served. Anyway, the telephone exchange tells us Miss Viljoen phoned Huilwater repeatedly that morning— from a cellphone. But she hung up each time Freddie answered. We'll be able to tell for sure that she was in the area when we go through her cellphone records."

"And De Kok? What about him?"

"Ja, well, Windvogel had realised something was going on with Masilela and Boet Pretorius—he'd been watching them for a while, working it out. But he didn't want to come to us, didn't trust us. But I reckon he might have told his old friend the housekeeper at Huilwater about his suspicions.

"So the two of them, they brought in the sangoma and his muti, and Freddie the painter enjoyed the exotic idea of him too. Outanna wanted to protect the farm, the people she loved. Maybe the old lady thought Freddie's murder was part of some devilish revenge—she was very frightened, scared of everything, wouldn't talk to us. Maybe she was scared of the crooked fairy, maybe of Masilela, maybe they knew she knew something. And after the old woman was killed, old Windvogel took De Kok to show him the whole operation in action—then De Kok lost it, attacked Masilela, the man he thought had killed the woman he loved."

Ghaap was dead quiet next to Beeslaar, who eventually checked to see whether he was still awake. "If you fall asleep, I'll klap you."

Ghaap's reply was a chortle. Then he asked, "And Viljoen and Pretorius?"

A cellphone rang and he scrabbled for it with clumsy fingers, his eyes already a bit glassy. "Sharp-sharp, my bru," he answered. "No, man, Ballies, I'm hanging with the inspector!" He listened for a moment, then, "Hey? In the BM? Where's he now?"

"Masilela," Ghaap said a moment later, putting his phone back in his pocket. "The helicopter got him. In Miss Millions's car, nogal. Stuck in the sand somewhere near the border. BMW—real rubbish for the roads around here. Anyway, what's the rest of the story?"

"Okay, well, Viljoen was the financier for Pretorius's big dreams—initially. But like I said, her greed eventually became clear to him too. She wasn't happy with just the Red Sands project. She wanted *more*. And she hijacked Pretorius's dreams by using her money. She wanted more land, to get even richer. And if people stood in her way—Jesus, she even began to bring in weapons for Hanekom. You see, the more he destabilised the area, the sooner she hoped she could buy up all the land—and she'd get it for next to nothing. The land claims were a spanner in her works—she sure wasn't planning to give up her investment in Karrikamma all because of some historic claims. Pretorius reckons she stole the will from the archive herself. And I think that's when Freddie started to smell a rat, as well as seeing her jealousy and obsessiveness—it's clear from her diary, anyway, where she describes her one-time friend as evil."

"Jissie, that's a big word, that."

"Mmm. But there was a weak link in Ms Viljoen's plan—Pretorius. She hadn't banked on him buckling so pathetically under pressure. Stock theft was one thing, but when the woman he loved was killed, and killed like *that*—hell, it cracked him up completely. He knew it wasn't Masilela—he figured out right at the start it was Viljoen. There was just one way out for him, and it meant teaching her a lesson for good. And then he strangled her and left her for dead in the veld. But big man that he is, he wasn't as effective a murderer as the woman he tried to kill."

He turned to Ghaap, who was snoring lightly, the empty brandy glass toppled over on his stomach. Beeslaar got up quietly. In the kitchen he threw what was left of his drink down the sink and poured himself a big glass of water. He was past caring about the taste. He took it to the lounge, where he sank gratefully into the couch. He took out his cellphone, scrolled down to "G" and pressed Call when he found Gerda's number.

She answered immediately. He could hear she was wide awake.

"I've been thinking," he said. "If I bought you and Kleinpiet a plane ticket to Upington. You could come visit me then?"

She didn't answer, but he heard her breathing. He was acutely aware of the sound of his own heartbeat. "It doesn't have to be right away, you know. It's still very hot here, anyway. Maybe towards the end of March or something."

She exhaled slowly. He could almost feel the warmth of her breath, see her red hair tousled on the pillow, the cool green of her eyes staring dreamily out the window. He could sense her—warm vanilla and musk rising from the soft curves of her breasts, her belly, her generous thighs.

"Will you think about it?"

She made a sound. "Albertus?"

"Yes?"

"I don't want to remember."

"I'll help you forget."

Silence.

"Gerda?"

"Nobody can help me to forget. Especially not you . . . "

The line went dead.

The phone slipped from his hand. She was right, he knew. Of all people, it was him. *He* had started it all . . .

Beeslaar swung his legs onto the couch, and lay back. He closed his eyes and felt the weariness washing over him. Soon, sleep came, a tender hand brushing away the pain.

Acknowledgements

Most sincere thanks to Isobel Dixon of Blake Friedmann Literary Agency who set the ball rolling, did the translation from Afrikaans together with Maya Fowler, and kept chiselling to turn this work into a novel. Isobel's inexhaustible energy, enthusiasm, grace and commitment has been a source of constant inspiration.

Special thanks to Lynda Gilfillan for the extraordinary editing job. She magically gave the story wings.

It has been such an amazing experience to work with you ladies. And what a learning curve for me.

Also, special thanks to the production team at Penguin for taking on this job, and for executing it so professionally under the baton of Fourie Botha. And to Frederik de Jager, in particular, for his part in bringing this work to Penguin. You guys rock.

Several people were instrumental in the research for this book: Wessel van der Vyver and his wife, Anne-Marie, of the farm Cairntop in the Griekwastad district. Wessel's stories about the area, plants, animals and agriculture were a great help. The Van der Vyvers also opened doors to other sources, including Hetta Hager of the Griekwastad Museum, who knows everything there is to know about Griqua history; Sanna van Wyk of Rainbow Valley, who patiently informed me about old Griqua customs regarding water divining; Robbie Philips, headmaster at Griekwastad School, who, together with Bennie Beukes of Campbell, enlightened me with regard to the tragic history of the Griqua people, the loss of their land, and the subsequent impoverishment of a once proud people. Thank you, too, for helping me to understand the dilemma of "minority cultures" in the very complex politics of post-colonial, post-apartheid South Africa.

I am grateful also to Koos and Amanda Geldenhuys of the farm Kliplaagte in the Lichtenburg district. They introduced me to countless victims as well as family members of victims of farm attacks. Koos ran a column about farm safety for *Landbouweekblad*, the contents of which he generously shared with me.

Everything I learnt about falconeering was provided by Jannes Kruger, who ran the Eagle Encounters programme at the Spier wine estate outside Stellenbosch, and Hank Chalmers, who demonstrated the feeding and hunting patterns of birds of prey.

Ex-detective De Vries Vermeulen of Bellville provided much information regarding police work. Thanks also to private detective Christian Botha of East-London for his insights, as well as Dr Ansie Adendorff, a general practitioner in Stellenbosch, who provided crucial forensic information.

I made extensive use of the web pages of, inter alia, *Die Burger*, *Volksblad*, *Beeld*, *Rapport*, *Landbouweekblad* and the *Mail & Guardian*, and I also made use of several research facilities, including the Institute for Security Studies, the Helen Suzman Foundation and AgriSA. I researched the history of the South African Police Service, and I also investigated the agenda and activities of various international far-right organisations.

Among the numerous books I consulted are: *Flowering Plants of the Kalahari Dunes* by Noel van Rooyen, *The Kalahari and its Plants* by Elias le Riche and Pieter van der Walt, and *Frontiers* by Noel Mostert.

My thanks are also due to photographer Ansie du Toit. And to the family of the late Donald Rieckert for permission to translate and use Donald's poem, "Die Oog."

In creating the original Afrikaans *Plaasmoord*, I owe a big thank you to Deon Meyer, an author I greatly admire, and Hettie Scholtz, whose wise counsel always resulted in major improvements.

And finally, I wish to thank Etienne Bloemhof, managing editor at NB Publishers, who believed in the story right from the start and assisted in its development.